STEVEN UNIVERSE

AND THE CRYSTAL GEMS

WWW.BOOM-STUDIOS.COM

STEVEN UNIVERSE AND THE CRYSTAL GEMS, September 2019. Published by KaBOOM!, a division of Boom Entertainment, Inc. STEVEN UNIVERSE, CARTOON NETWORK, the logos, and all related characters and elements are trademarks of and © Cartoon Network. A WarnerMedia Company. All rights reserved. (S19) Originally published in single magazine form as STEVEN UNIVERSE AND THE CRYSTAL GEMS No. 1-4. © Cartoon Network. A WarnerMedia Company. All rights reserved. (S16) KaBOOM!™ and the KaBOOM! logo are trademarks of Boom Entertainment, Inc., registered in various countries and categories. All characters, events, and institutions depicted herein are fictional. Any similarity between any of the names, characters, persons, events, and/ or institutions in this publication to actual names, characters, and persons, whether living or dead, events, and/or institutions is unintended and purely coincidental. KaBOOM! does not read or accept unsolicited submissions of ideas, stories, or artwork.

BOOM! Studios, 5670 Wilshire Boulevard, Suite 400, Los Angeles, CA 90036-5679. Printed in China. Second Printing.

ISBN: 978-1-60886-921-3, eISBN: 978-1-61398-592-2

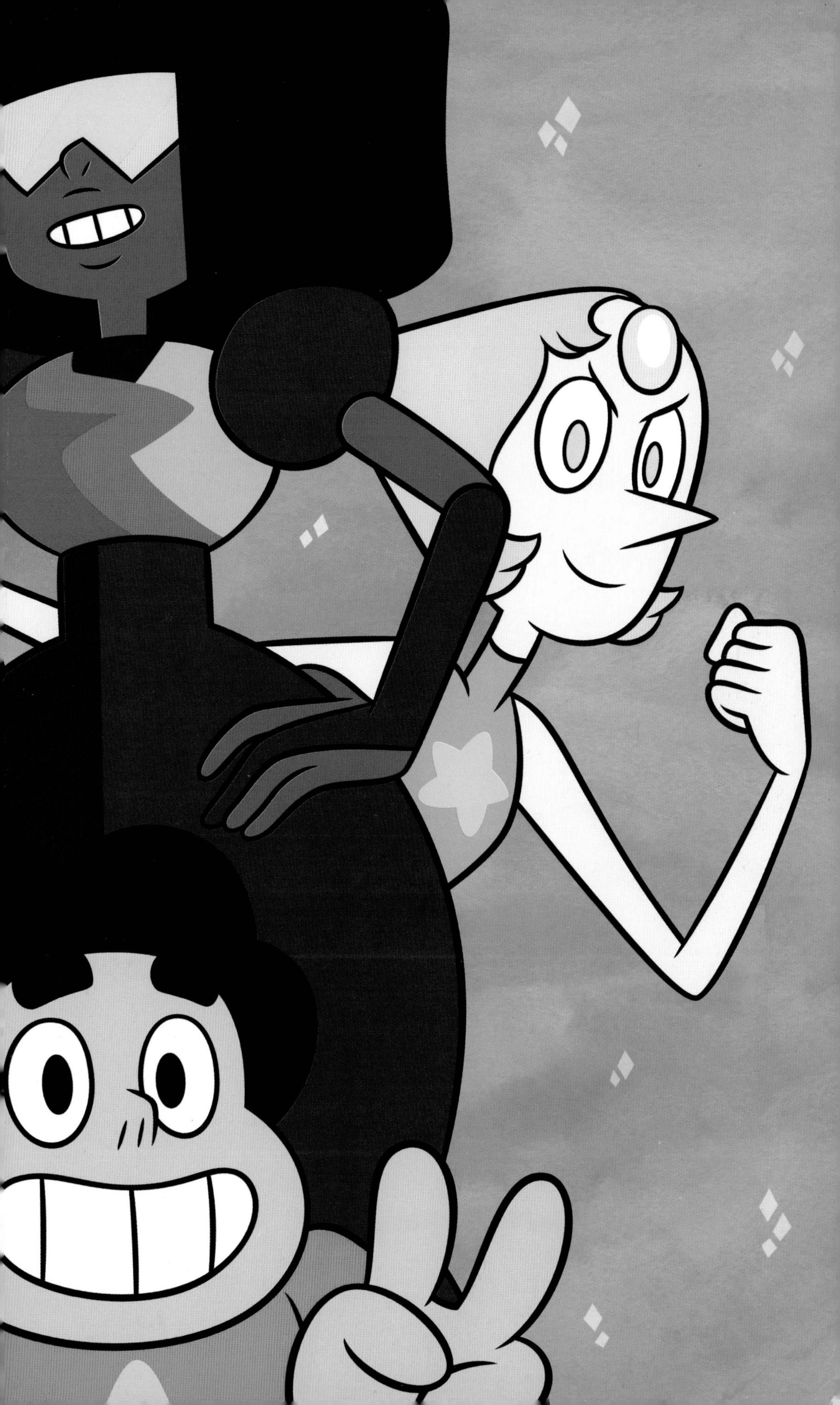

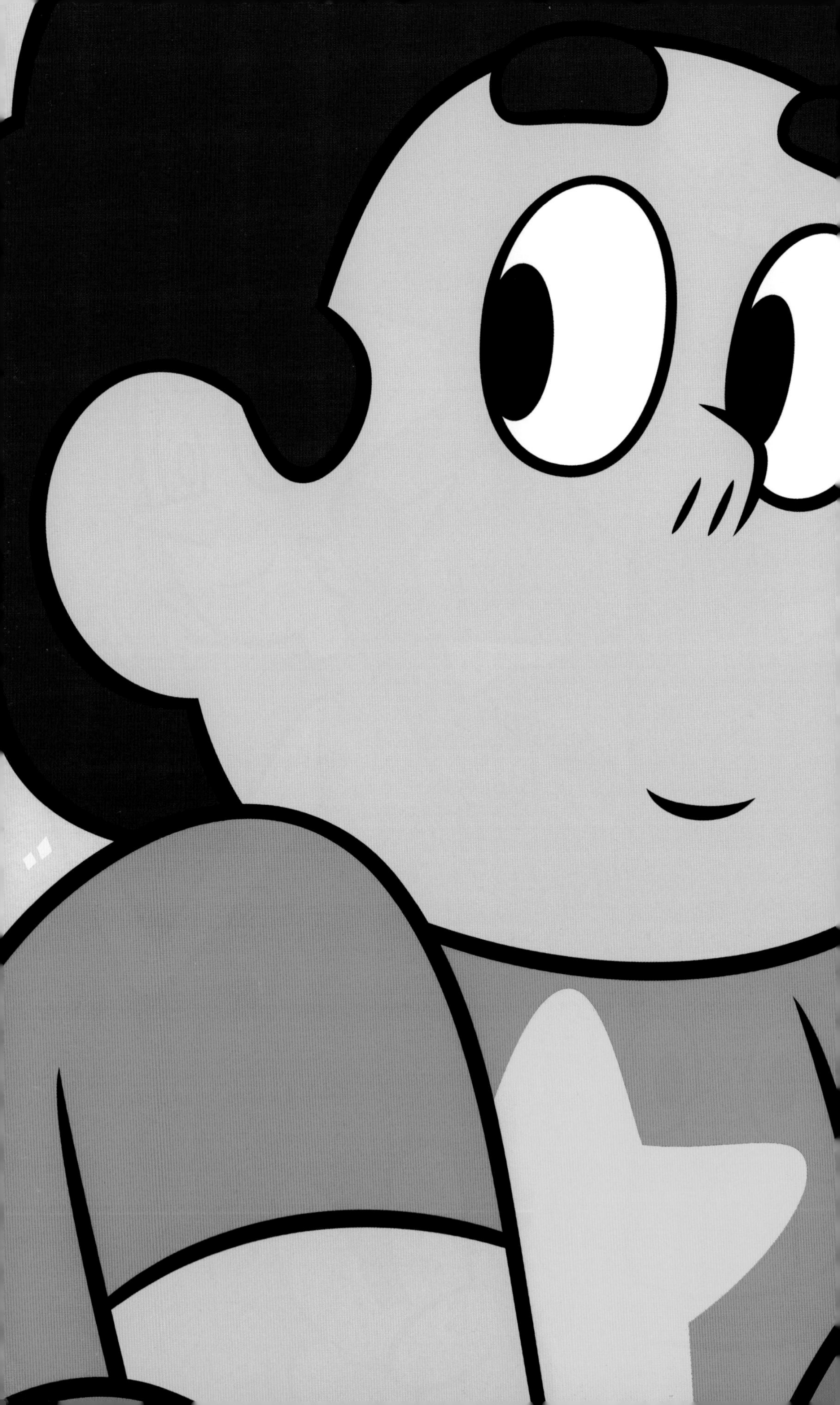

STEVEN UNIVERSE
AND THE CRYSTAL GEMS

created by
REBECCA SUGAR

written by
JOSCELINE FENTON

illustrated by
CHRYSTIN GARLAND

colors by
LEIGH LUNA

letters by
JIM CAMPBELL

cover by
KAT LEYH

designer
JILLIAN CRAB

associate editor
CHRIS ROSA

editor
SHANNON WATTERS

Special thanks to
Marisa Marionakis, Rick Blanco, Jim Valeri,
Curtis Lelash, Conrad Montgomery,
Meghan Bradley, Jackie Buscarino, Alan Pasman
and the wonderful folks at **Cartoon Network**.

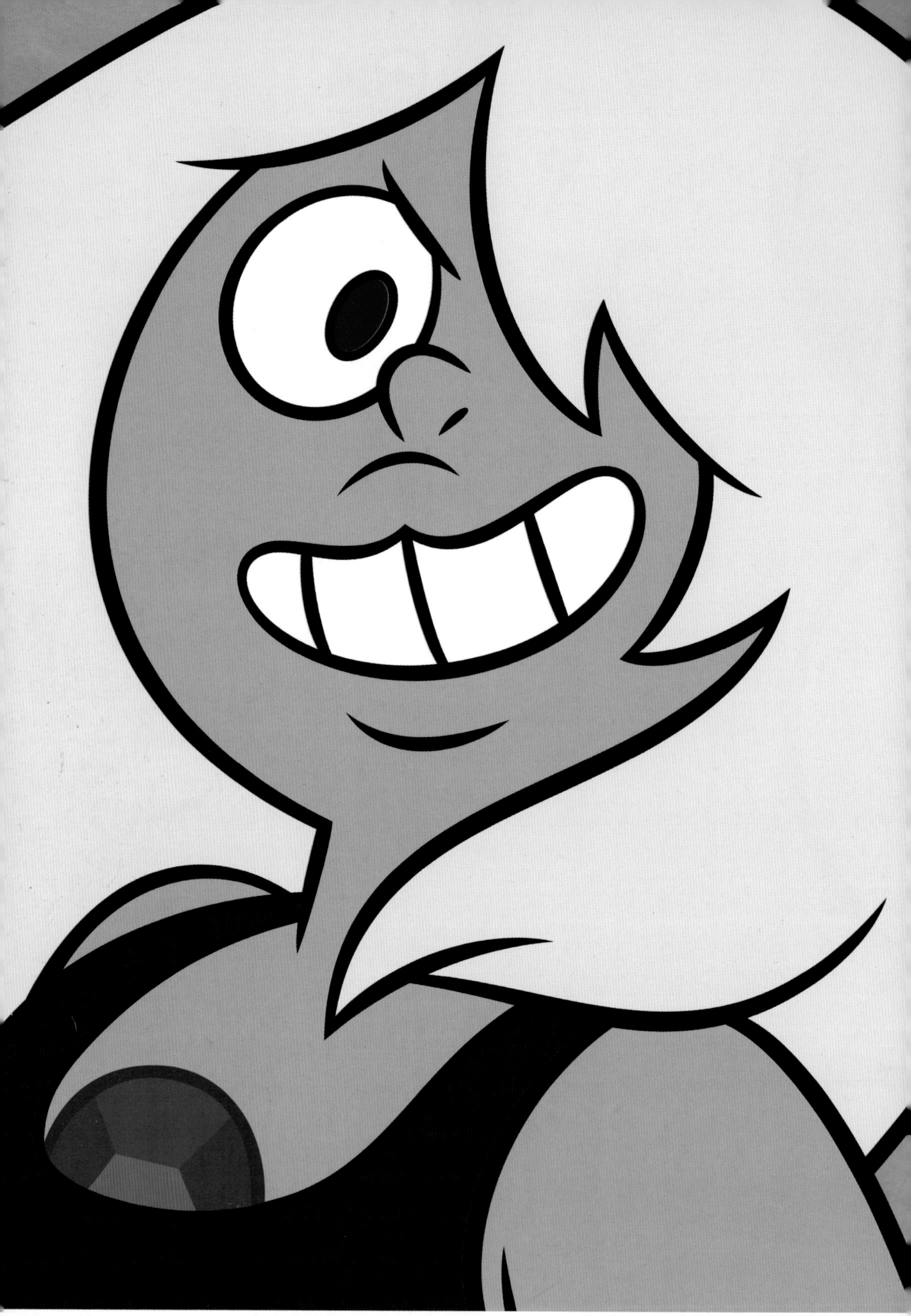

CHAPTER ONE

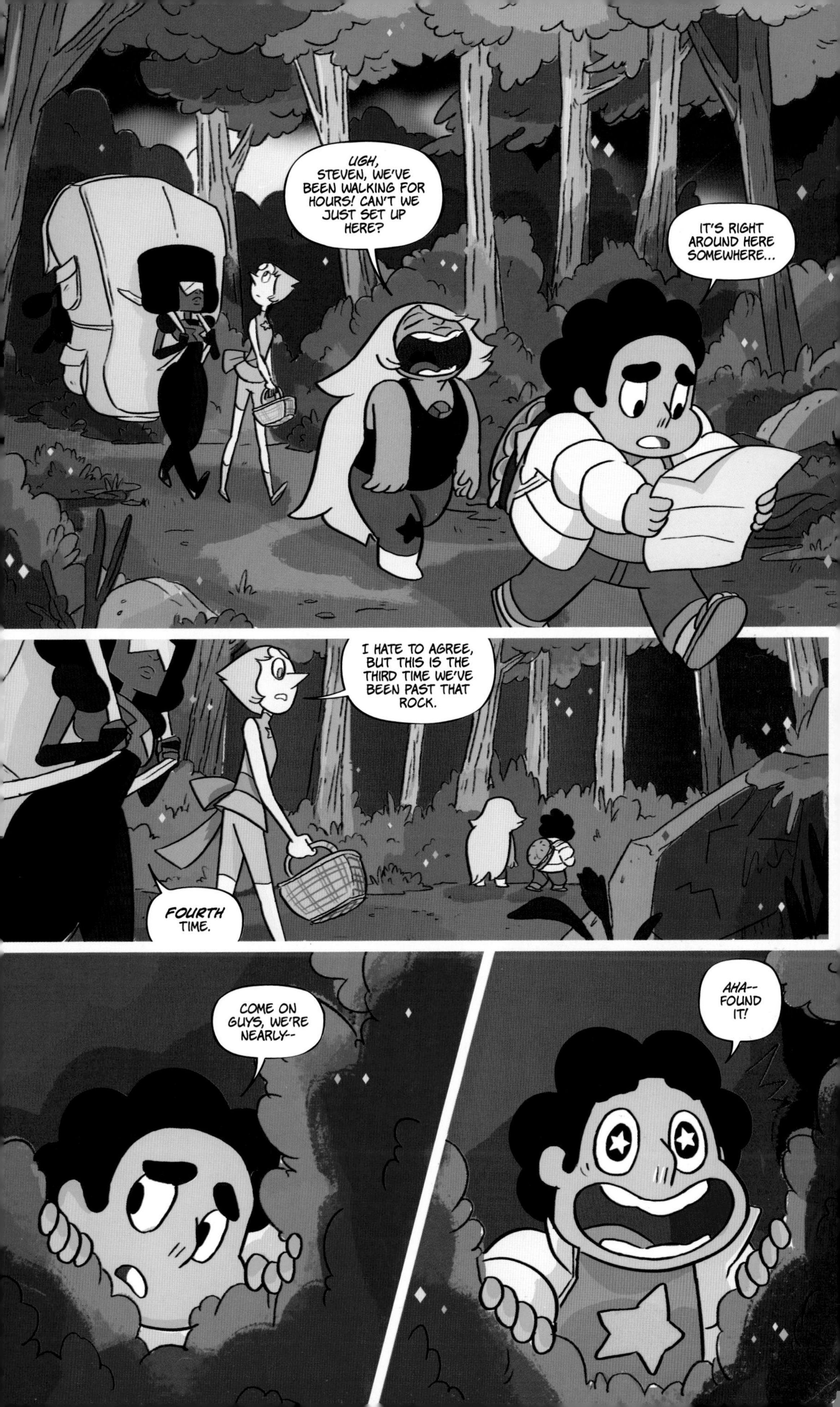
UGH, STEVEN, WE'VE BEEN WALKING FOR HOURS! CAN'T WE JUST SET UP HERE?
IT'S RIGHT AROUND HERE SOMEWHERE...
I HATE TO AGREE, BUT THIS IS THE THIRD TIME WE'VE BEEN PAST THAT ROCK.
FOURTH TIME.
COME ON GUYS, WE'RE NEARLY--
AHA-- FOUND IT!

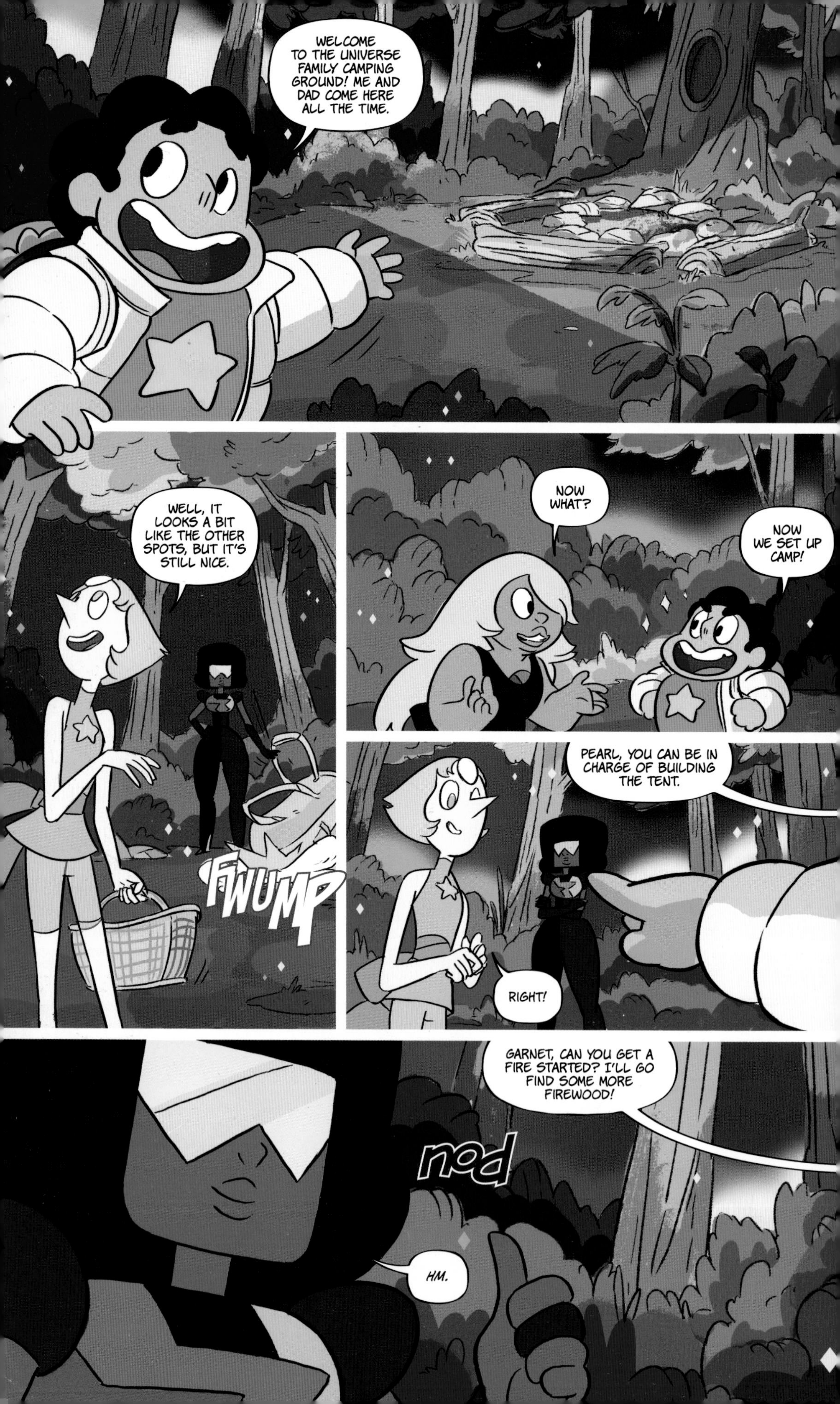
WELCOME TO THE UNIVERSE FAMILY CAMPING GROUND! ME AND DAD COME HERE ALL THE TIME.
WELL, IT LOOKS A BIT LIKE THE OTHER SPOTS, BUT IT'S STILL NICE.
FWUMP
NOW WHAT?
NOW WE SET UP CAMP!
PEARL, YOU CAN BE IN CHARGE OF BUILDING THE TENT.
RIGHT!
GARNET, CAN YOU GET A FIRE STARTED? I'LL GO FIND SOME MORE FIREWOOD!
nod
HM.

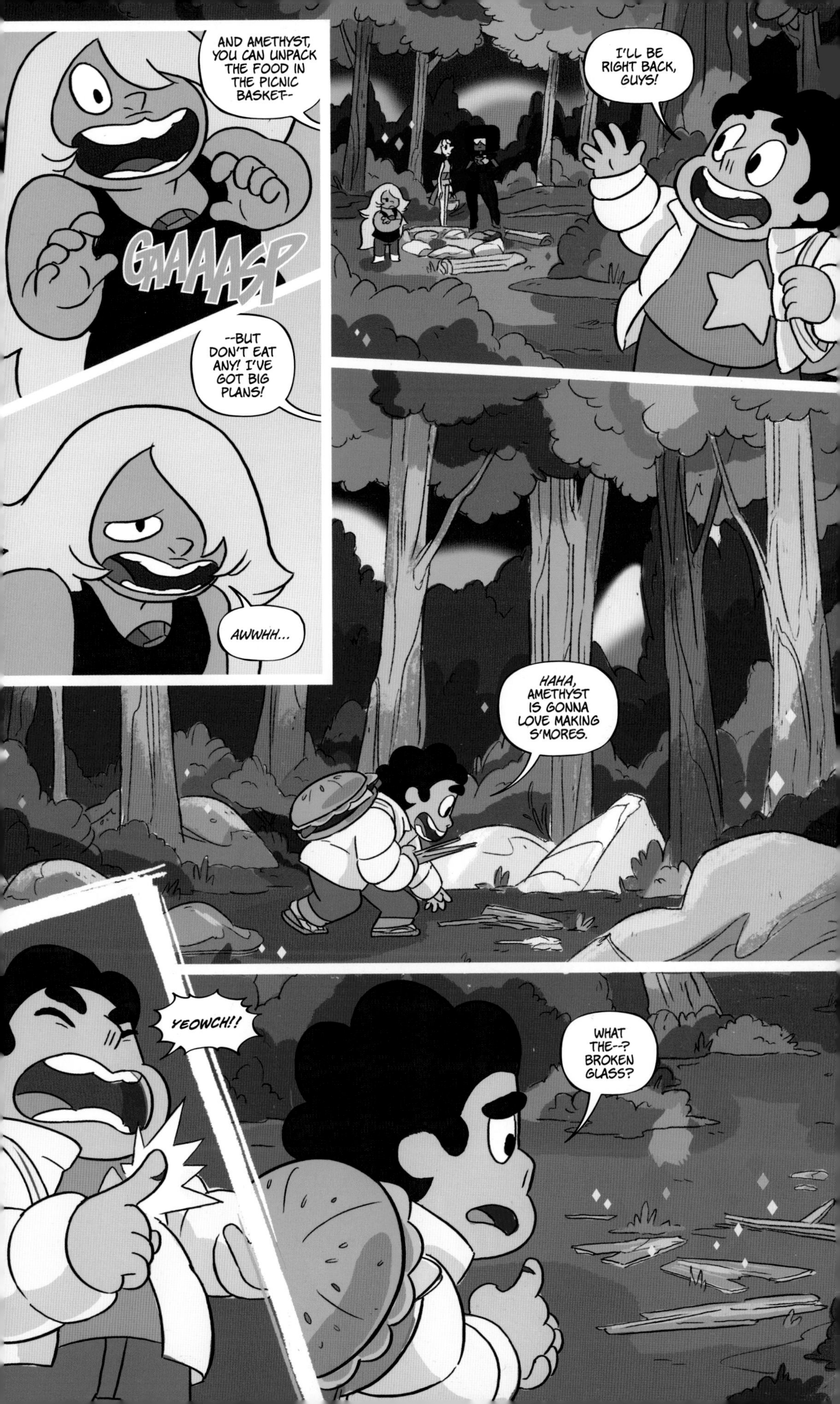
AND AMETHYST, YOU CAN UNPACK THE FOOD IN THE PICNIC BASKET--
GAAAASP
--BUT DON'T EAT ANY! I'VE GOT BIG PLANS!
AWWHH...
I'LL BE RIGHT BACK, GUYS!
HAHA, AMETHYST IS GONNA LOVE MAKING S'MORES.
YEOWCH!!
WHAT THE--? BROKEN GLASS?

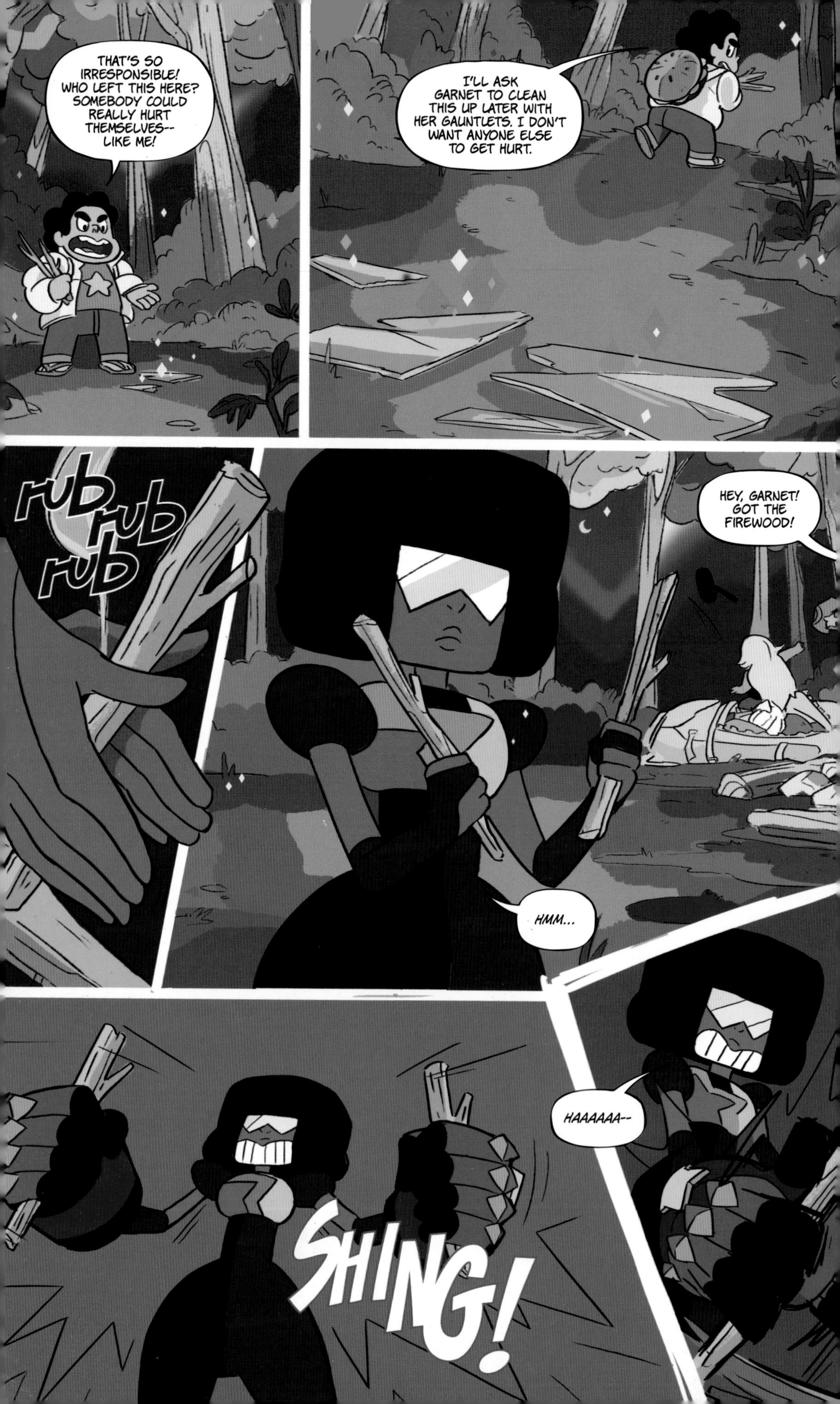
THAT'S SO IRRESPONSIBLE! WHO LEFT THIS HERE? SOMEBODY COULD REALLY HURT THEMSELVES-- LIKE ME!
I'LL ASK GARNET TO CLEAN THIS UP LATER WITH HER GAUNTLETS. I DON'T WANT ANYONE ELSE TO GET HURT.
rub rub rub
HEY, GARNET! GOT THE FIREWOOD!
HMM...
HAAAAAA--
SHING!

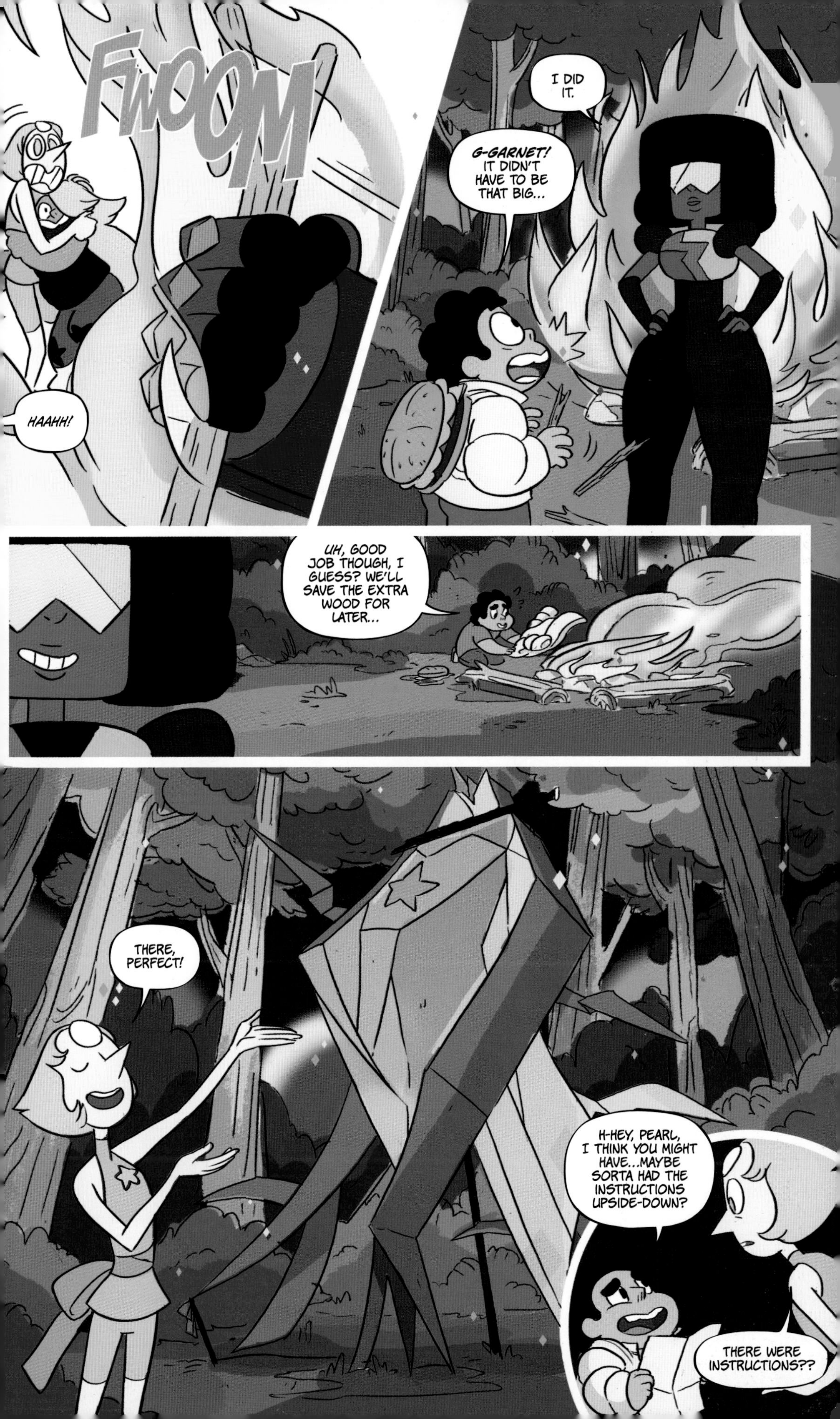
FWOOM
HAAHH!
I DID IT.
G-GARNET! IT DIDN'T HAVE TO BE THAT BIG...
UH, GOOD JOB THOUGH, I GUESS? WE'LL SAVE THE EXTRA WOOD FOR LATER...
THERE, PERFECT!
H-HEY, PEARL, I THINK YOU MIGHT HAVE...MAYBE SORTA HAD THE INSTRUCTIONS UPSIDE-DOWN?
THERE WERE INSTRUCTIONS??

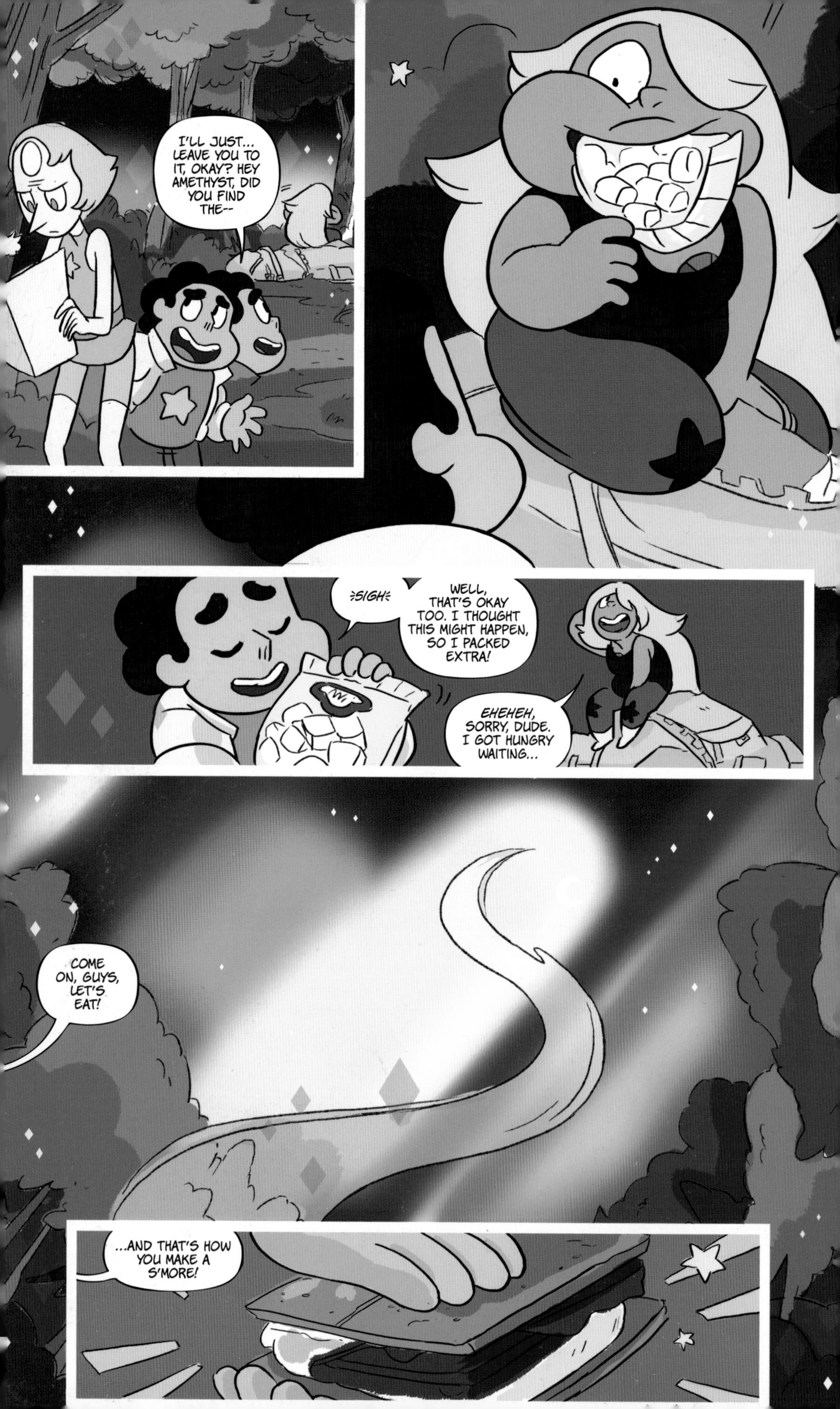

I'LL JUST... LEAVE YOU TO IT, OKAY? HEY AMETHYST, DID YOU FIND THE--
≈SIGH≈
WELL, THAT'S OKAY TOO. I THOUGHT THIS MIGHT HAPPEN, SO I PACKED EXTRA!
EHEHEH, SORRY, DUDE. I GOT HUNGRY WAITING...
COME ON, GUYS, LET'S EAT!
...AND THAT'S HOW YOU MAKE A S'MORE!

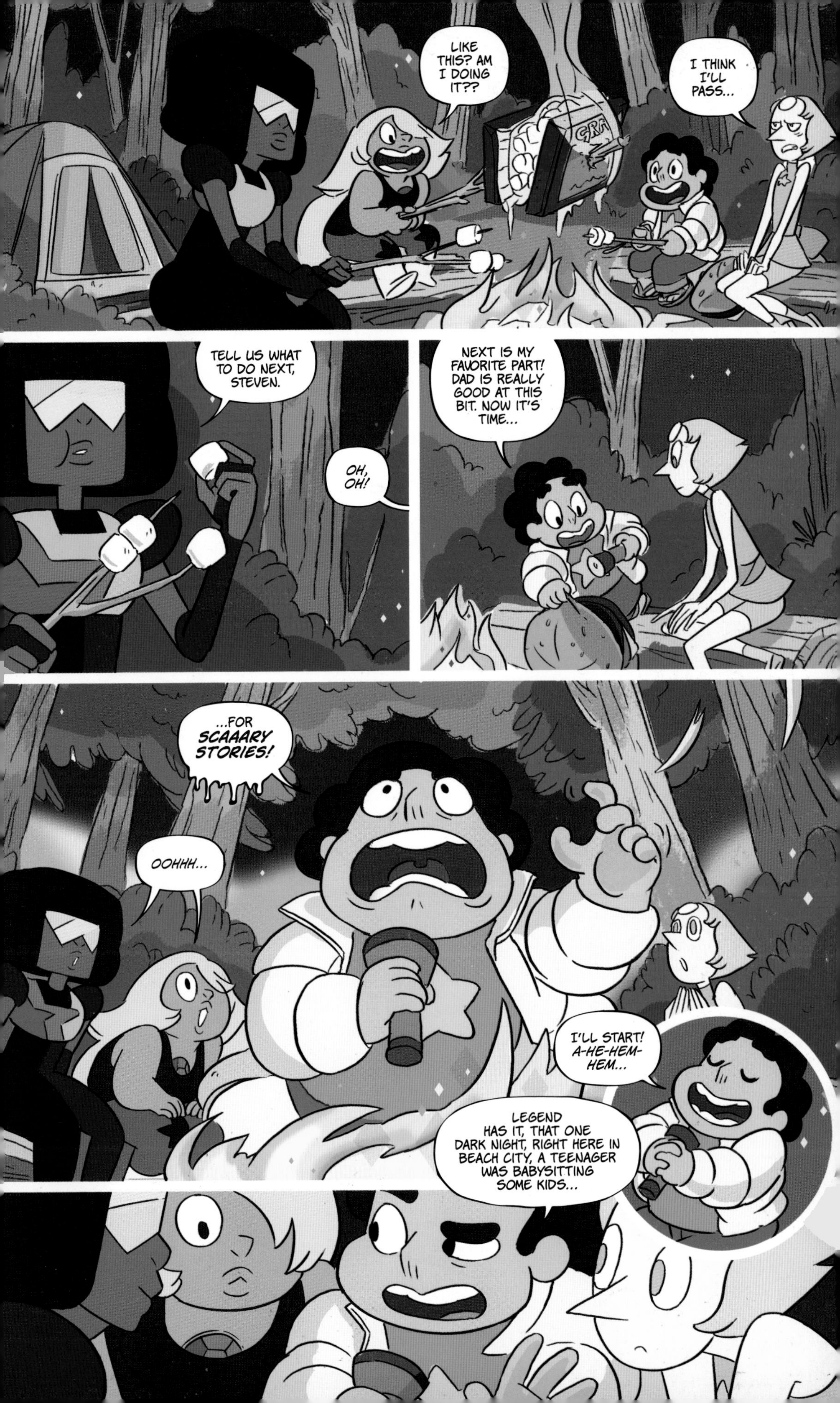

LIKE THIS? AM I DOING IT??
I THINK I'LL PASS...
TELL US WHAT TO DO NEXT, STEVEN.
OH, OH!
NEXT IS MY FAVORITE PART! DAD IS REALLY GOOD AT THIS BIT. NOW IT'S TIME...
...FOR SCAAARY STORIES!
OOHHH...
I'LL START! A-HE-HEM-HEM...
LEGEND HAS IT, THAT ONE DARK NIGHT, RIGHT HERE IN BEACH CITY, A TEENAGER WAS BABYSITTING SOME KIDS...

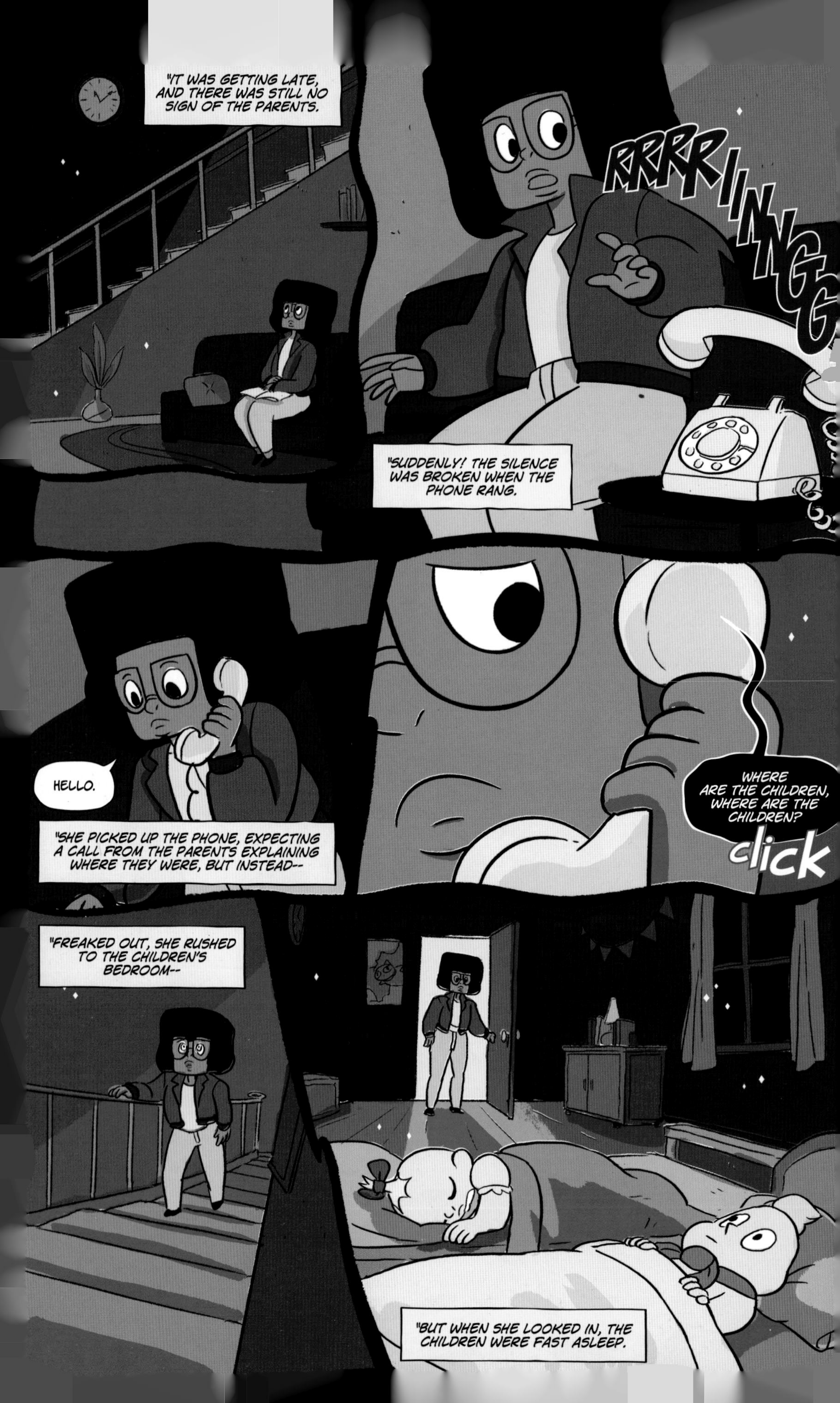
"IT WAS GETTING LATE, AND THERE WAS STILL NO SIGN OF THE PARENTS.
RRRRIINNGG
"SUDDENLY! THE SILENCE WAS BROKEN WHEN THE PHONE RANG.
HELLO.
"SHE PICKED UP THE PHONE, EXPECTING A CALL FROM THE PARENTS EXPLAINING WHERE THEY WERE, BUT INSTEAD--
WHERE ARE THE CHILDREN, WHERE ARE THE CHILDREN?
click
"FREAKED OUT, SHE RUSHED TO THE CHILDREN'S BEDROOM--
"BUT WHEN SHE LOOKED IN, THE CHILDREN WERE FAST ASLEEP.

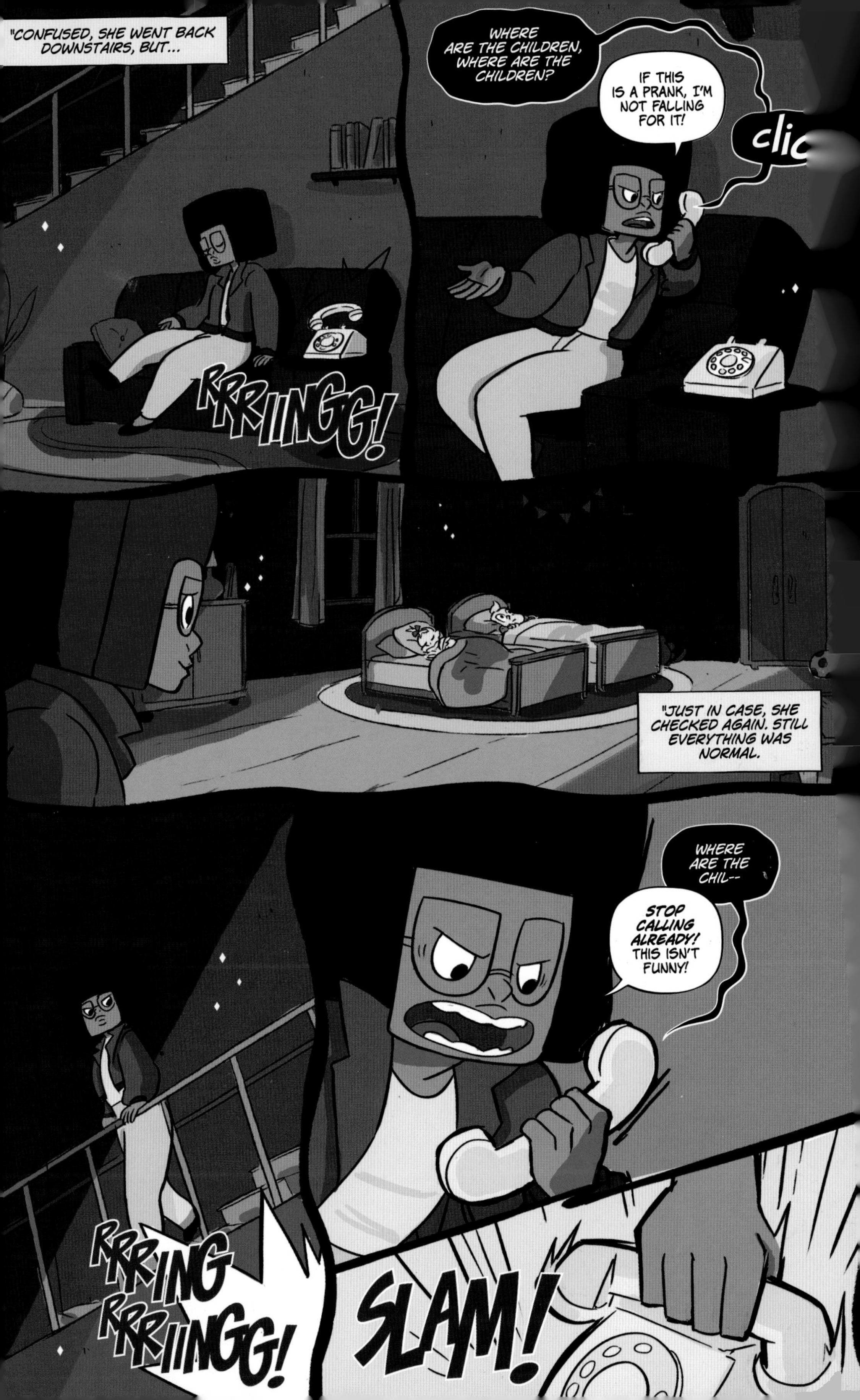
"CONFUSED, SHE WENT BACK DOWNSTAIRS, BUT...
RRRIINGG!
WHERE ARE THE CHILDREN, WHERE ARE THE CHILDREN?
IF THIS IS A PRANK, I'M NOT FALLING FOR IT!
"JUST IN CASE, SHE CHECKED AGAIN. STILL EVERYTHING WAS NORMAL.
RRRING RRRIINGG!
WHERE ARE THE CHIL--
STOP CALLING ALREADY! THIS ISN'T FUNNY!
SLAM!

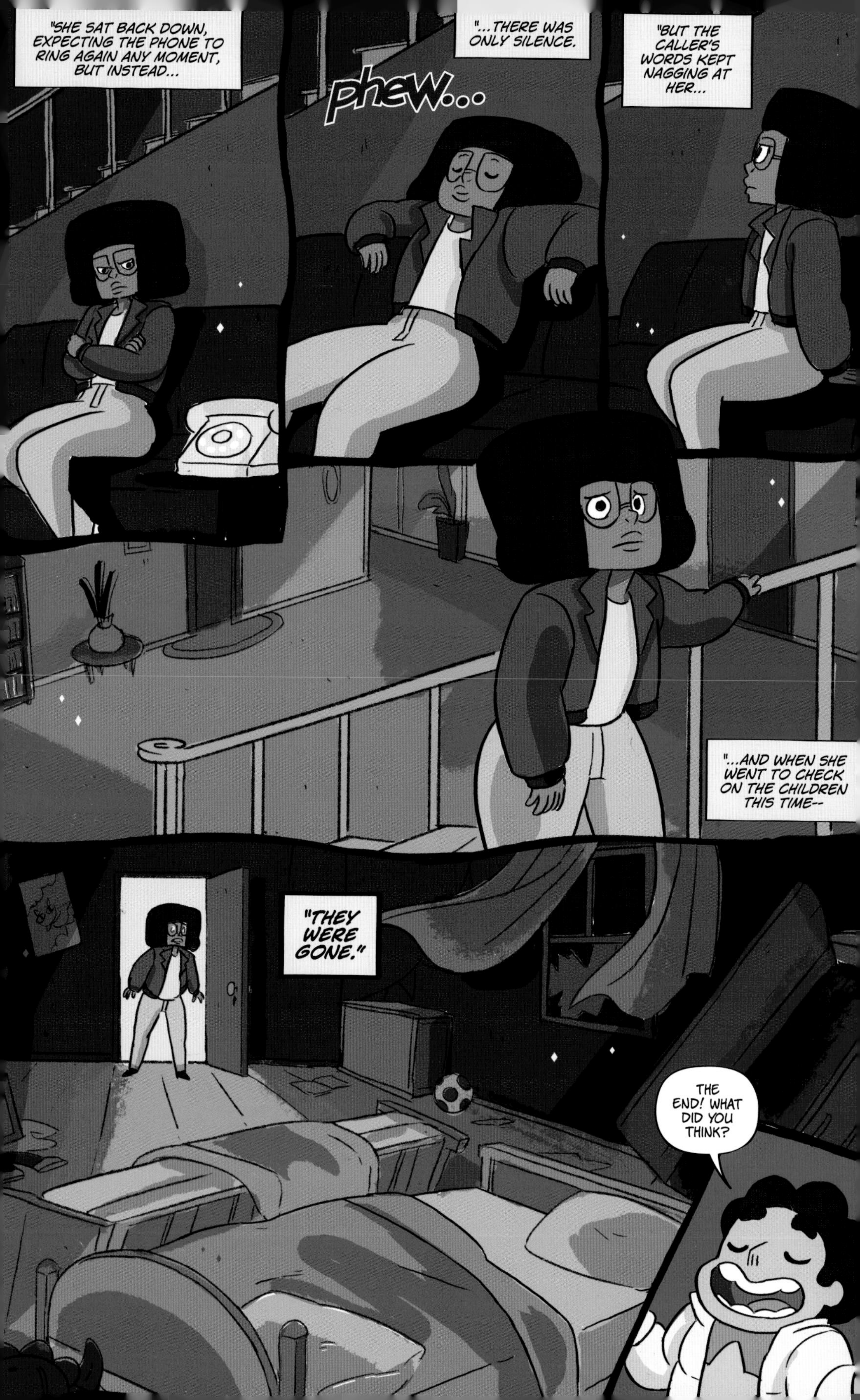
"SHE SAT BACK DOWN, EXPECTING THE PHONE TO RING AGAIN ANY MOMENT, BUT INSTEAD...
"...THERE WAS ONLY SILENCE.
phew...
"BUT THE CALLER'S WORDS KEPT NAGGING AT HER...
"...AND WHEN SHE WENT TO CHECK ON THE CHILDREN THIS TIME--
"THEY WERE GONE."
THE END! WHAT DID YOU THINK?

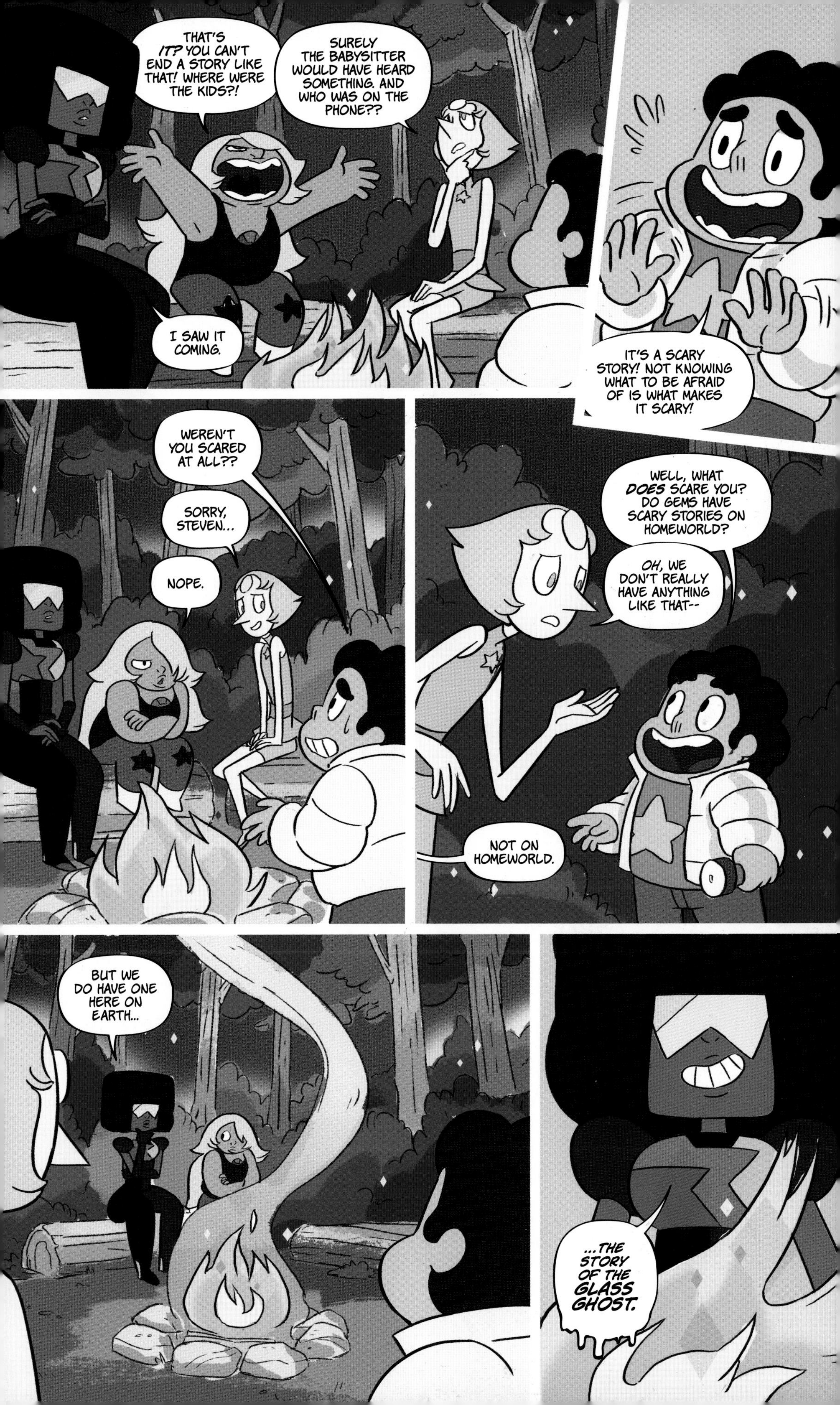
THAT'S *IT?* YOU CAN'T END A STORY LIKE THAT! WHERE WERE THE KIDS?!
SURELY THE BABYSITTER WOULD HAVE HEARD SOMETHING. AND WHO WAS ON THE PHONE??
I SAW IT COMING.
IT'S A SCARY STORY! NOT KNOWING WHAT TO BE AFRAID OF IS WHAT MAKES IT SCARY!
WEREN'T YOU SCARED AT ALL??
SORRY, STEVEN...
NOPE.
WELL, WHAT *DOES* SCARE YOU? DO GEMS HAVE SCARY STORIES ON HOMEWORLD?
OH, WE DON'T REALLY HAVE ANYTHING LIKE THAT--
NOT ON HOMEWORLD.
BUT WE DO HAVE ONE HERE ON EARTH...
...THE STORY OF THE GLASS GHOST.

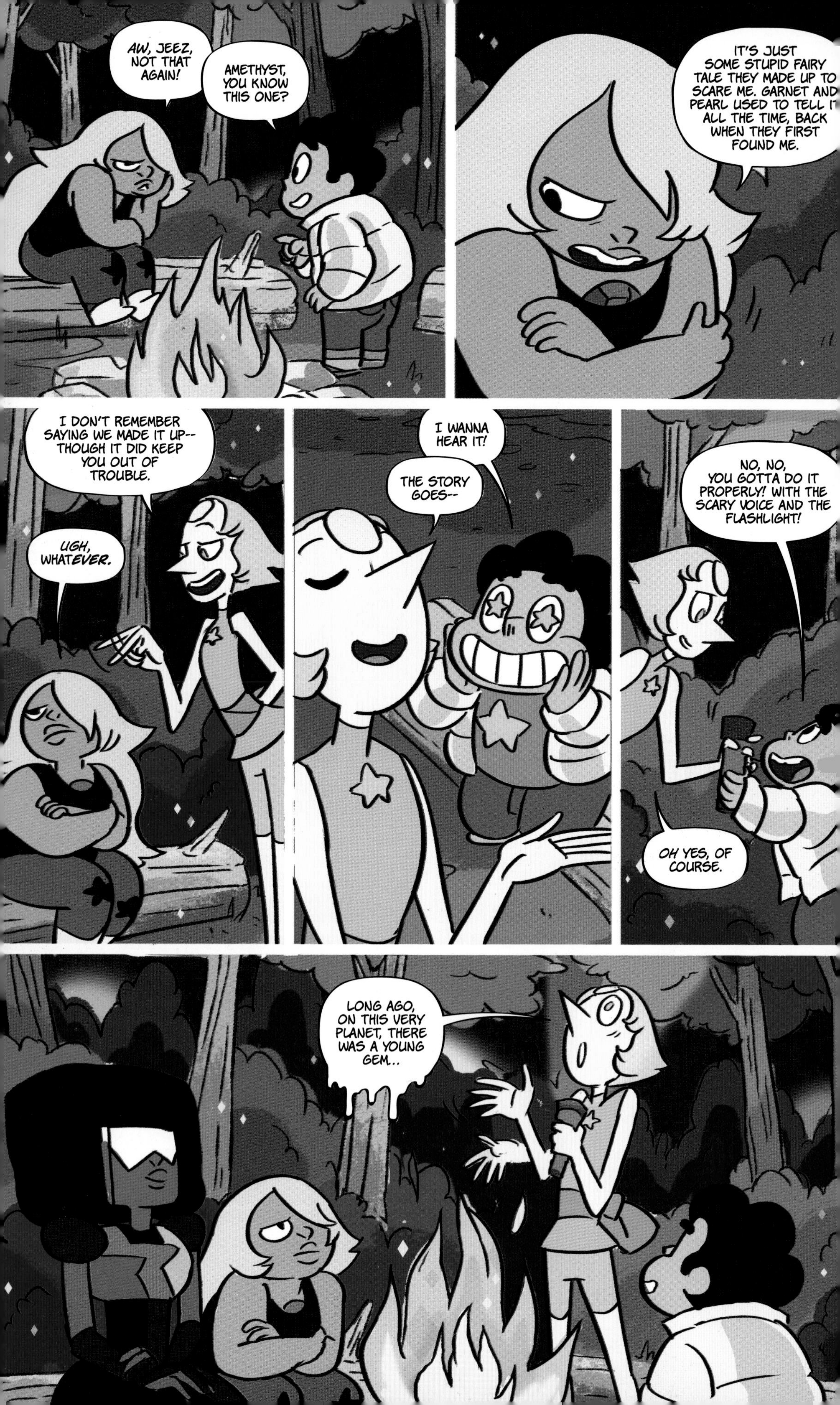
AW, JEEZ, NOT THAT AGAIN!
AMETHYST, YOU KNOW THIS ONE?
IT'S JUST SOME STUPID FAIRY TALE THEY MADE UP TO SCARE ME. GARNET AND PEARL USED TO TELL IT ALL THE TIME, BACK WHEN THEY FIRST FOUND ME.
I DON'T REMEMBER SAYING WE MADE IT UP-- THOUGH IT DID KEEP YOU OUT OF TROUBLE.
UGH, WHATEVER.
I WANNA HEAR IT!
THE STORY GOES--
NO, NO, YOU GOTTA DO IT PROPERLY! WITH THE SCARY VOICE AND THE FLASHLIGHT!
OH YES, OF COURSE.
LONG AGO, ON THIS VERY PLANET, THERE WAS A YOUNG GEM...

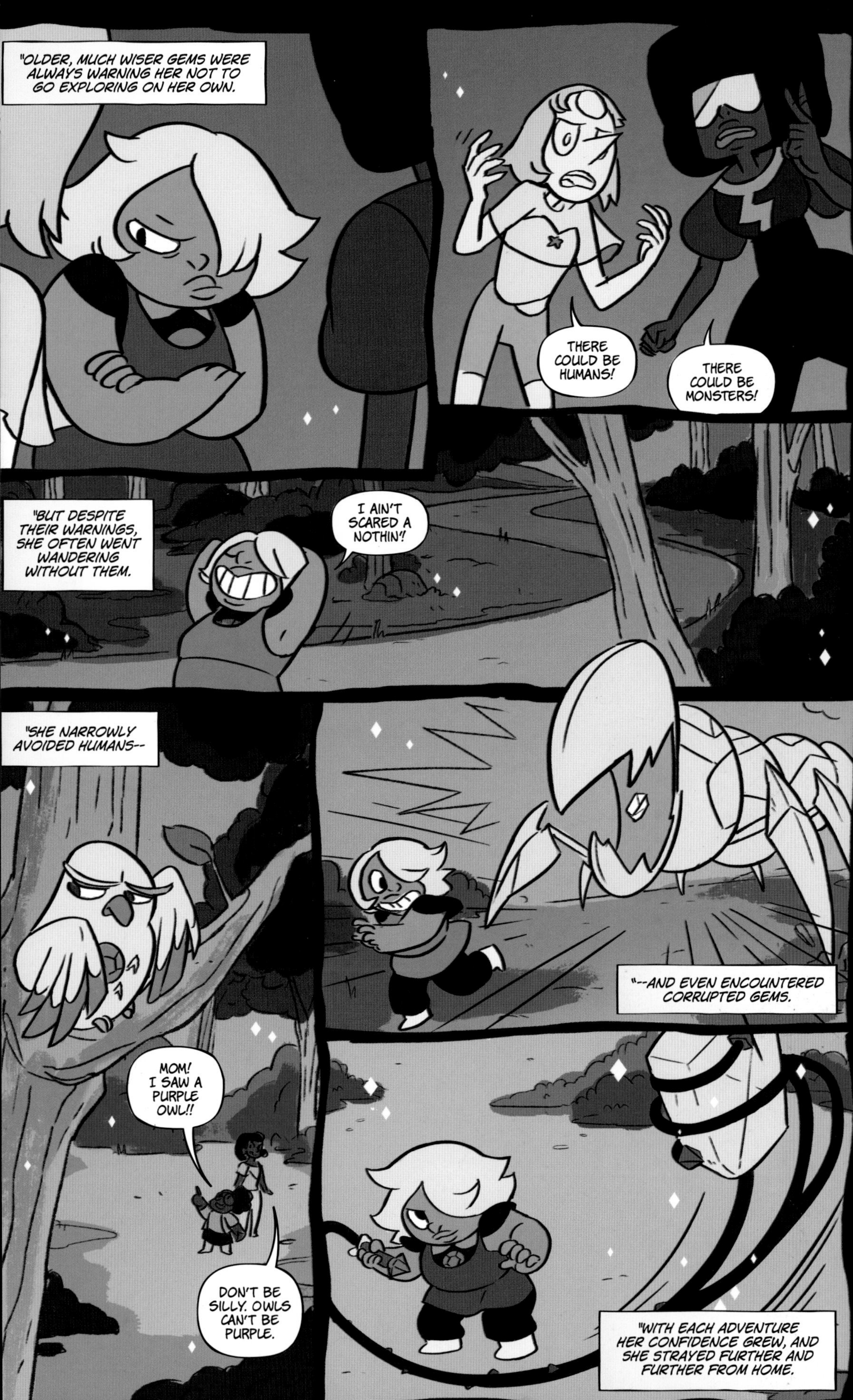
"OLDER, MUCH WISER GEMS WERE ALWAYS WARNING HER NOT TO GO EXPLORING ON HER OWN.
THERE COULD BE HUMANS!
THERE COULD BE MONSTERS!
"BUT DESPITE THEIR WARNINGS, SHE OFTEN WENT WANDERING WITHOUT THEM.
I AIN'T SCARED A NOTHIN'!
"SHE NARROWLY AVOIDED HUMANS--
MOM! I SAW A PURPLE OWL!!
DON'T BE SILLY. OWLS CAN'T BE PURPLE.
"--AND EVEN ENCOUNTERED CORRUPTED GEMS.
"WITH EACH ADVENTURE HER CONFIDENCE GREW, AND SHE STRAYED FURTHER AND FURTHER FROM HOME.

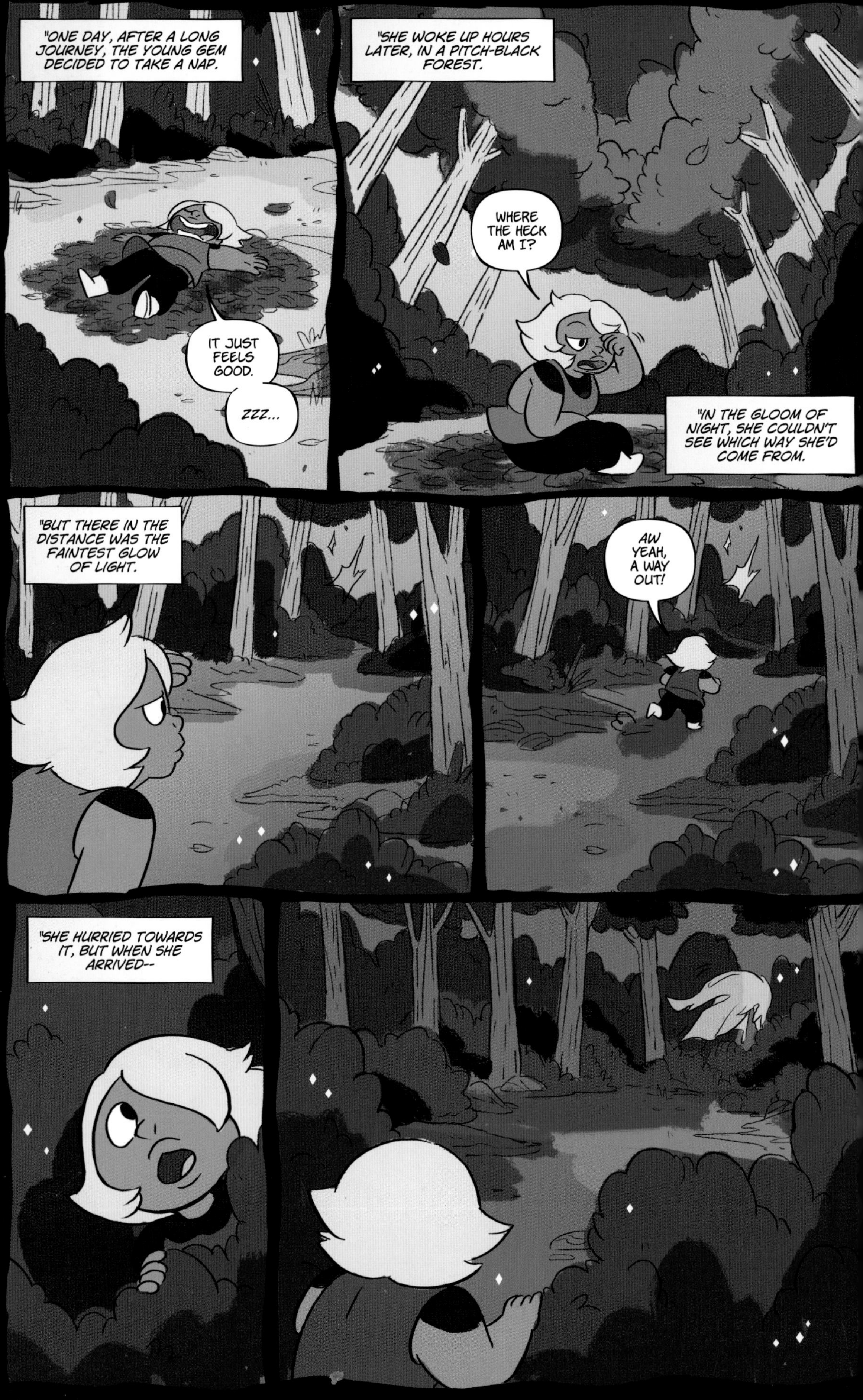

"ONE DAY, AFTER A LONG JOURNEY, THE YOUNG GEM DECIDED TO TAKE A NAP.
IT JUST FEELS GOOD.
ZZZ...
"SHE WOKE UP HOURS LATER, IN A PITCH-BLACK FOREST.
WHERE THE HECK AM I?
"IN THE GLOOM OF NIGHT, SHE COULDN'T SEE WHICH WAY SHE'D COME FROM.
"BUT THERE IN THE DISTANCE WAS THE FAINTEST GLOW OF LIGHT.
AW YEAH, A WAY OUT!
"SHE HURRIED TOWARDS IT, BUT WHEN SHE ARRIVED--

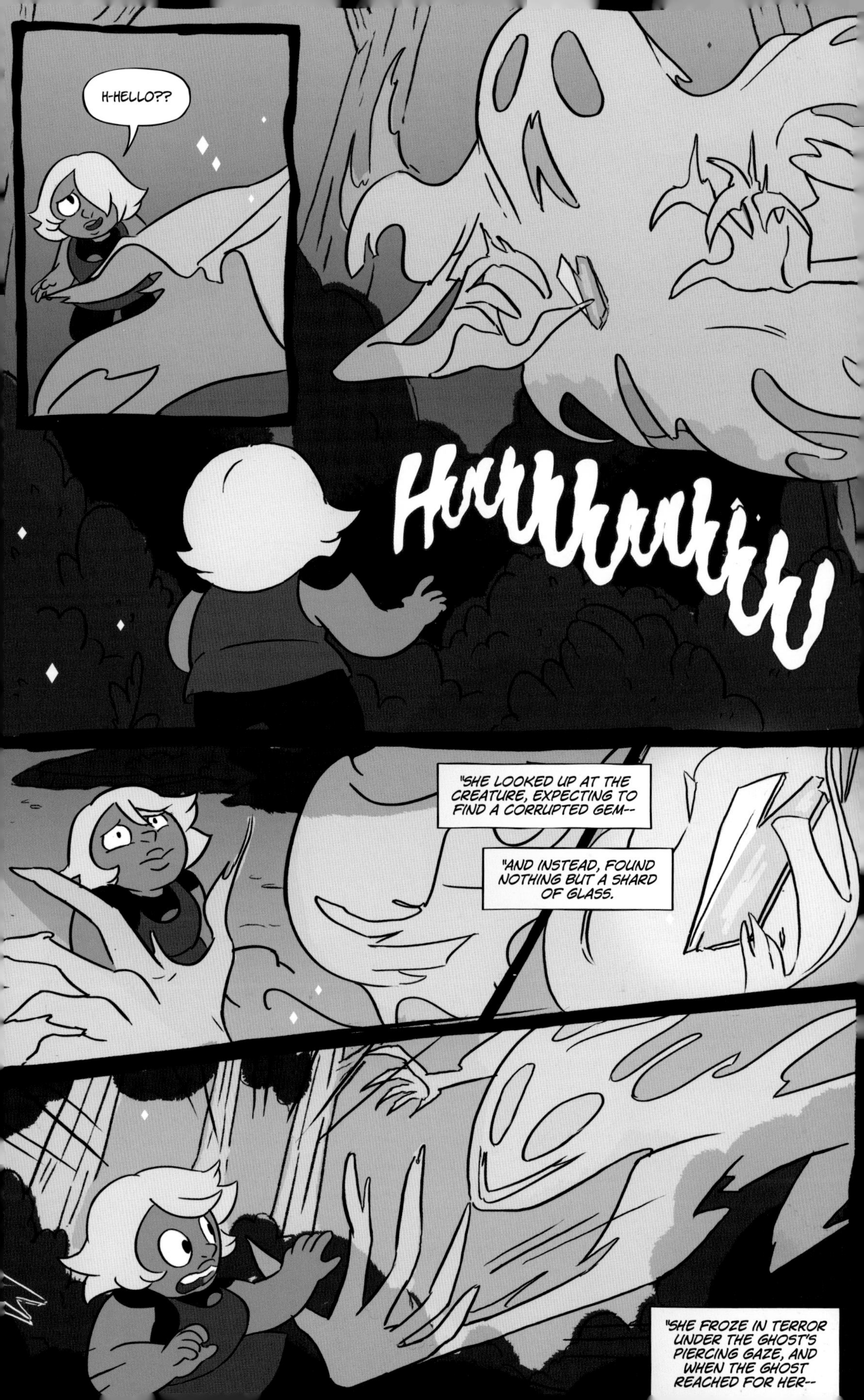
H-HELLO??
Hrrrhhhhhhhw
"SHE LOOKED UP AT THE CREATURE, EXPECTING TO FIND A CORRUPTED GEM--
"AND INSTEAD, FOUND NOTHING BUT A SHARD OF GLASS.
"SHE FROZE IN TERROR UNDER THE GHOST'S PIERCING GAZE, AND WHEN THE GHOST REACHED FOR HER--

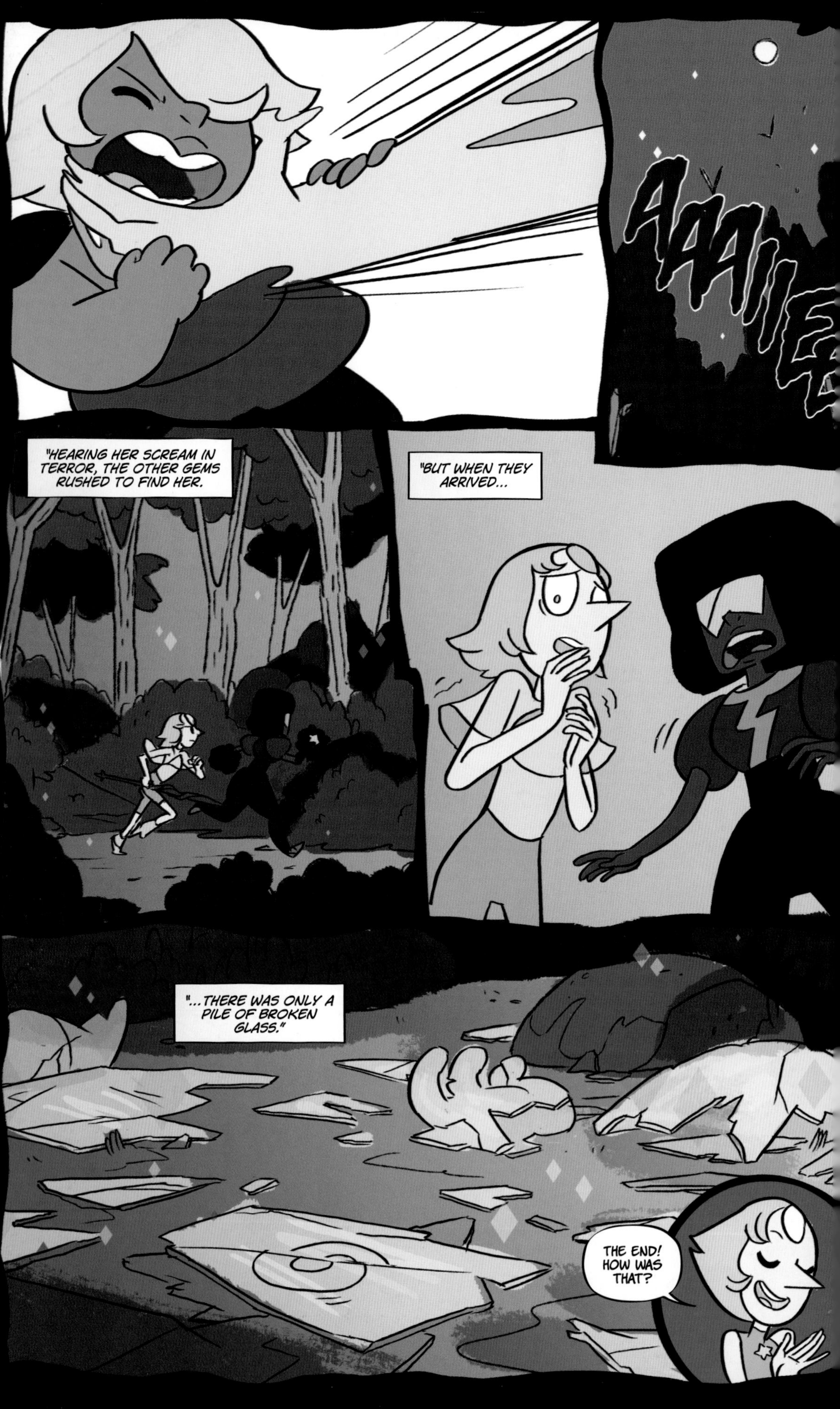
AAAIIEE
"HEARING HER SCREAM IN TERROR, THE OTHER GEMS RUSHED TO FIND HER.
"BUT WHEN THEY ARRIVED...
"...THERE WAS ONLY A PILE OF BROKEN GLASS."
THE END! HOW WAS THAT?

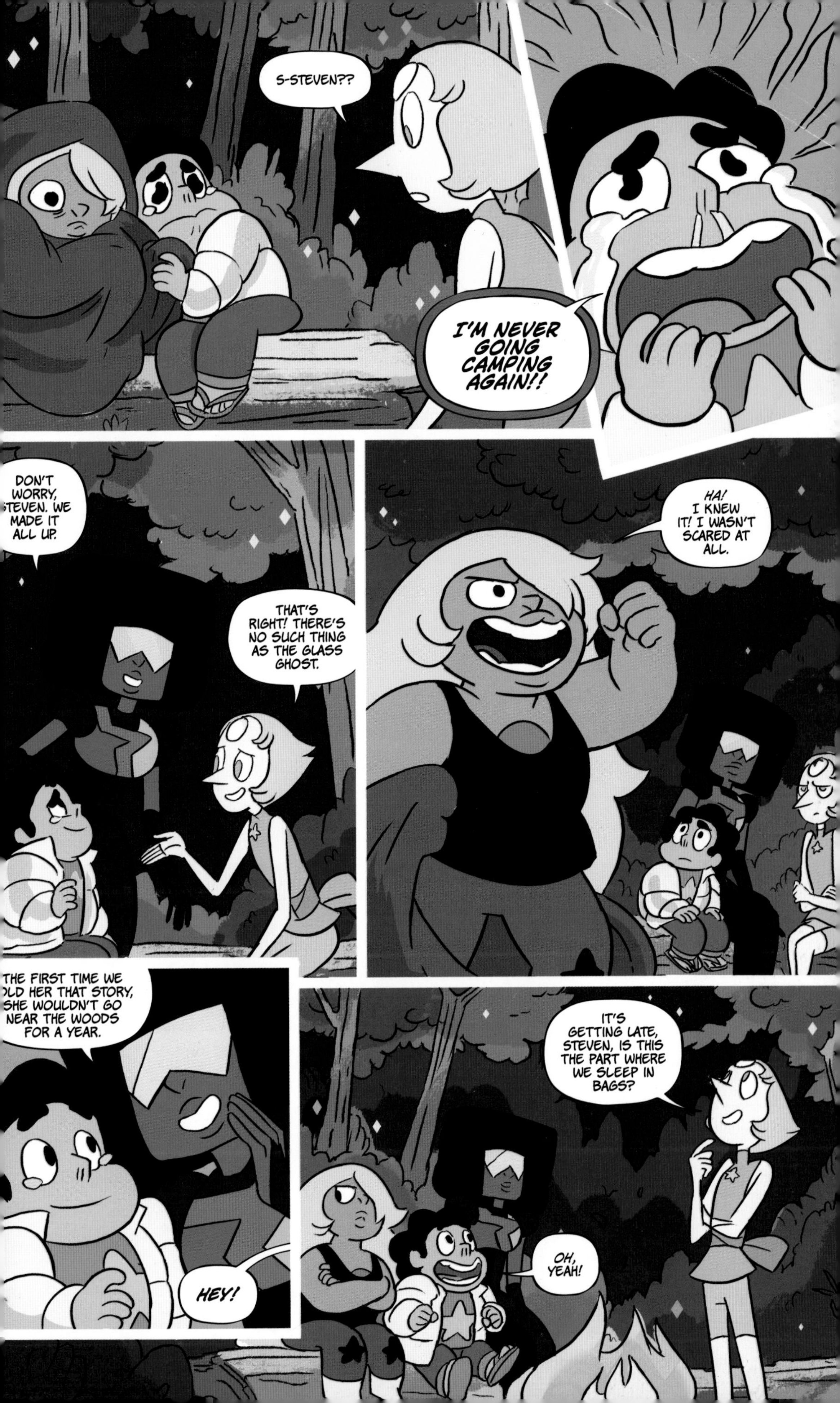
S-STEVEN??
I'M NEVER GOING CAMPING AGAIN!!
DON'T WORRY, STEVEN. WE MADE IT ALL UP.
THAT'S RIGHT! THERE'S NO SUCH THING AS THE GLASS GHOST.
HA! I KNEW IT! I WASN'T SCARED AT ALL.
THE FIRST TIME WE TOLD HER THAT STORY, SHE WOULDN'T GO NEAR THE WOODS FOR A YEAR.
HEY!
IT'S GETTING LATE, STEVEN, IS THIS THE PART WHERE WE SLEEP IN BAGS?
OH, YEAH!

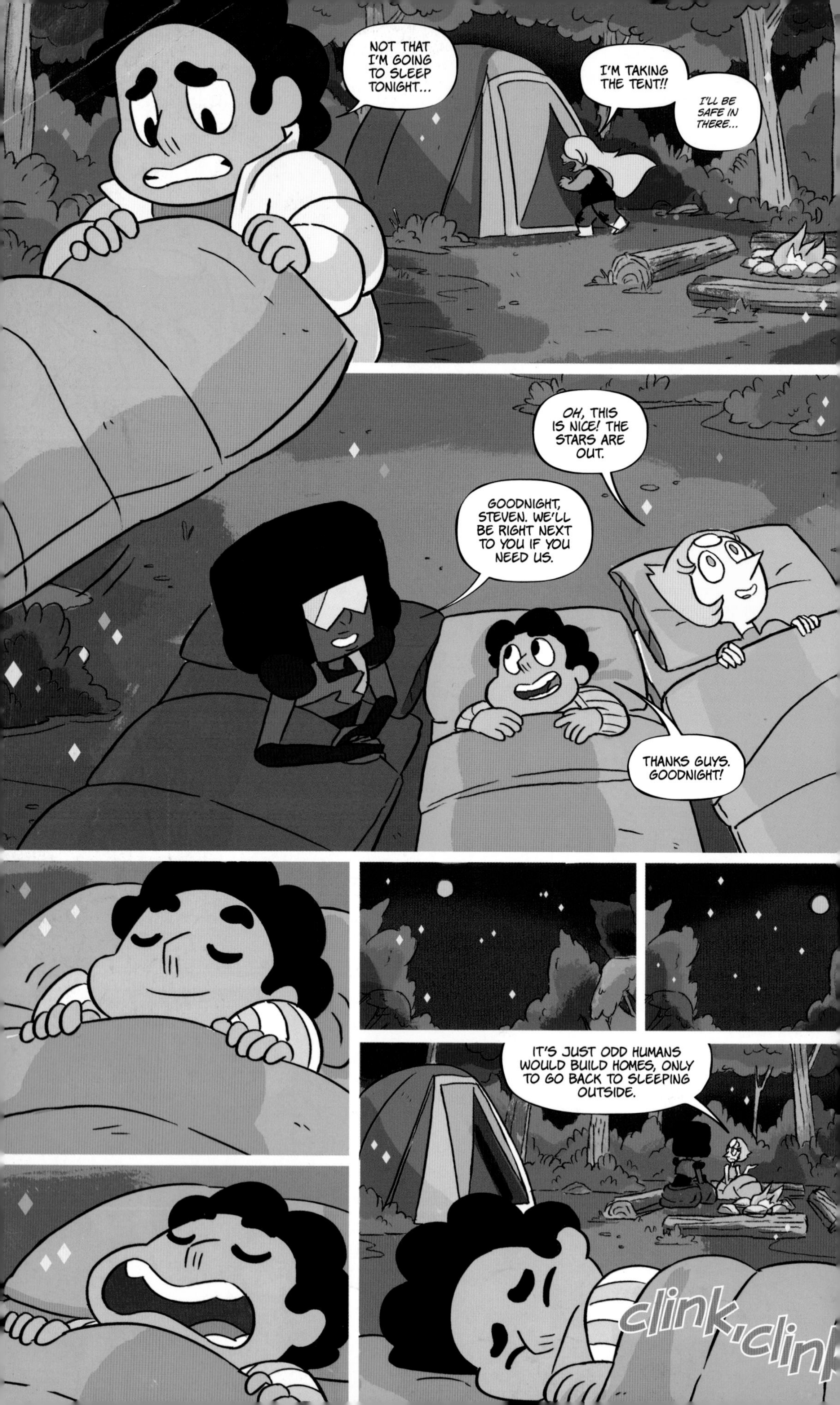
NOT THAT I'M GOING TO SLEEP TONIGHT...
I'M TAKING THE TENT!!
I'LL BE SAFE IN THERE...
OH, THIS IS NICE! THE STARS ARE OUT.
GOODNIGHT, STEVEN. WE'LL BE RIGHT NEXT TO YOU IF YOU NEED US.
THANKS GUYS. GOODNIGHT!
IT'S JUST ODD HUMANS WOULD BUILD HOMES, ONLY TO GO BACK TO SLEEPING OUTSIDE.
clink, clin

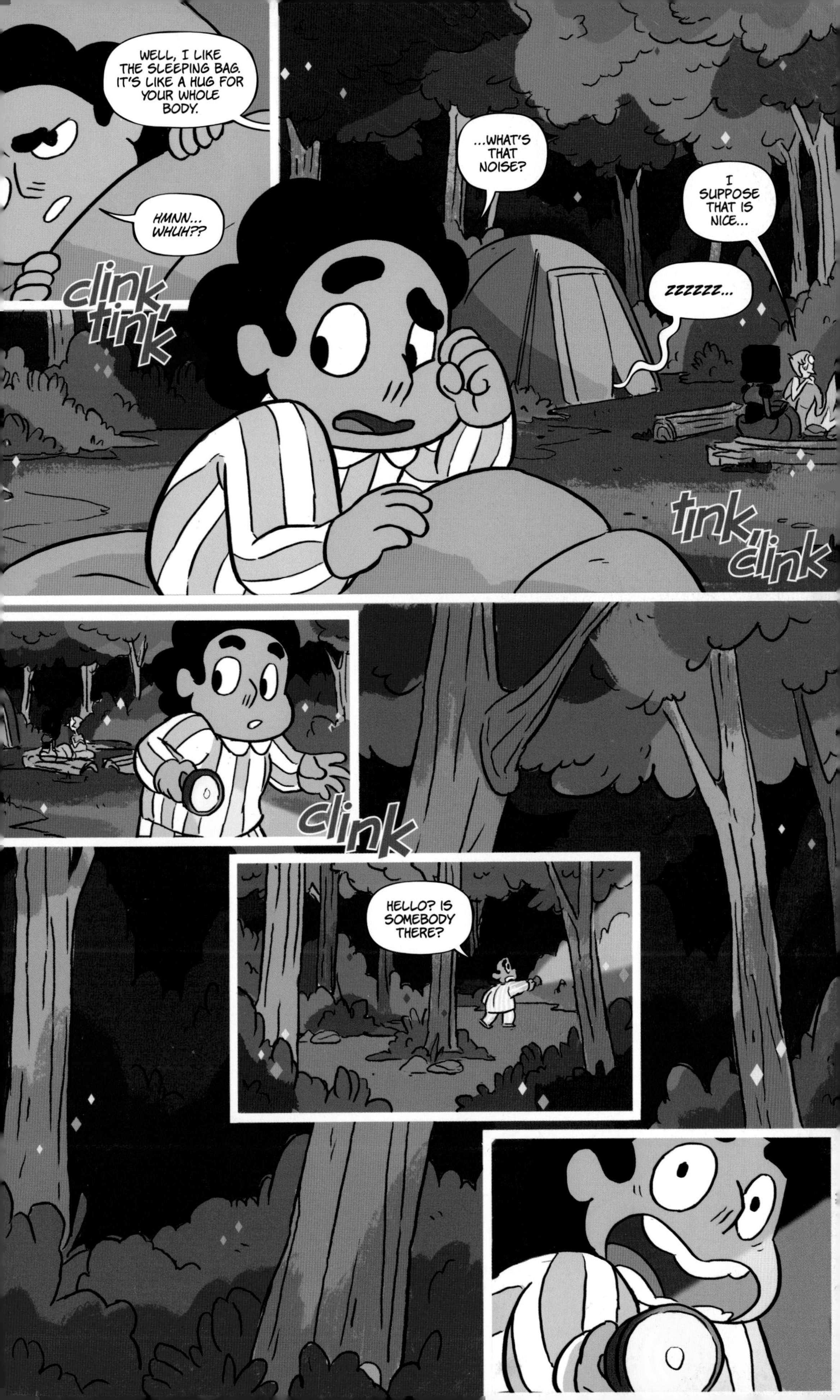
WELL, I LIKE THE SLEEPING BAG. IT'S LIKE A HUG FOR YOUR WHOLE BODY.
HMNN... WHUH??
clink, tink,
...WHAT'S THAT NOISE?
I SUPPOSE THAT IS NICE...
ZZZZZZ...
tink, clink
clink
HELLO? IS SOMEBODY THERE?

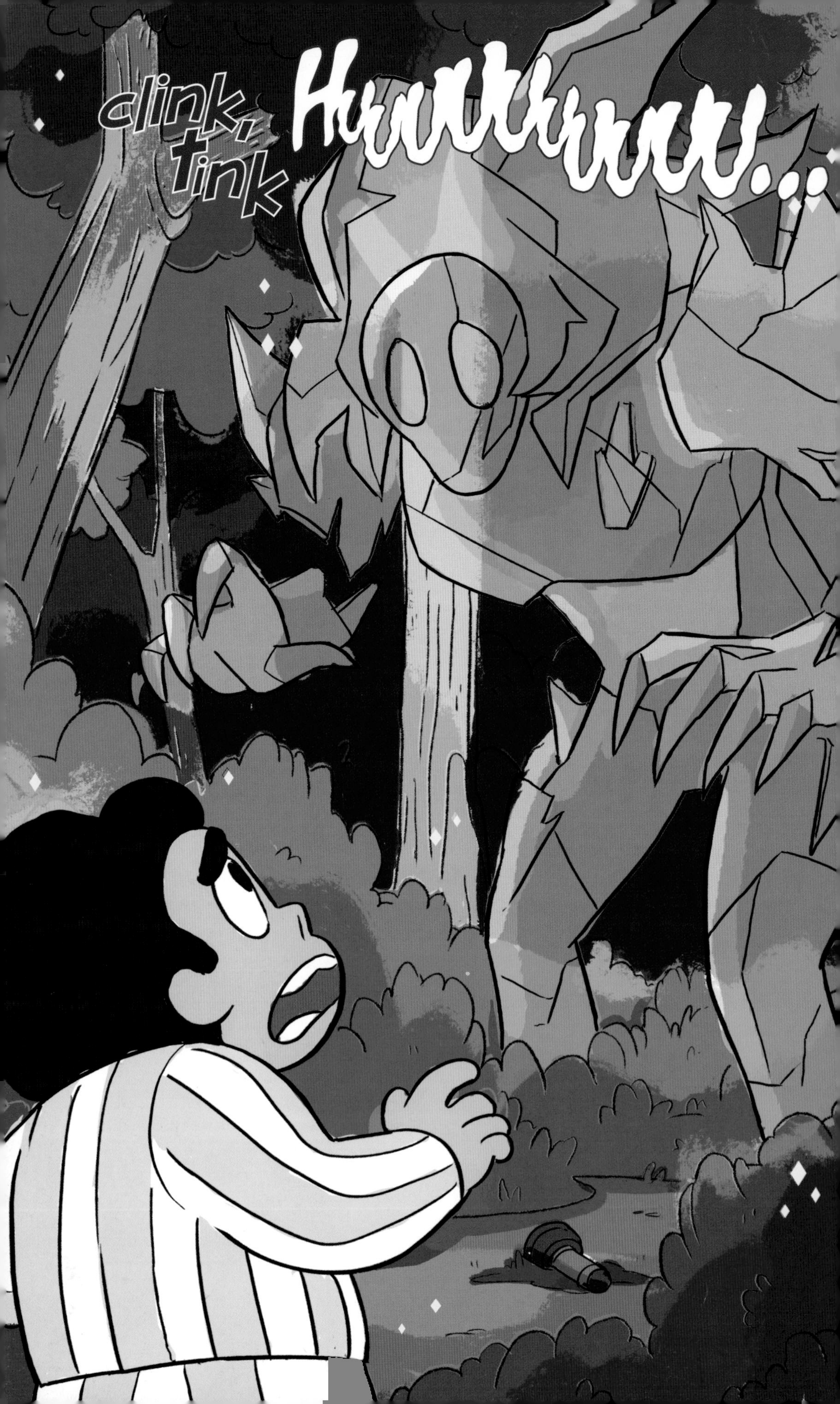
clink, tink
Hrrrhhrrrrr...

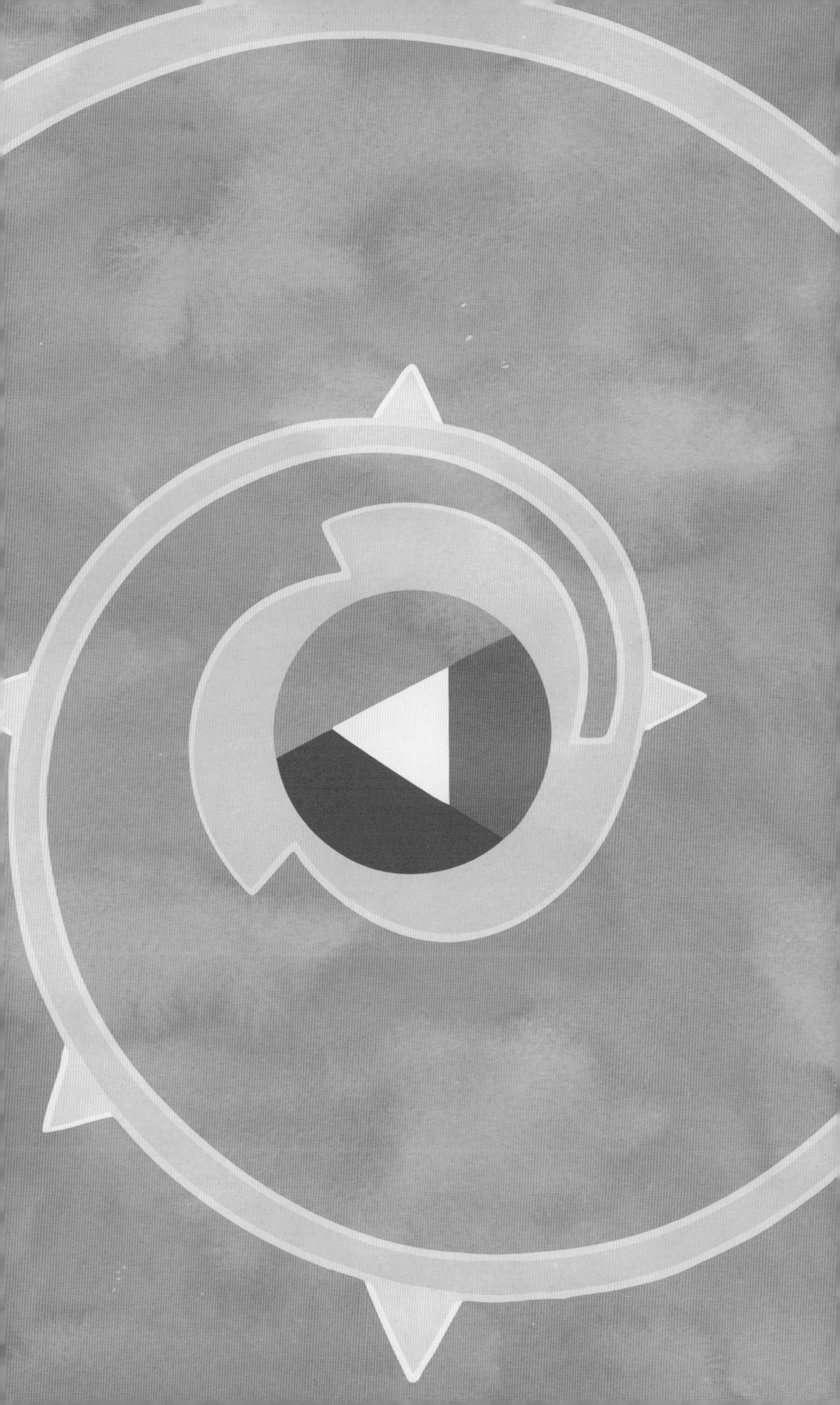

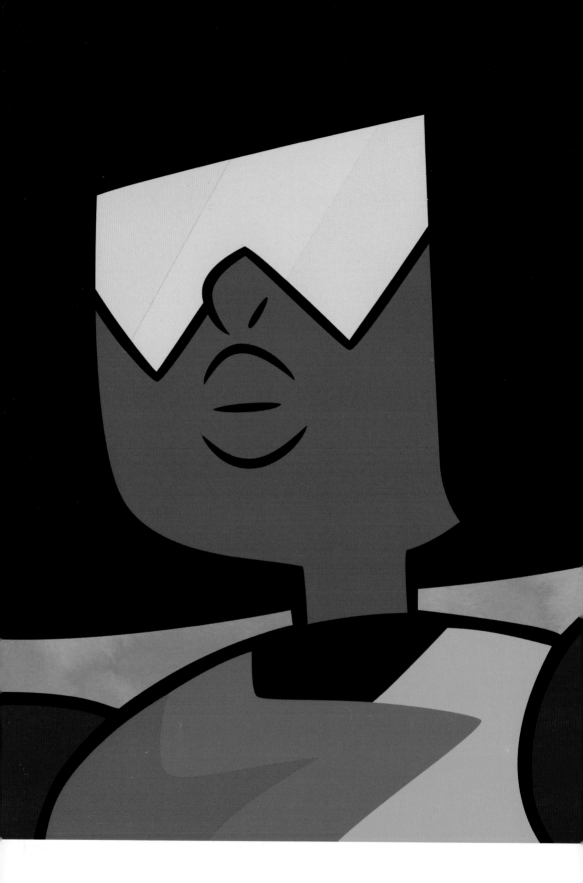

CHAPTER TWO

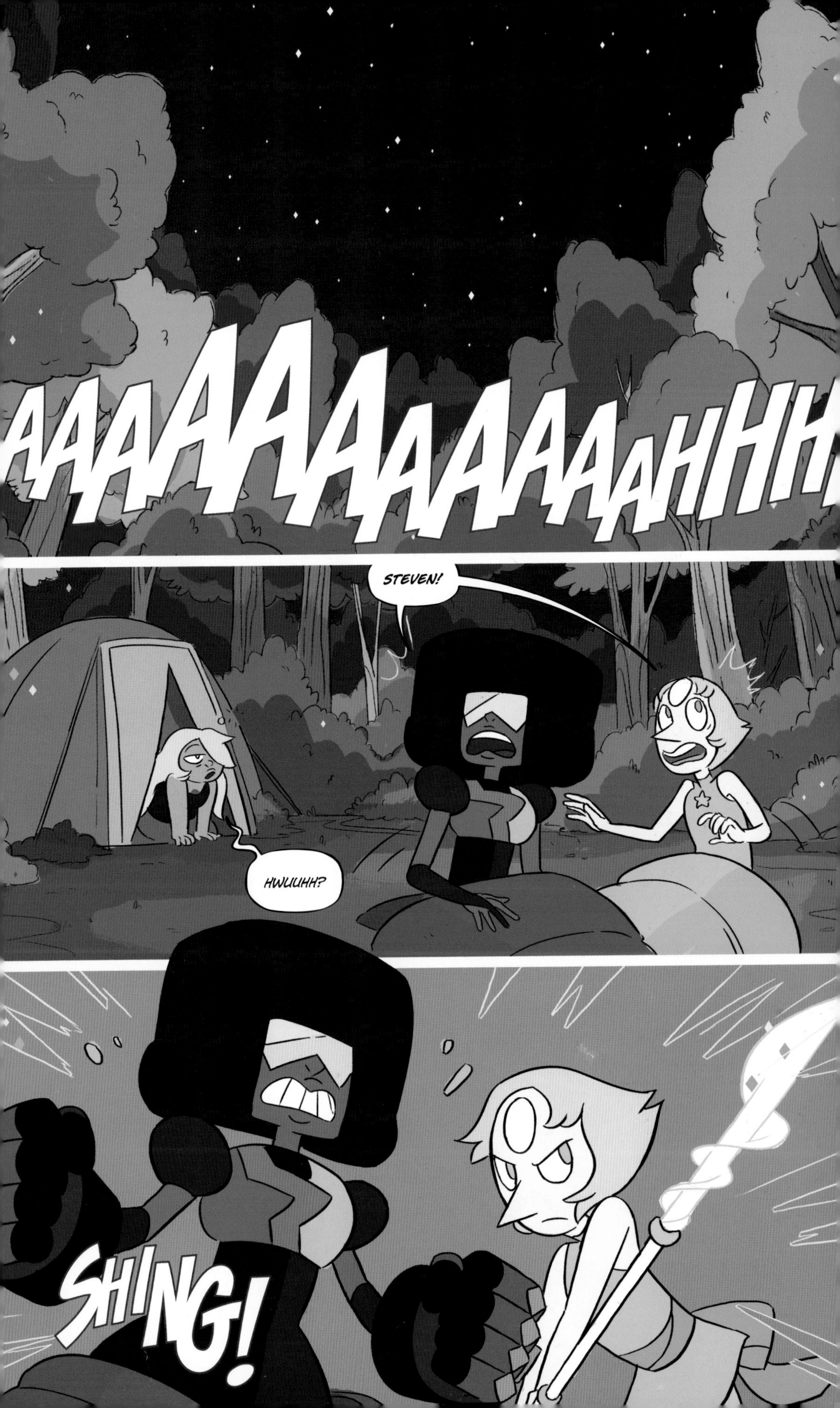

AAAAAAAAAAAAAAAHHHH
STEVEN!
HWUUHH?
SHING!

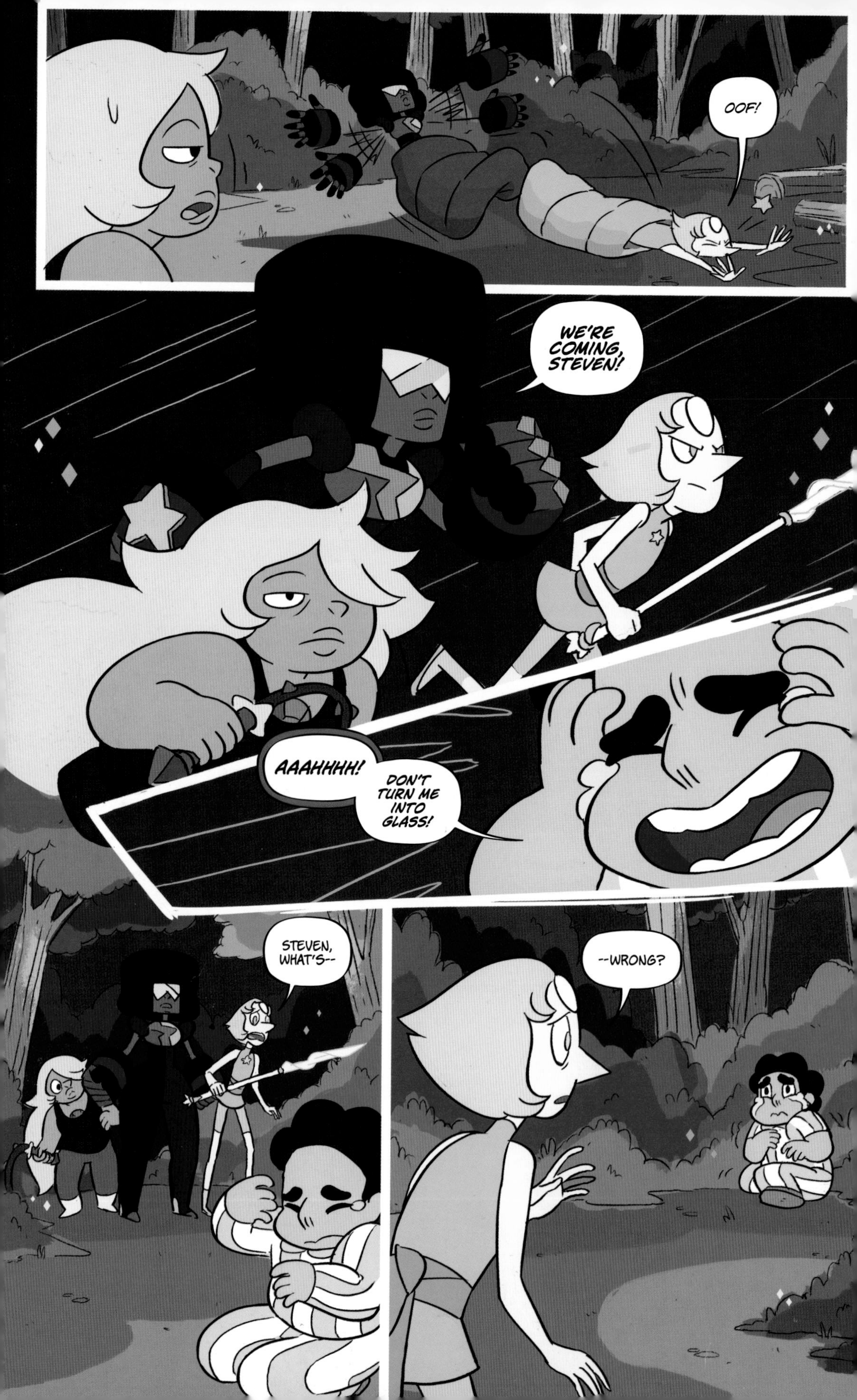
OOF!
WE'RE COMING, STEVEN!
AAAHHHH!
DON'T TURN ME INTO GLASS!
STEVEN, WHAT'S--
--WRONG?

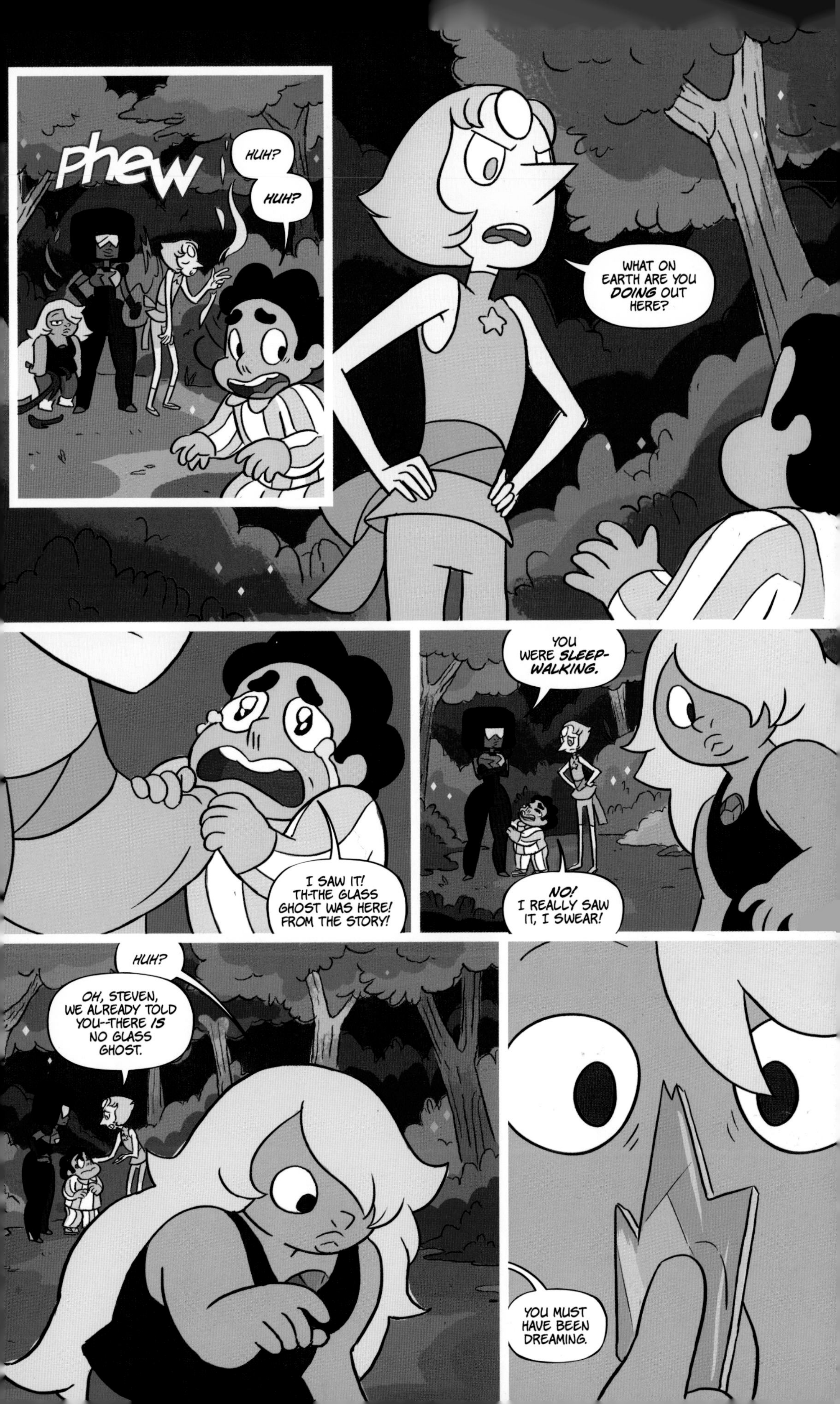

PHEW
HUH?
HUH?
WHAT ON EARTH ARE YOU DOING OUT HERE?
I SAW IT! TH-THE GLASS GHOST WAS HERE! FROM THE STORY!
YOU WERE SLEEP-WALKING.
NO! I REALLY SAW IT, I SWEAR!
HUH?
OH, STEVEN, WE ALREADY TOLD YOU--THERE IS NO GLASS GHOST.
YOU MUST HAVE BEEN DREAMING.

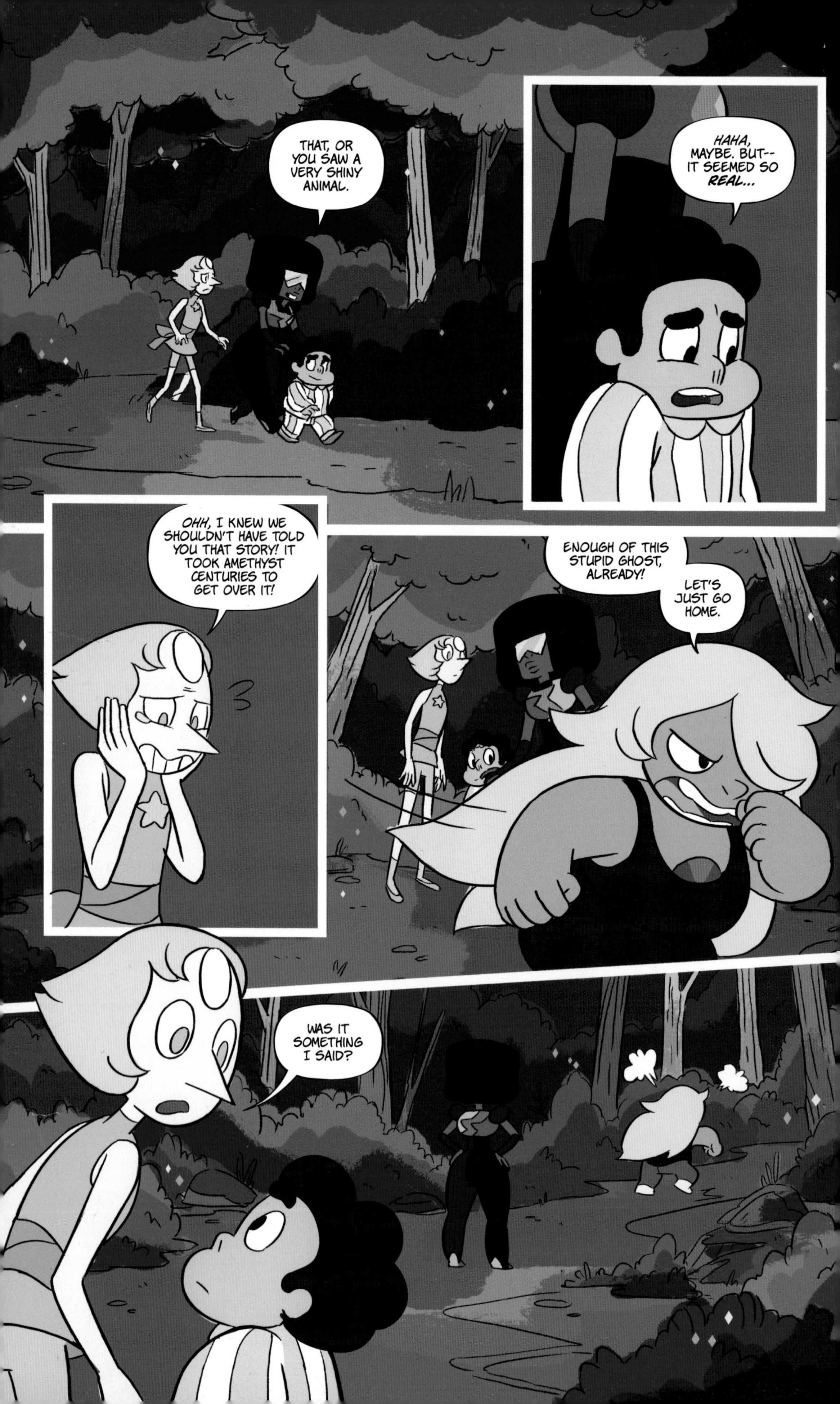
THAT, OR YOU SAW A VERY SHINY ANIMAL.
HAHA, MAYBE. BUT-- IT SEEMED SO ***REAL...***
OHH, I KNEW WE SHOULDN'T HAVE TOLD YOU THAT STORY! IT TOOK AMETHYST CENTURIES TO GET OVER IT!
ENOUGH OF THIS STUPID GHOST, ALREADY!
LET'S JUST GO HOME.
WAS IT SOMETHING I SAID?

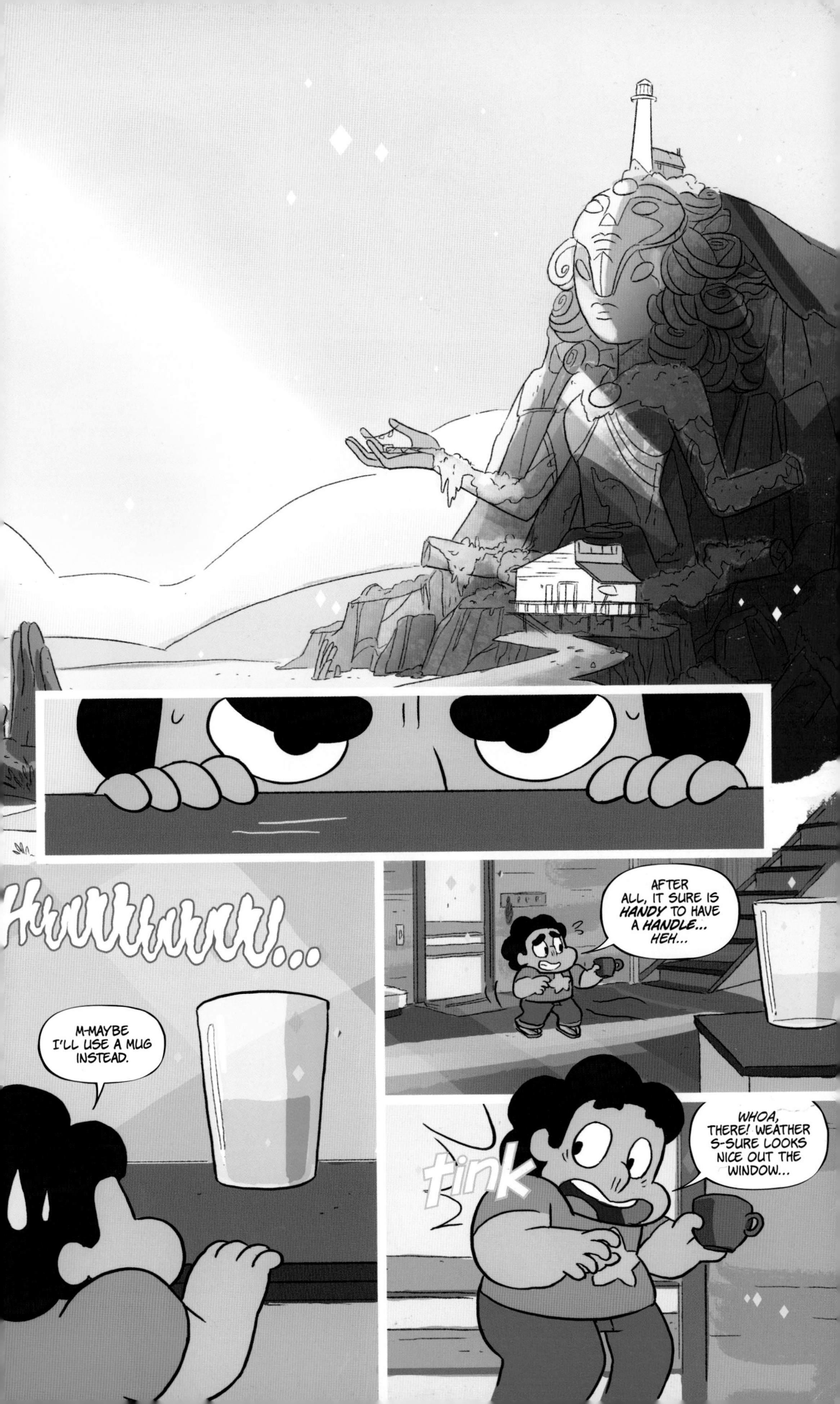

HRRRRRRRRR...
M-MAYBE I'LL USE A MUG INSTEAD.
AFTER ALL, IT SURE IS HANDY TO HAVE A HANDLE... HEH...
tink
WHOA, THERE! WEATHER S-SURE LOOKS NICE OUT THE WINDOW...

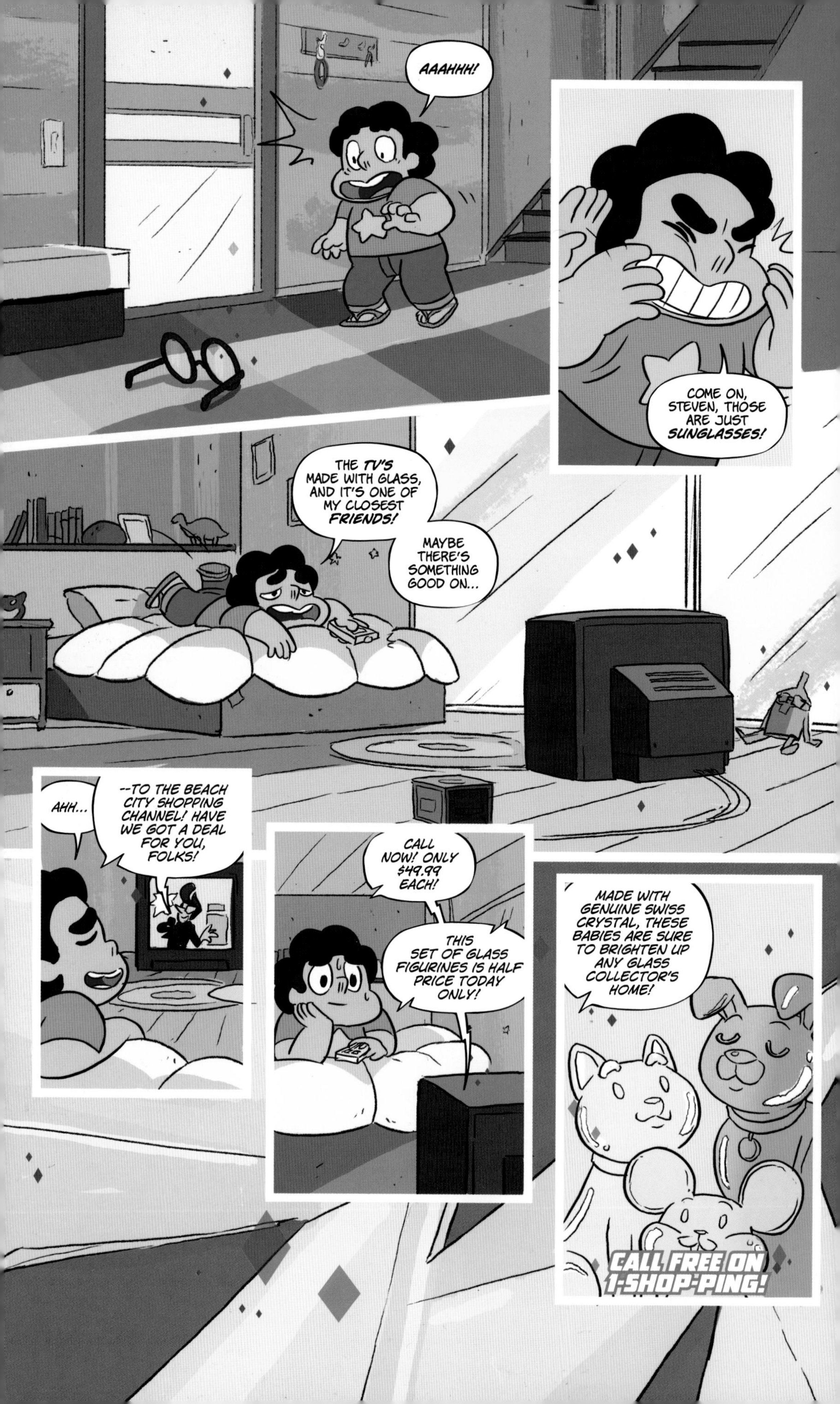

AAAHHH!
COME ON, STEVEN, THOSE ARE JUST SUNGLASSES!
THE TV'S MADE WITH GLASS, AND IT'S ONE OF MY CLOSEST FRIENDS!
MAYBE THERE'S SOMETHING GOOD ON...
AHH...
--TO THE BEACH CITY SHOPPING CHANNEL! HAVE WE GOT A DEAL FOR YOU, FOLKS!
CALL NOW! ONLY $49.99 EACH!
THIS SET OF GLASS FIGURINES IS HALF PRICE TODAY ONLY!
MADE WITH GENUINE SWISS CRYSTAL, THESE BABIES ARE SURE TO BRIGHTEN UP ANY GLASS COLLECTOR'S HOME!
CALL FREE ON 1-SHOP-PING!

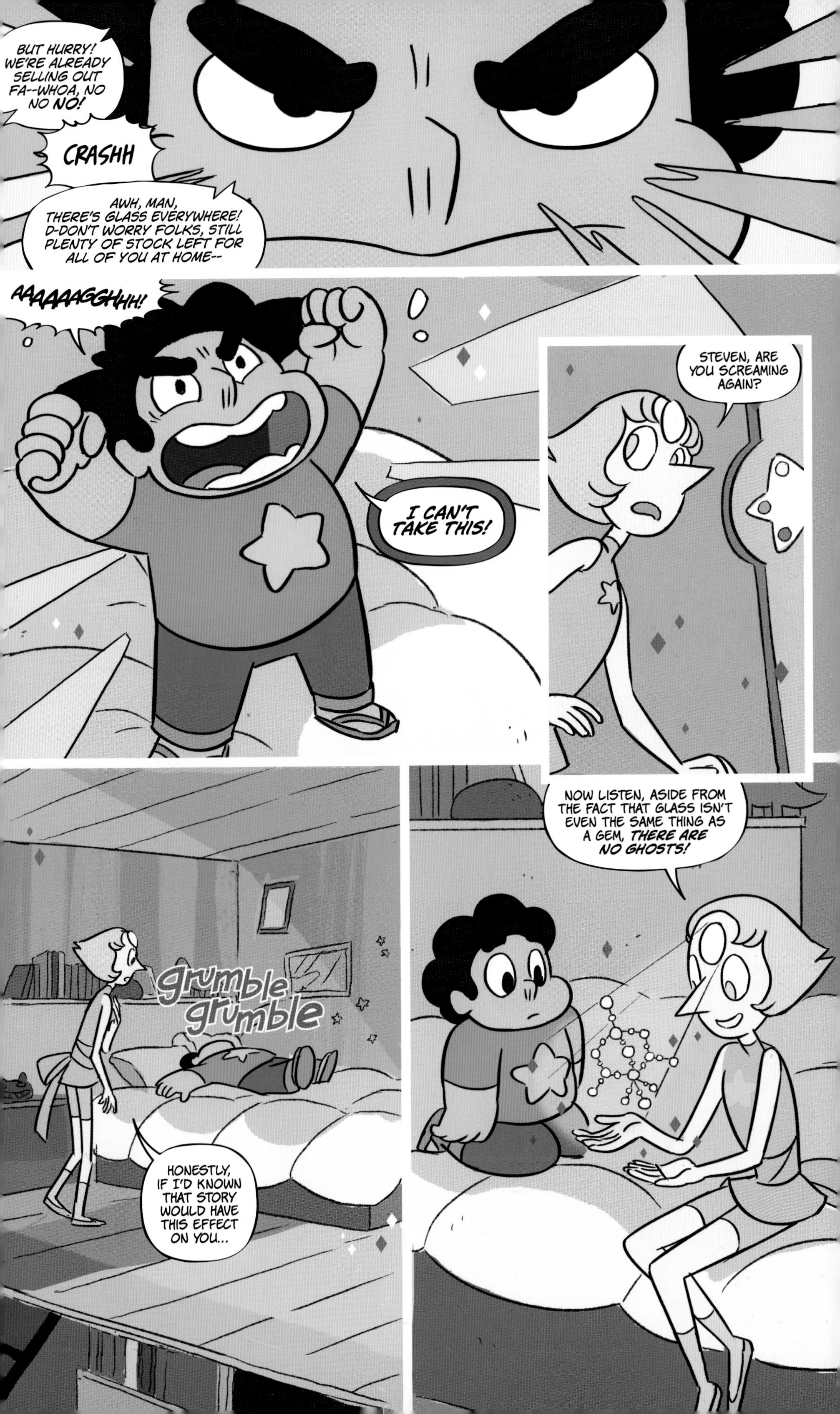
BUT HURRY! WE'RE ALREADY SELLING OUT FA--WHOA, NO NO **NO!**
CRASHH
AWH, MAN, THERE'S GLASS EVERYWHERE! D-DON'T WORRY FOLKS, STILL PLENTY OF STOCK LEFT FOR ALL OF YOU AT HOME--
AAAAAAGGHHH!
I CAN'T TAKE THIS!
STEVEN, ARE YOU SCREAMING AGAIN?
grumble grumble
HONESTLY, IF I'D KNOWN THAT STORY WOULD HAVE THIS EFFECT ON YOU...
NOW LISTEN, ASIDE FROM THE FACT THAT GLASS ISN'T EVEN THE SAME THING AS A GEM, *THERE ARE NO GHOSTS!*

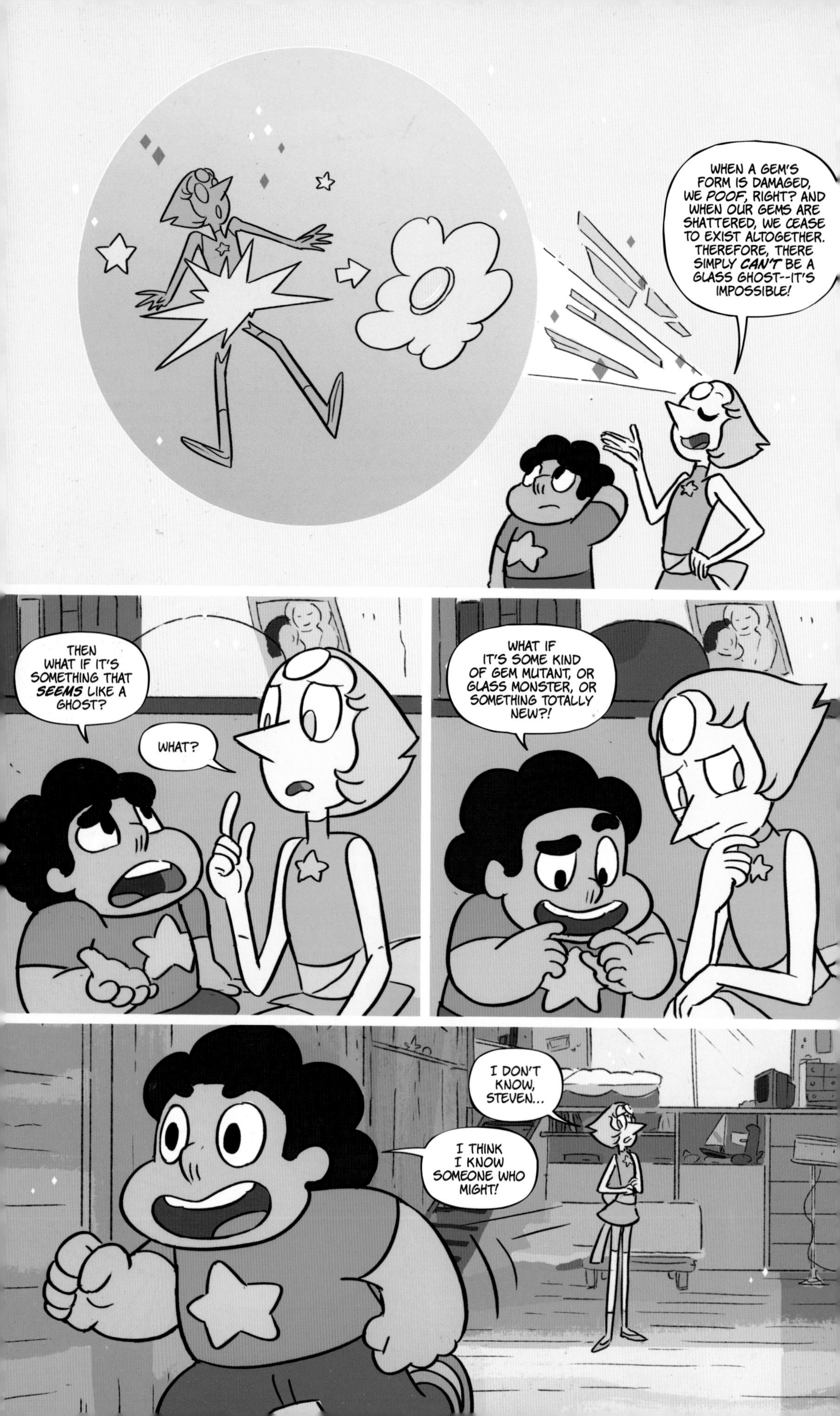
WHEN A GEM'S FORM IS DAMAGED, WE *POOF*, RIGHT? AND WHEN OUR GEMS ARE SHATTERED, WE CEASE TO EXIST ALTOGETHER. THEREFORE, THERE SIMPLY ***CAN'T*** BE A GLASS GHOST--IT'S IMPOSSIBLE!
THEN WHAT IF IT'S SOMETHING THAT ***SEEMS*** LIKE A GHOST?
WHAT?
WHAT IF IT'S SOME KIND OF GEM MUTANT, OR GLASS MONSTER, OR SOMETHING TOTALLY NEW?!
I DON'T KNOW, STEVEN...
I THINK I KNOW SOMEONE WHO MIGHT!

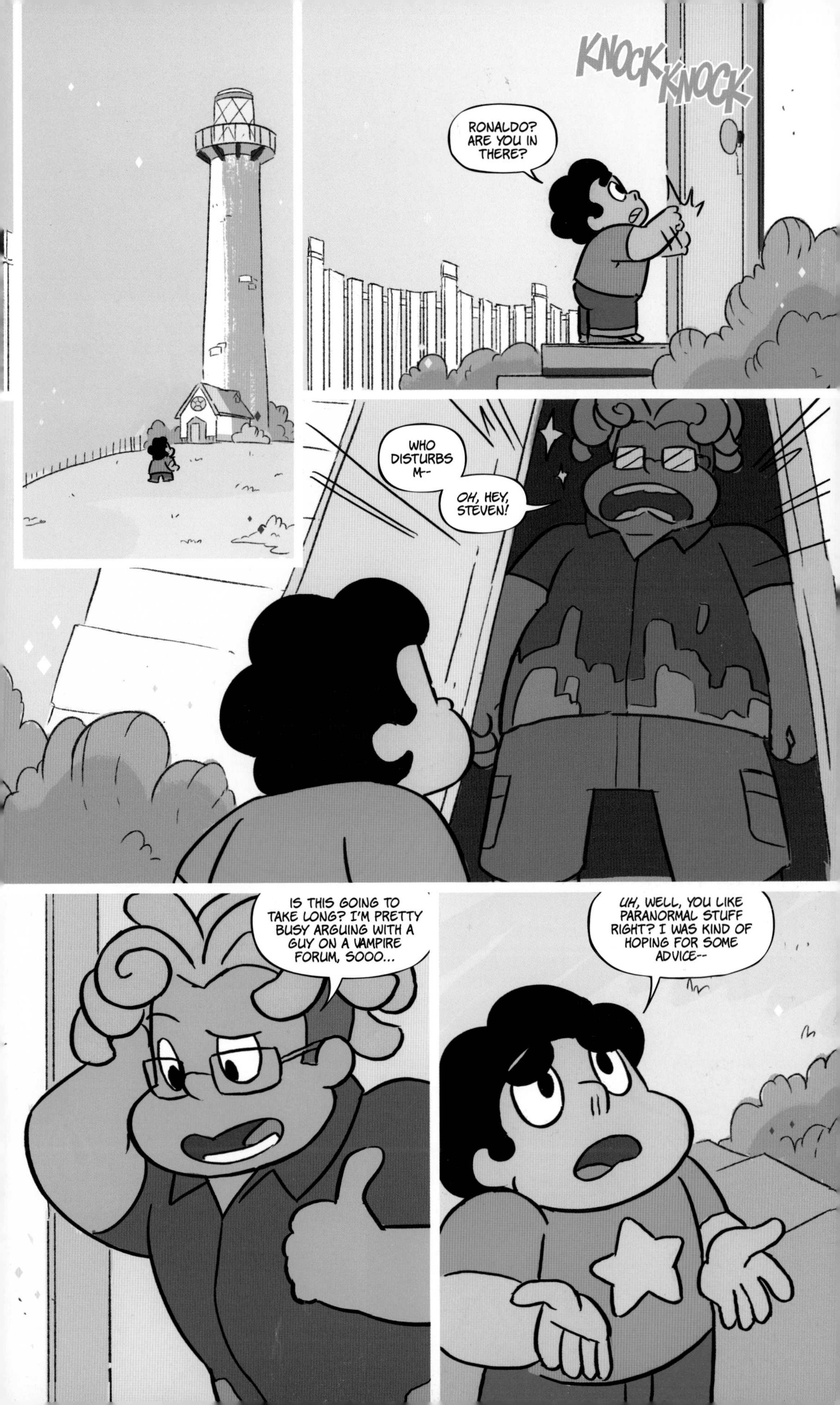
KNOCK KNOCK
RONALDO? ARE YOU IN THERE?
WHO DISTURBS M--
OH, HEY, STEVEN!
IS THIS GOING TO TAKE LONG? I'M PRETTY BUSY ARGUING WITH A GUY ON A VAMPIRE FORUM, SOOO...
UH, WELL, YOU LIKE PARANORMAL STUFF RIGHT? I WAS KIND OF HOPING FOR SOME ADVICE--

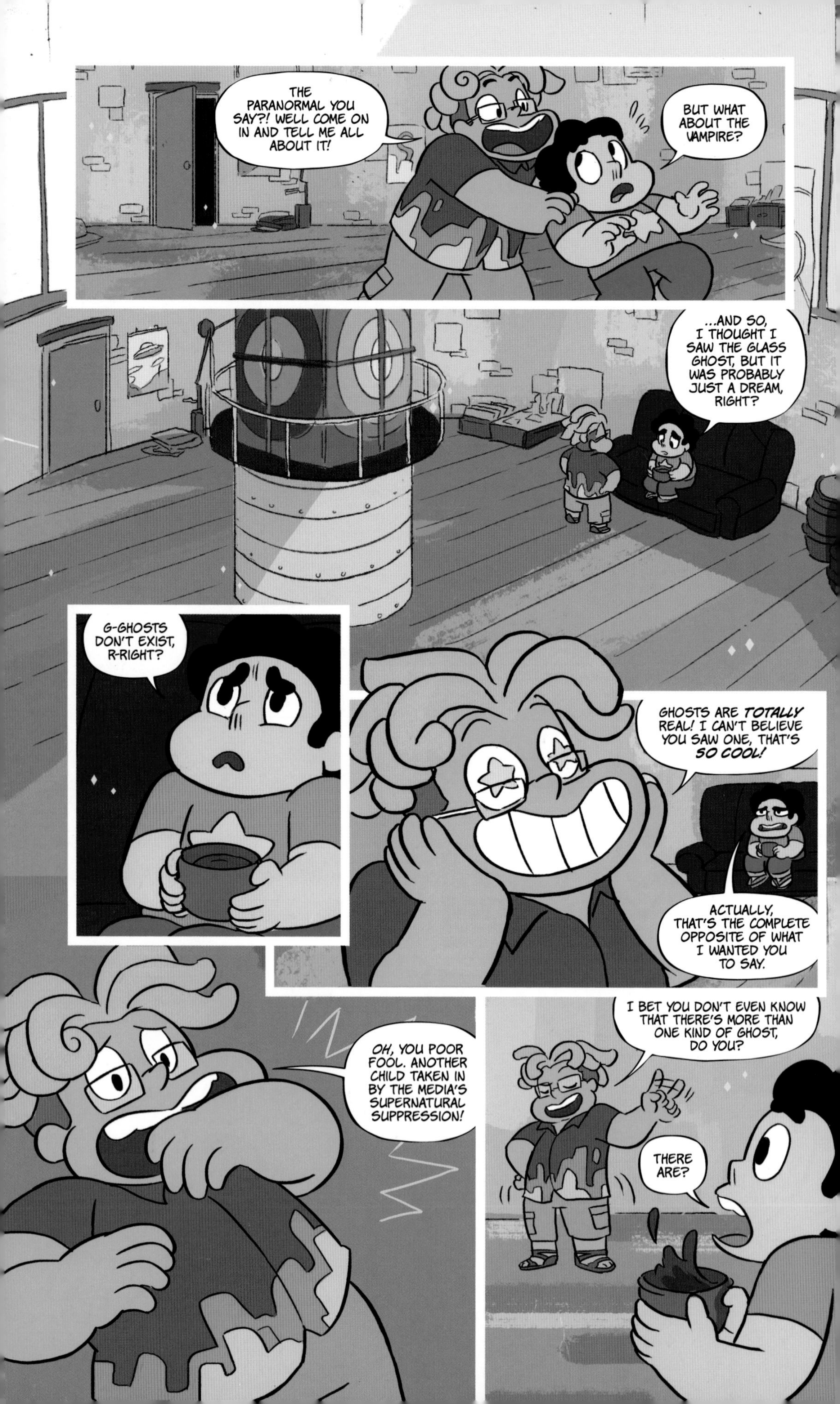
THE PARANORMAL YOU SAY?! WELL COME ON IN AND TELL ME ALL ABOUT IT!
BUT WHAT ABOUT THE VAMPIRE?
...AND SO, I THOUGHT I SAW THE GLASS GHOST, BUT IT WAS PROBABLY JUST A DREAM, RIGHT?
G-GHOSTS DON'T EXIST, R-RIGHT?
GHOSTS ARE *TOTALLY* REAL! I CAN'T BELIEVE YOU SAW ONE, THAT'S ***SO COOL!***
ACTUALLY, THAT'S THE COMPLETE OPPOSITE OF WHAT I WANTED YOU TO SAY.
OH, YOU POOR FOOL. ANOTHER CHILD TAKEN IN BY THE MEDIA'S SUPERNATURAL SUPPRESSION!
I BET YOU DON'T EVEN KNOW THAT THERE'S MORE THAN ONE KIND OF GHOST, DO YOU?
THERE ARE?

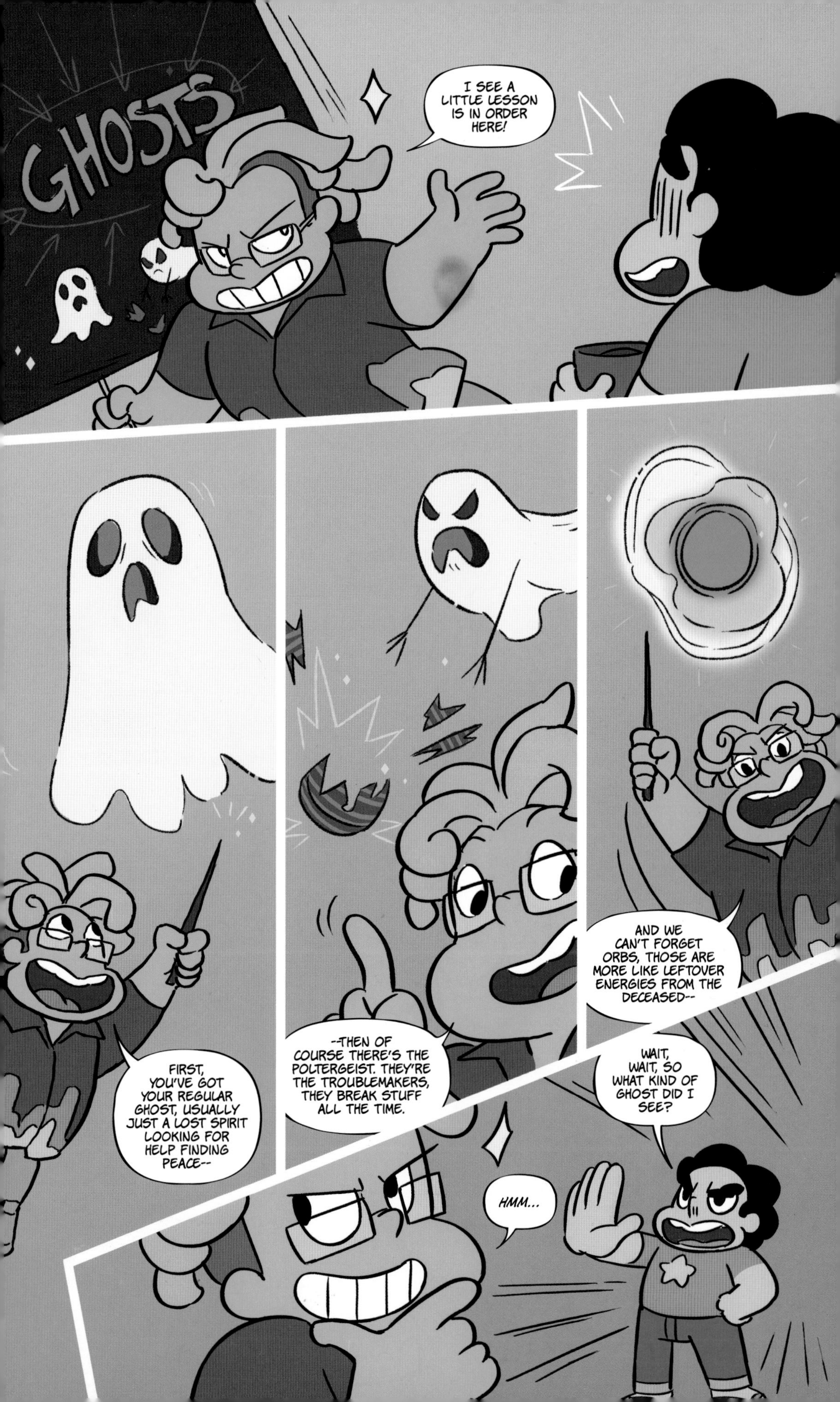
GHOSTS
I SEE A LITTLE LESSON IS IN ORDER HERE!
FIRST, YOU'VE GOT YOUR REGULAR GHOST, USUALLY JUST A LOST SPIRIT LOOKING FOR HELP FINDING PEACE--
--THEN OF COURSE THERE'S THE POLTERGEIST. THEY'RE THE TROUBLEMAKERS, THEY BREAK STUFF ALL THE TIME.
AND WE CAN'T FORGET ORBS, THOSE ARE MORE LIKE LEFTOVER ENERGIES FROM THE DECEASED--
WAIT, WAIT, SO WHAT KIND OF GHOST DID I SEE?
HMM...

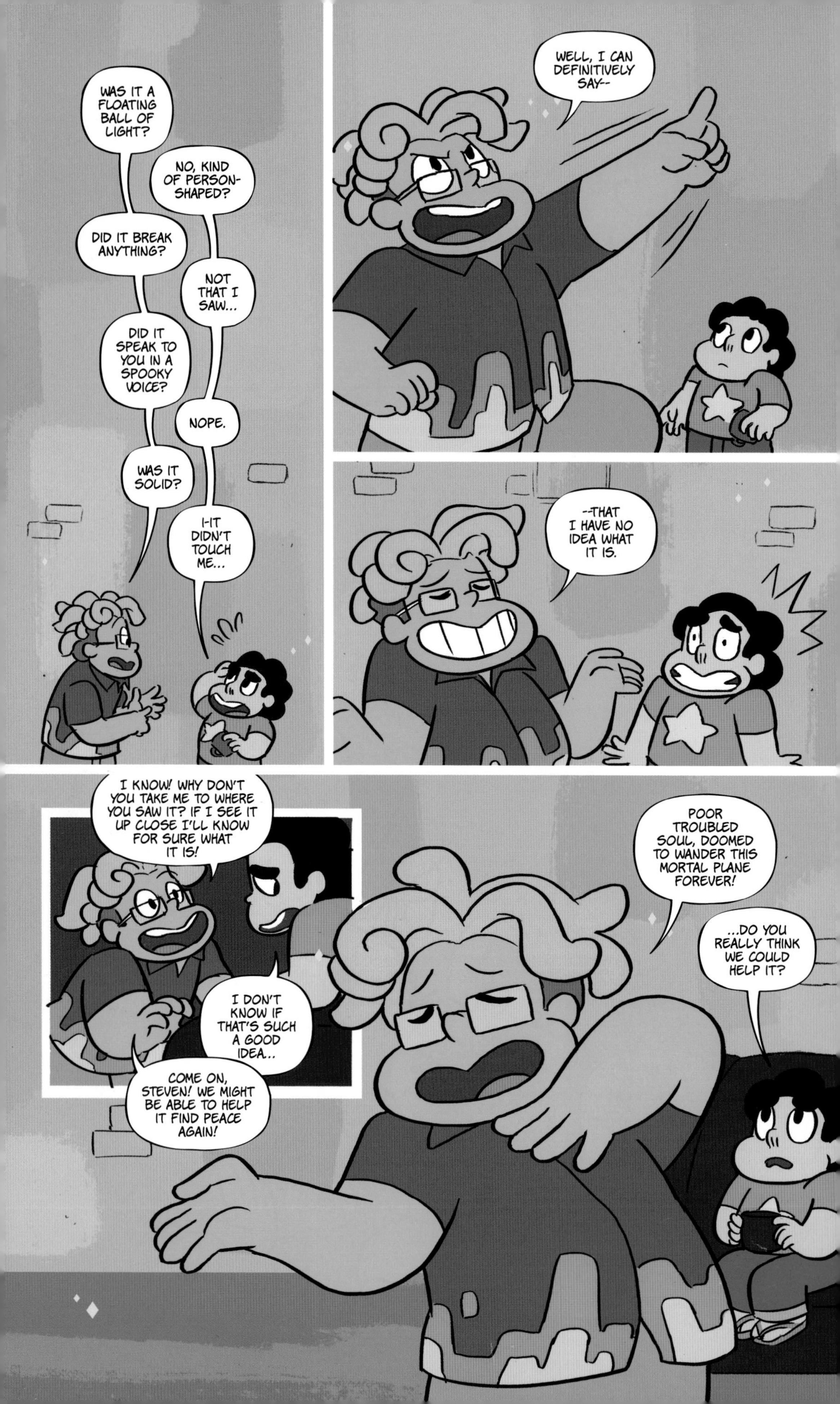
WAS IT A FLOATING BALL OF LIGHT?
NO, KIND OF PERSON-SHAPED?
DID IT BREAK ANYTHING?
NOT THAT I SAW...
DID IT SPEAK TO YOU IN A SPOOKY VOICE?
NOPE.
WAS IT SOLID?
I-IT DIDN'T TOUCH ME...
WELL, I CAN DEFINITIVELY SAY--
--THAT I HAVE NO IDEA WHAT IT IS.
I KNOW! WHY DON'T YOU TAKE ME TO WHERE YOU SAW IT? IF I SEE IT UP CLOSE I'LL KNOW FOR SURE WHAT IT IS!
I DON'T KNOW IF THAT'S SUCH A GOOD IDEA...
COME ON, STEVEN! WE MIGHT BE ABLE TO HELP IT FIND PEACE AGAIN!
POOR TROUBLED SOUL, DOOMED TO WANDER THIS MORTAL PLANE FOREVER!
...DO YOU REALLY THINK WE COULD HELP IT?

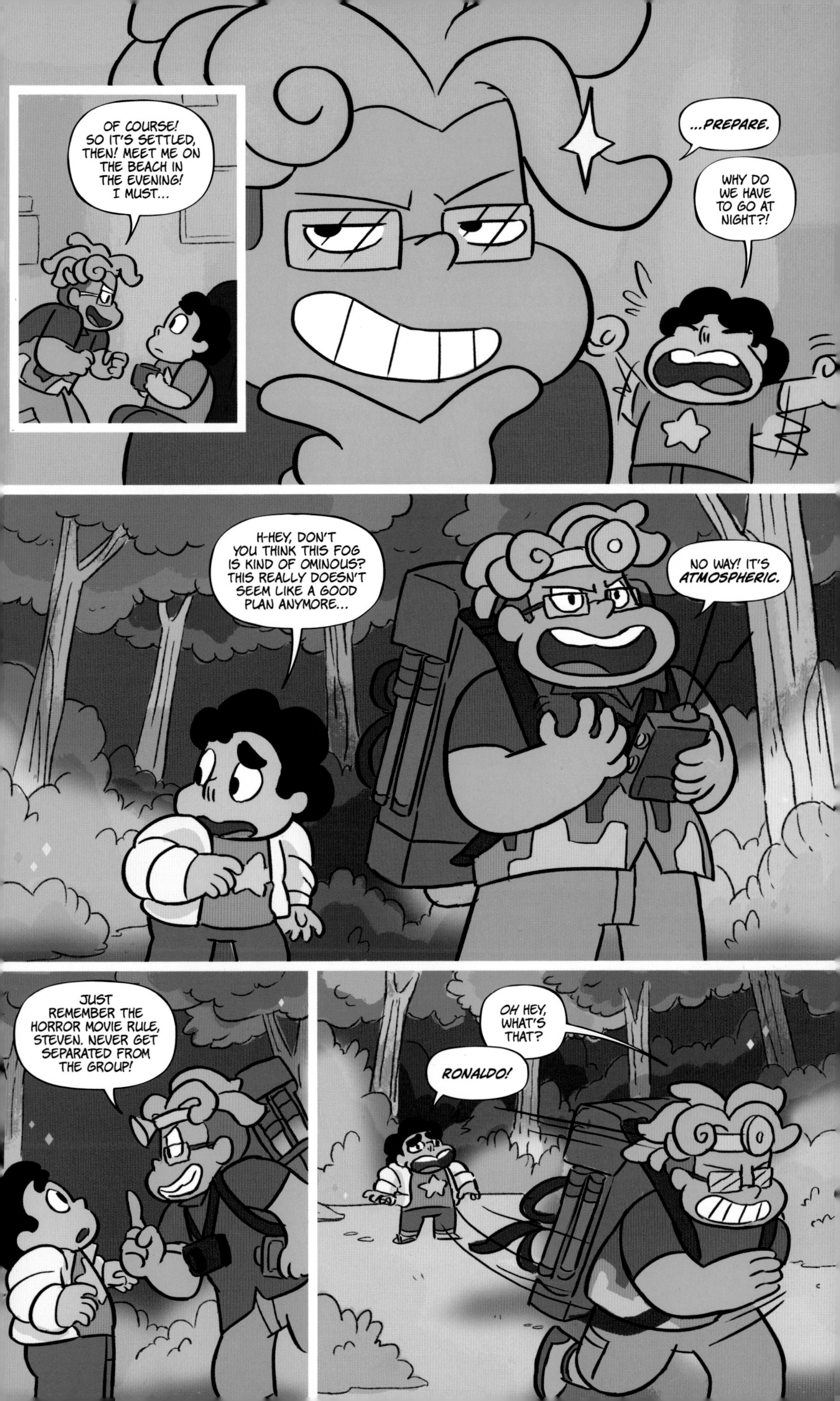
OF COURSE! SO IT'S SETTLED, THEN! MEET ME ON THE BEACH IN THE EVENING! I MUST...
...PREPARE.
WHY DO WE HAVE TO GO AT NIGHT?!
H-HEY, DON'T YOU THINK THIS FOG IS KIND OF OMINOUS? THIS REALLY DOESN'T SEEM LIKE A GOOD PLAN ANYMORE...
NO WAY! IT'S ATMOSPHERIC.
JUST REMEMBER THE HORROR MOVIE RULE, STEVEN. NEVER GET SEPARATED FROM THE GROUP!
OH HEY, WHAT'S THAT?
RONALDO!

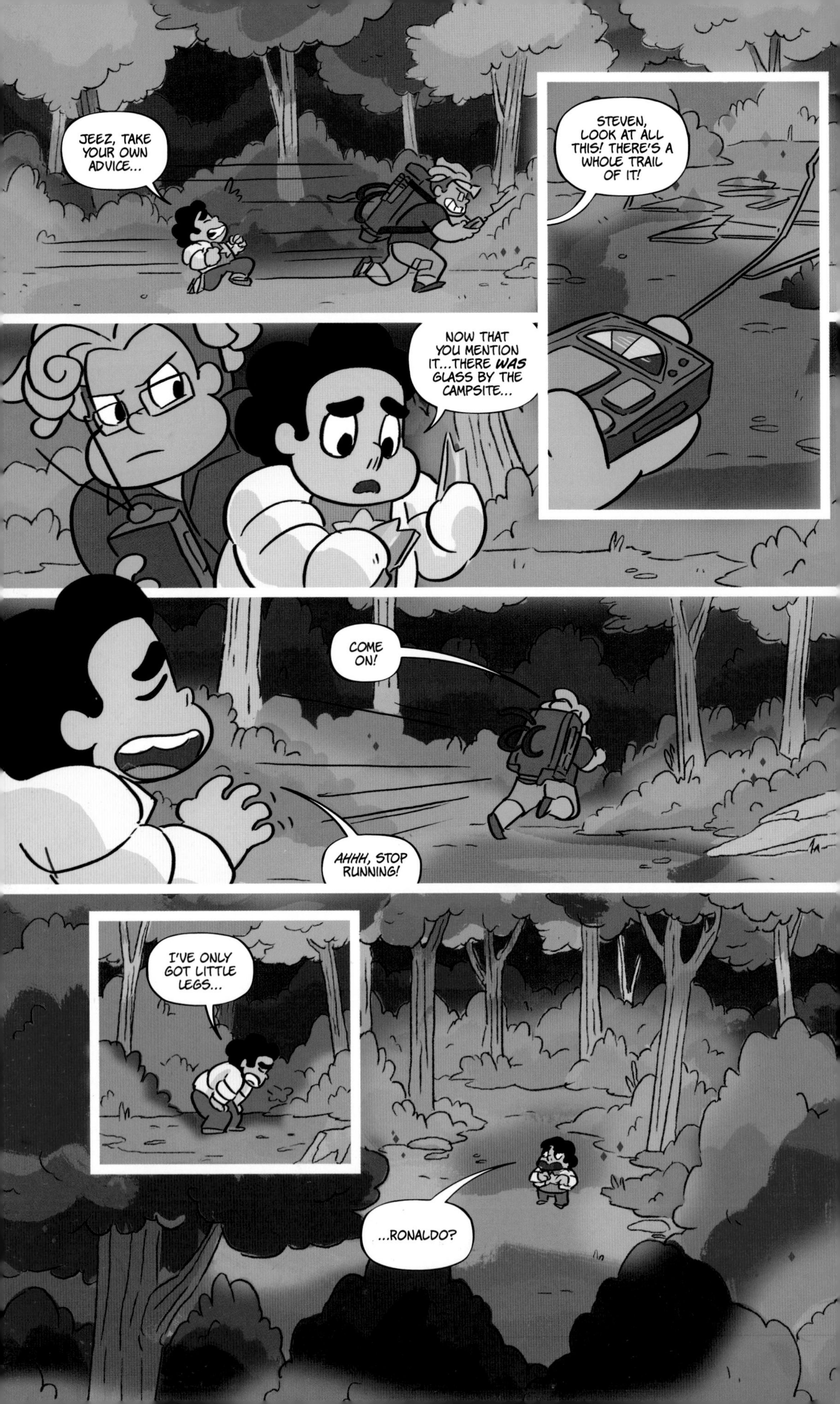
JEEZ, TAKE YOUR OWN ADVICE...
STEVEN, LOOK AT ALL THIS! THERE'S A WHOLE TRAIL OF IT!
NOW THAT YOU MENTION IT...THERE *WAS* GLASS BY THE CAMPSITE...
COME ON!
AHHH, STOP RUNNING!
I'VE ONLY GOT LITTLE LEGS...
...RONALDO?

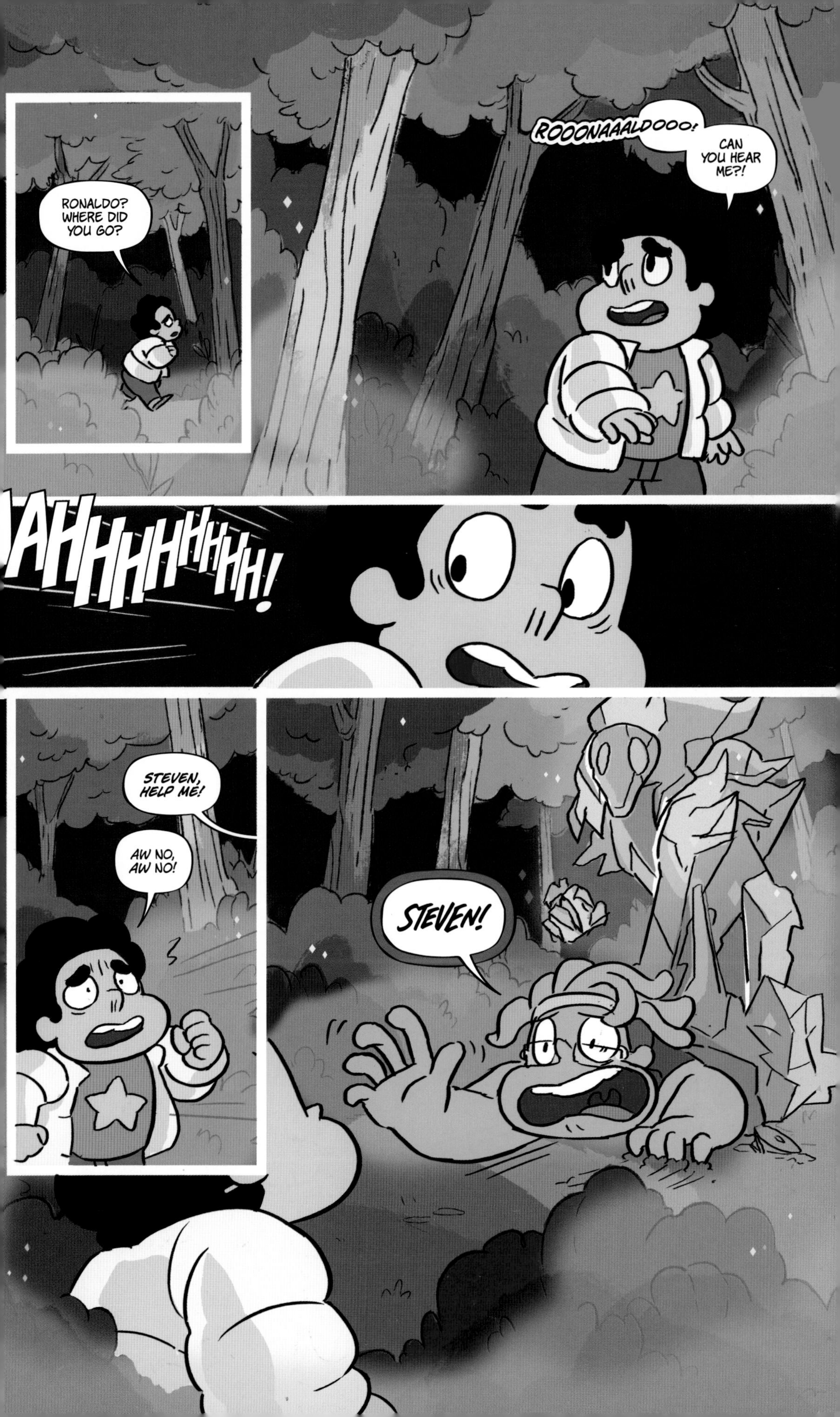
RONALDO? WHERE DID YOU GO?
ROOONAAALDOOO!
CAN YOU HEAR ME?!
AHHHHHHHHHH!
STEVEN, HELP ME!
AW NO, AW NO!
STEVEN!

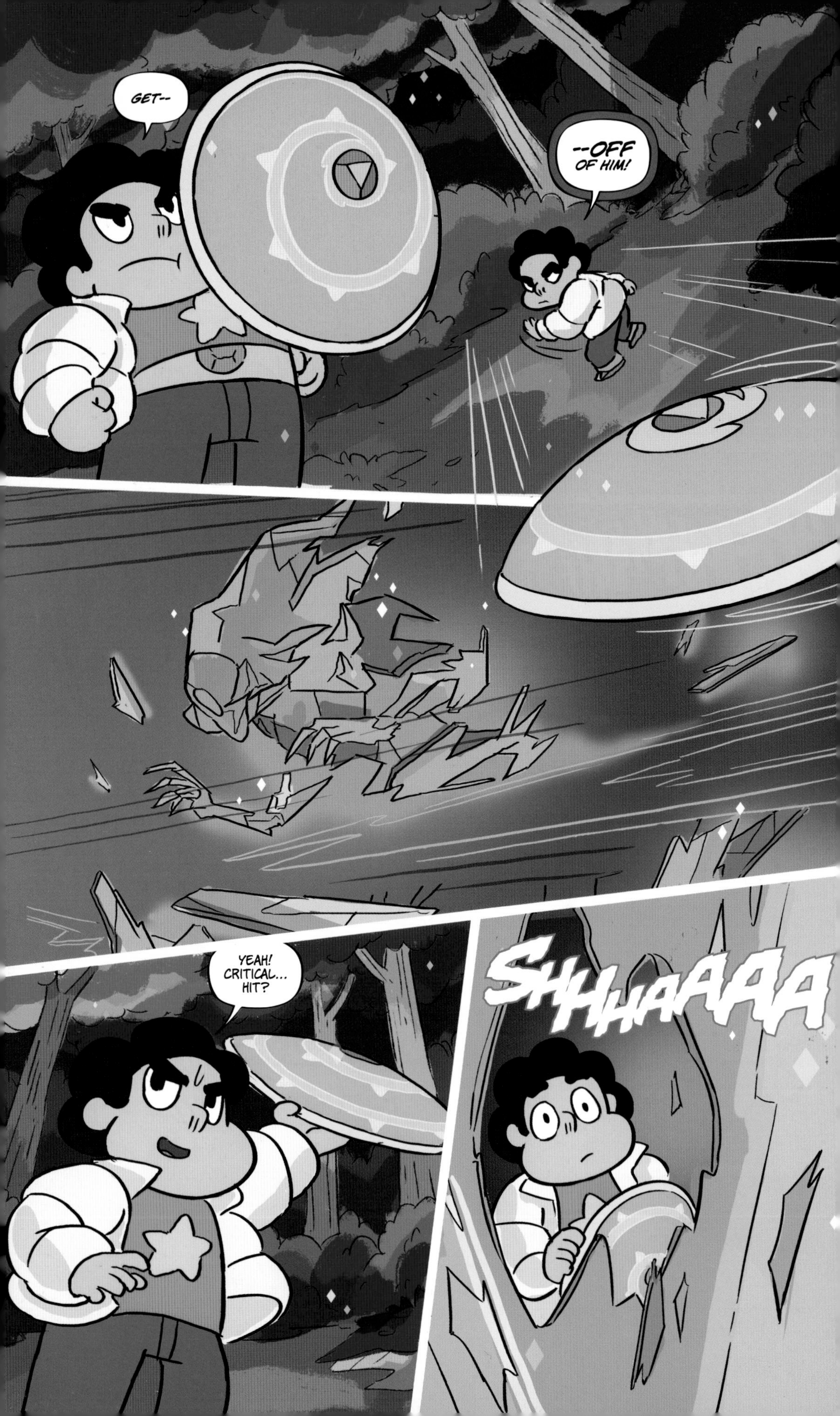
GET--
--OFF OF HIM!
YEAH! CRITICAL... HIT?
SHHHAAAAA

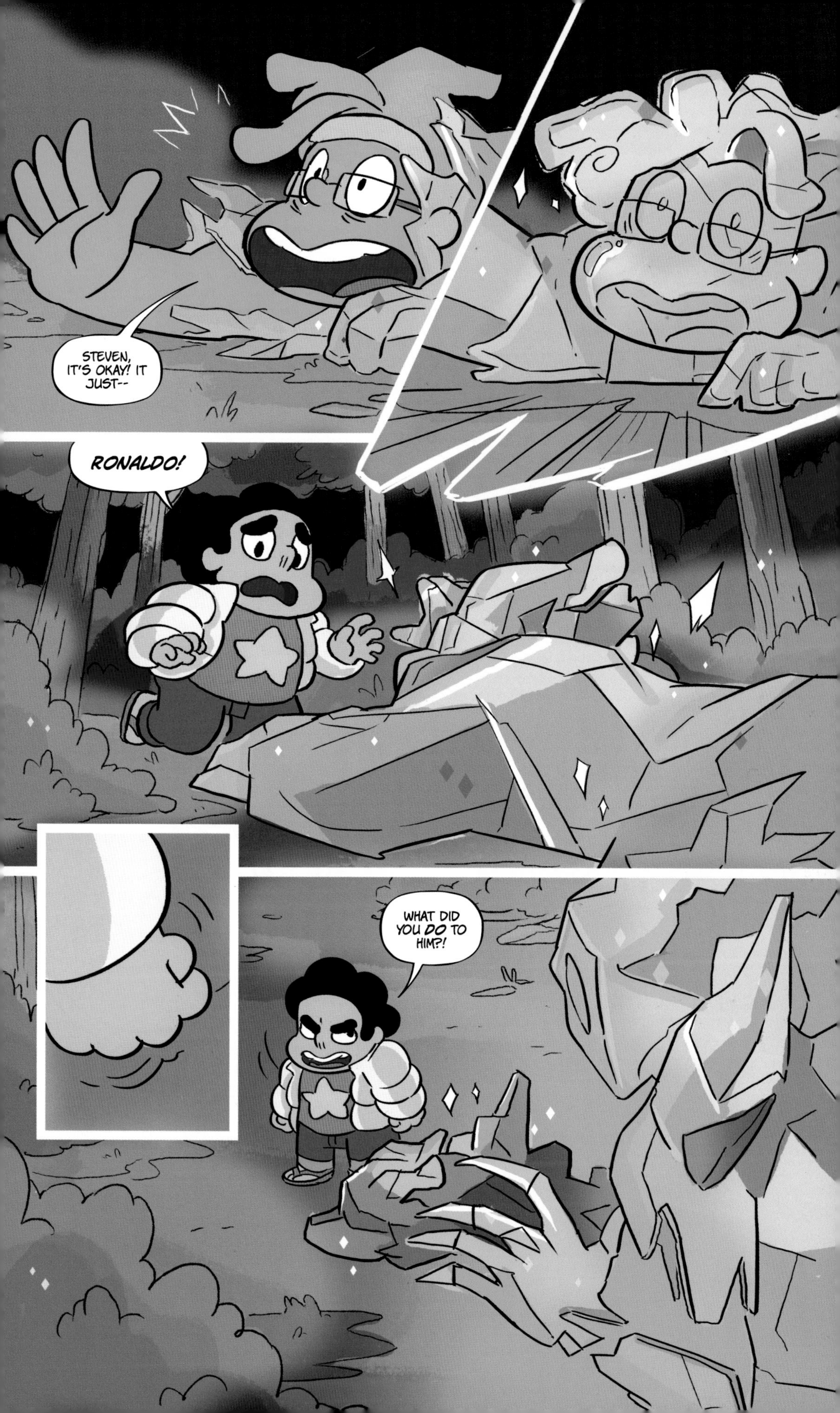
STEVEN, IT'S OKAY! IT JUST--
RONALDO!
WHAT DID YOU DO TO HIM?!

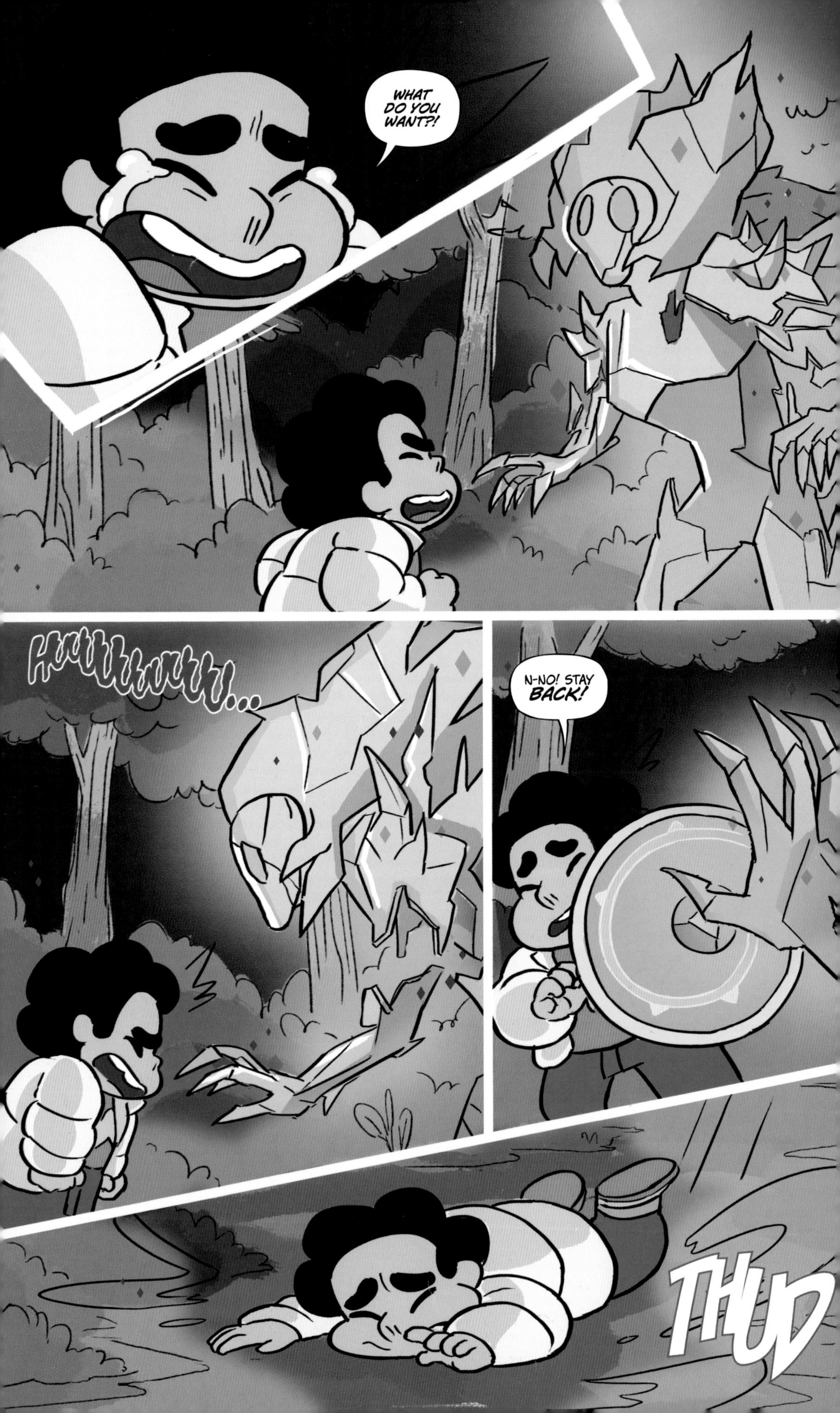
WHAT DO YOU WANT?!
N-NO! STAY BACK!
THUD

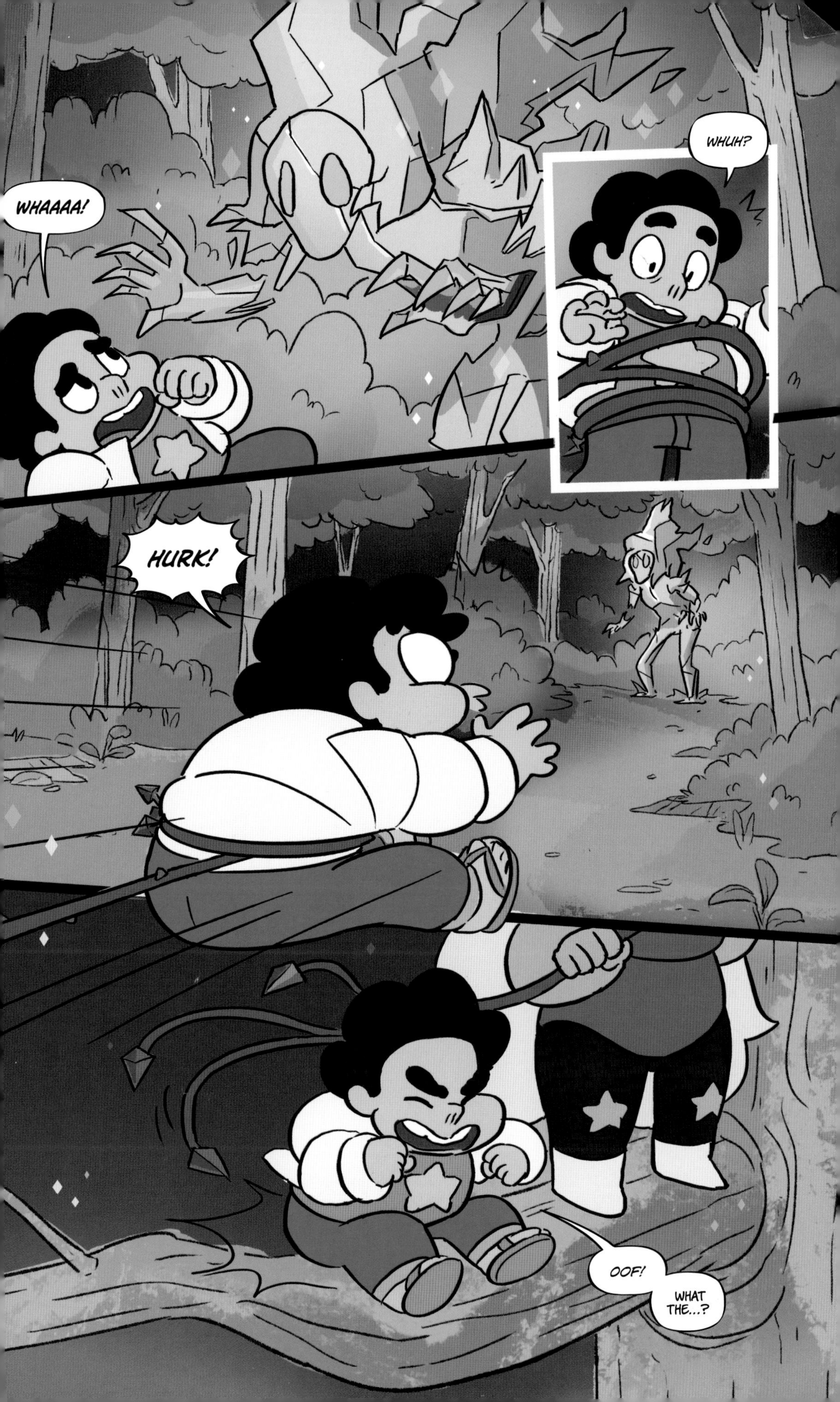
WHAAAA!
WHUH?
HURK!
OOF!
WHAT THE...?

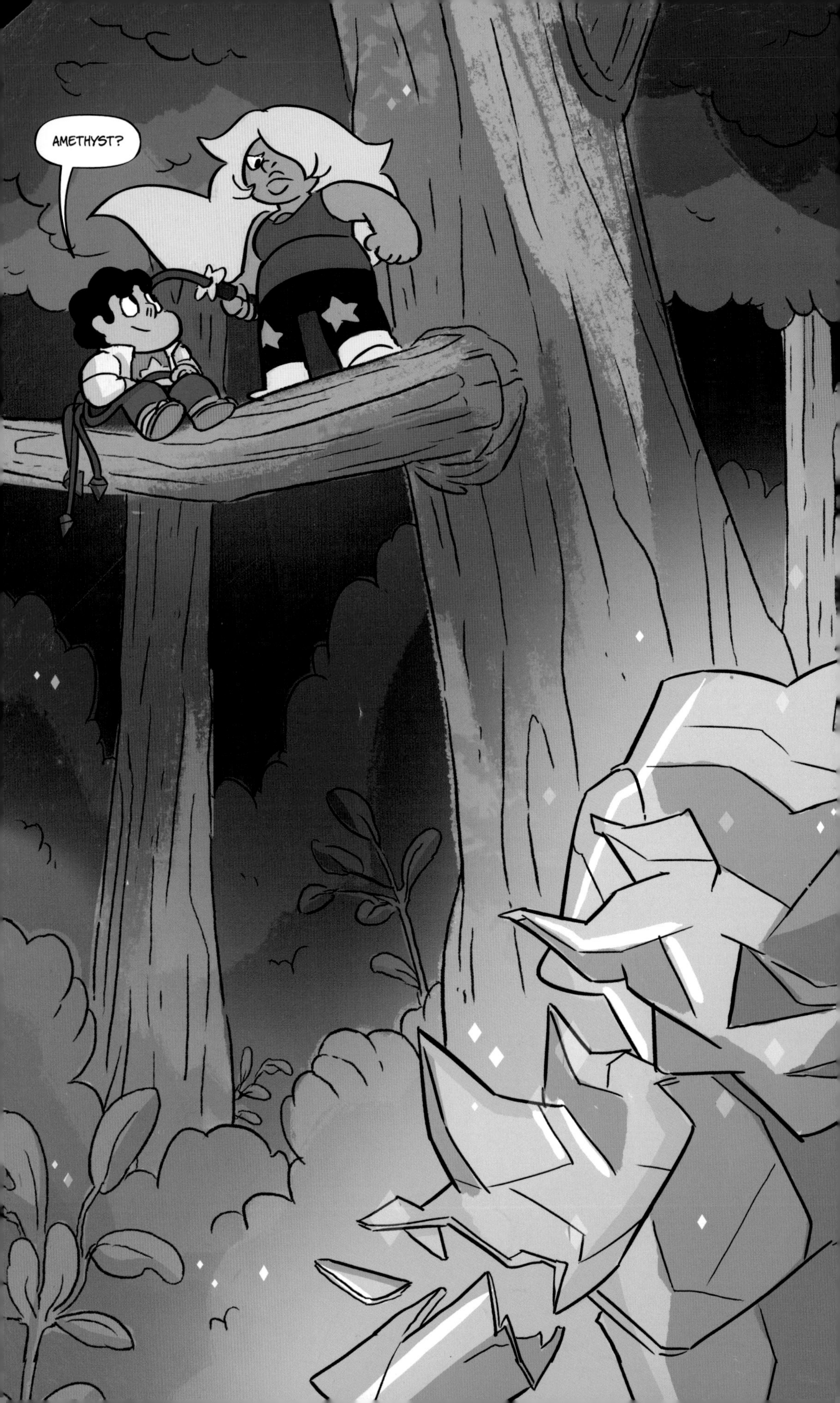
AMETHYST?

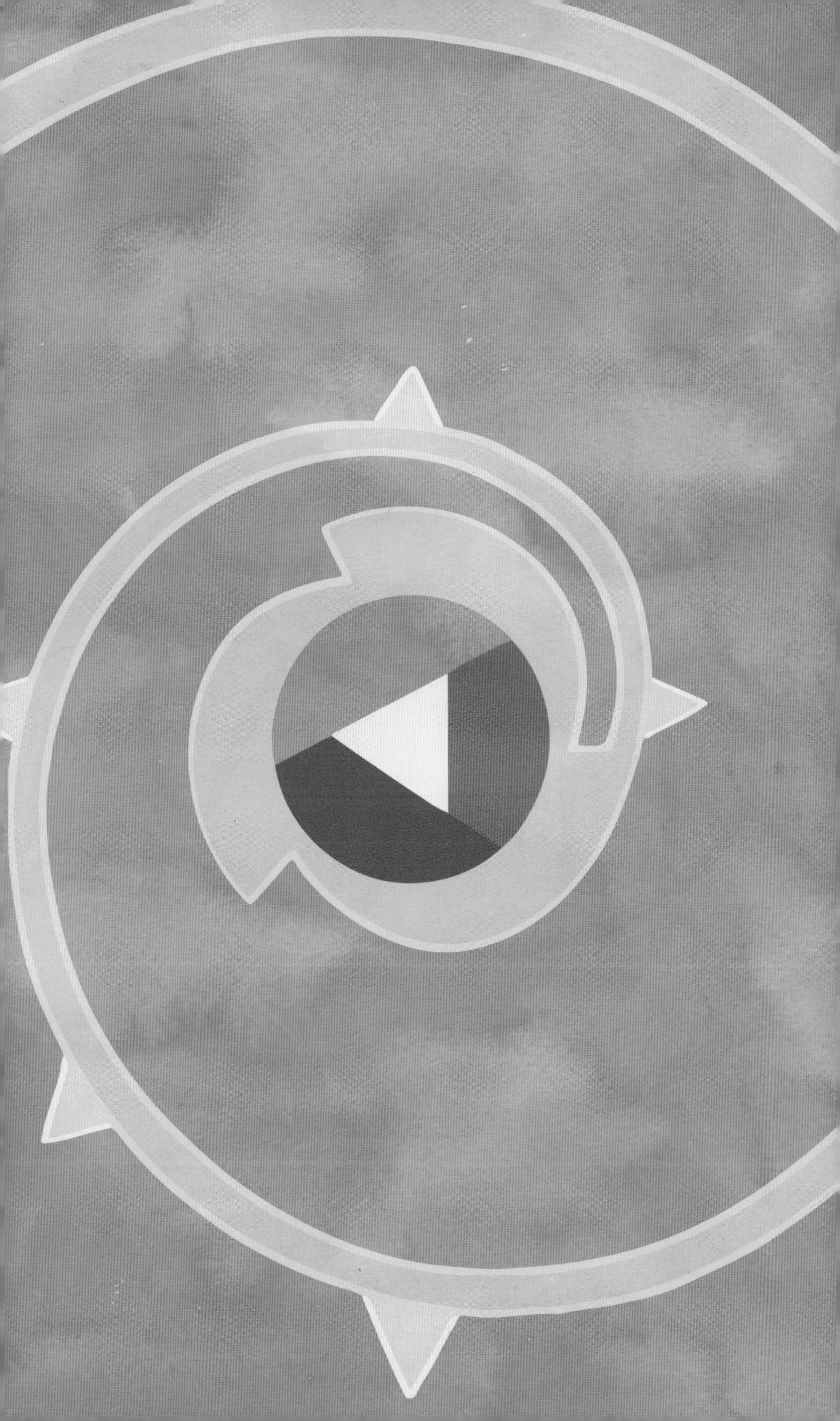

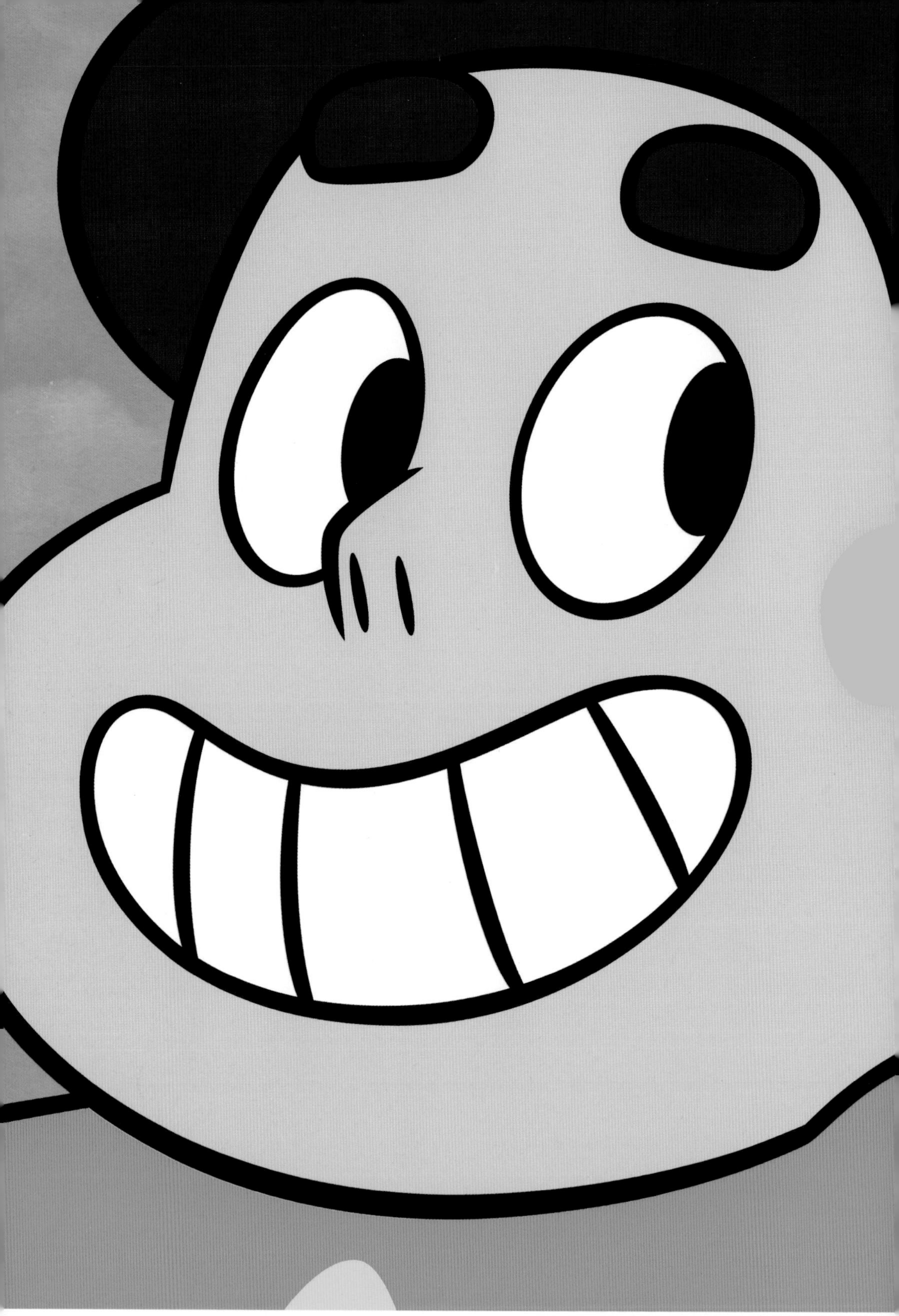

CHAPTER THREE

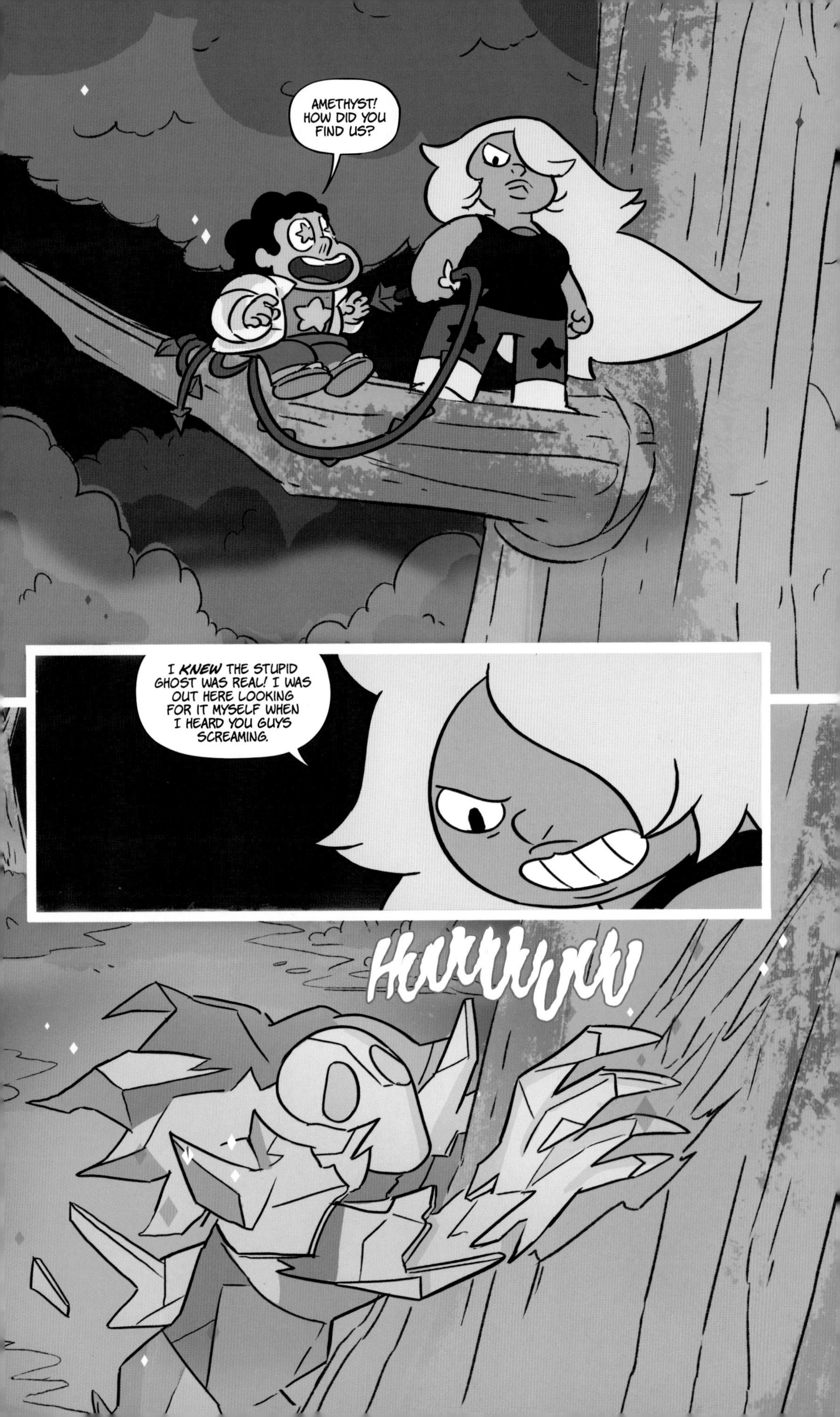
AMETHYST! HOW DID YOU FIND US?
I KNEW THE STUPID GHOST WAS REAL! I WAS OUT HERE LOOKING FOR IT MYSELF WHEN I HEARD YOU GUYS SCREAMING.
HRRRRWRRR

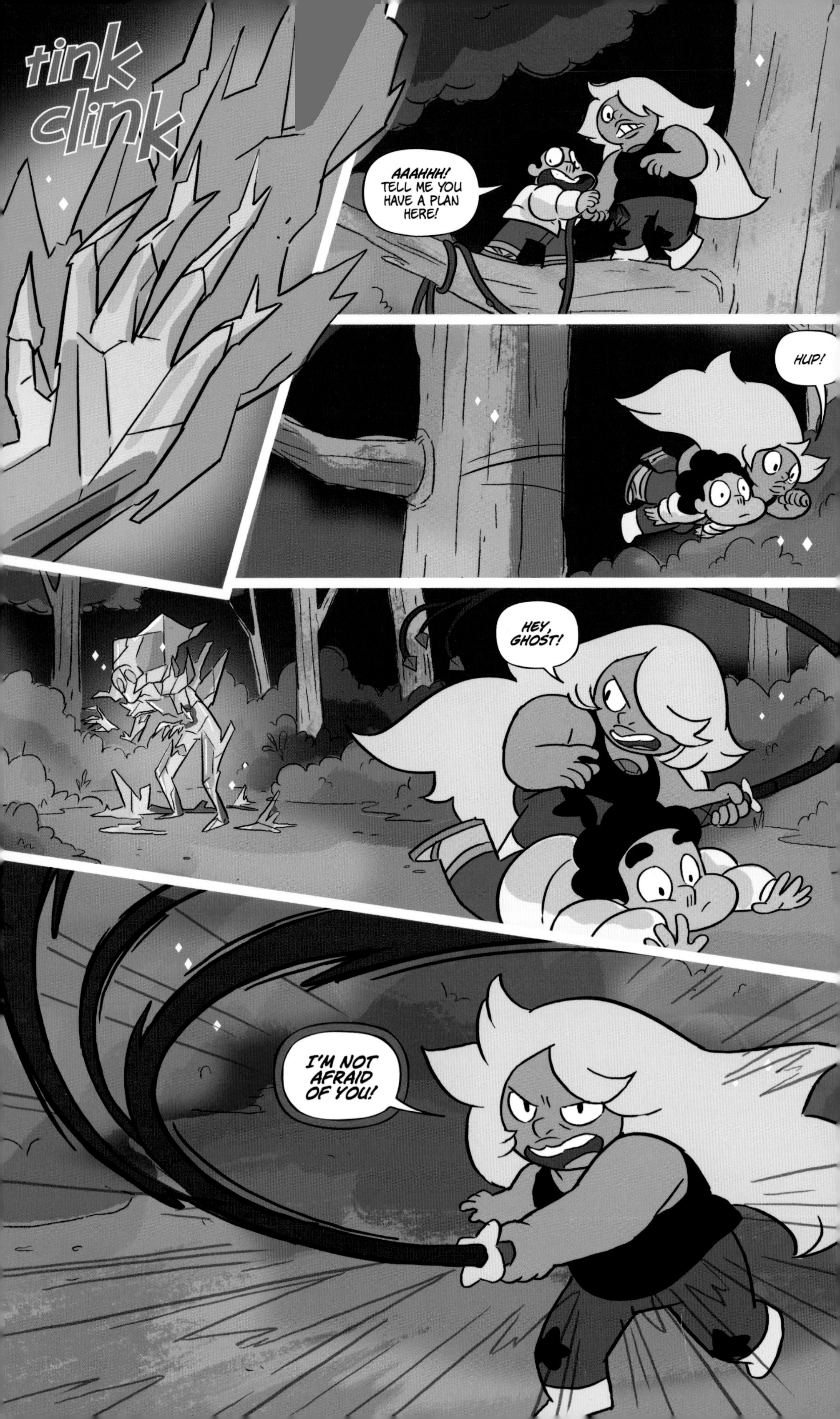
tink
clink
AAAHHH! TELL ME YOU HAVE A PLAN HERE!
HUP!
HEY, GHOST!
I'M NOT AFRAID OF YOU!

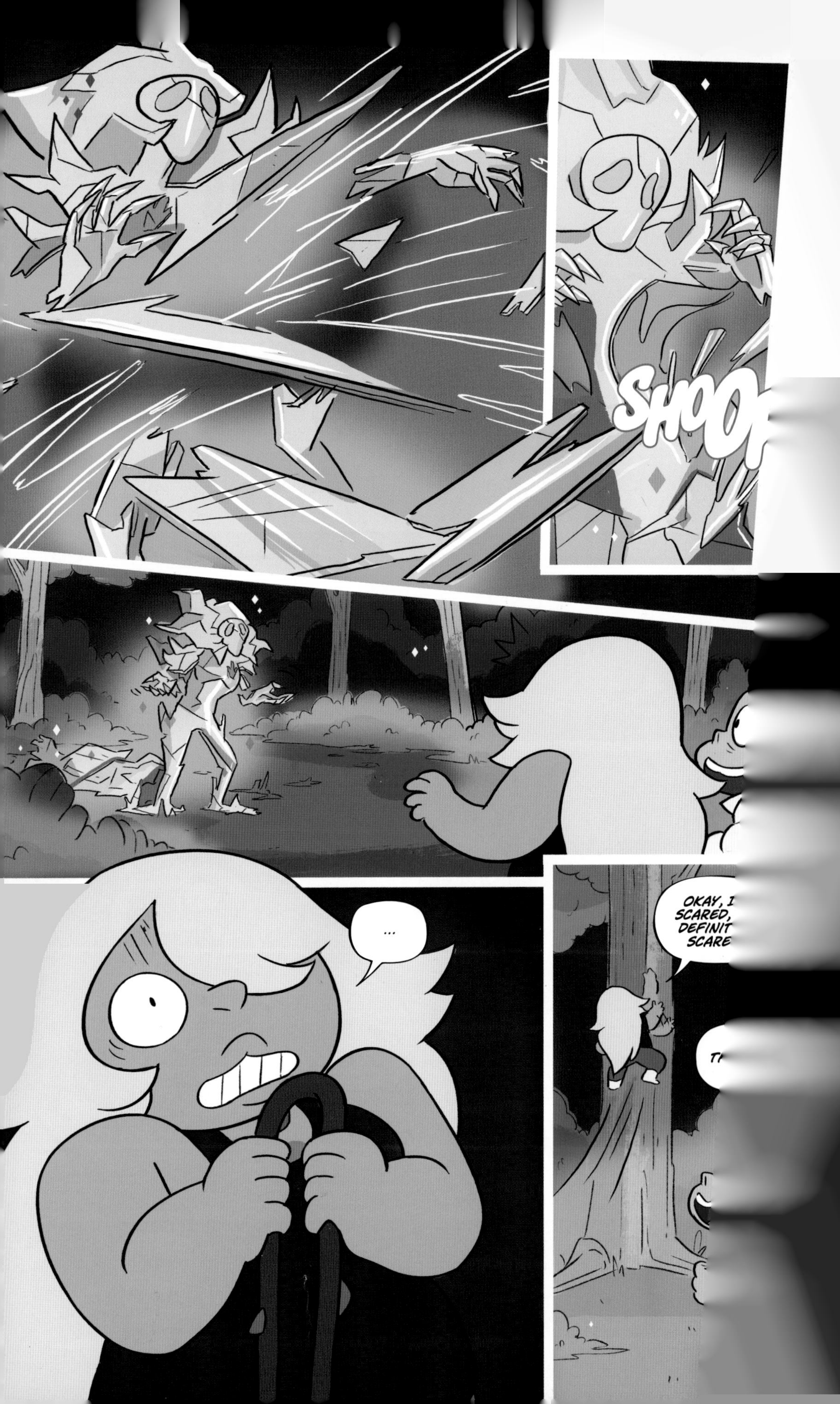

SHOO
...
OKAY, I
SCARED,
DEFINIT
SCARE

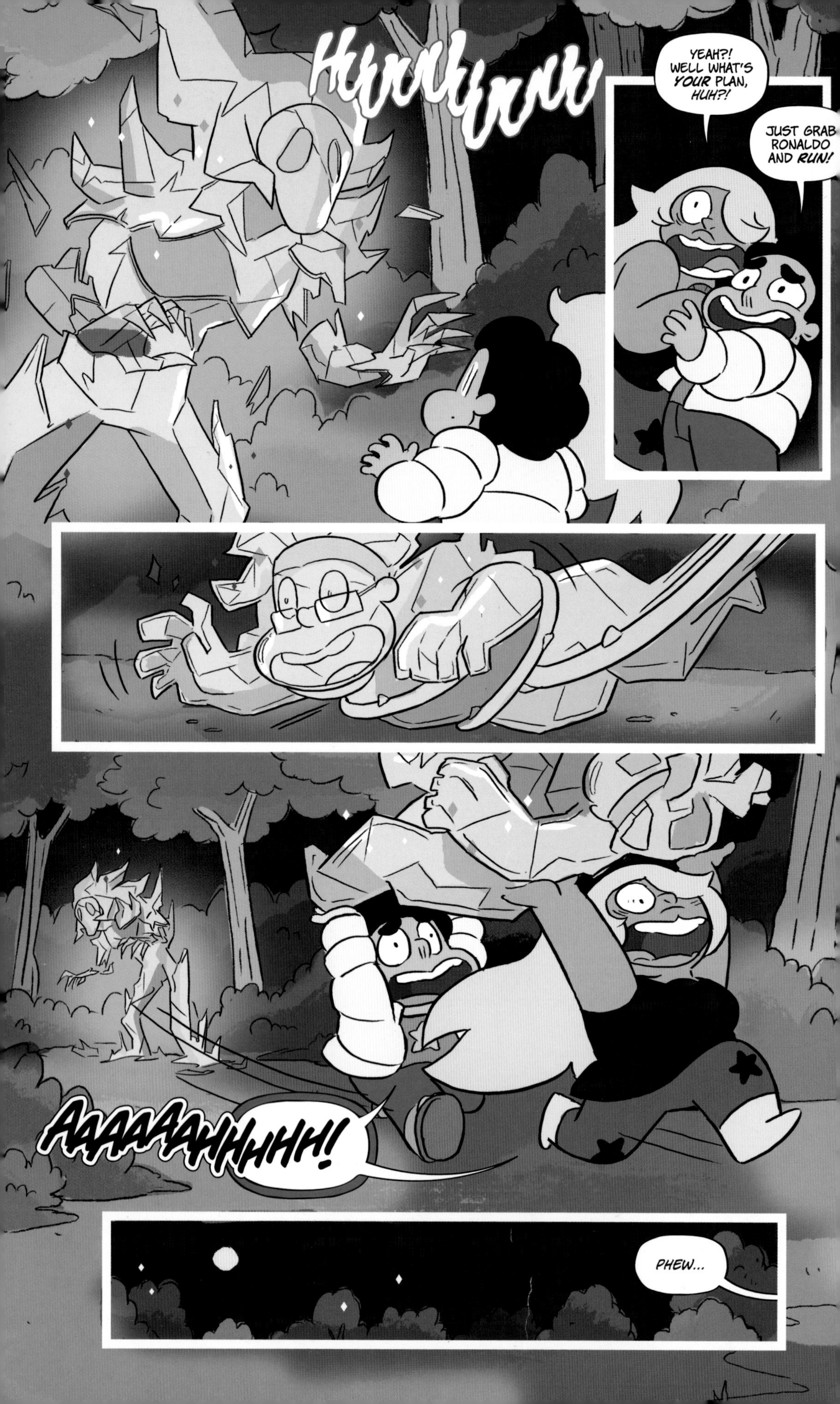
HRRRRRRRRR
YEAH?! WELL WHAT'S *YOUR* PLAN, HUH?!
JUST GRAB RONALDO AND *RUN!*
AAAAAAHHHHHH!
PHEW...

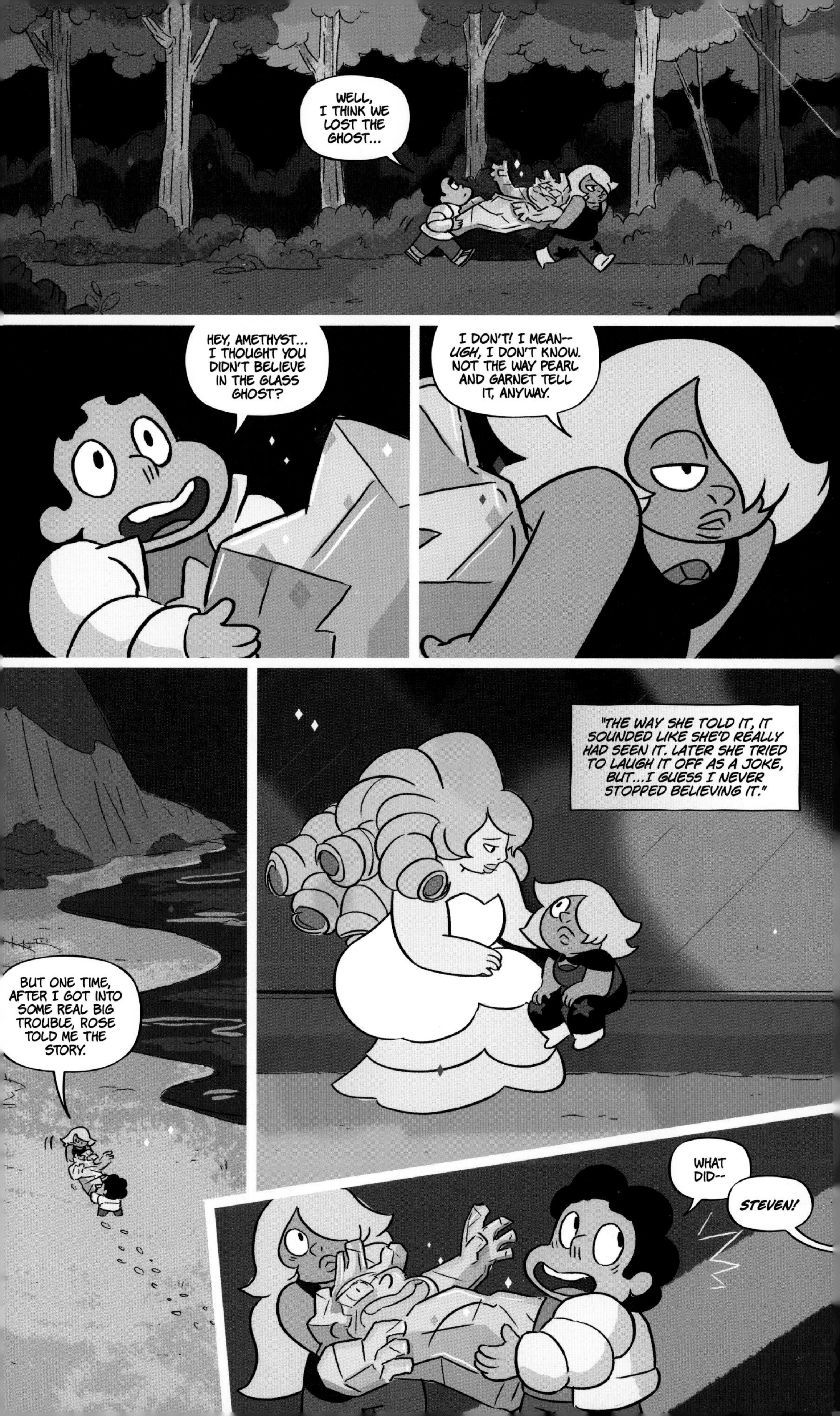
WELL, I THINK WE LOST THE GHOST...
HEY, AMETHYST... I THOUGHT YOU DIDN'T BELIEVE IN THE GLASS GHOST?
I DON'T! I MEAN-- UGH, I DON'T KNOW. NOT THE WAY PEARL AND GARNET TELL IT, ANYWAY.
BUT ONE TIME, AFTER I GOT INTO SOME REAL BIG TROUBLE, ROSE TOLD ME THE STORY.
"THE WAY SHE TOLD IT, IT SOUNDED LIKE SHE'D REALLY HAD SEEN IT. LATER SHE TRIED TO LAUGH IT OFF AS A JOKE, BUT...I GUESS I NEVER STOPPED BELIEVING IT."
WHAT DID--
STEVEN!

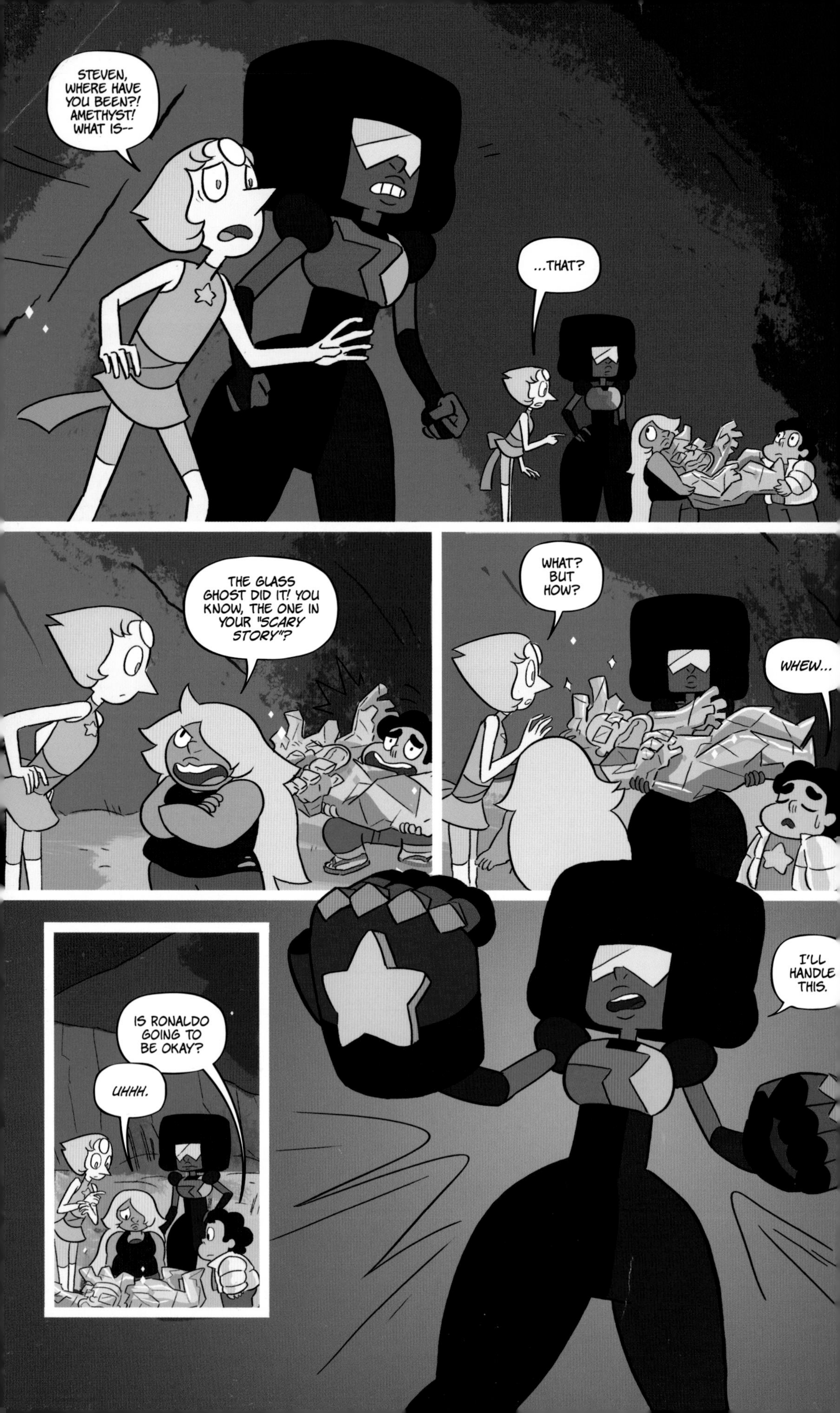

STEVEN, WHERE HAVE YOU BEEN?! AMETHYST! WHAT IS--
...THAT?
THE GLASS GHOST DID IT! YOU KNOW, THE ONE IN YOUR "SCARY STORY"?
WHAT? BUT HOW?
WHEW...
IS RONALDO GOING TO BE OKAY?
UHHH.
I'LL HANDLE THIS.

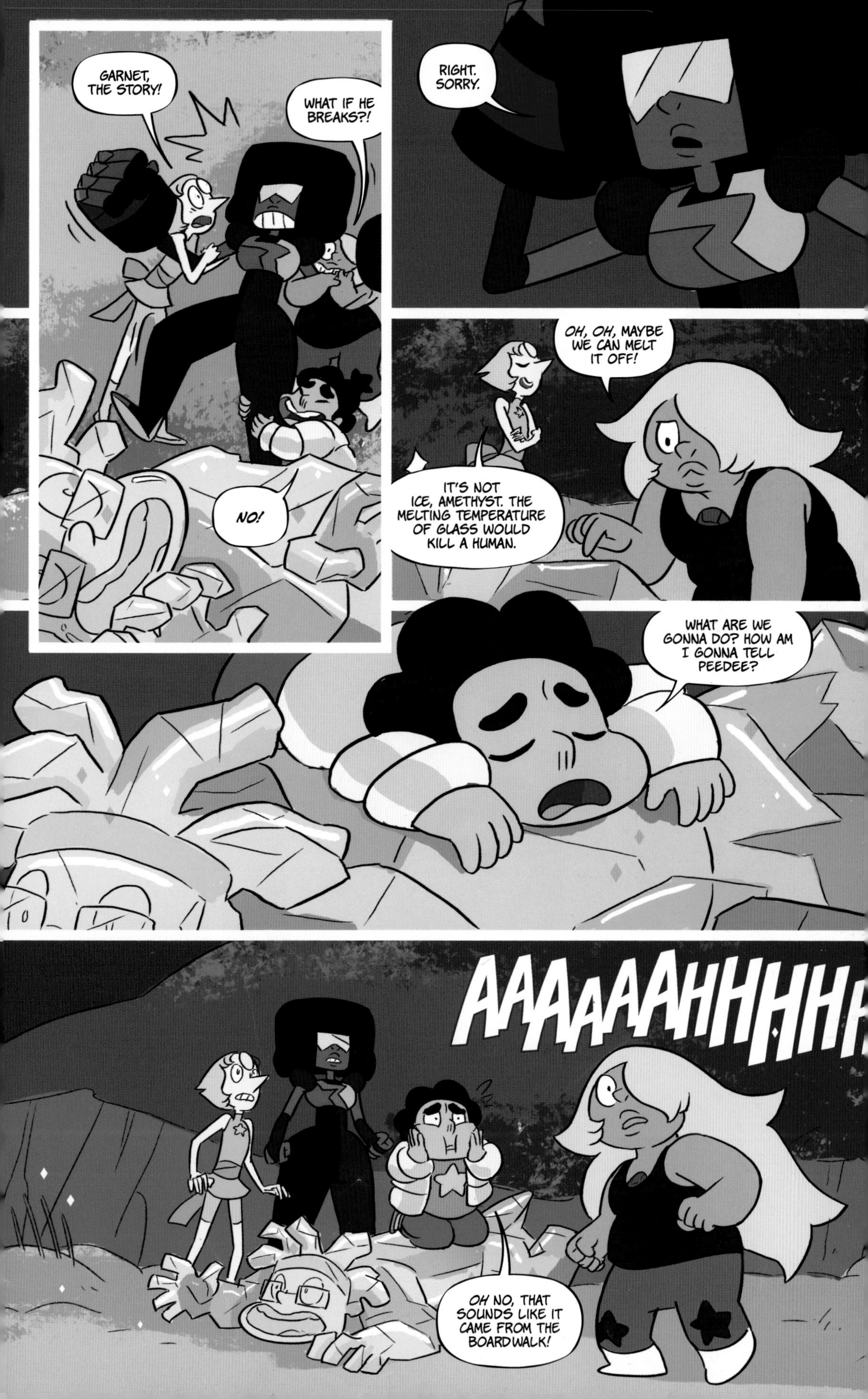

GARNET, THE STORY!
WHAT IF HE BREAKS?!
NO!
RIGHT. SORRY.
OH, OH, MAYBE WE CAN MELT IT OFF!
IT'S NOT ICE, AMETHYST. THE MELTING TEMPERATURE OF GLASS WOULD KILL A HUMAN.
WHAT ARE WE GONNA DO? HOW AM I GONNA TELL PEEDEE?
AAAAAAHHHHH
OH NO, THAT SOUNDS LIKE IT CAME FROM THE BOARDWALK!

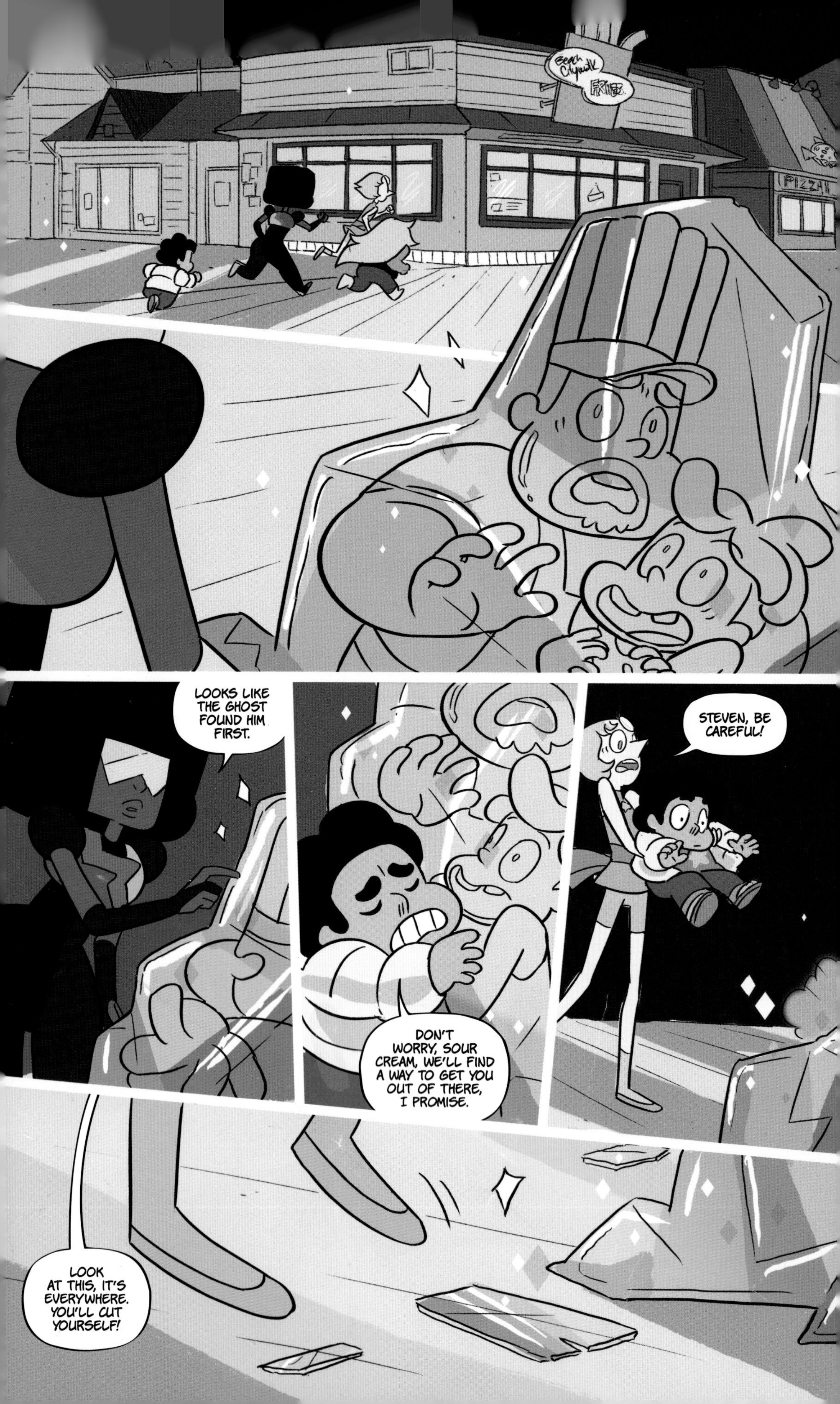
Beach Citywalk Fries
PIZZA
LOOKS LIKE THE GHOST FOUND HIM FIRST.
DON'T WORRY, SOUR CREAM, WE'LL FIND A WAY TO GET YOU OUT OF THERE, I PROMISE.
STEVEN, BE CAREFUL!
LOOK AT THIS, IT'S EVERYWHERE. YOU'LL CUT YOURSELF!

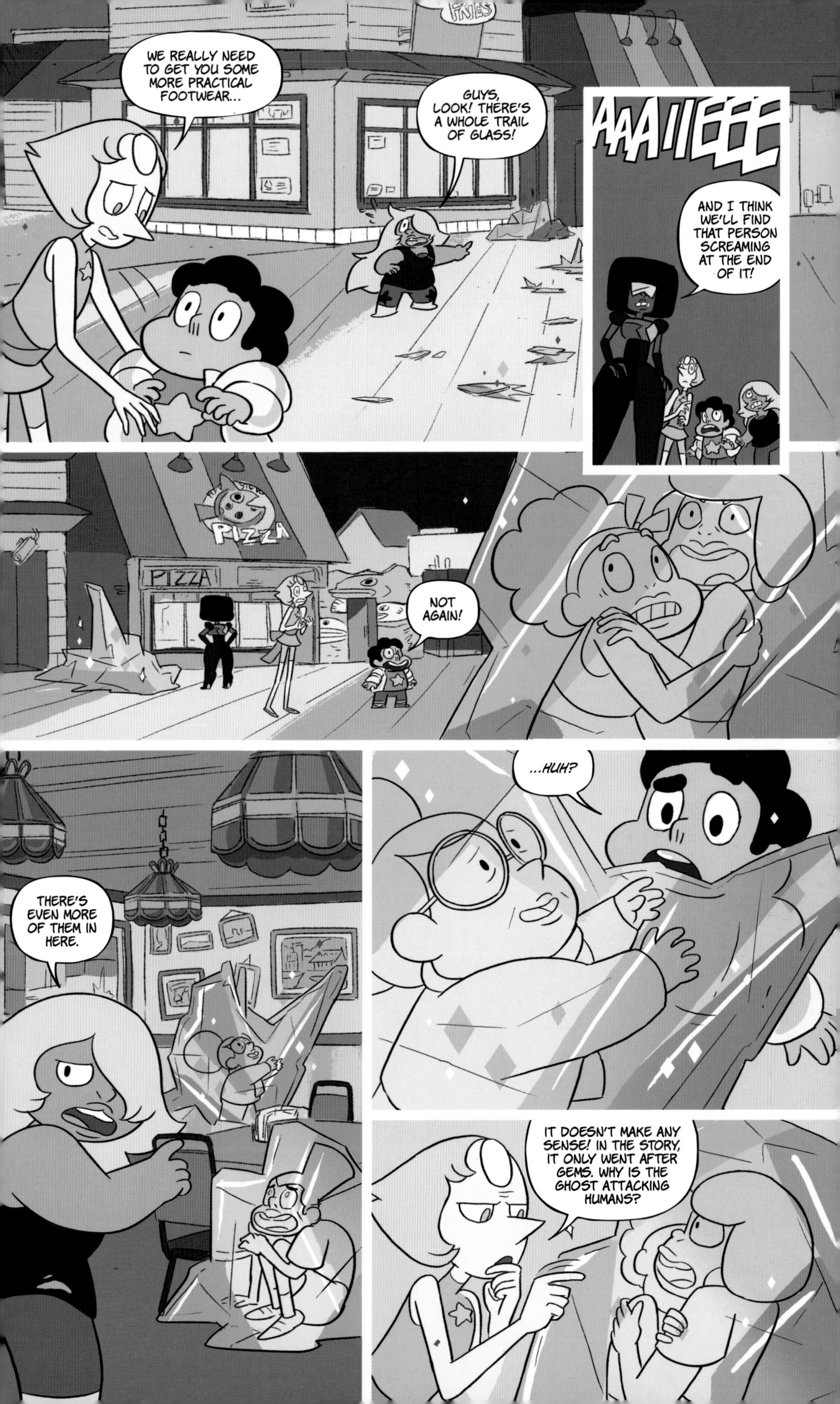
WE REALLY NEED TO GET YOU SOME MORE PRACTICAL FOOTWEAR...
GUYS, LOOK! THERE'S A WHOLE TRAIL OF GLASS!
AAAIIEEEE
AND I THINK WE'LL FIND THAT PERSON SCREAMING AT THE END OF IT!
PIZZA
PIZZA
NOT AGAIN!
THERE'S EVEN MORE OF THEM IN HERE.
...HUH?
IT DOESN'T MAKE ANY SENSE! IN THE STORY, IT ONLY WENT AFTER GEMS. WHY IS THE GHOST ATTACKING HUMANS?

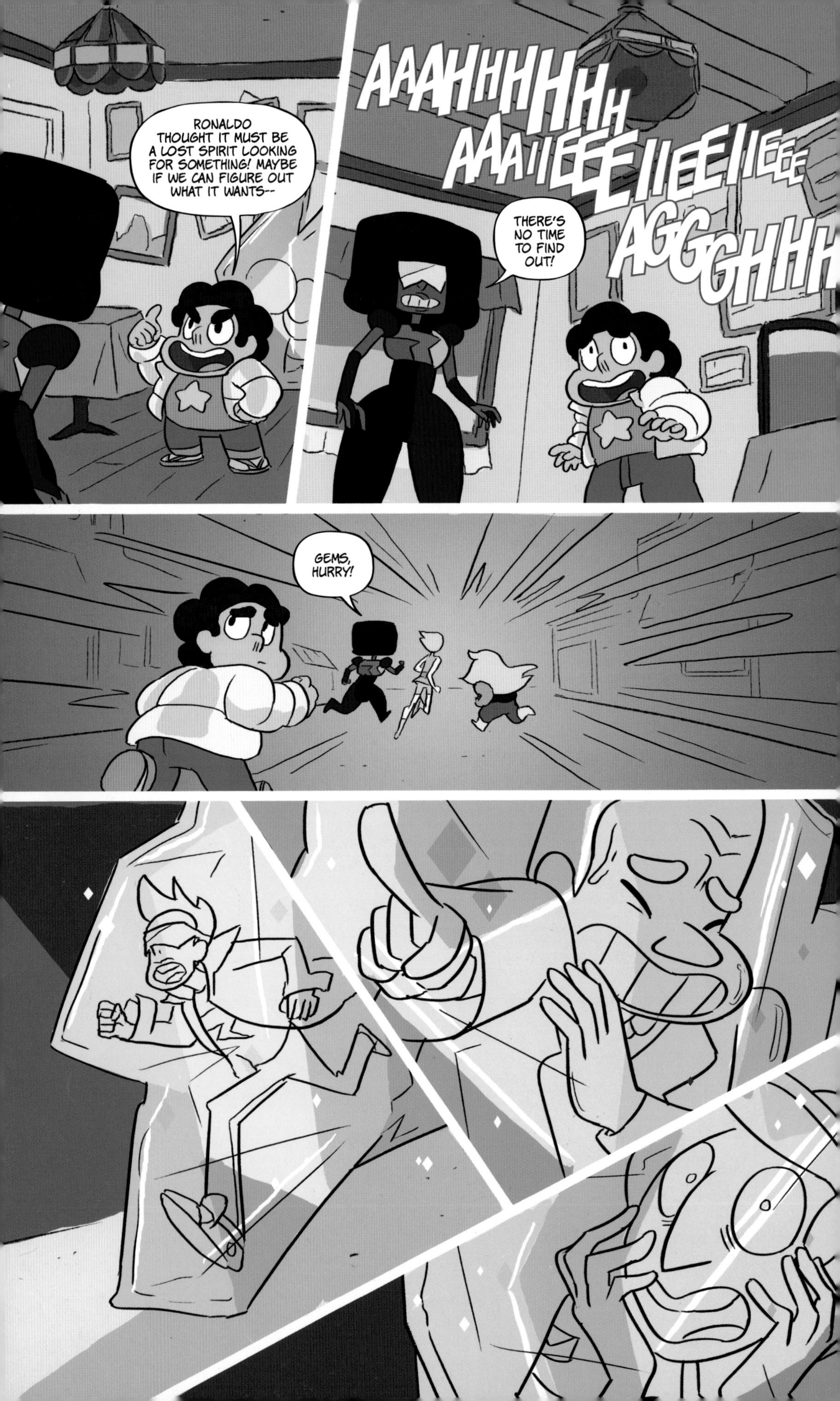
RONALDO THOUGHT IT MUST BE A LOST SPIRIT LOOKING FOR SOMETHING! MAYBE IF WE CAN FIGURE OUT WHAT IT WANTS--
AAAHHHHHHh AAAIIEEEEIIEEIIEEE AGGGHHH
THERE'S NO TIME TO FIND OUT!
GEMS, HURRY!

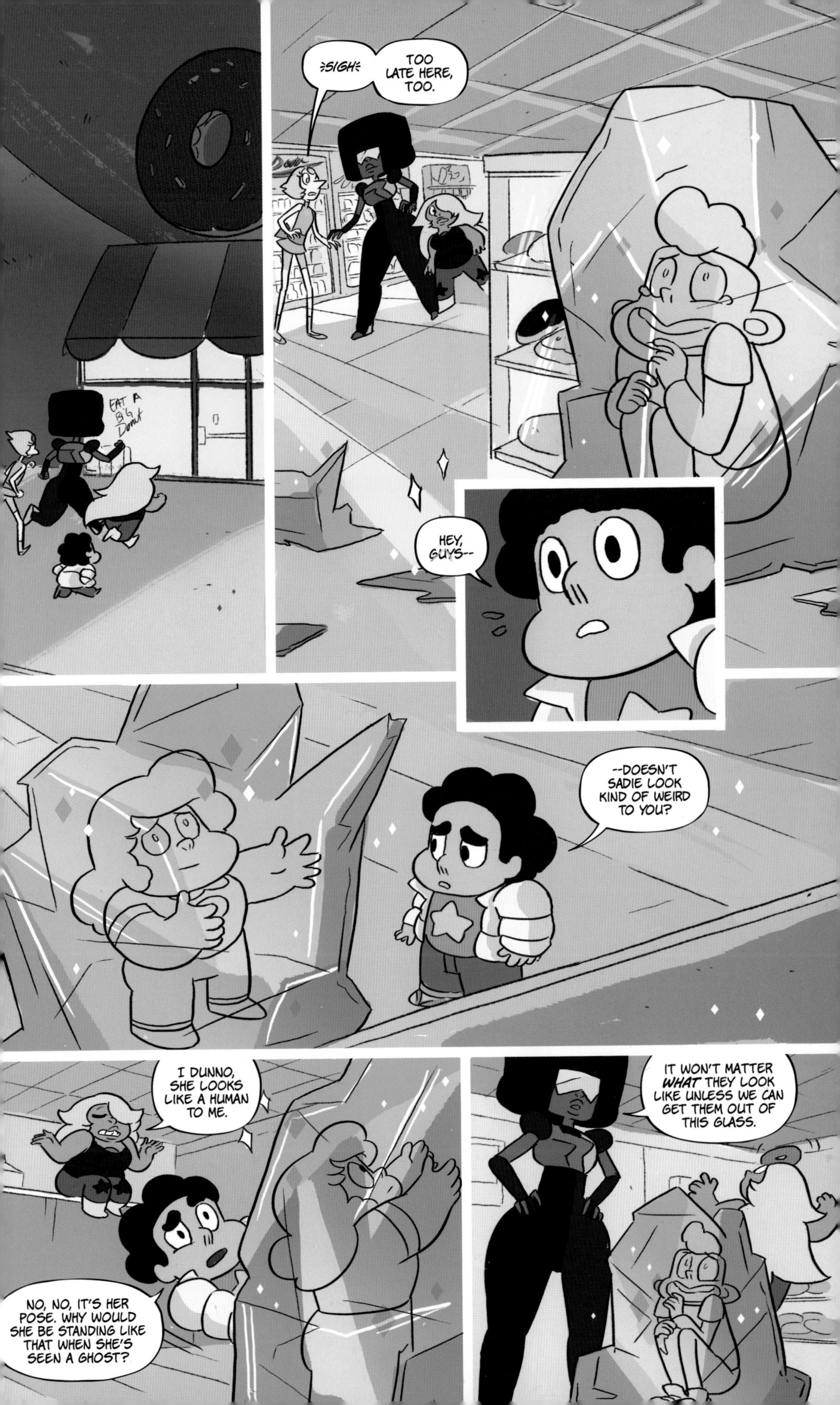

EAT A BIG Donut
≈SIGH≈
TOO LATE HERE, TOO.
HEY, GUYS--
--DOESN'T SADIE LOOK KIND OF WEIRD TO YOU?
I DUNNO, SHE LOOKS LIKE A HUMAN TO ME.
NO, NO, IT'S HER POSE. WHY WOULD SHE BE STANDING LIKE THAT WHEN SHE'S SEEN A GHOST?
IT WON'T MATTER *WHAT* THEY LOOK LIKE UNLESS WE CAN GET THEM OUT OF THIS GLASS.

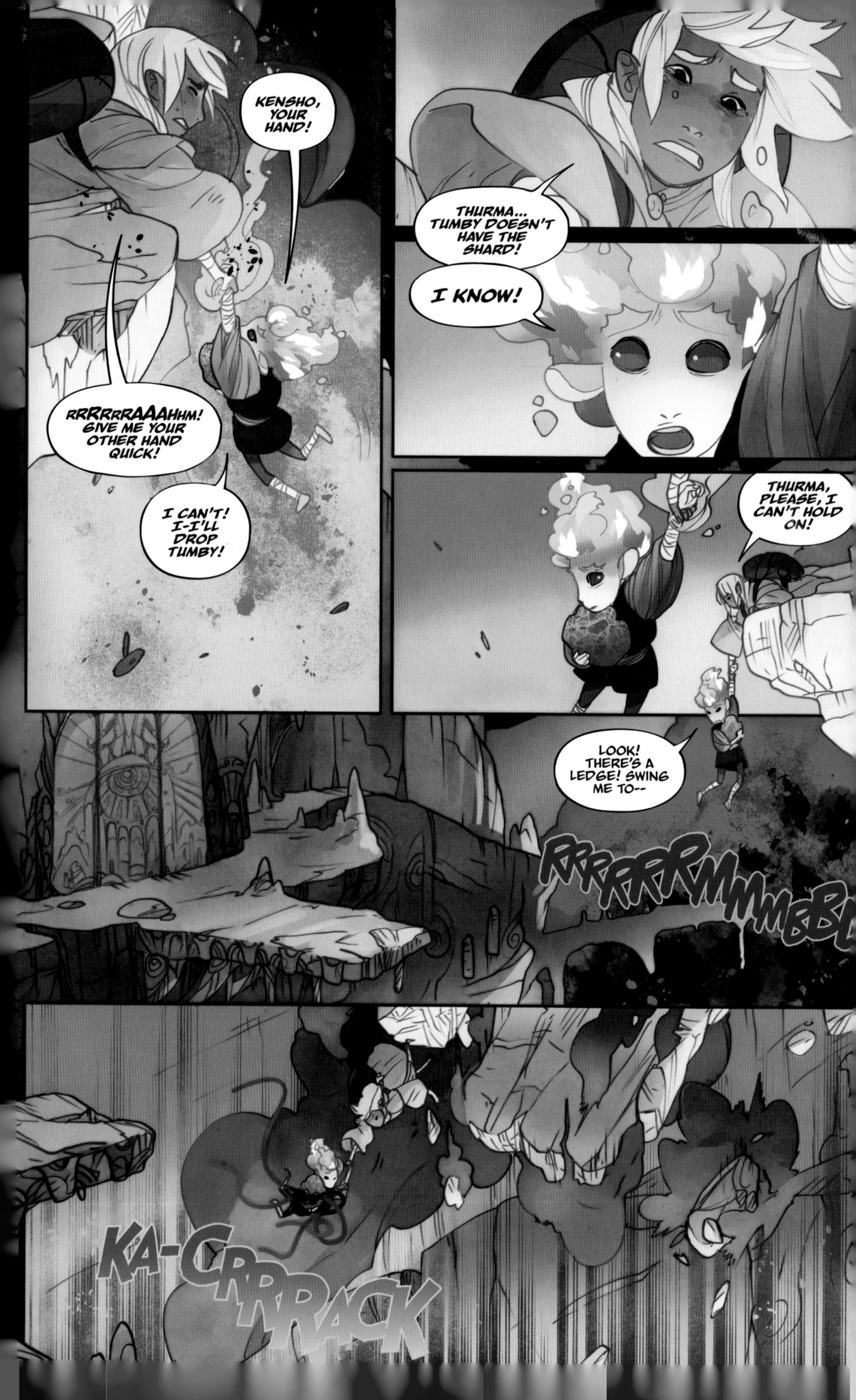
KENSHO, YOUR HAND!
RRRRRRAAAHHM! GIVE ME YOUR OTHER HAND QUICK!
I CAN'T! I-I'LL DROP TUMBY!
THURMA... TUMBY DOESN'T HAVE THE SHARD!
I KNOW!
THURMA, PLEASE, I CAN'T HOLD ON!
LOOK! THERE'S A LEDGE! SWING ME TO--
RRRRRRMMMBBL
KA-CRRRACK

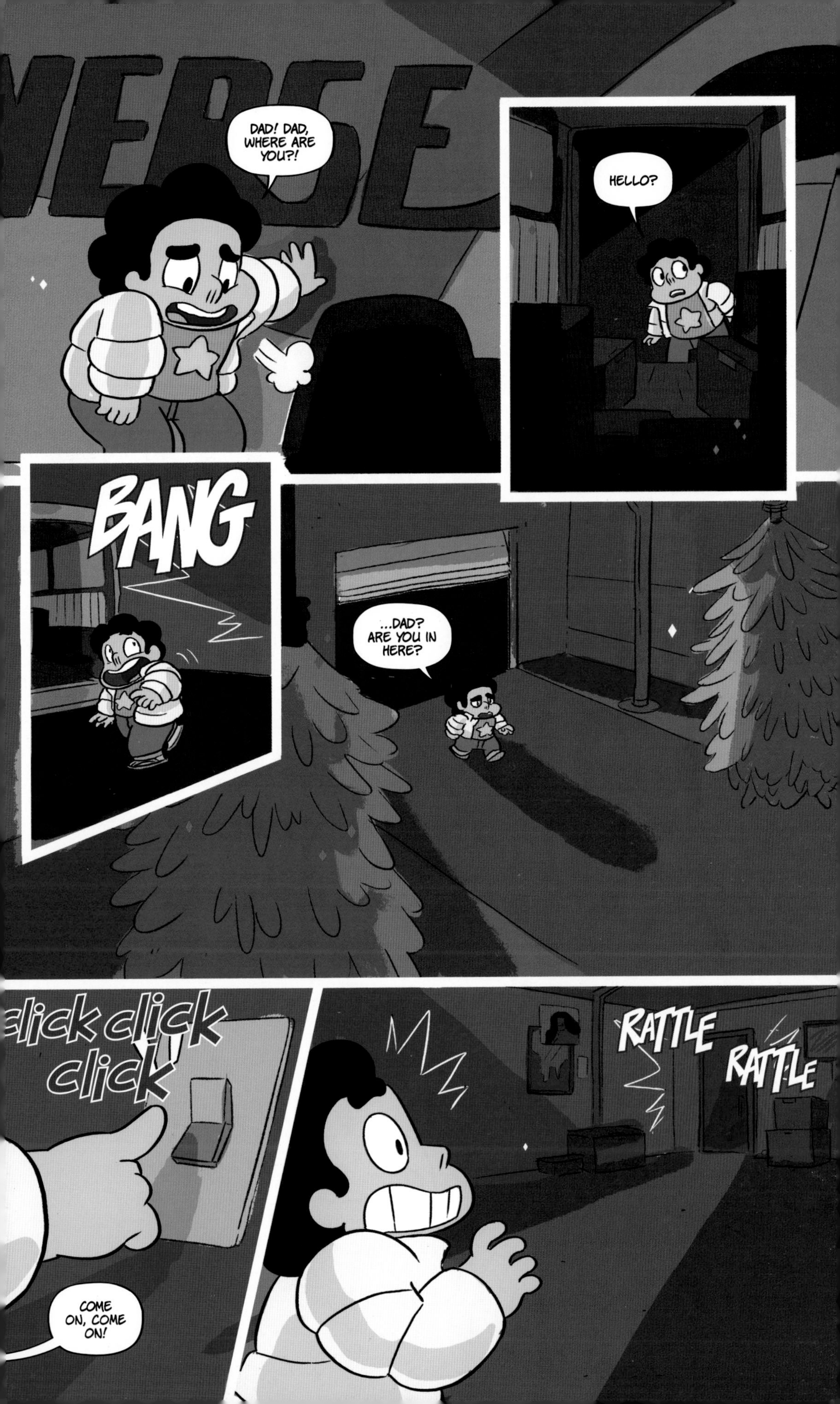
DAD! DAD, WHERE ARE YOU?!
HELLO?
BANG
...DAD? ARE YOU IN HERE?
click click click
COME ON, COME ON!
RATTLE RATTLE

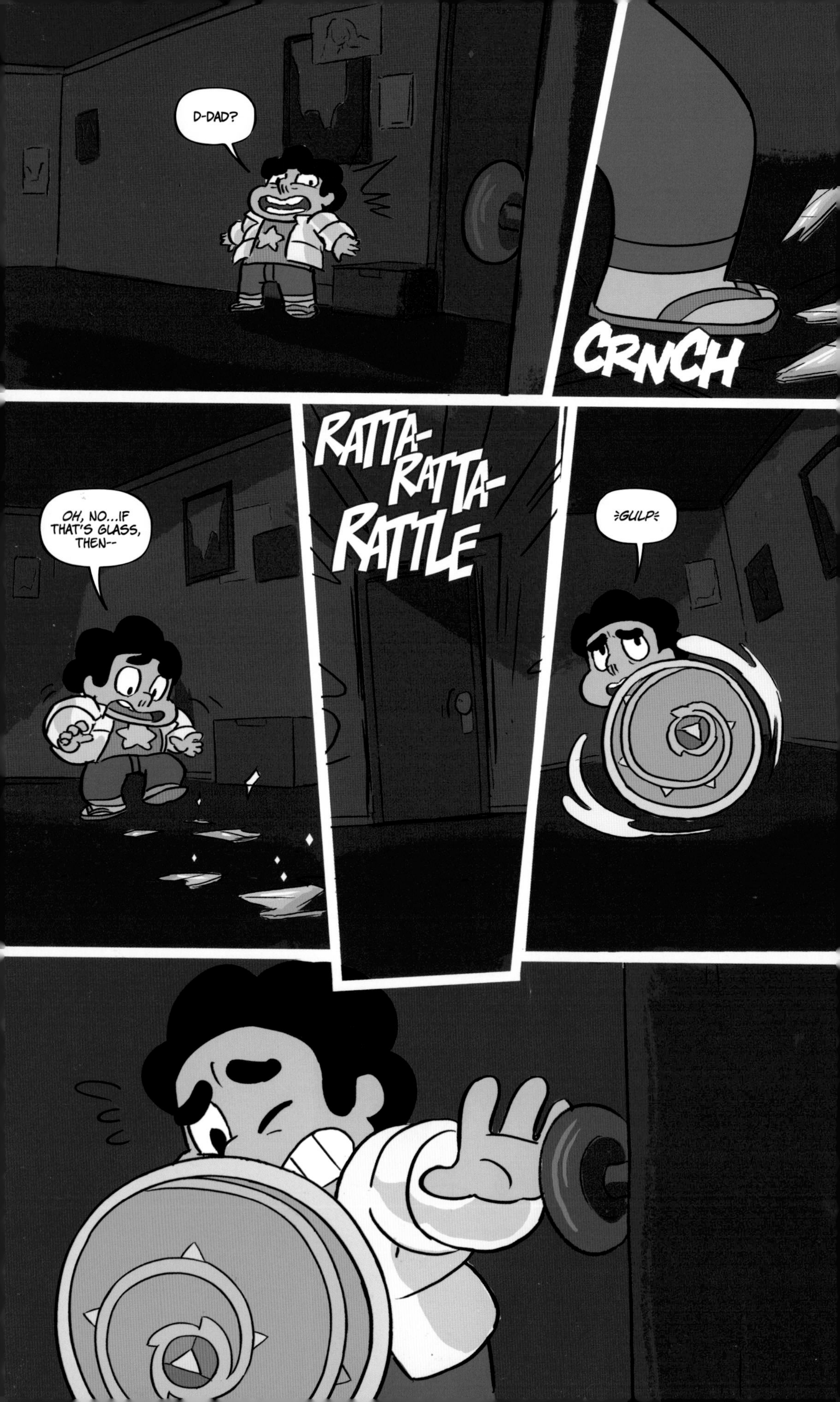
D-DAD?
CRNCH
OH, NO...IF THAT'S GLASS, THEN--
RATTA-RATTA-RATTLE
GULP

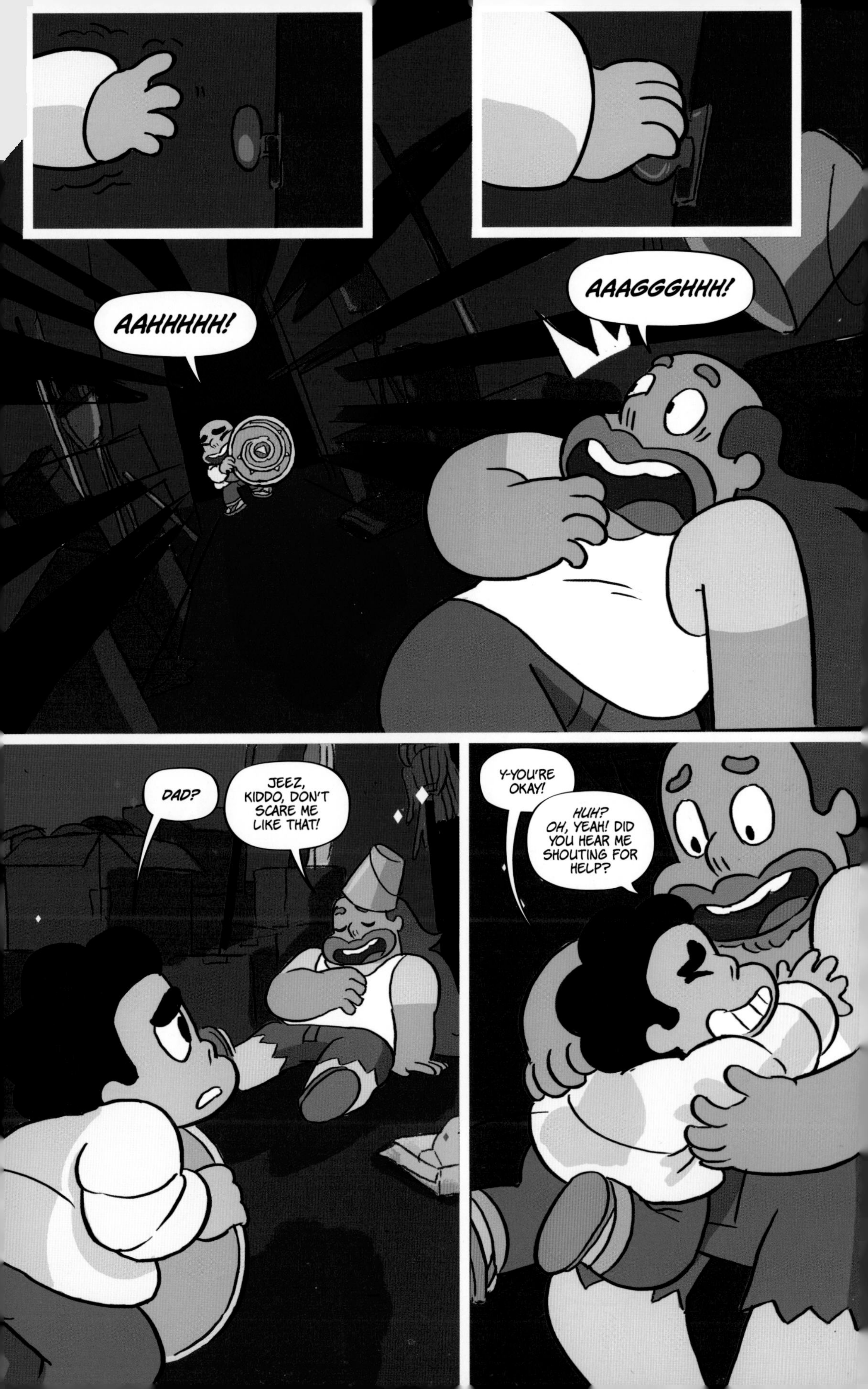
AHHHHHH!
AAAGGGHHH!
DAD?
JEEZ, KIDDO, DON'T SCARE ME LIKE THAT!
Y-YOU'RE OKAY!
HUH? OH, YEAH! DID YOU HEAR ME SHOUTING FOR HELP?

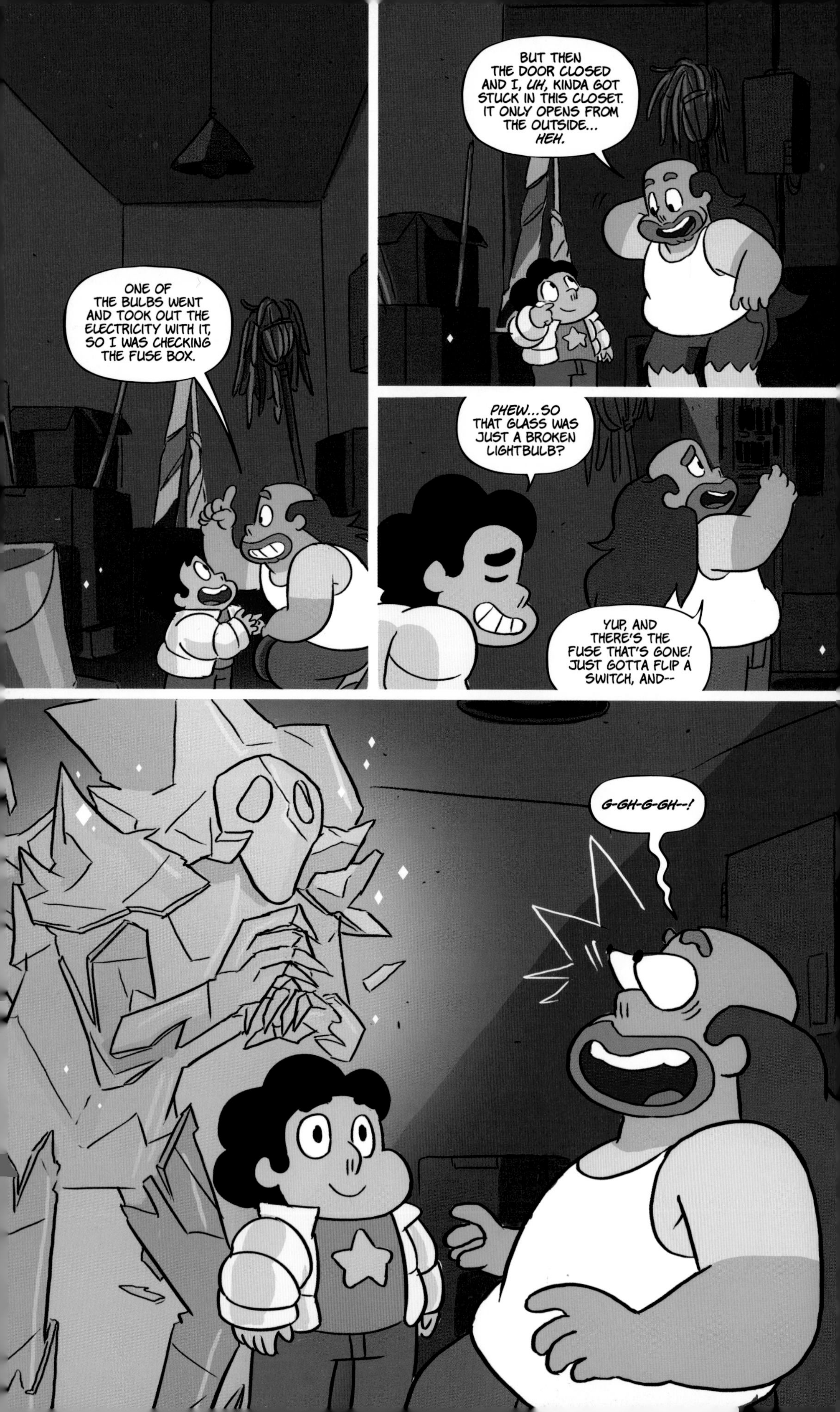
ONE OF THE BULBS WENT AND TOOK OUT THE ELECTRICITY WITH IT, SO I WAS CHECKING THE FUSE BOX.
BUT THEN THE DOOR CLOSED AND I, UH, KINDA GOT STUCK IN THIS CLOSET. IT ONLY OPENS FROM THE OUTSIDE... HEH.
PHEW...SO THAT GLASS WAS JUST A BROKEN LIGHTBULB?
YUP, AND THERE'S THE FUSE THAT'S GONE! JUST GOTTA FLIP A SWITCH, AND--
G-GH-G-GH--!

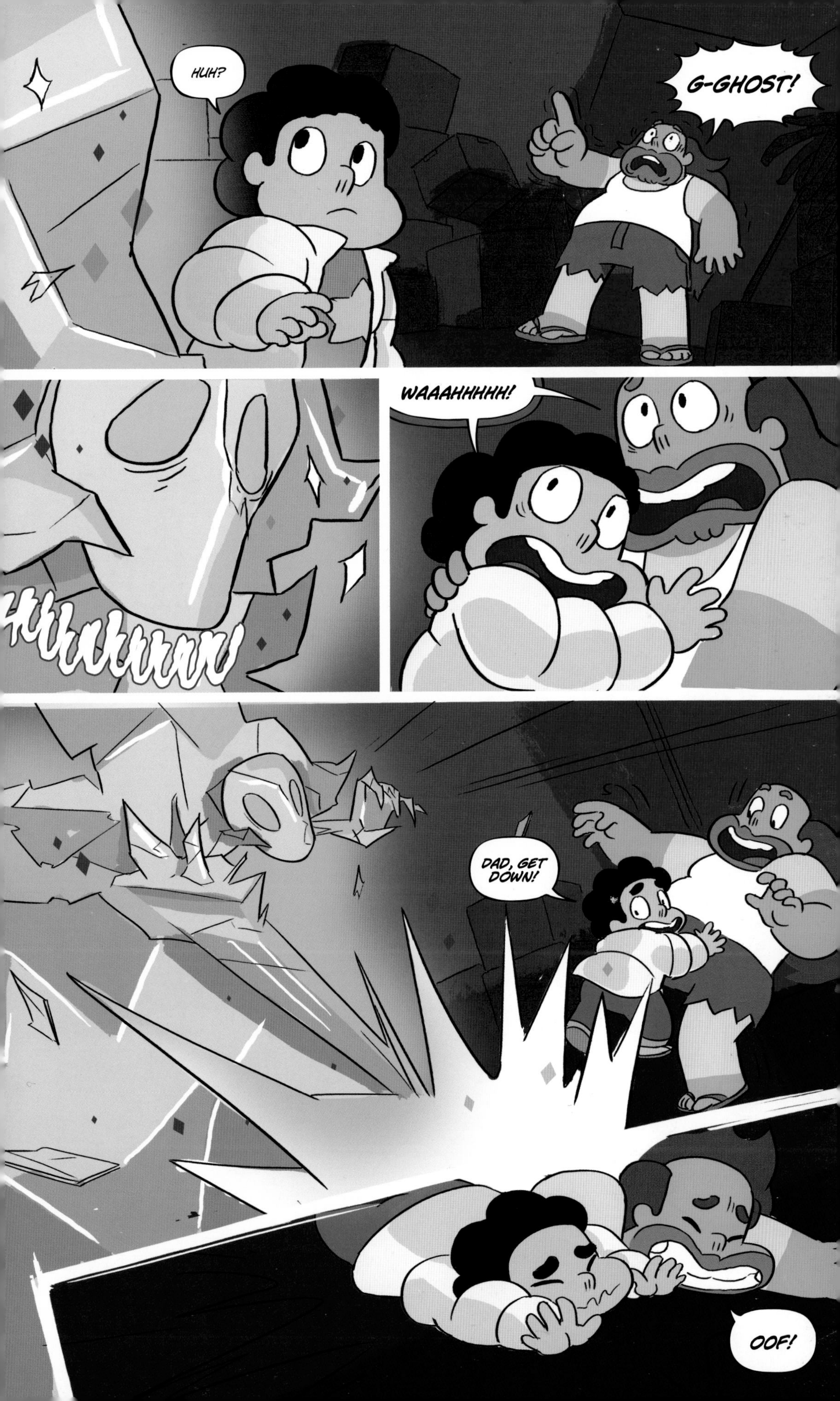
HUH?
G-GHOST!
WAAAHHHHH!
Hrrrhrrrrrr!
DAD, GET DOWN!
OOF!

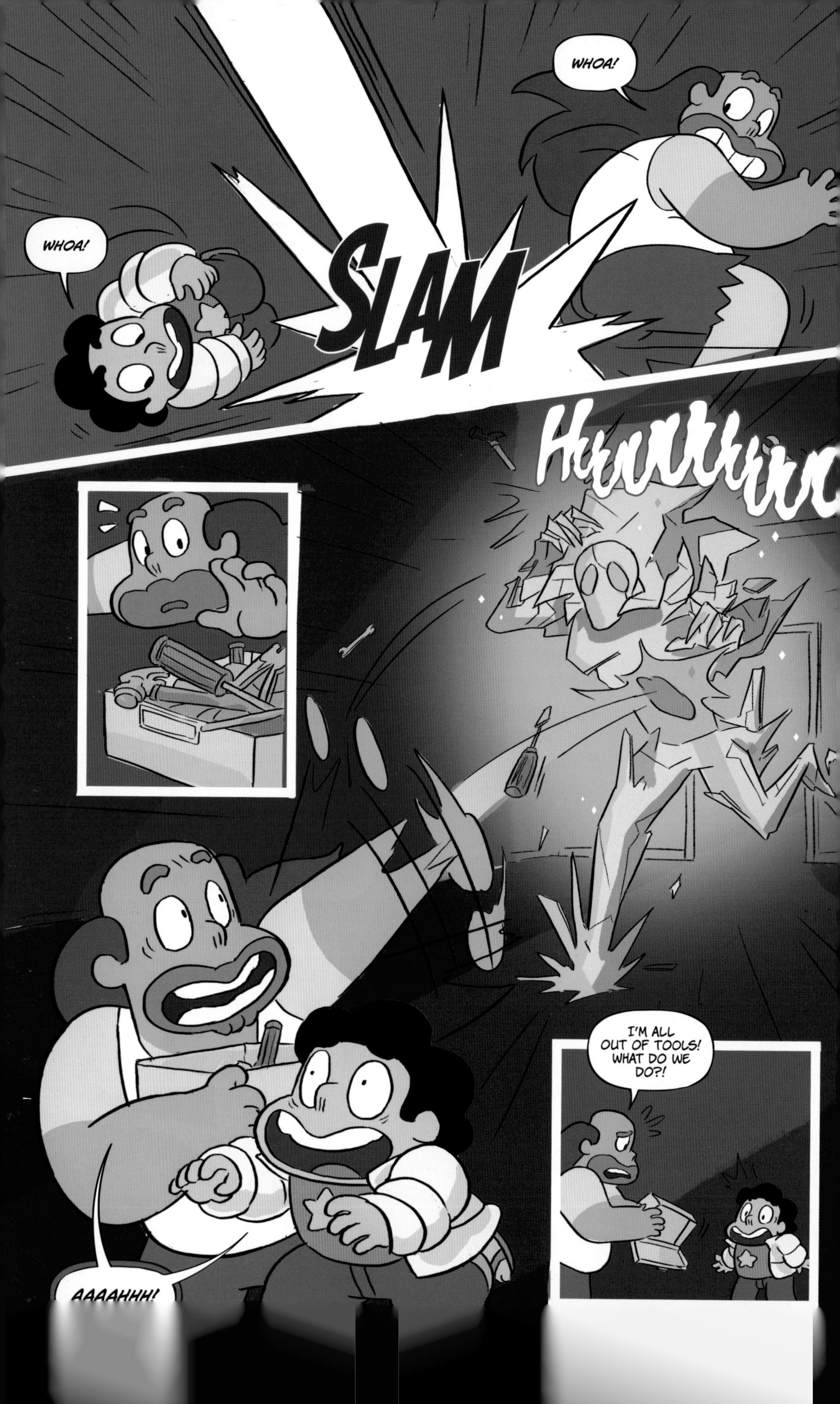

WHOA!
WHOA!
SLAM
Hrrrrrrrrrrrrrrr
AAAAHHH!
I'M ALL OUT OF TOOLS! WHAT DO WE DO?!

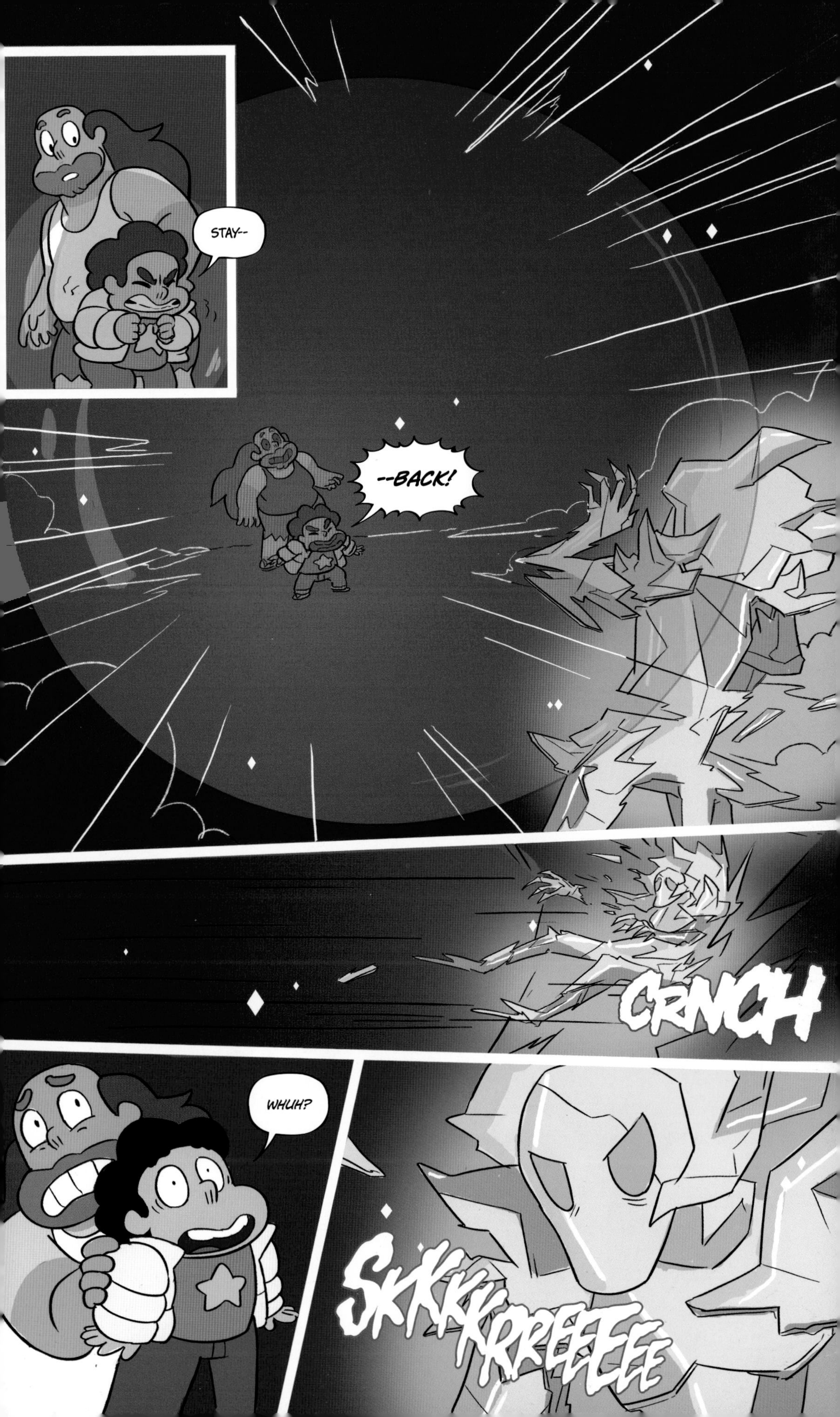
STAY--
--BACK!
CRNCH
WHUH?
SKKKKRREEEEEE

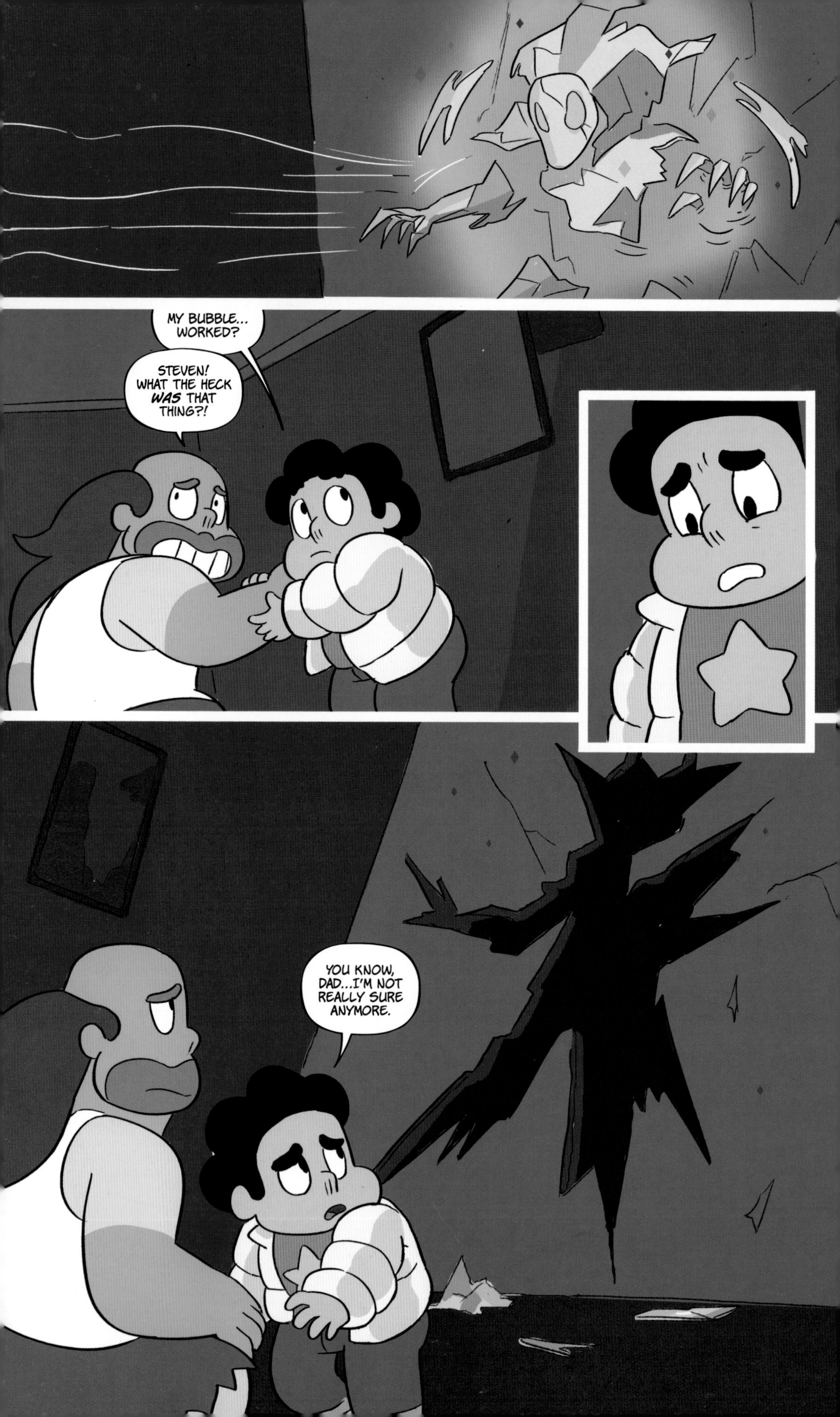
MY BUBBLE... WORKED?
STEVEN! WHAT THE HECK *WAS* THAT THING?!
YOU KNOW, DAD...I'M NOT REALLY SURE ANYMORE.

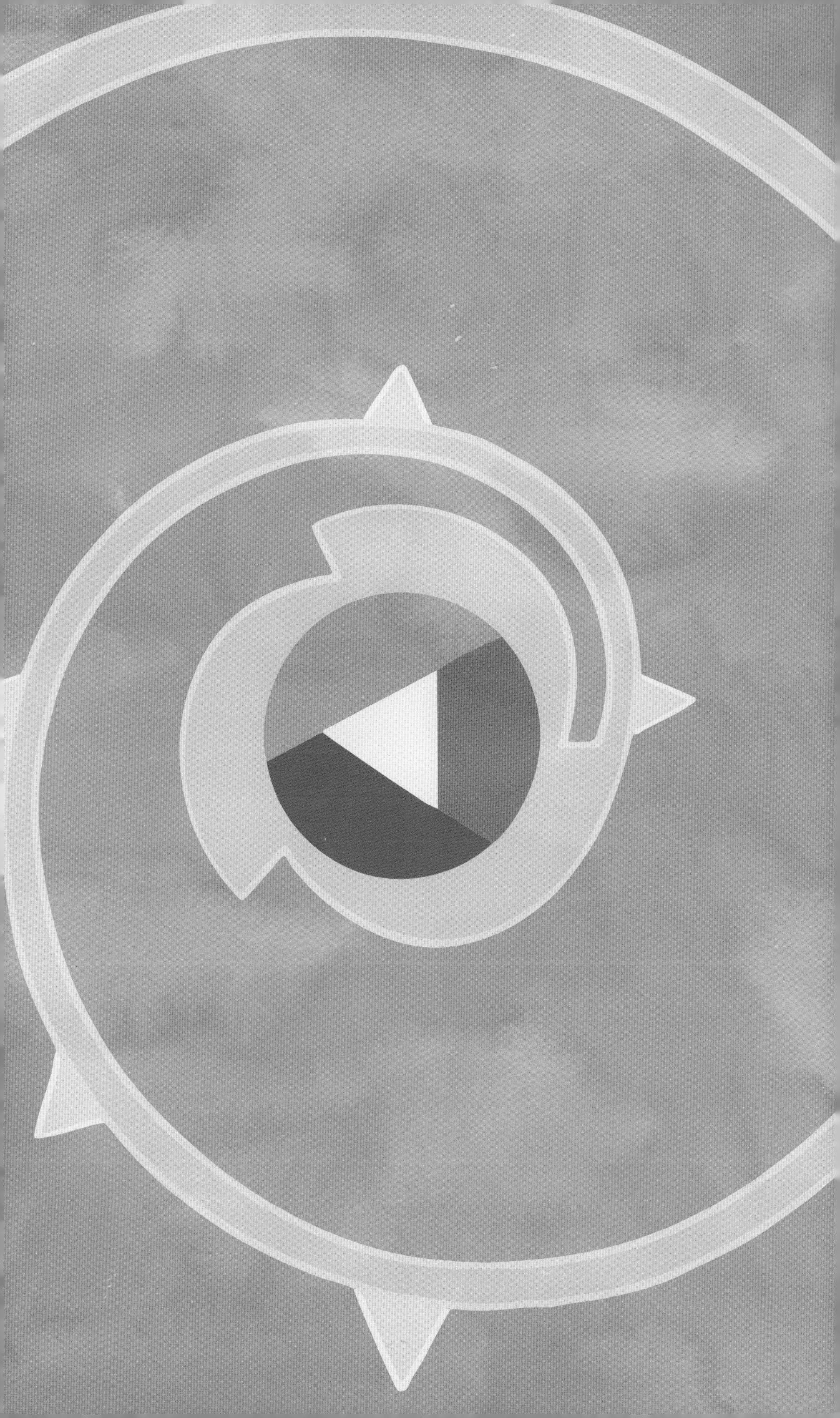

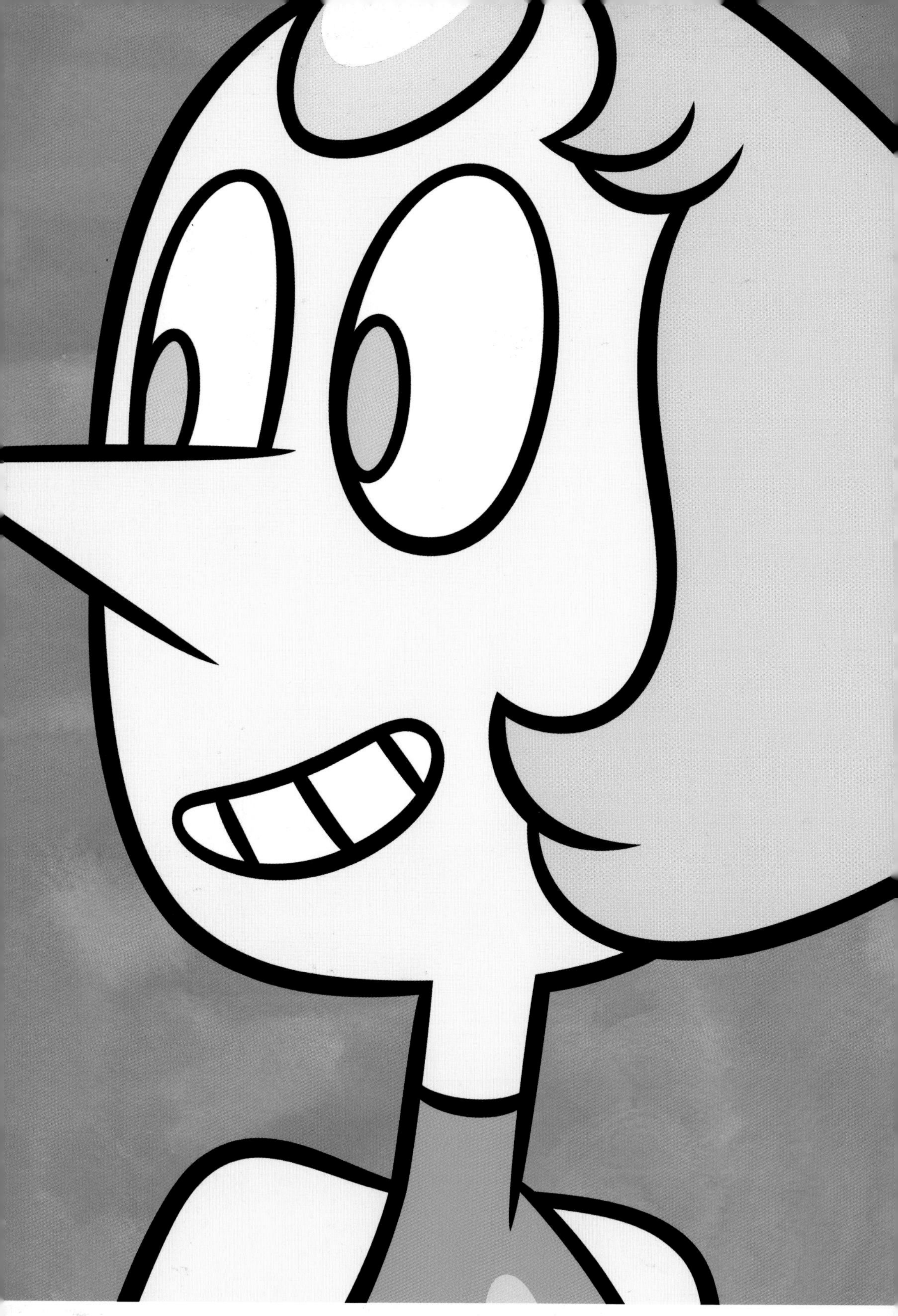

CHAPTER FOUR

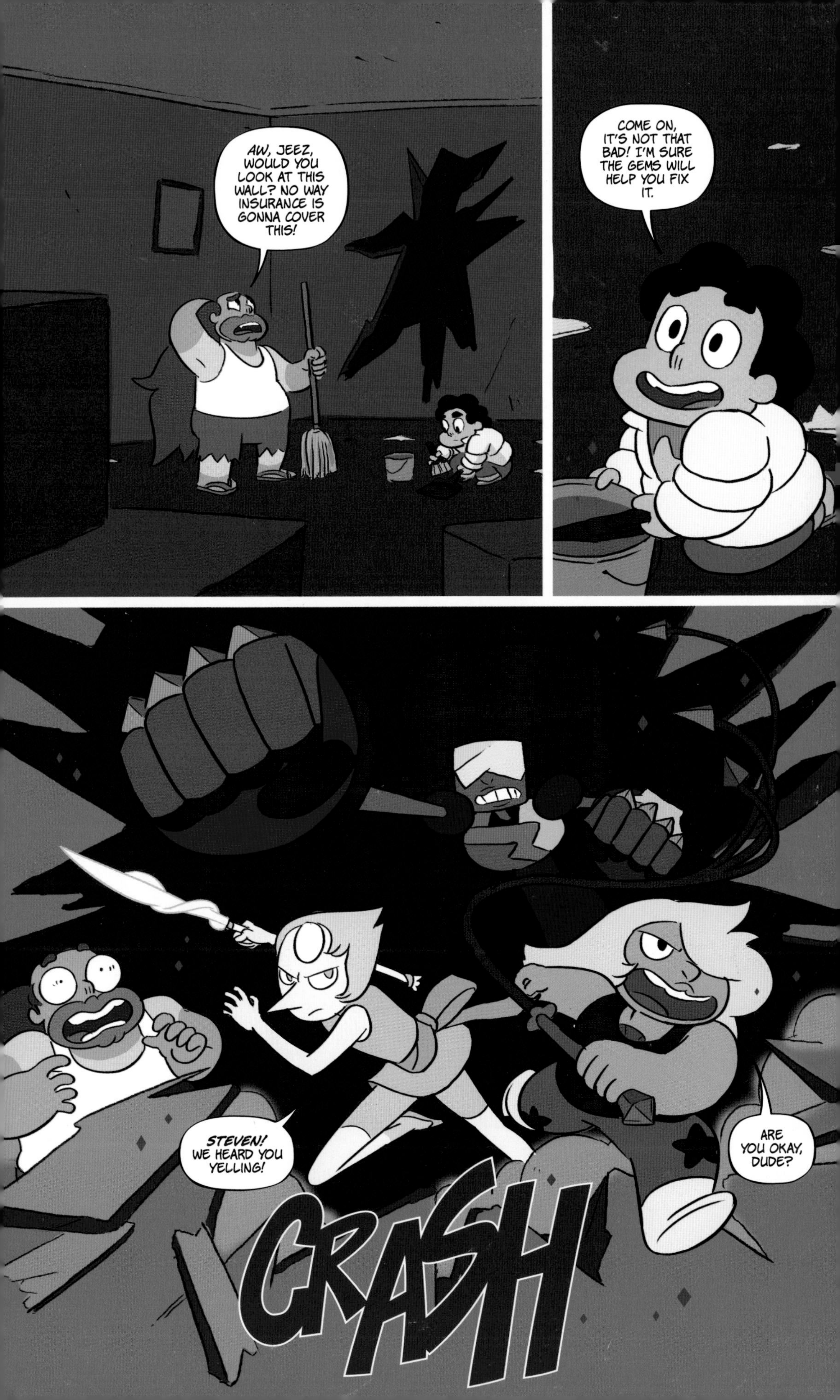
AW, JEEZ, WOULD YOU LOOK AT THIS WALL? NO WAY INSURANCE IS GONNA COVER THIS!
COME ON, IT'S NOT THAT BAD! I'M SURE THE GEMS WILL HELP YOU FIX IT.
STEVEN! WE HEARD YOU YELLING!
ARE YOU OKAY, DUDE?
CRASH

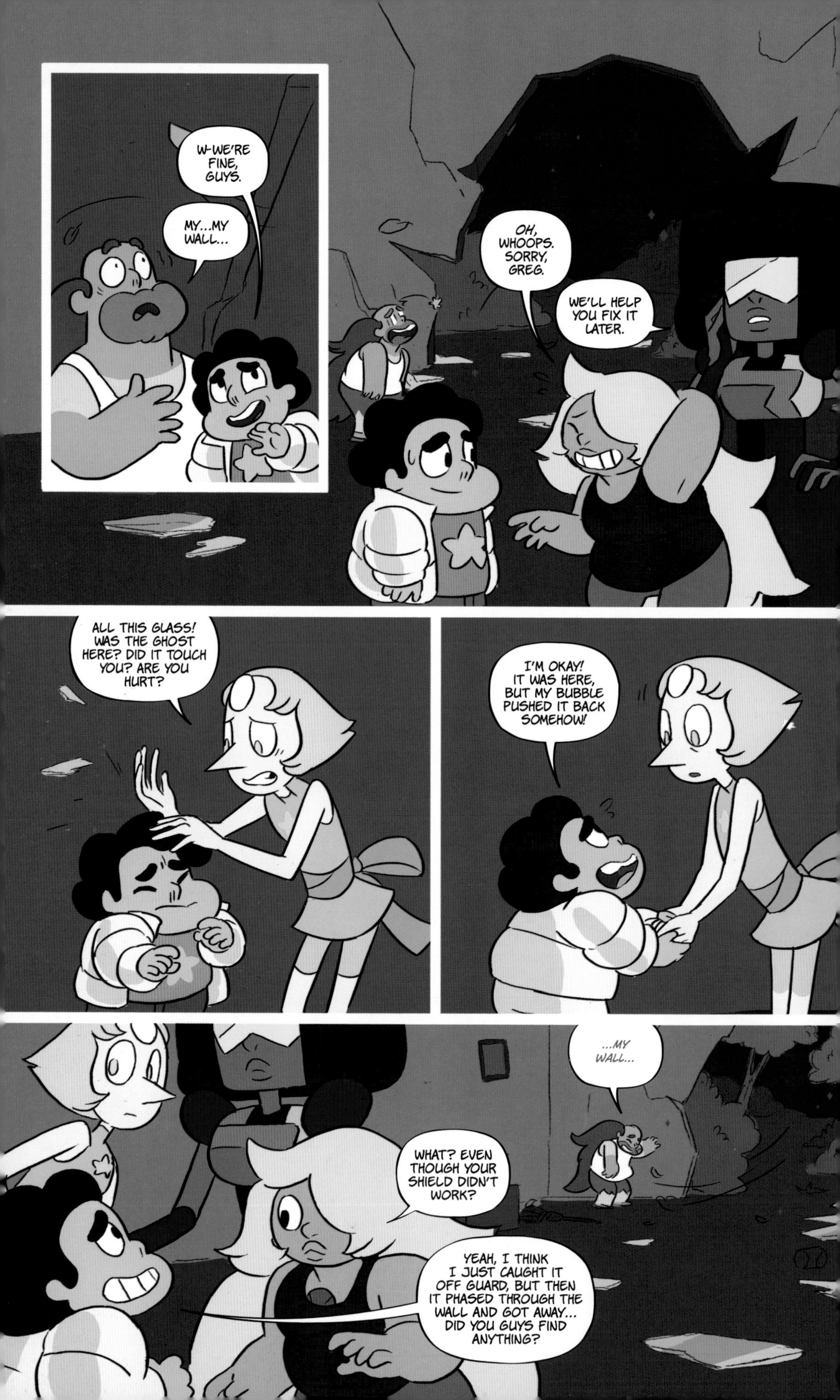
W-WE'RE FINE, GUYS.
MY...MY WALL...
OH, WHOOPS. SORRY, GREG.
WE'LL HELP YOU FIX IT LATER.
ALL THIS GLASS! WAS THE GHOST HERE? DID IT TOUCH YOU? ARE YOU HURT?
I'M OKAY! IT WAS HERE, BUT MY BUBBLE PUSHED IT BACK SOMEHOW!
...MY WALL...
WHAT? EVEN THOUGH YOUR SHIELD DIDN'T WORK?
YEAH, I THINK I JUST CAUGHT IT OFF GUARD, BUT THEN IT PHASED THROUGH THE WALL AND GOT AWAY... DID YOU GUYS FIND ANYTHING?

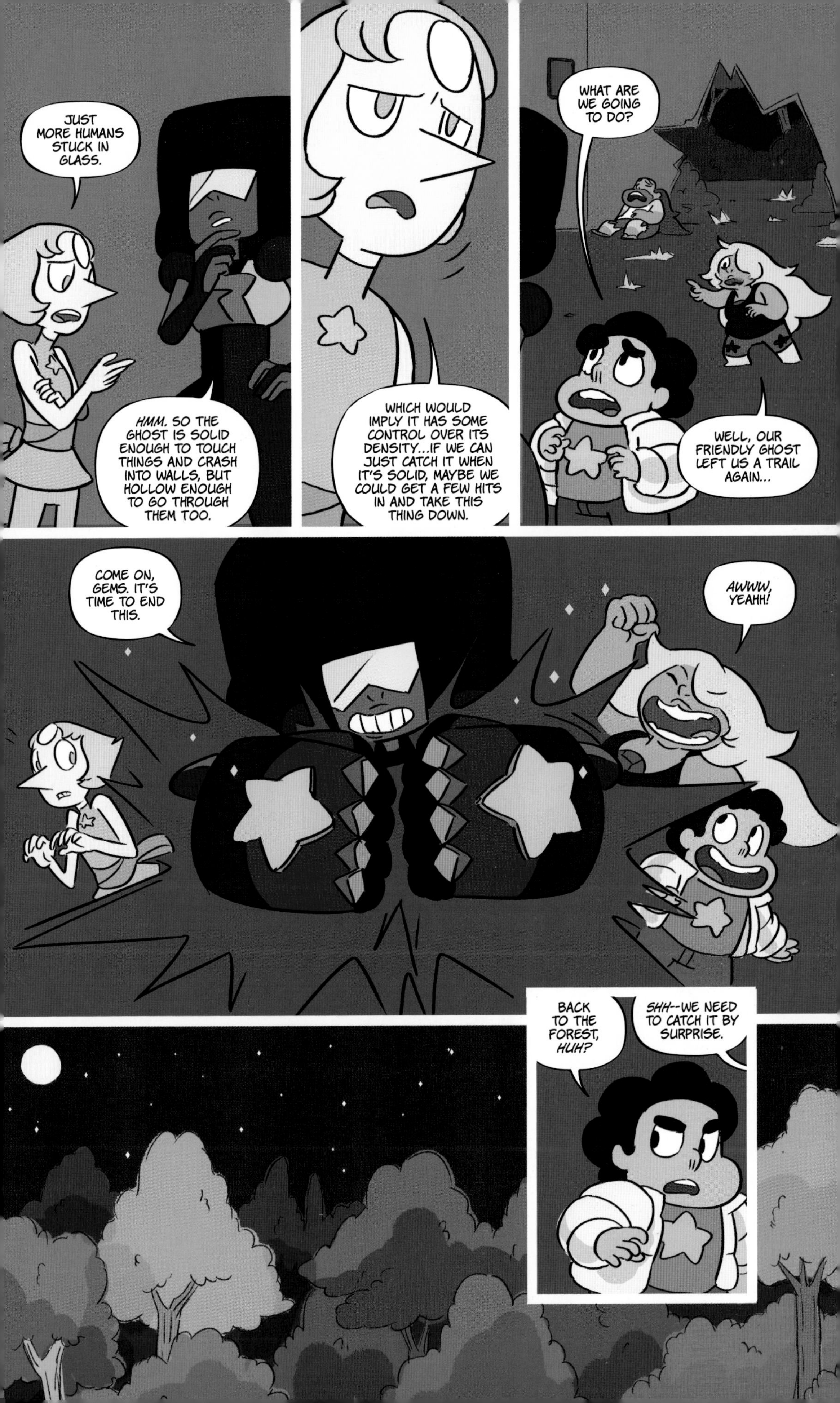
JUST MORE HUMANS STUCK IN GLASS.
HMM. SO THE GHOST IS SOLID ENOUGH TO TOUCH THINGS AND CRASH INTO WALLS, BUT HOLLOW ENOUGH TO GO THROUGH THEM TOO.
WHICH WOULD IMPLY IT HAS SOME CONTROL OVER ITS DENSITY...IF WE CAN JUST CATCH IT WHEN IT'S SOLID, MAYBE WE COULD GET A FEW HITS IN AND TAKE THIS THING DOWN.
WHAT ARE WE GOING TO DO?
WELL, OUR FRIENDLY GHOST LEFT US A TRAIL AGAIN...
COME ON, GEMS. IT'S TIME TO END THIS.
AWWW, YEAHH!
BACK TO THE FOREST, *HUH?*
*SHH--*WE NEED TO CATCH IT BY SURPRISE.

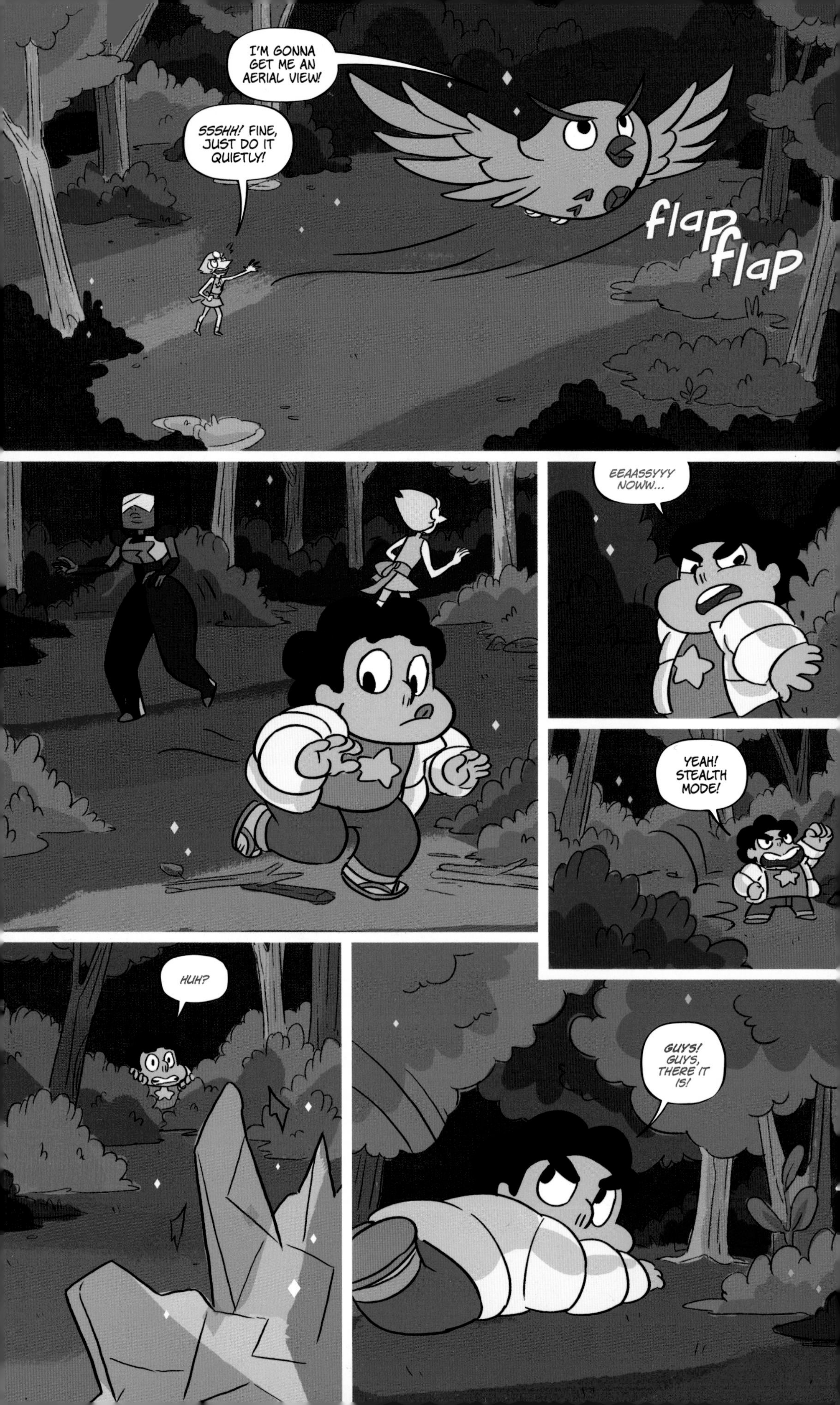
I'M GONNA GET ME AN AERIAL VIEW!
SSSHH! FINE, JUST DO IT QUIETLY!
flap flap
EEAASSYYY NOWW...
YEAH! STEALTH MODE!
HUH?
GUYS! GUYS, THERE IT IS!

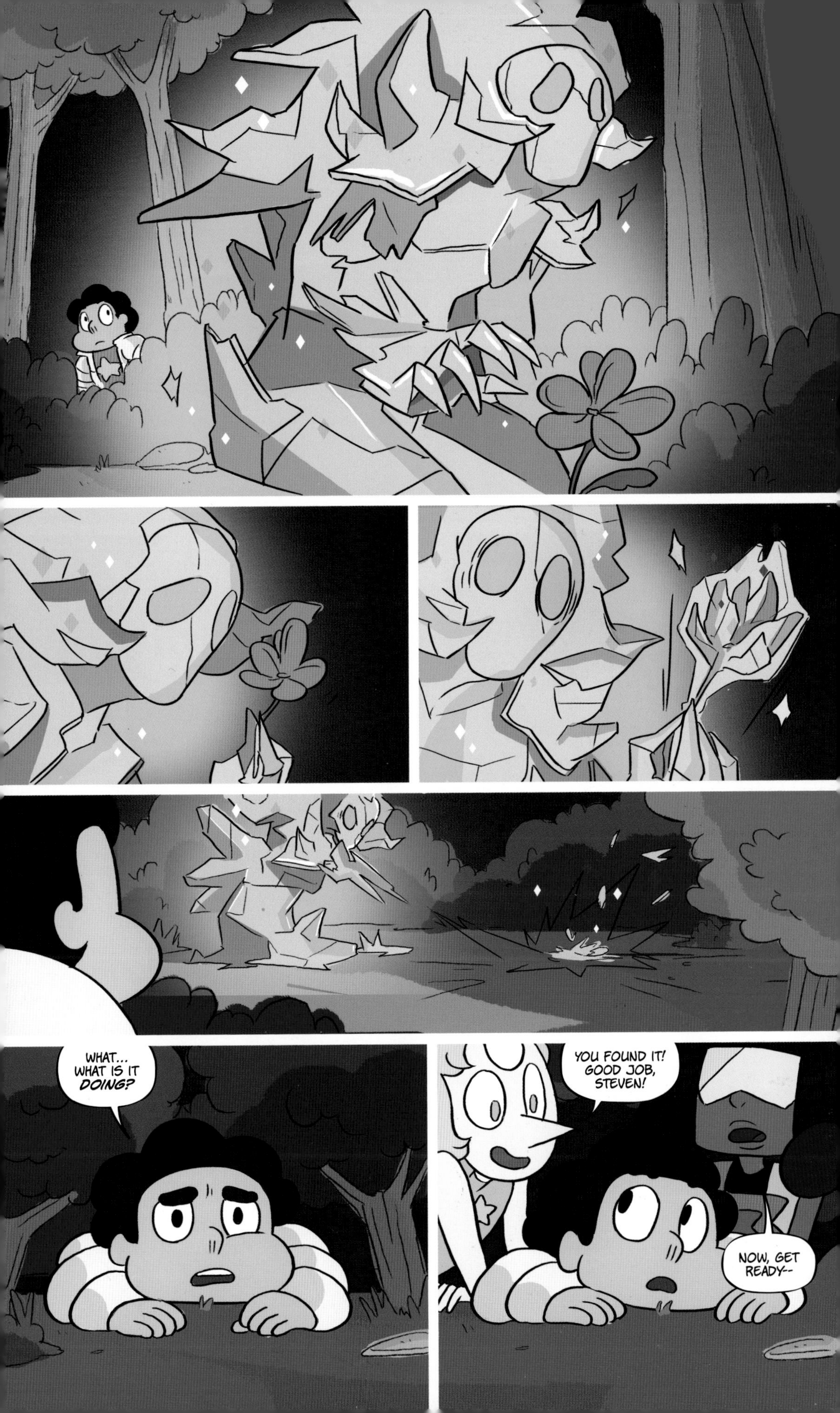
WHAT... WHAT IS IT *DOING?*
YOU FOUND IT! GOOD JOB, STEVEN!
NOW, GET READY--

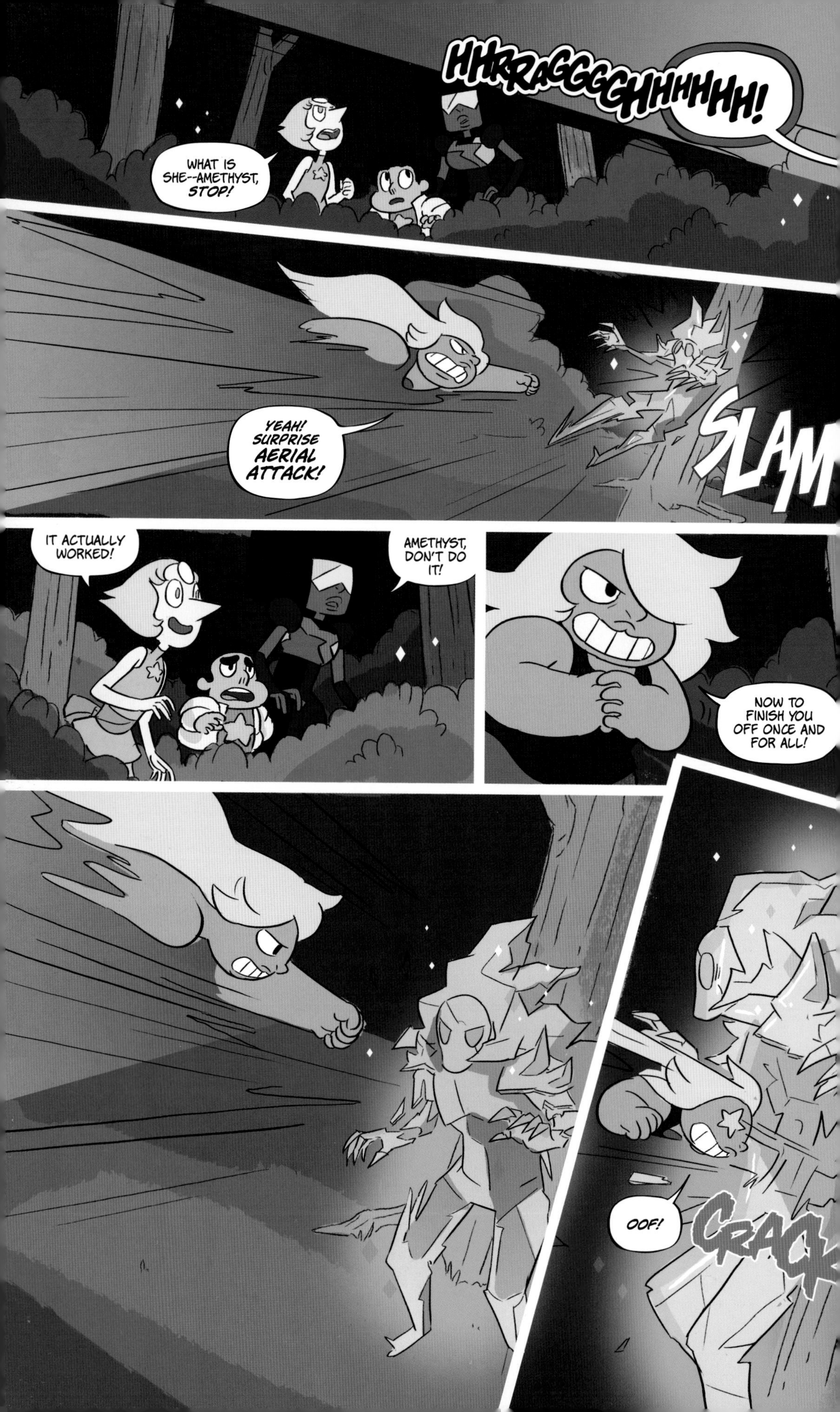
HHRRAGGGGHHHHHH!
WHAT IS SHE--AMETHYST, STOP!
YEAH! SURPRISE AERIAL ATTACK!
SLAM
IT ACTUALLY WORKED!
AMETHYST, DON'T DO IT!
NOW TO FINISH YOU OFF ONCE AND FOR ALL!
OOF!
CRAC

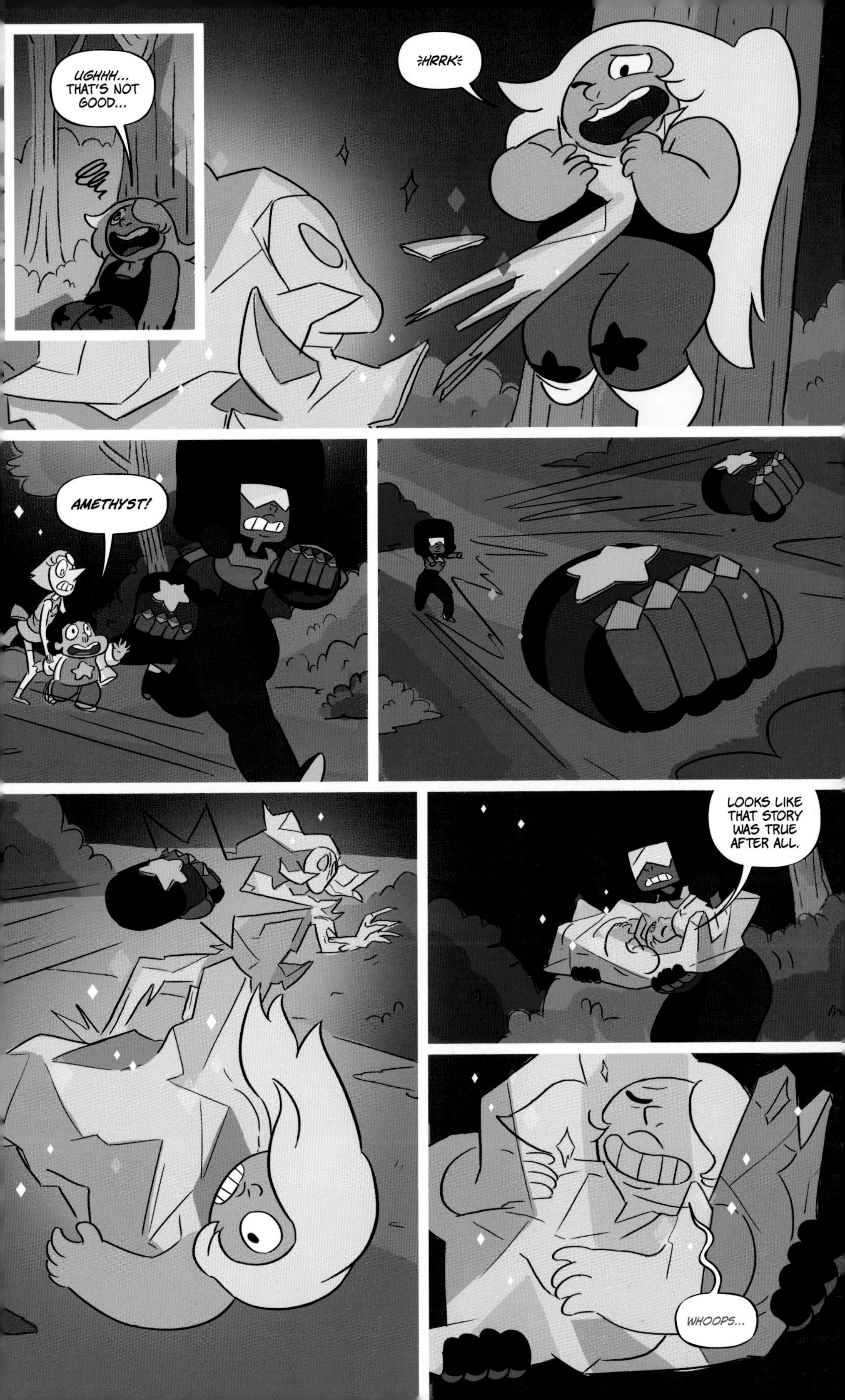
UGHHH... THAT'S NOT GOOD...
HRRK
AMETHYST!
LOOKS LIKE THAT STORY WAS TRUE AFTER ALL.
WHOOPS...

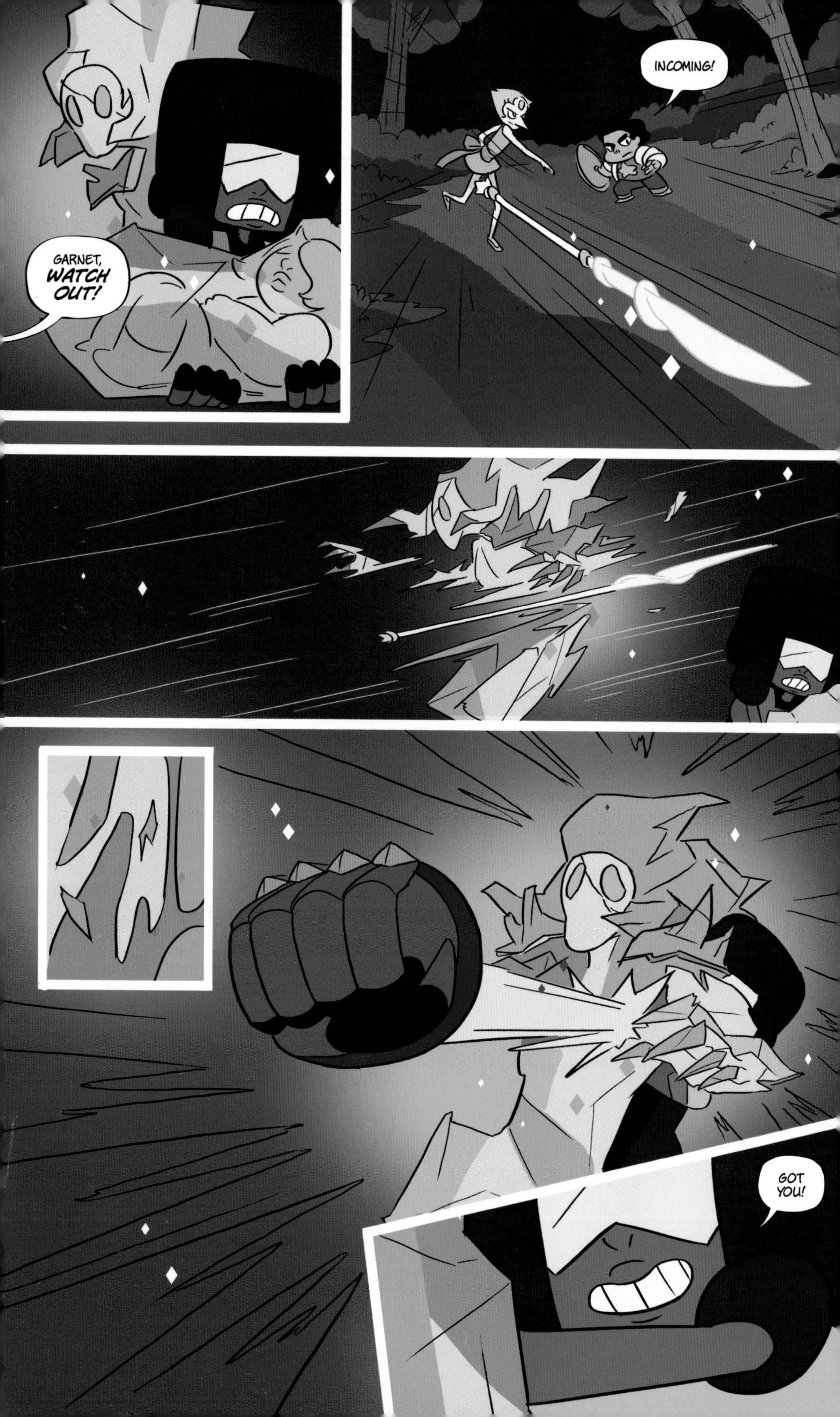
INCOMING!
GARNET, WATCH OUT!
GOT YOU!

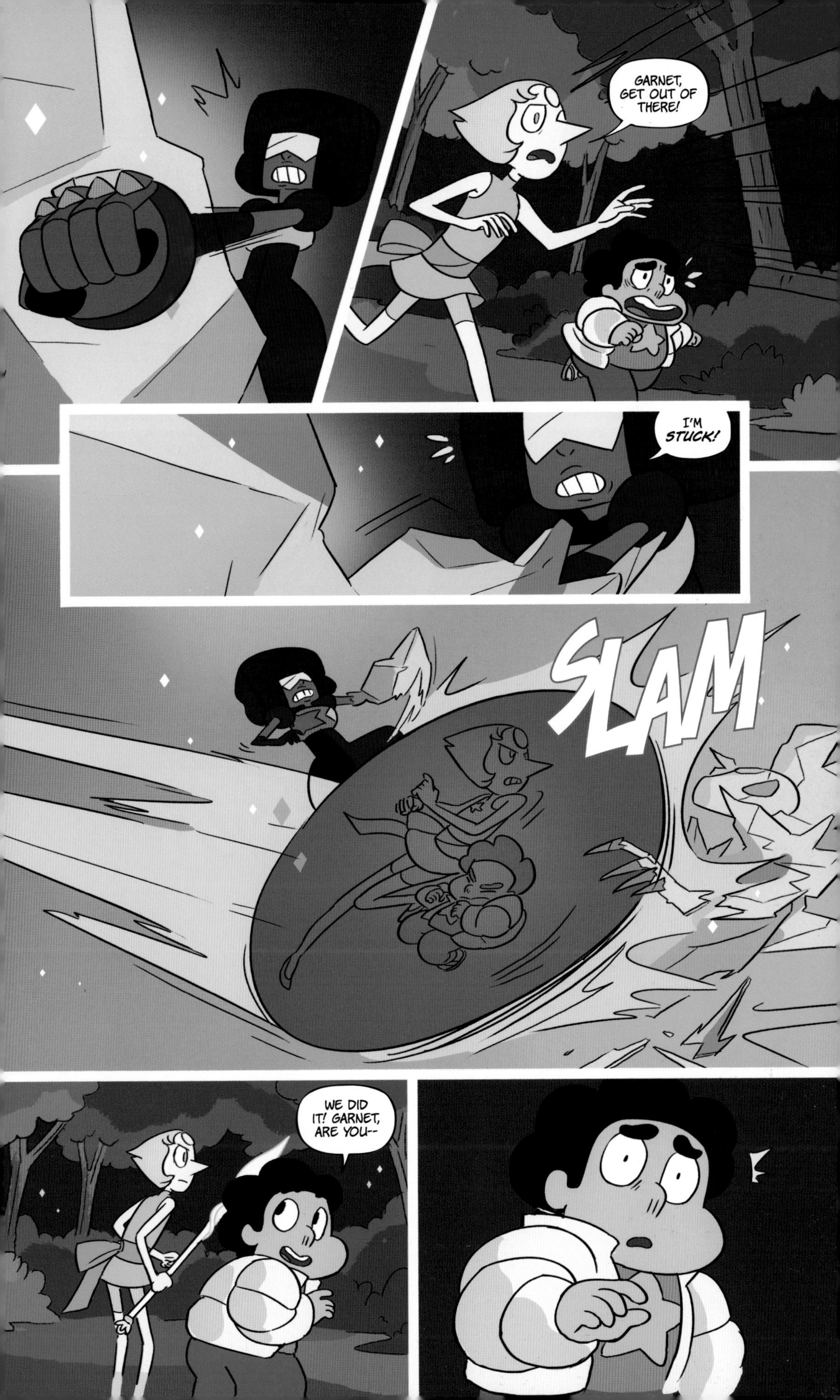
GARNET, GET OUT OF THERE!
I'M STUCK!
SLAM
WE DID IT! GARNET, ARE YOU--

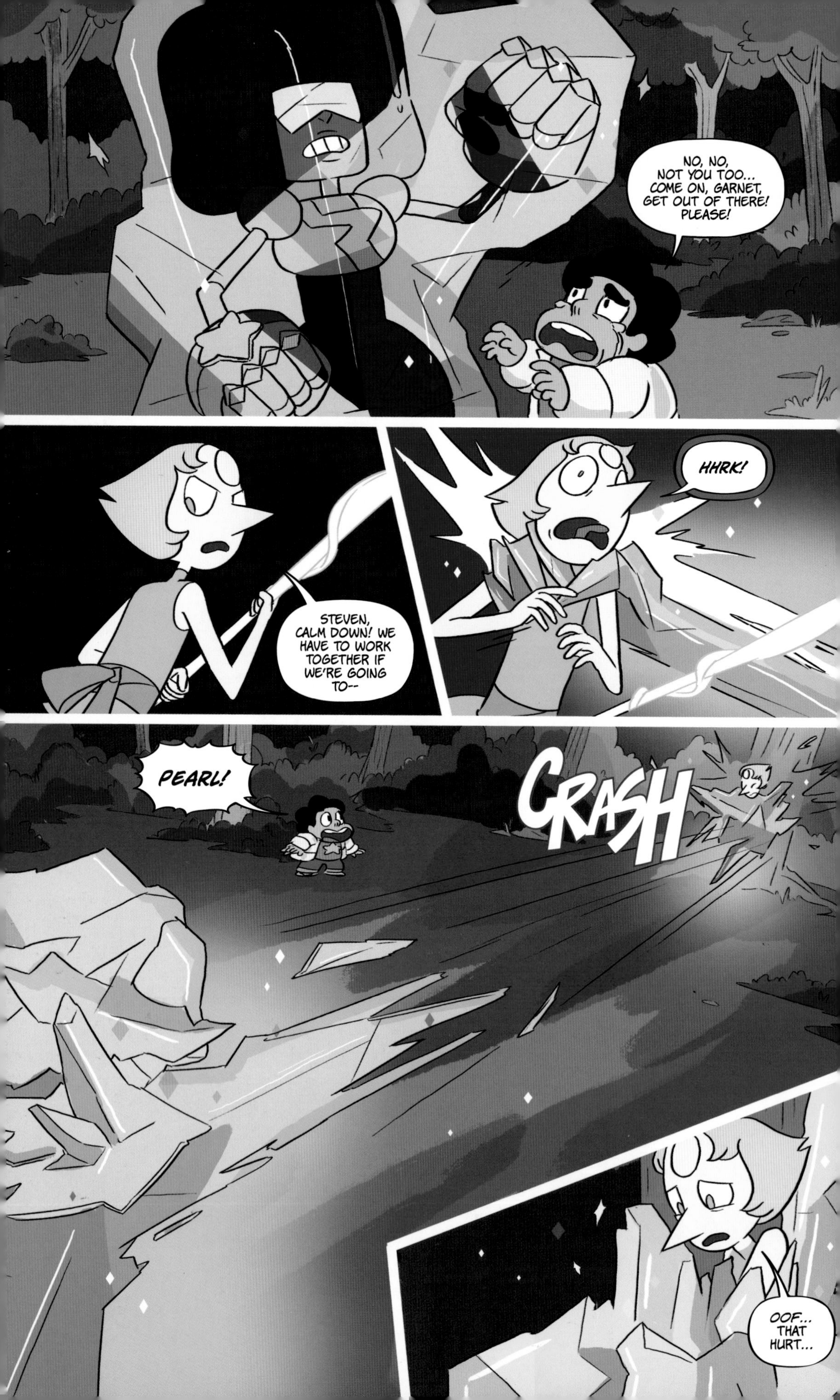
NO, NO, NOT YOU TOO... COME ON, GARNET, GET OUT OF THERE! PLEASE!
STEVEN, CALM DOWN! WE HAVE TO WORK TOGETHER IF WE'RE GOING TO--
HHRK!
PEARL!
CRASH
OOF... THAT HURT...

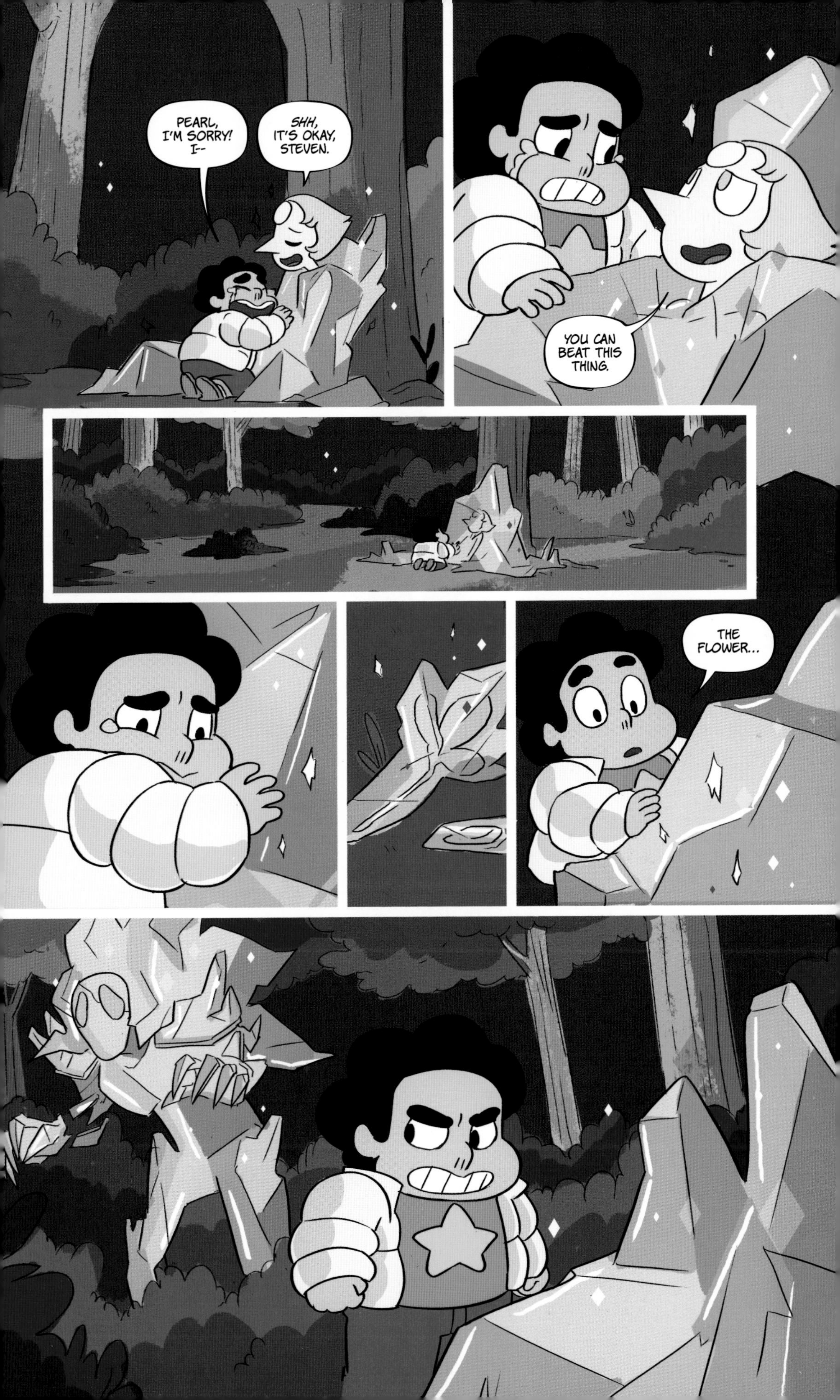
PEARL, I'M SORRY! I--
SHH, IT'S OKAY, STEVEN.
YOU CAN BEAT THIS THING.
THE FLOWER...

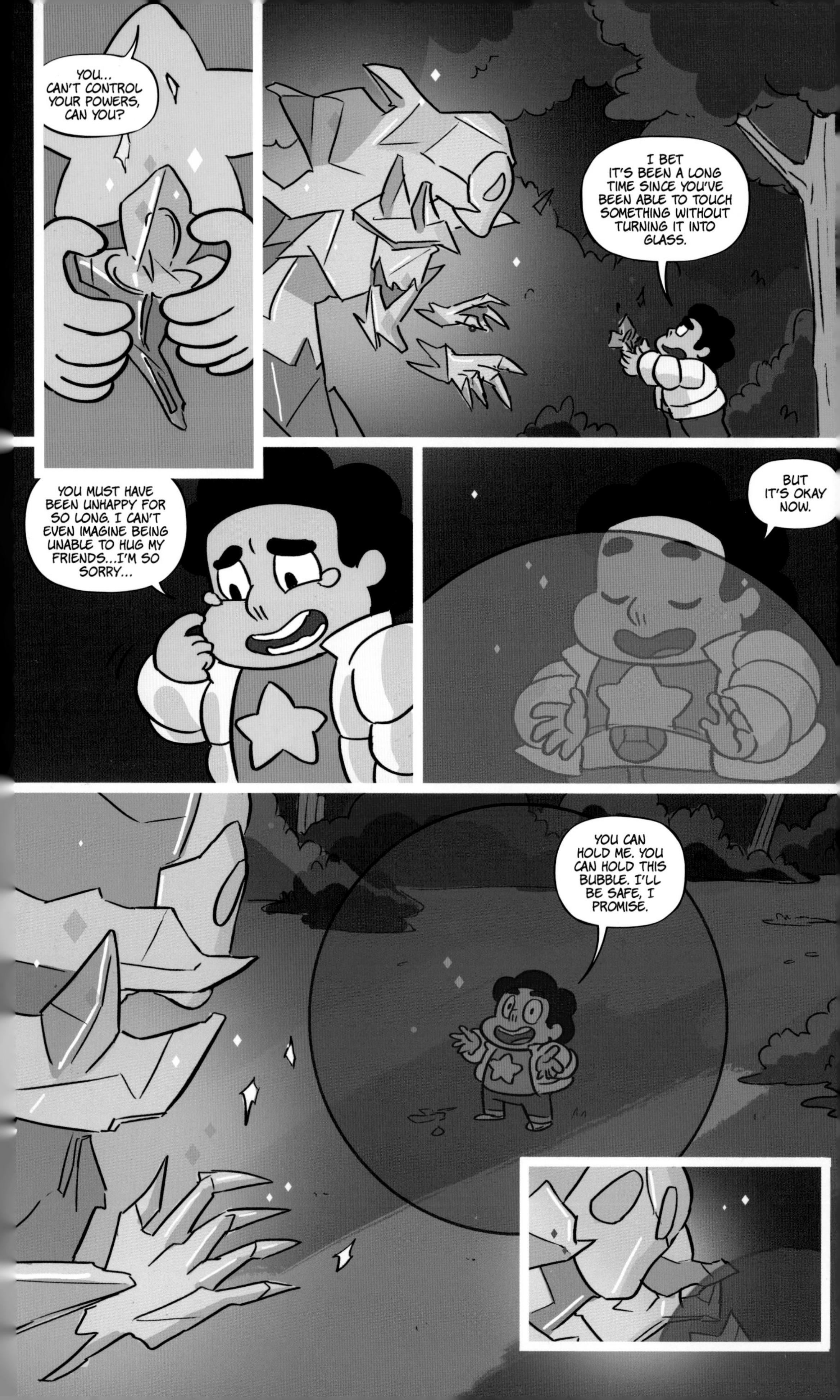

YOU... CAN'T CONTROL YOUR POWERS, CAN YOU?
I BET IT'S BEEN A LONG TIME SINCE YOU'VE BEEN ABLE TO TOUCH SOMETHING WITHOUT TURNING IT INTO GLASS.
YOU MUST HAVE BEEN UNHAPPY FOR SO LONG. I CAN'T EVEN IMAGINE BEING UNABLE TO HUG MY FRIENDS...I'M SO SORRY...
BUT IT'S OKAY NOW.
YOU CAN HOLD ME. YOU CAN HOLD THIS BUBBLE. I'LL BE SAFE, I PROMISE.

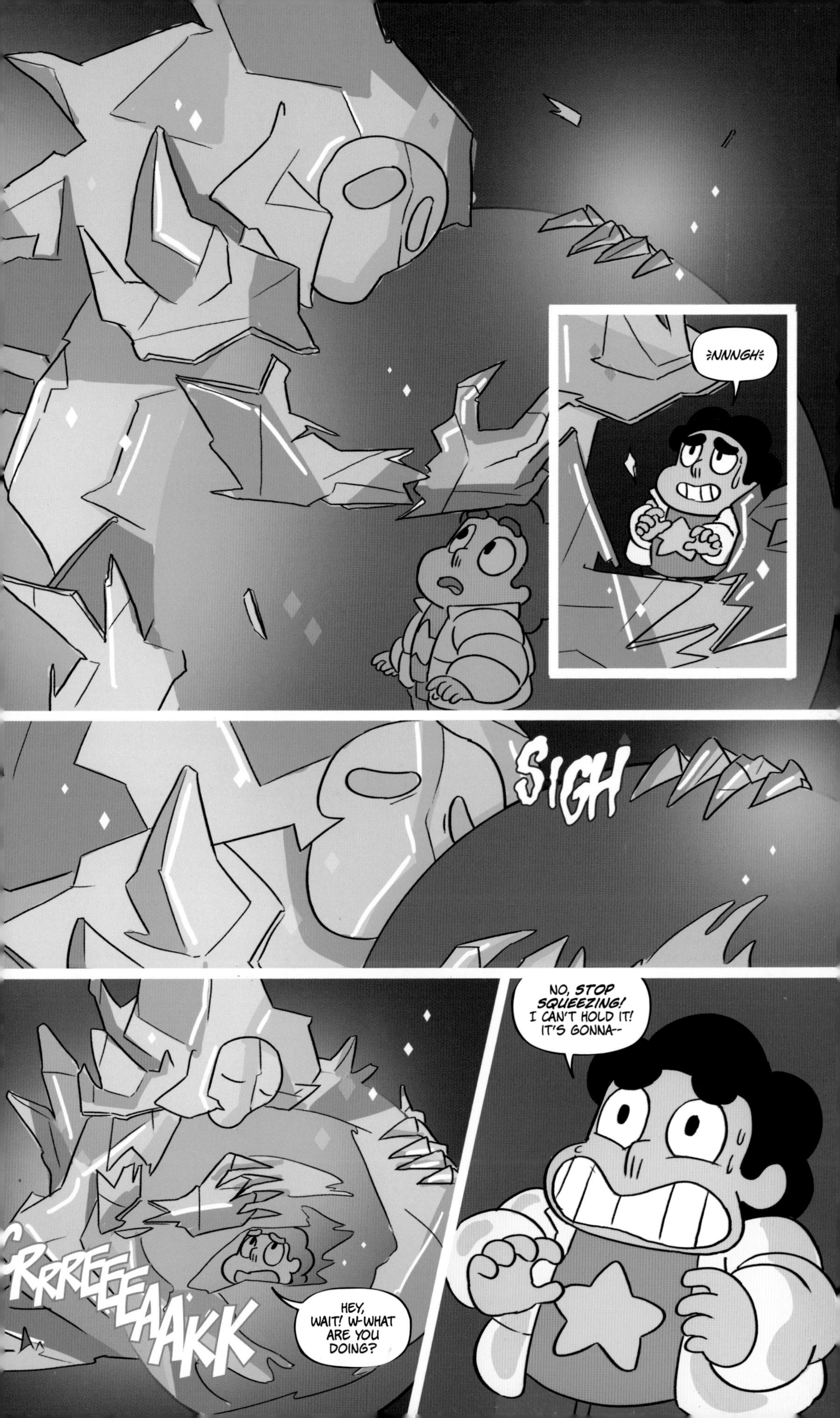
NNNGH
SIGH
CRRREEEEAAKK
HEY, WAIT! W-WHAT ARE YOU DOING?
NO, STOP SQUEEZING! I CAN'T HOLD IT! IT'S GONNA--

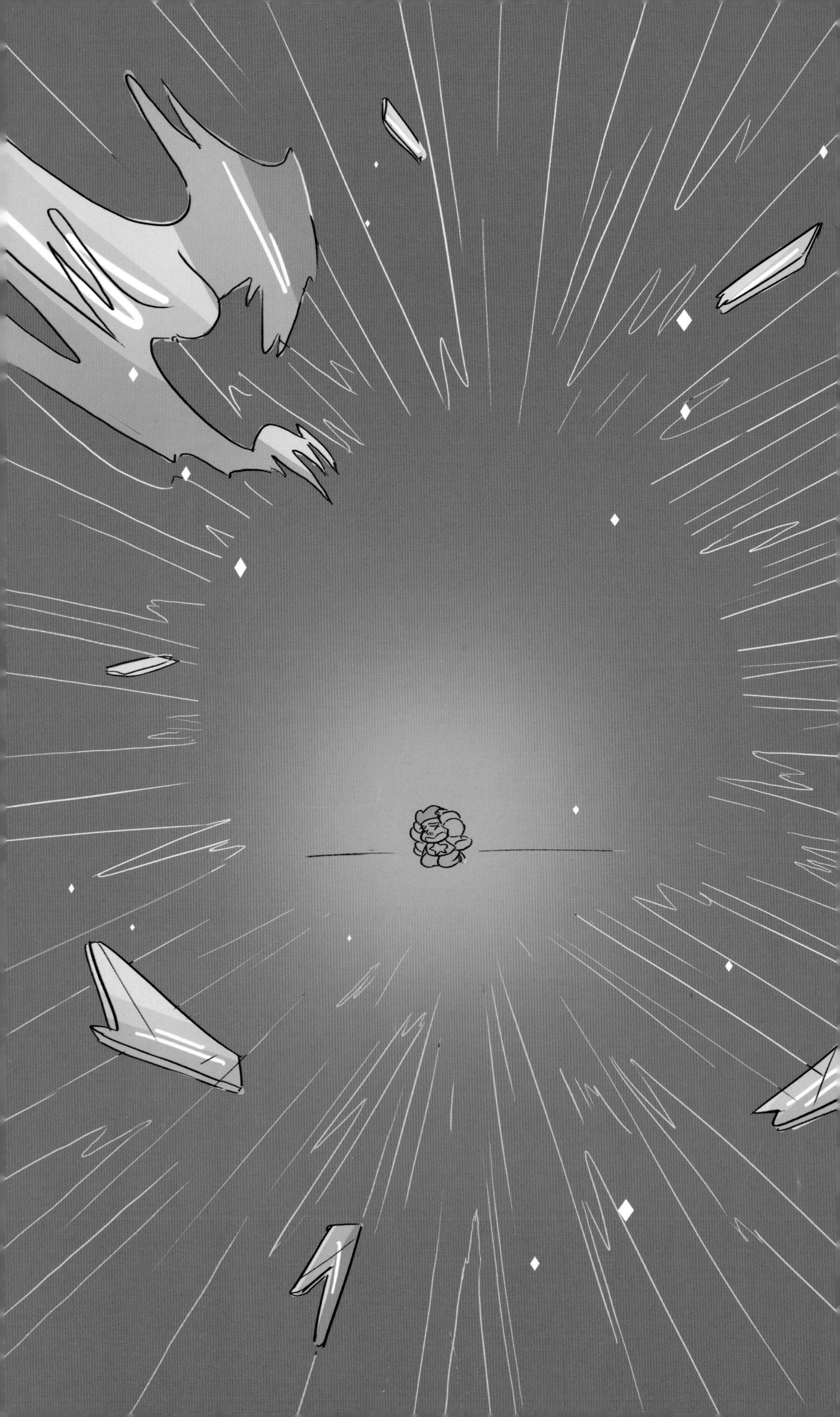

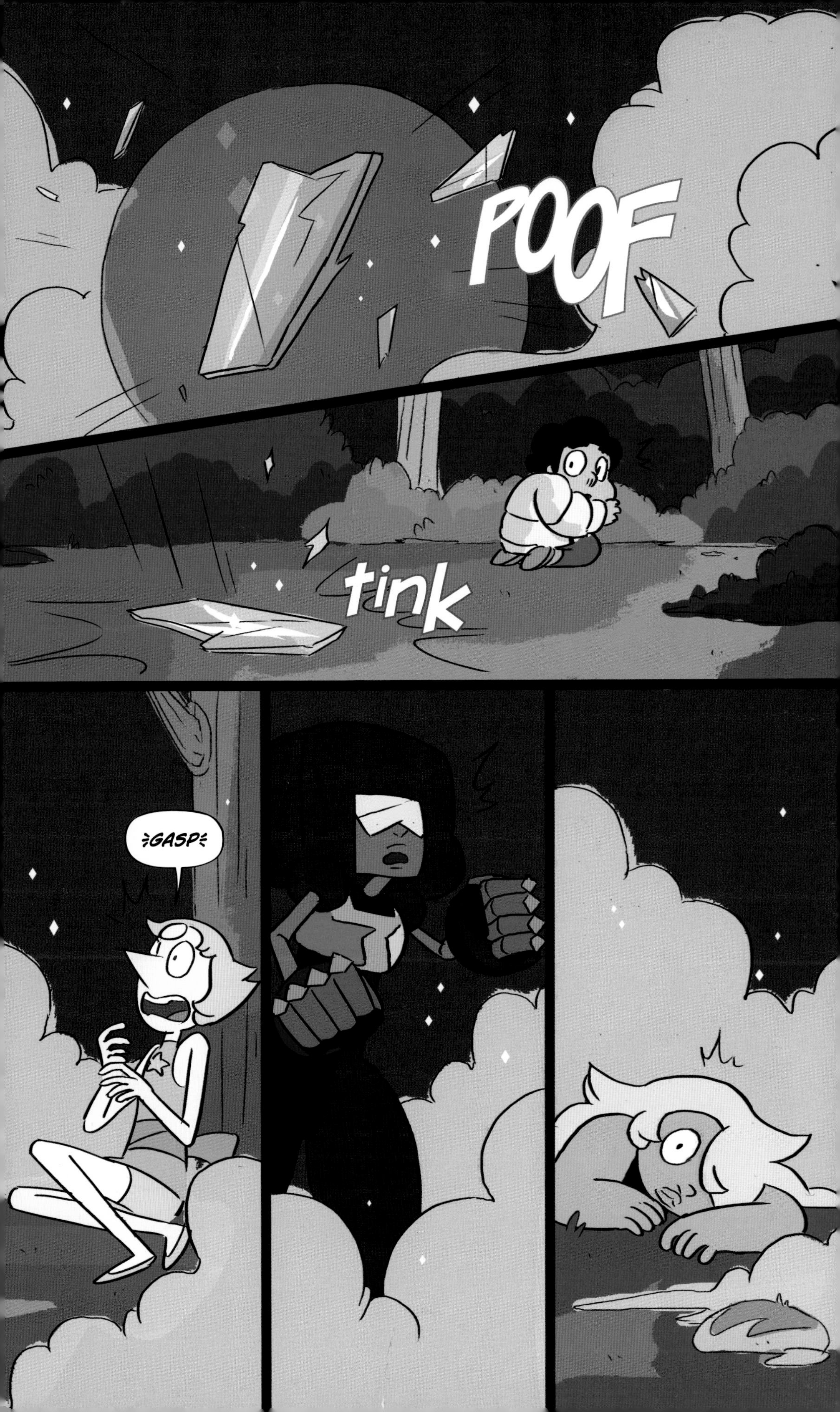
POOF
tink
GASP

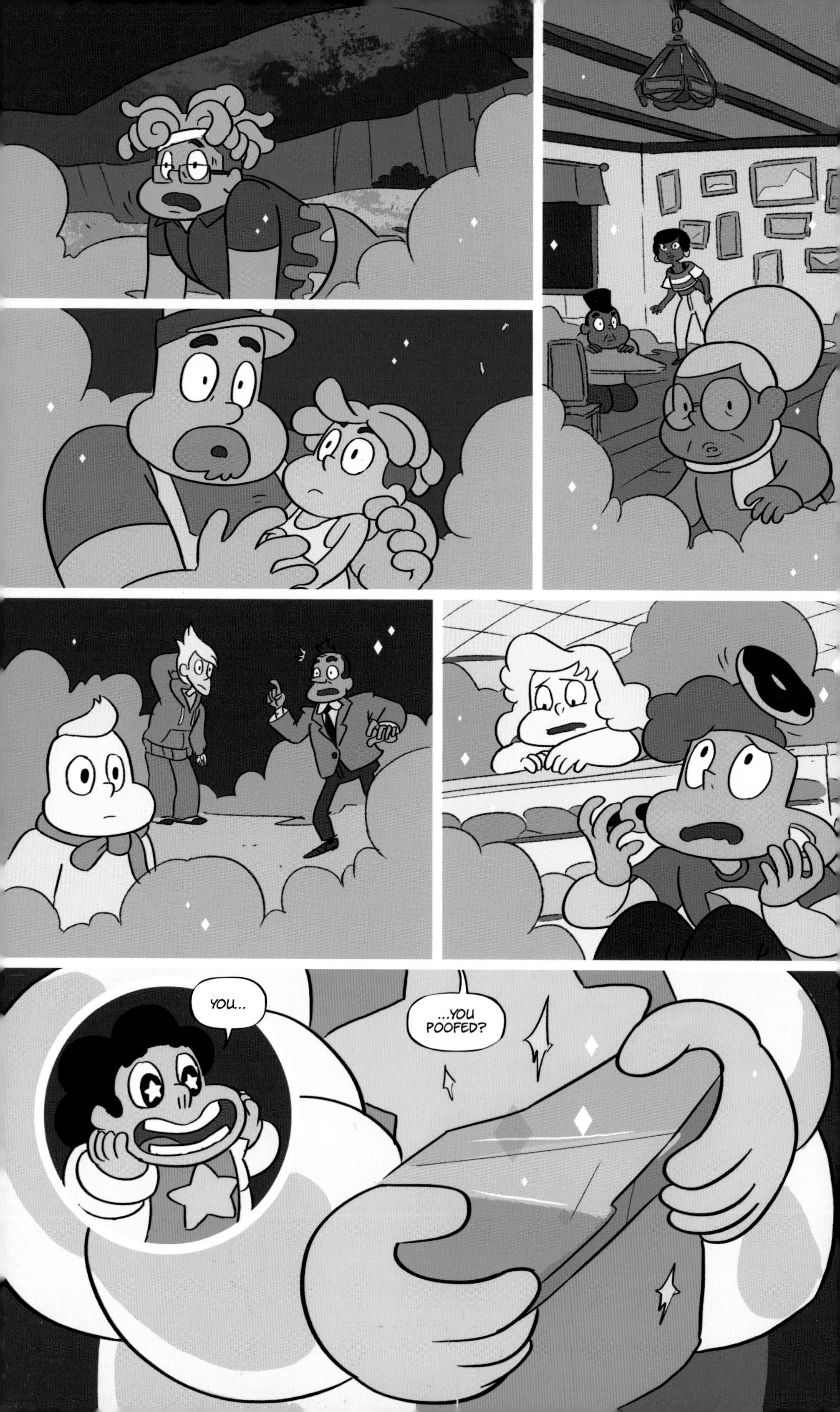
YOU...
...YOU POOFED?

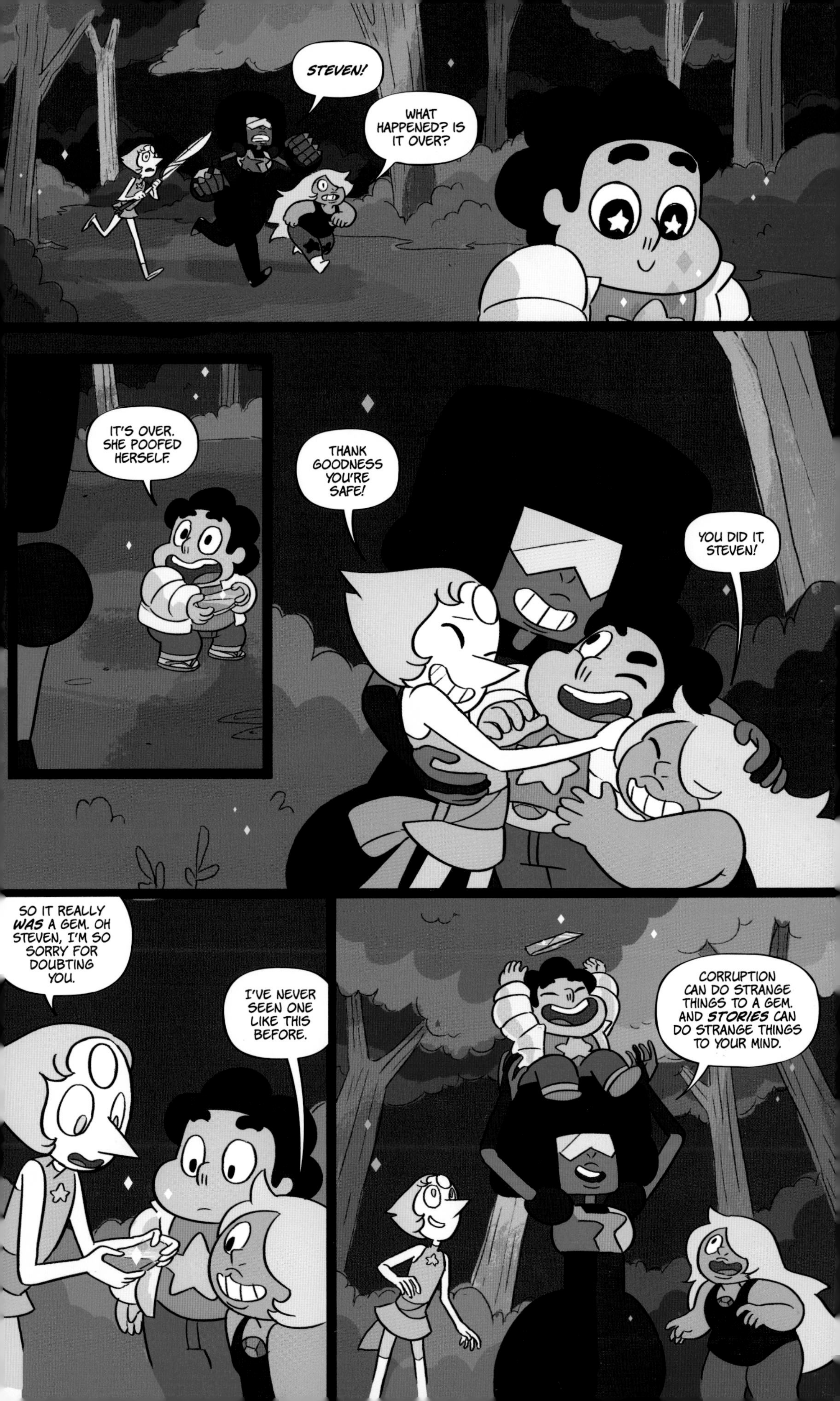
STEVEN!
WHAT HAPPENED? IS IT OVER?
IT'S OVER. SHE POOFED HERSELF.
THANK GOODNESS YOU'RE SAFE!
YOU DID IT, STEVEN!
SO IT REALLY *WAS* A GEM. OH STEVEN, I'M SO SORRY FOR DOUBTING YOU.
I'VE NEVER SEEN ONE LIKE THIS BEFORE.
CORRUPTION CAN DO STRANGE THINGS TO A GEM. AND *STORIES* CAN DO STRANGE THINGS TO YOUR MIND.

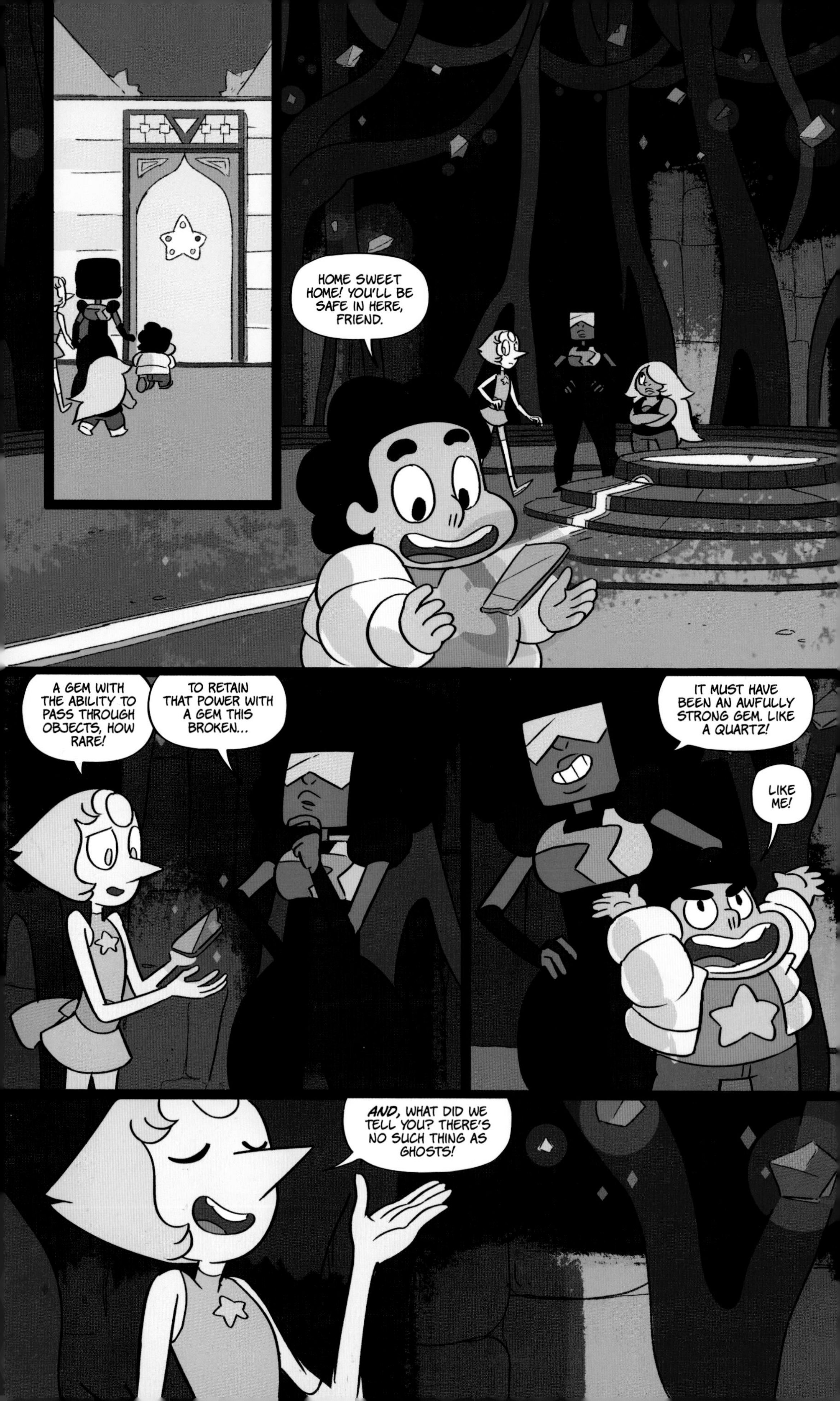
HOME SWEET HOME! YOU'LL BE SAFE IN HERE, FRIEND.
A GEM WITH THE ABILITY TO PASS THROUGH OBJECTS, HOW RARE!
TO RETAIN THAT POWER WITH A GEM THIS BROKEN...
IT MUST HAVE BEEN AN AWFULLY STRONG GEM. LIKE A QUARTZ!
LIKE ME!
AND, WHAT DID WE TELL YOU? THERE'S NO SUCH THING AS GHOSTS!

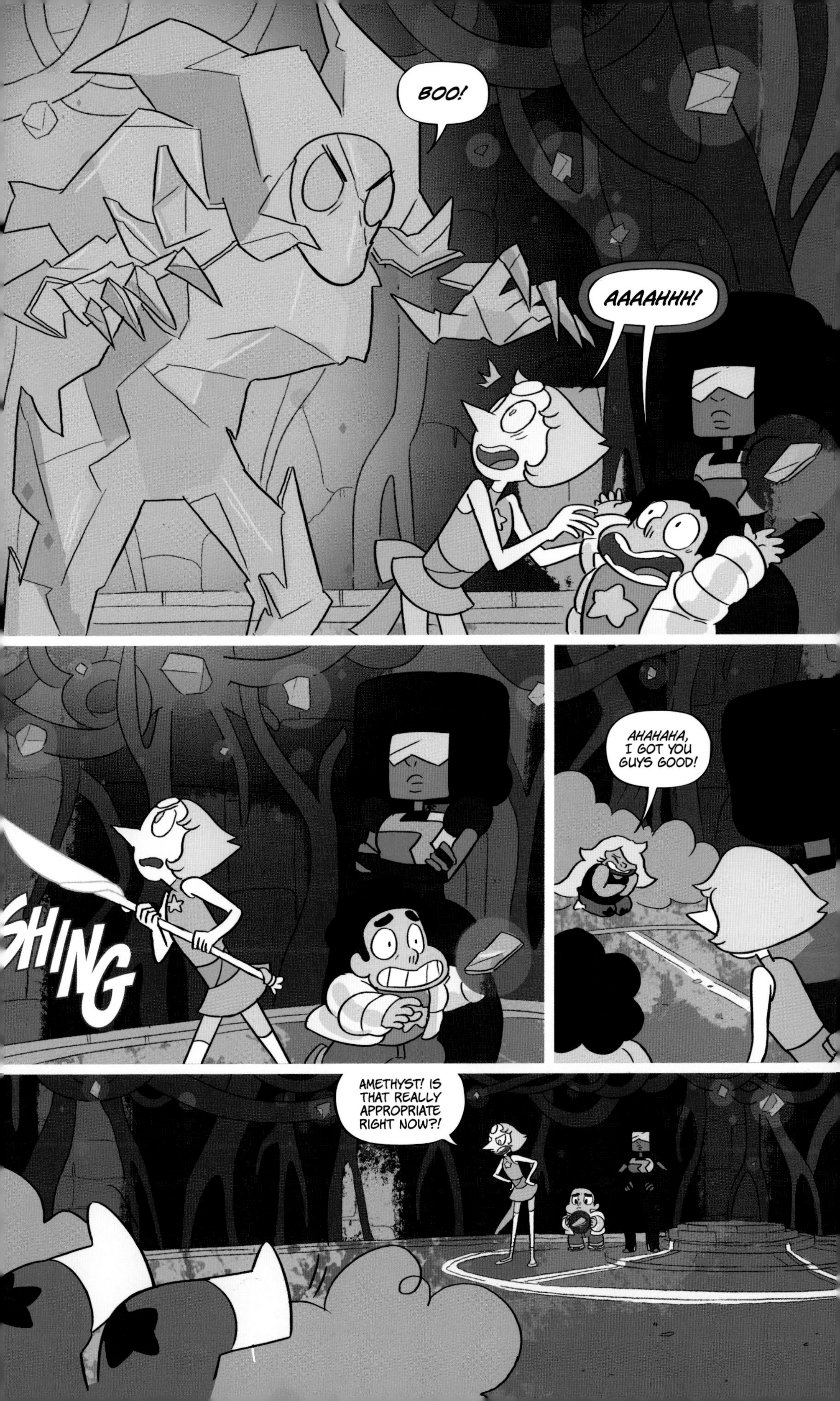
BOO!
AAAAHHH!
SHING
AHAHAHA, I GOT YOU GUYS GOOD!
AMETHYST! IS THAT REALLY APPROPRIATE RIGHT NOW?!

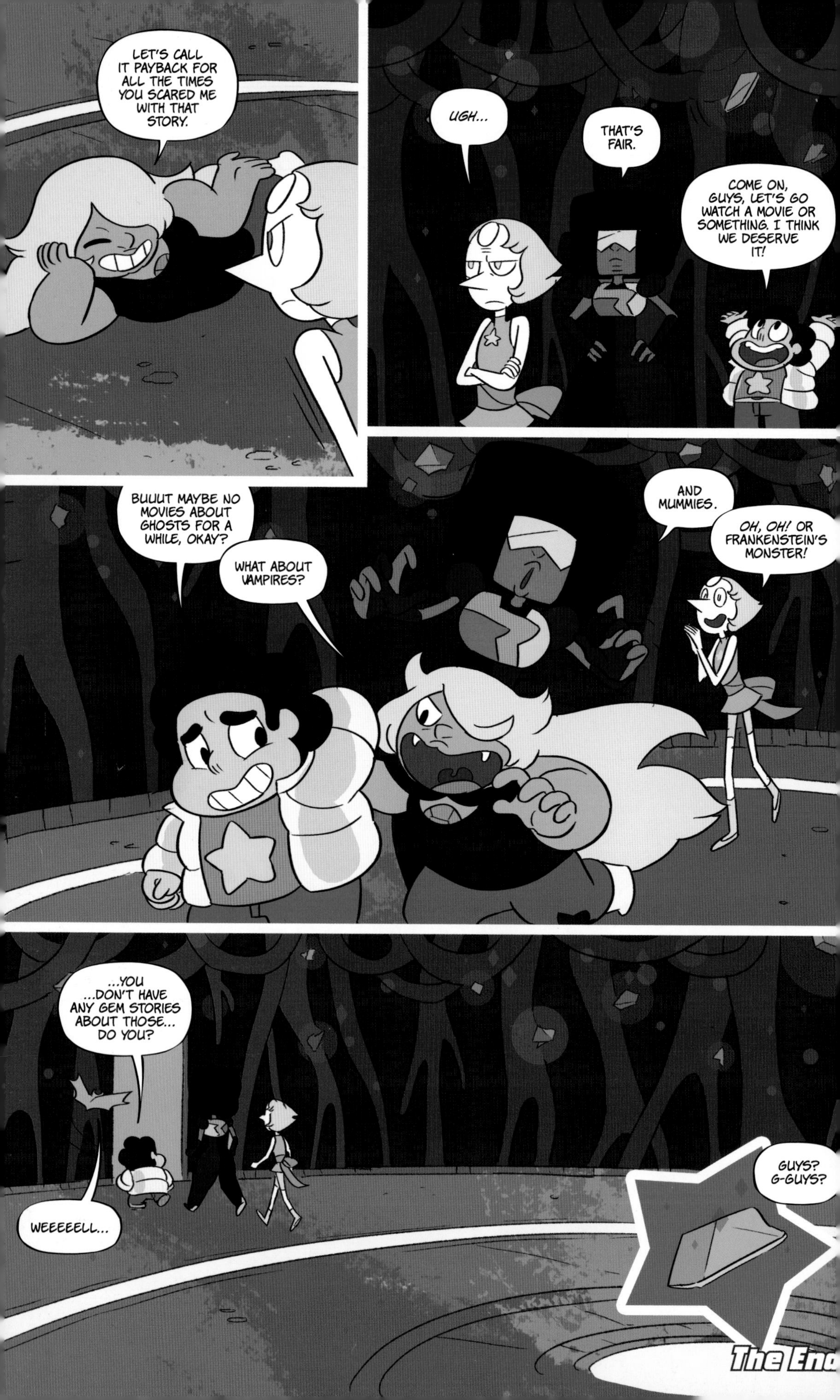
LET'S CALL IT PAYBACK FOR ALL THE TIMES YOU SCARED ME WITH THAT STORY.
UGH...
THAT'S FAIR.
COME ON, GUYS, LET'S GO WATCH A MOVIE OR SOMETHING. I THINK WE DESERVE IT!
BUUUT MAYBE NO MOVIES ABOUT GHOSTS FOR A WHILE, OKAY?
WHAT ABOUT VAMPIRES?
AND MUMMIES.
OH, OH! OR FRANKENSTEIN'S MONSTER!
...YOU ...DON'T HAVE ANY GEM STORIES ABOUT THOSE... DO YOU?
WEEEEELL...
GUYS? G-GUYS?
The End

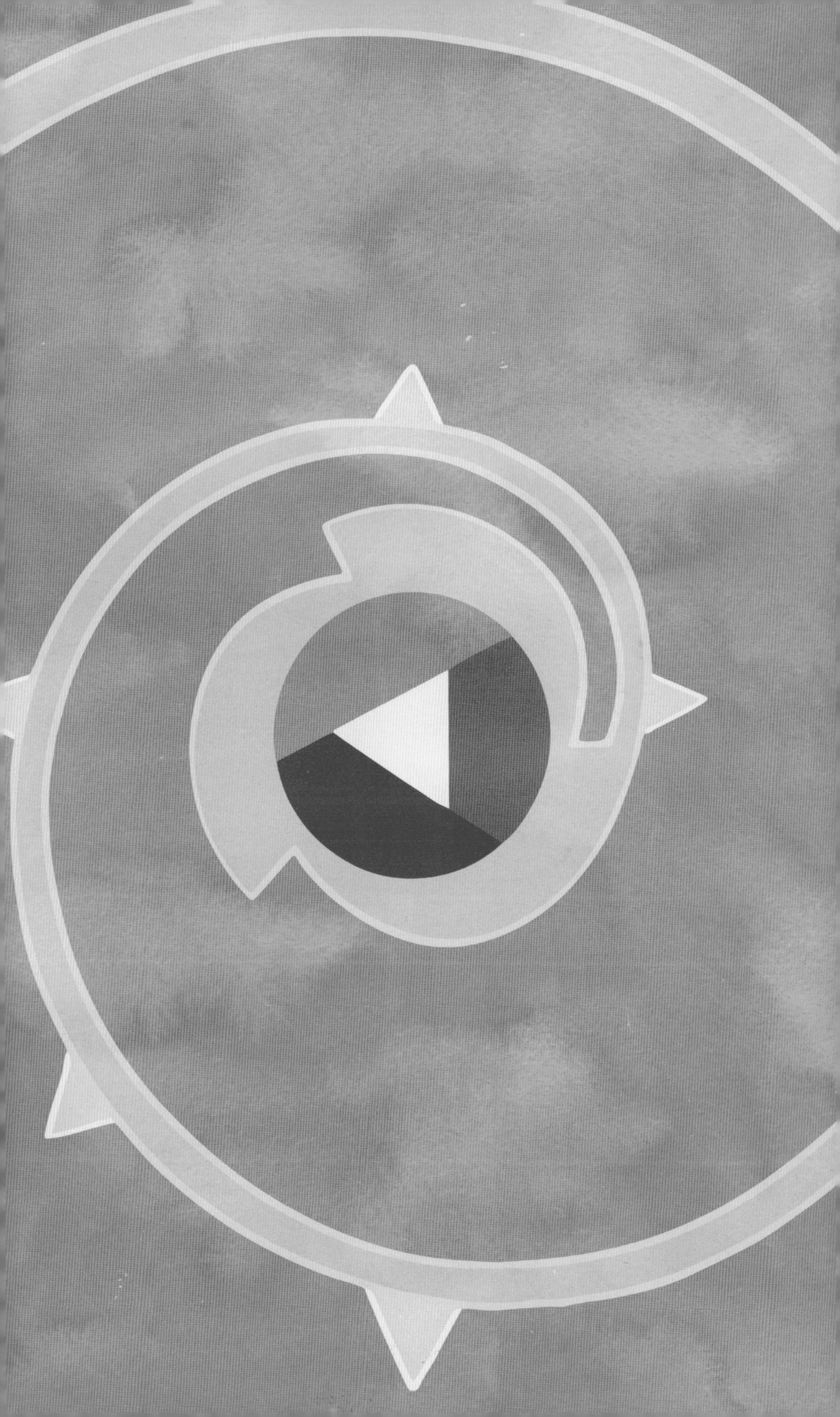

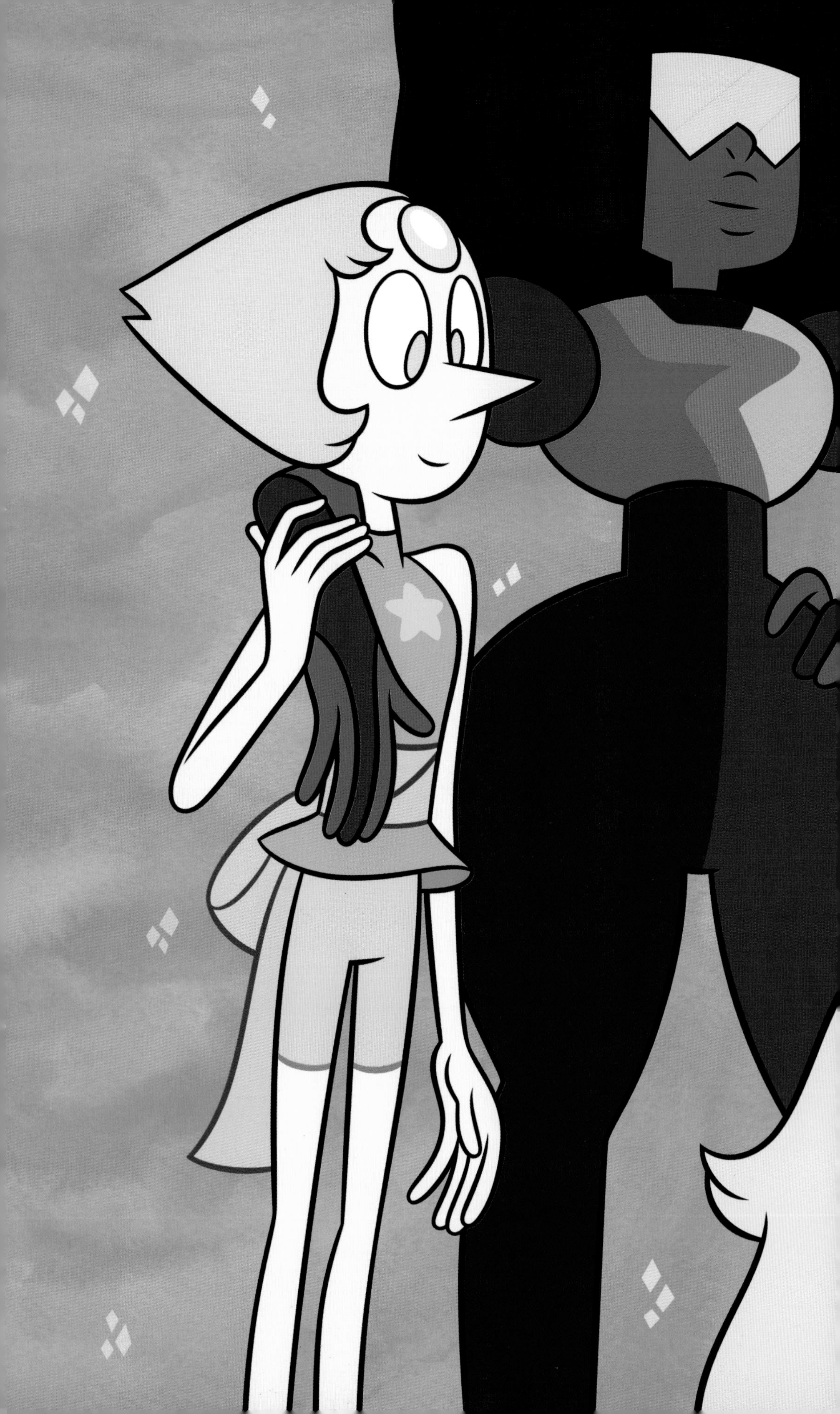

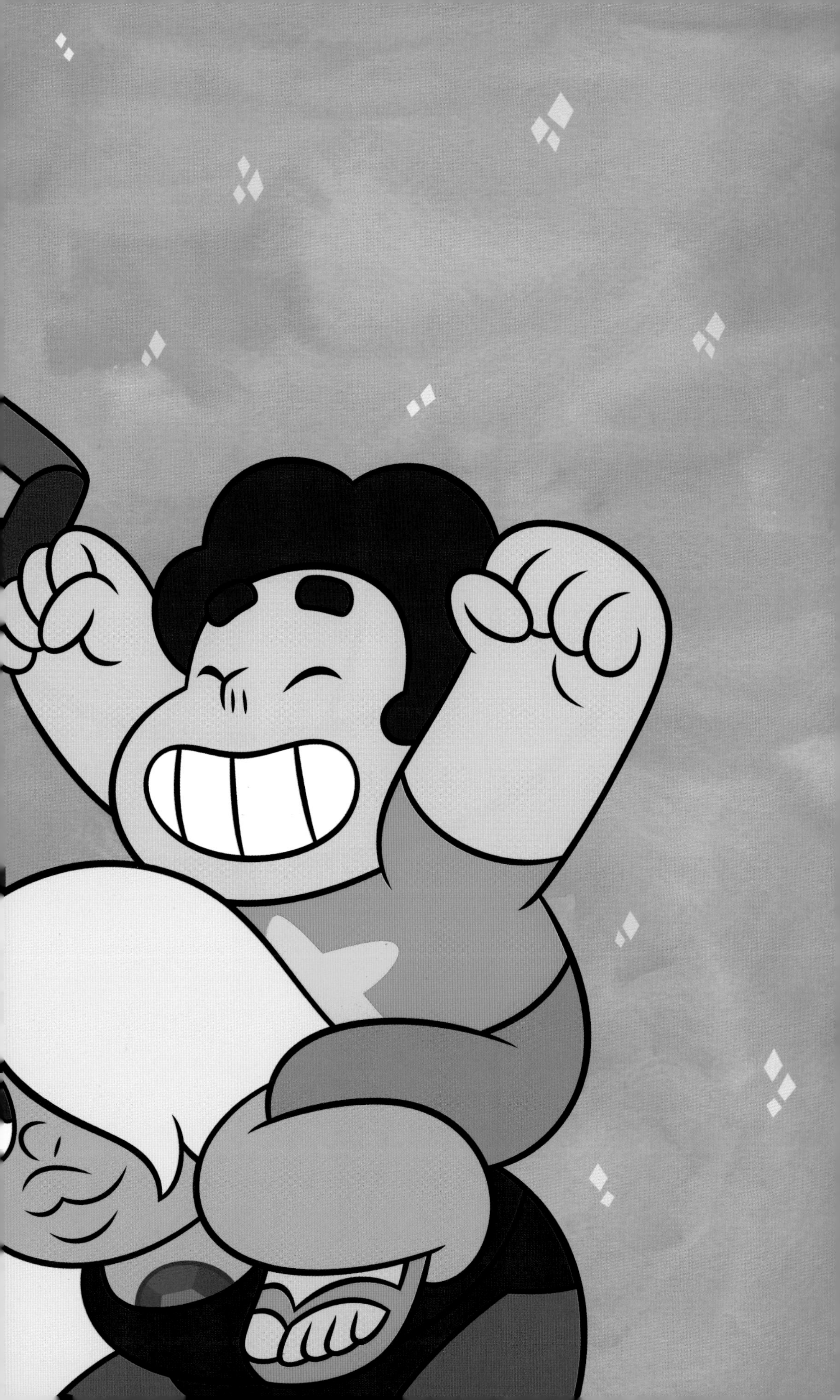

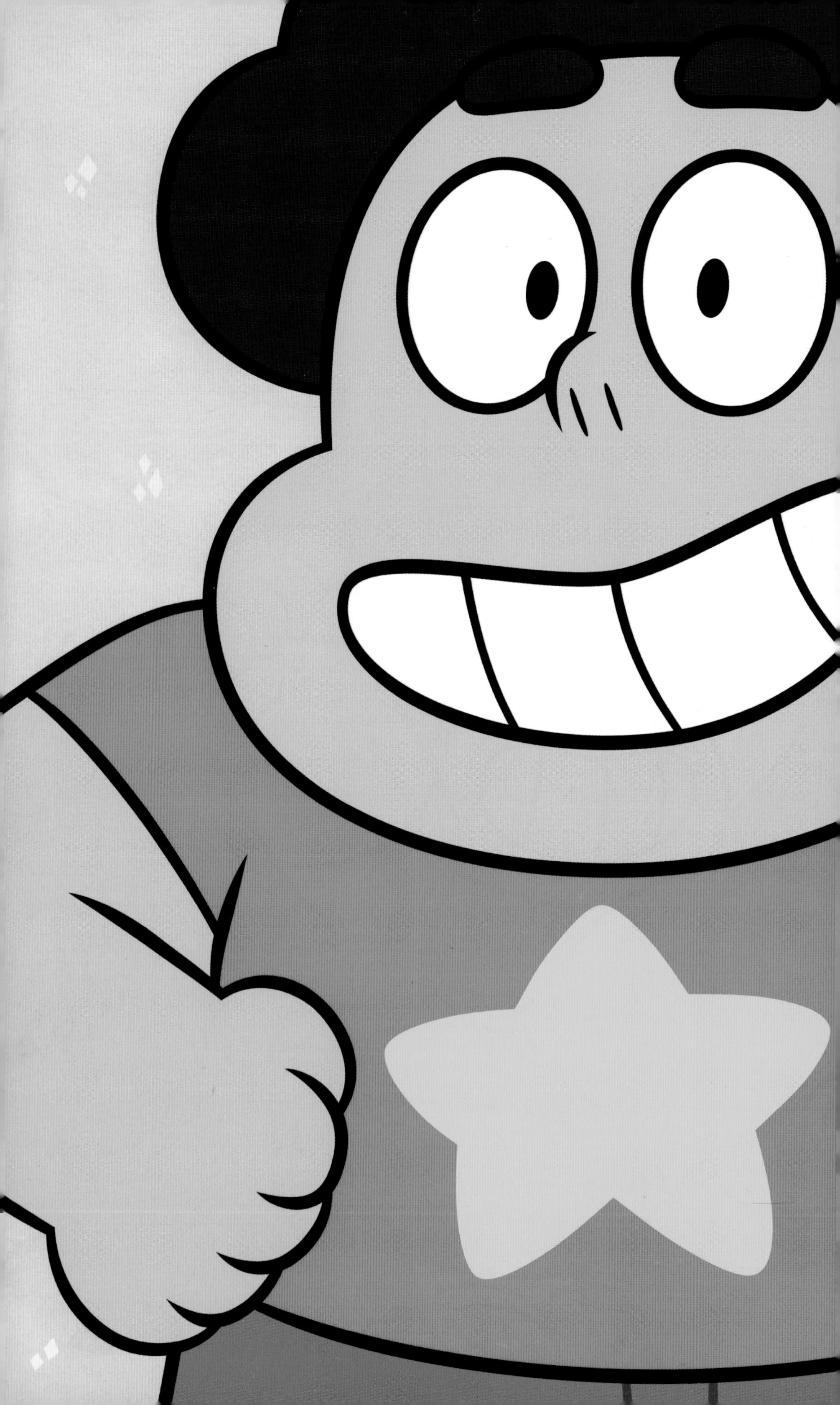

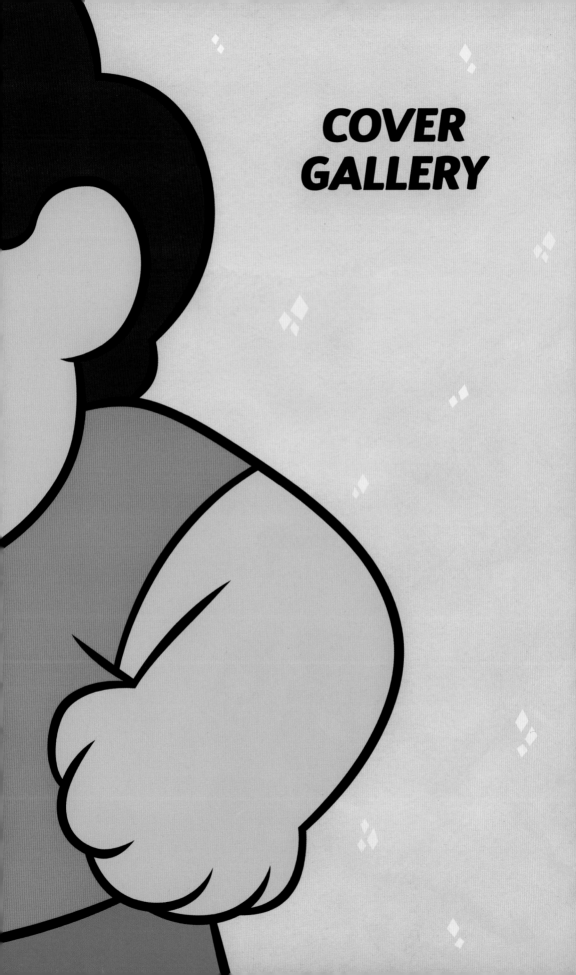

COVER GALLERY

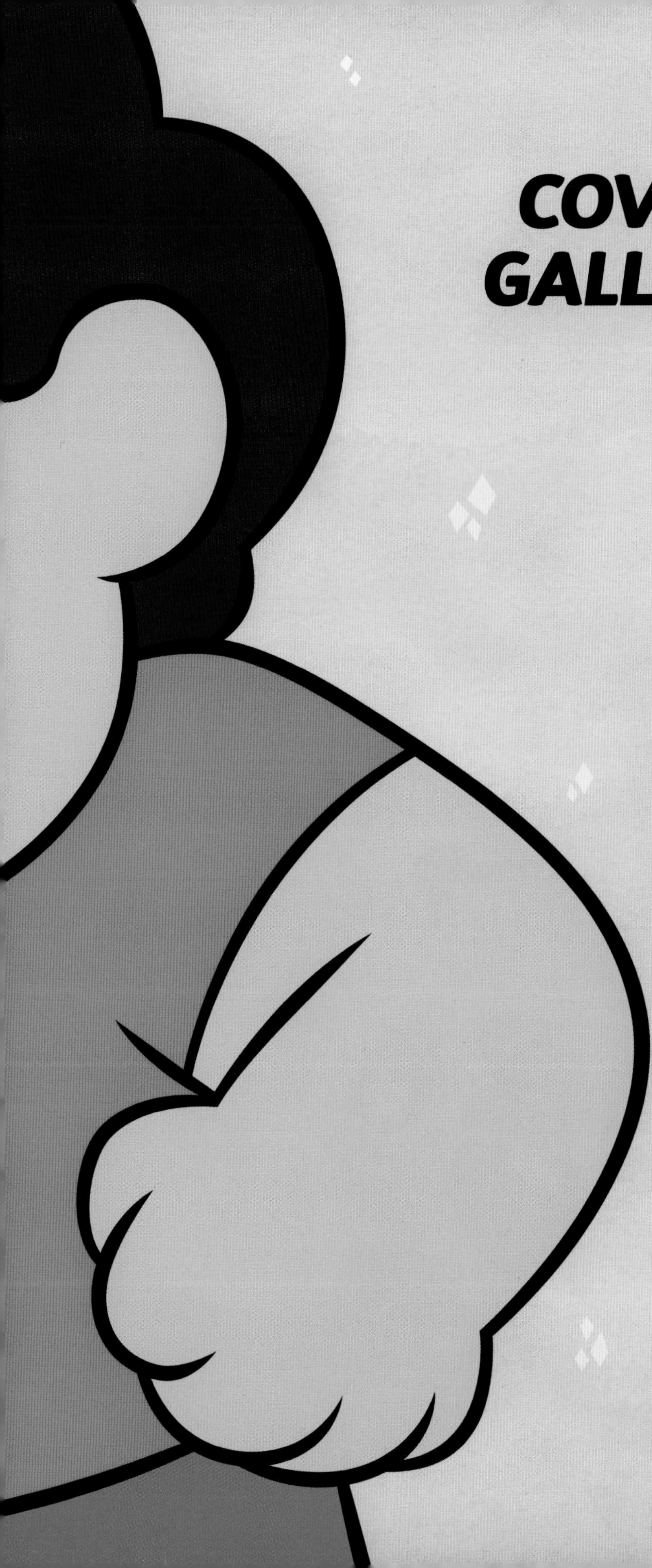

issue one main cover
KAT LEYH

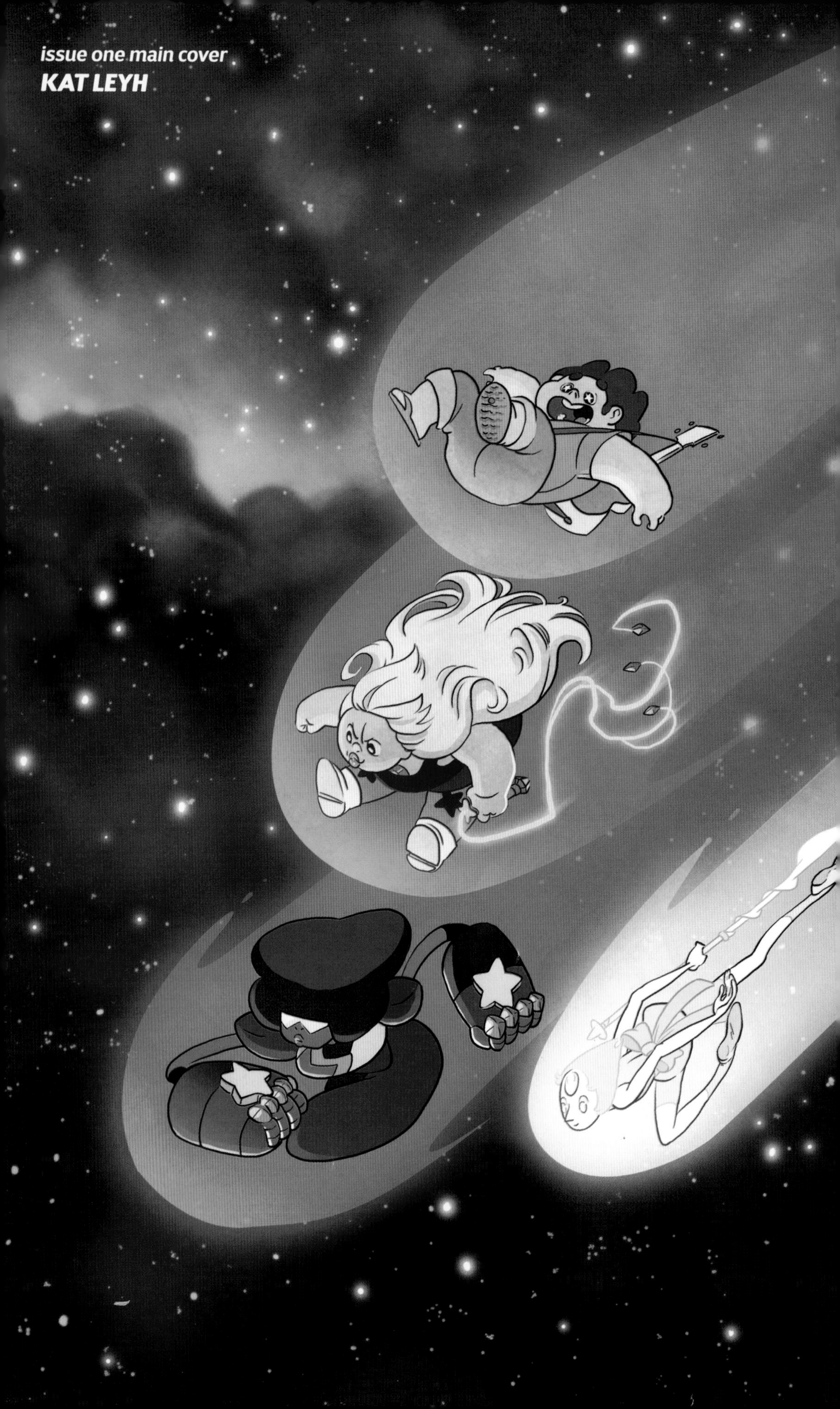

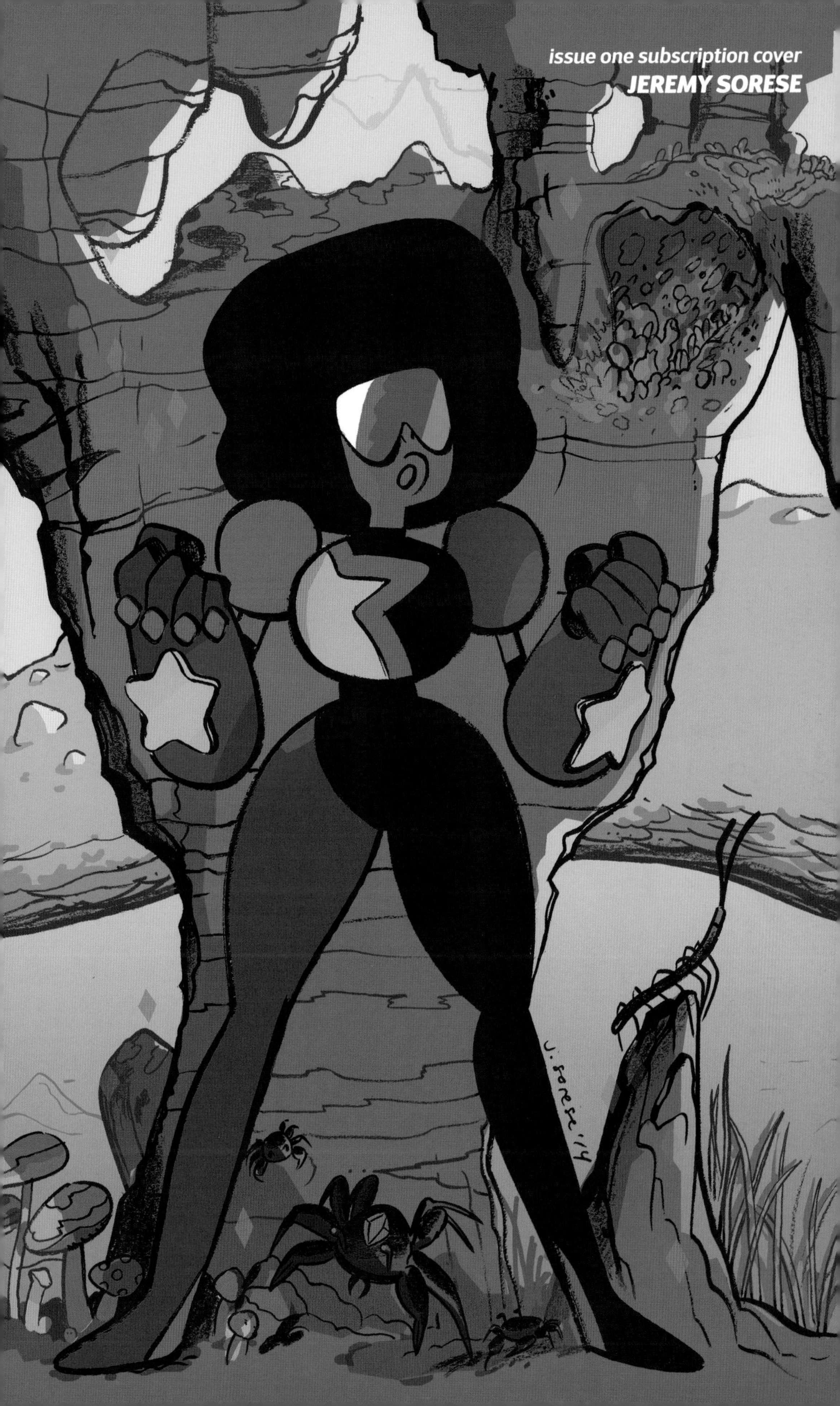
J. Sorese '14

issue one subscription cover
JEREMY SORESE

issue one variant cover
AMBER ROGERS

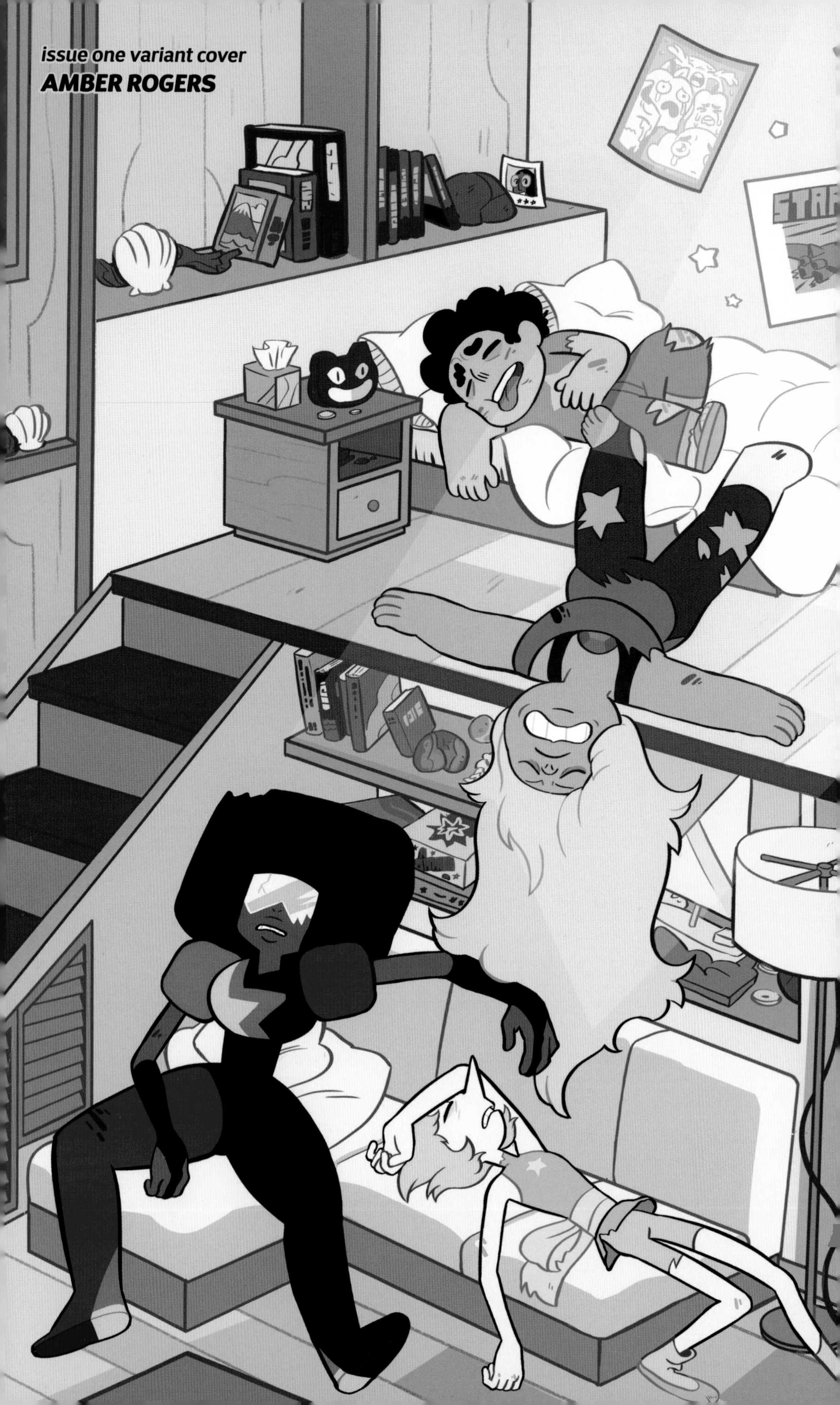

issue one fried pie exclusive cover
MISSY PEÑA

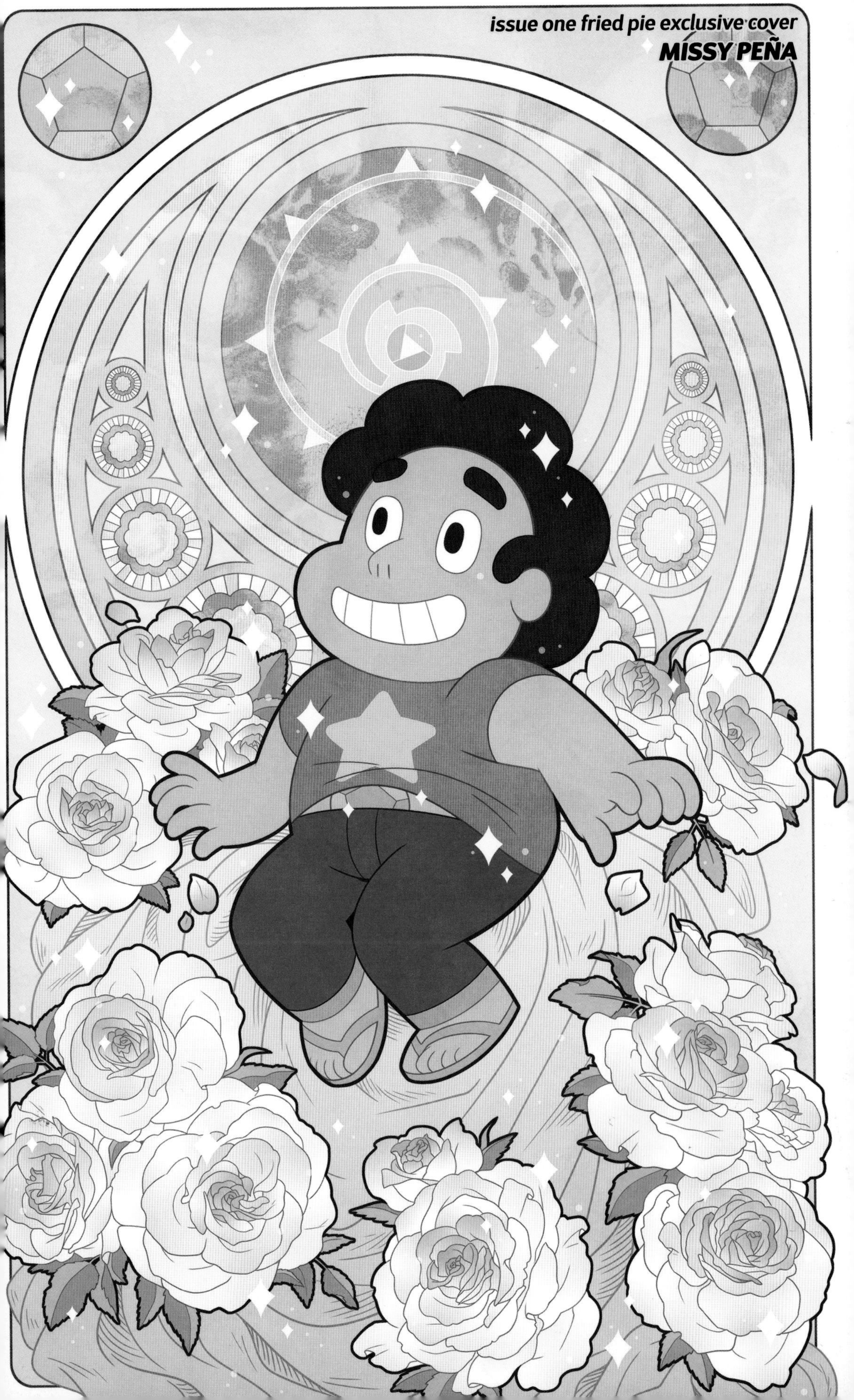

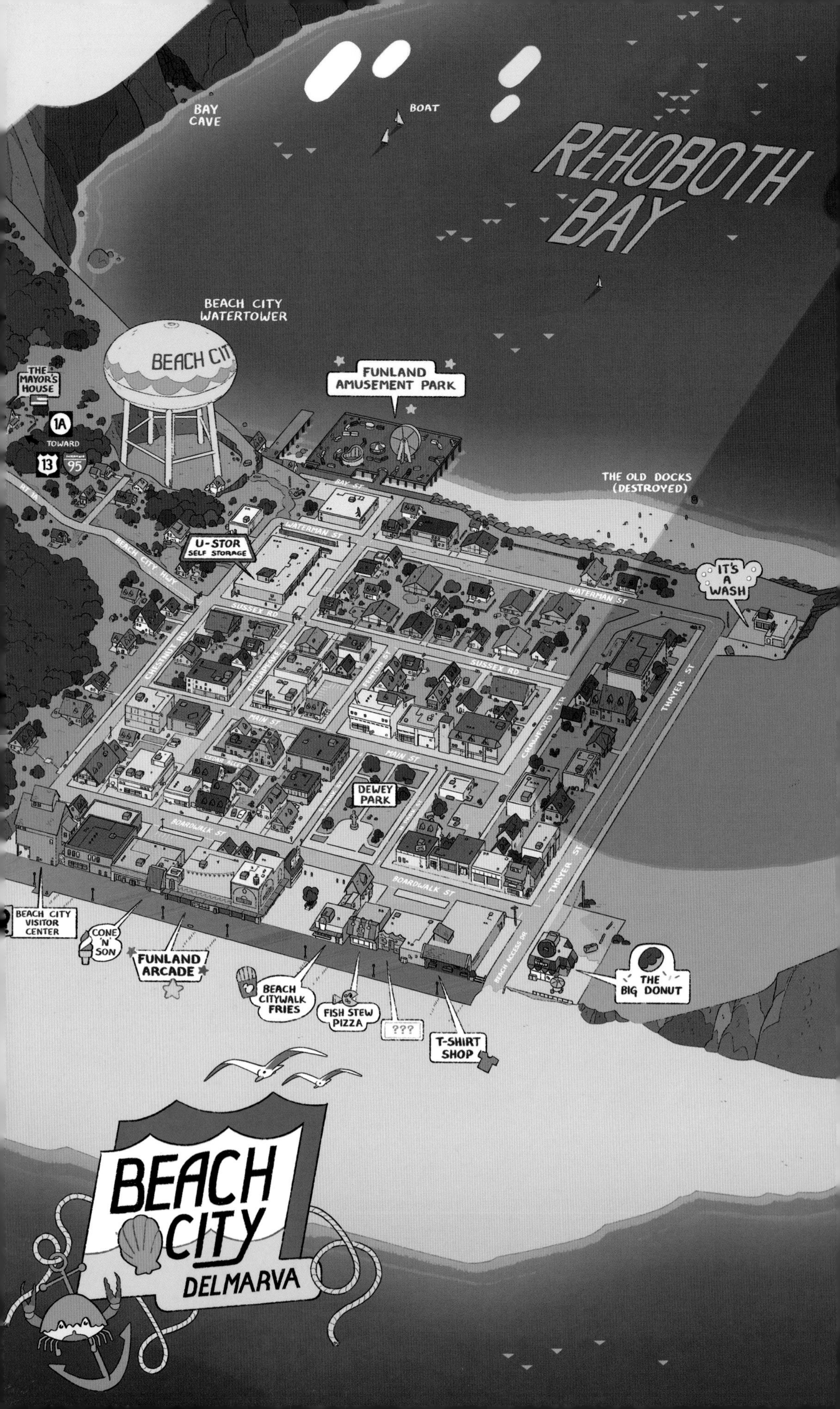

BAY CAVE
BOAT
REHOBOTH BAY
BEACH CITY WATERTOWER
BEACH CITY
THE MAYOR'S HOUSE
1A
TOWARD
13
95
FUNLAND AMUSEMENT PARK
THE OLD DOCKS (DESTROYED)
BAY ST
RT 1A
WATERMAN ST
BEACH CITY HWY
U-STOR SELF STORAGE
IT'S A WASH
SUSSEX RD
CHESTNUT RD
CHESAPEAKE ST
FENTON ST
SUSSEX RD
THAYER ST
CRAWFORD TER
MAIN ST
MAIN ST
CEDAR ALLEY
DEWEY PARK
BOARDWALK ST
BOARDWALK ST
THAYER ST
BEACH ACCESS DR
BEACH CITY VISITOR CENTER
CONE 'N' SON
FUNLAND ARCADE
BEACH CITYWALK FRIES
FISH STEW PIZZA
???
T-SHIRT SHOP
THE BIG DONUT
BEACH CITY
DELMARVA

issue one wondercon exclusive cover

STEVEN SUGAR

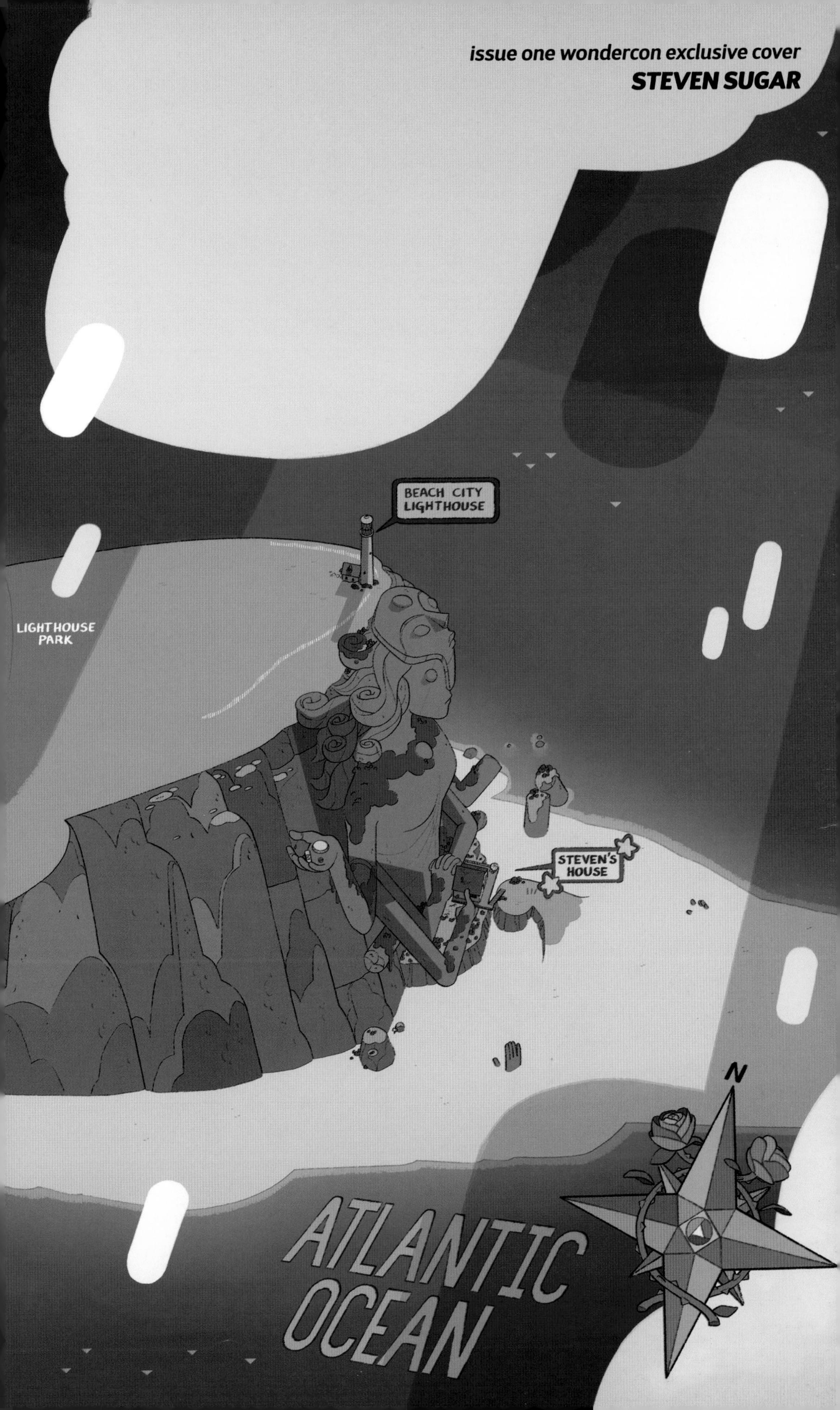

issue one newbury comics exclusive cover

ALLISON STREJLAU

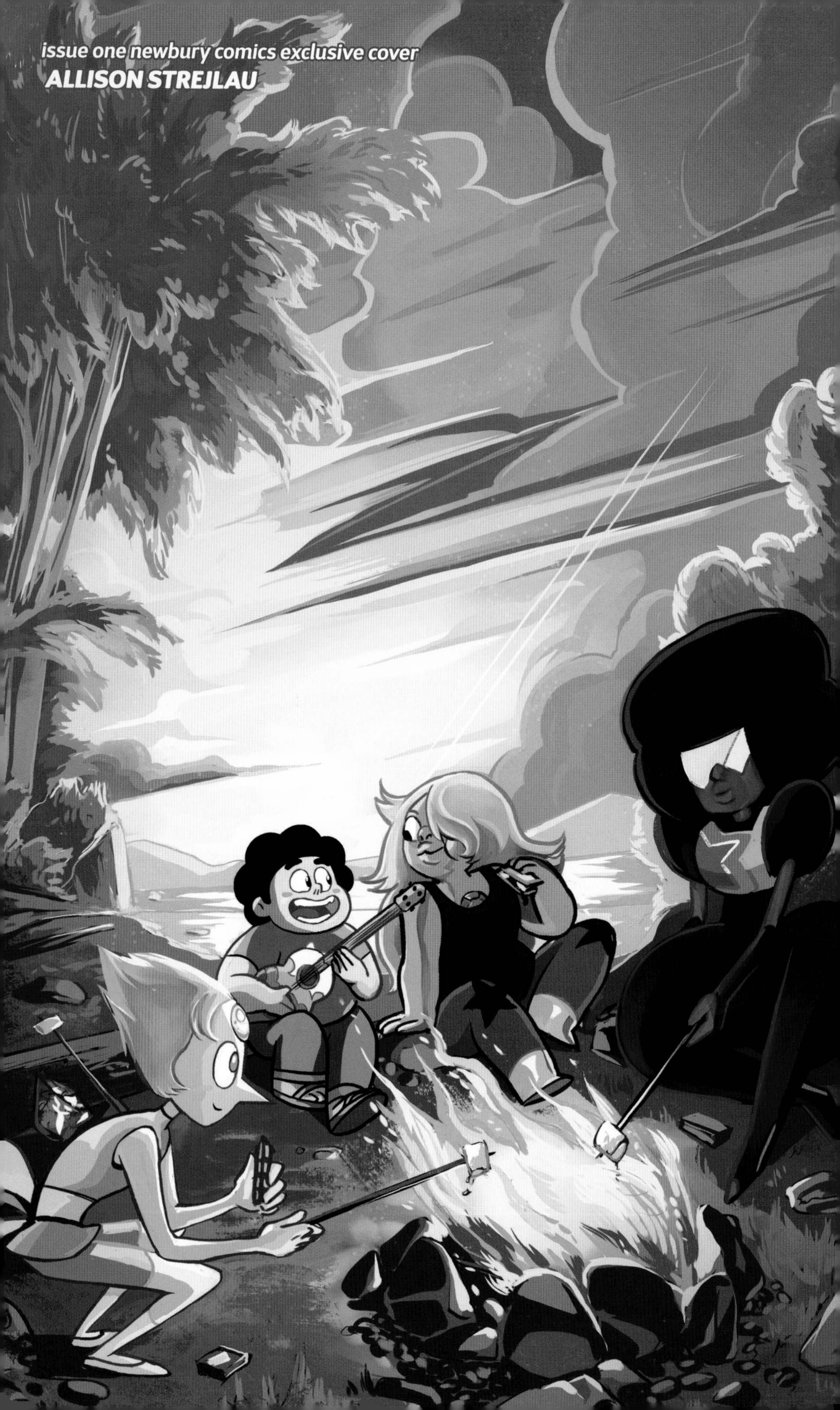

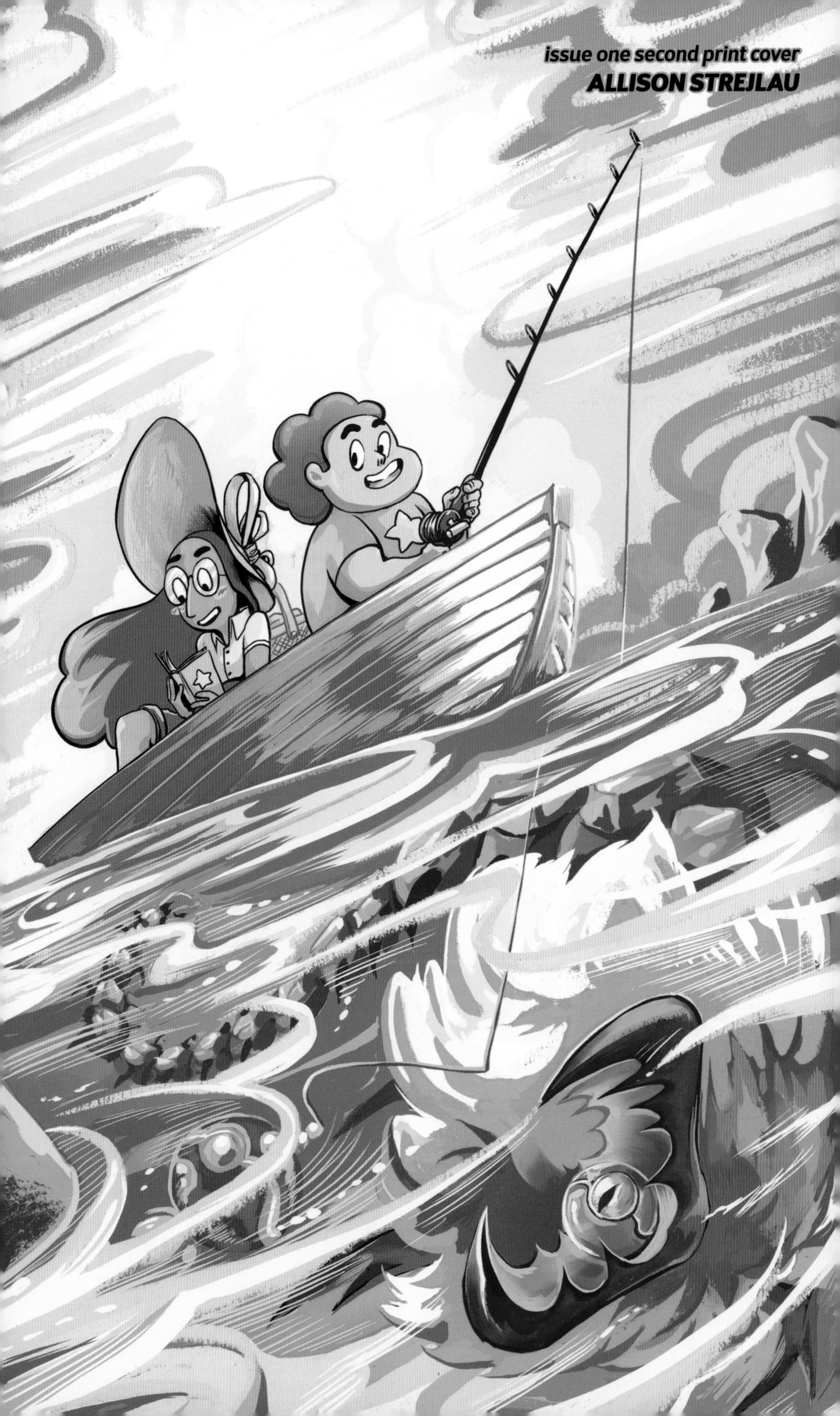

issue one second print cover
ALLISON STREJLAU

issue one third print cover

JOSCELINE FENTON

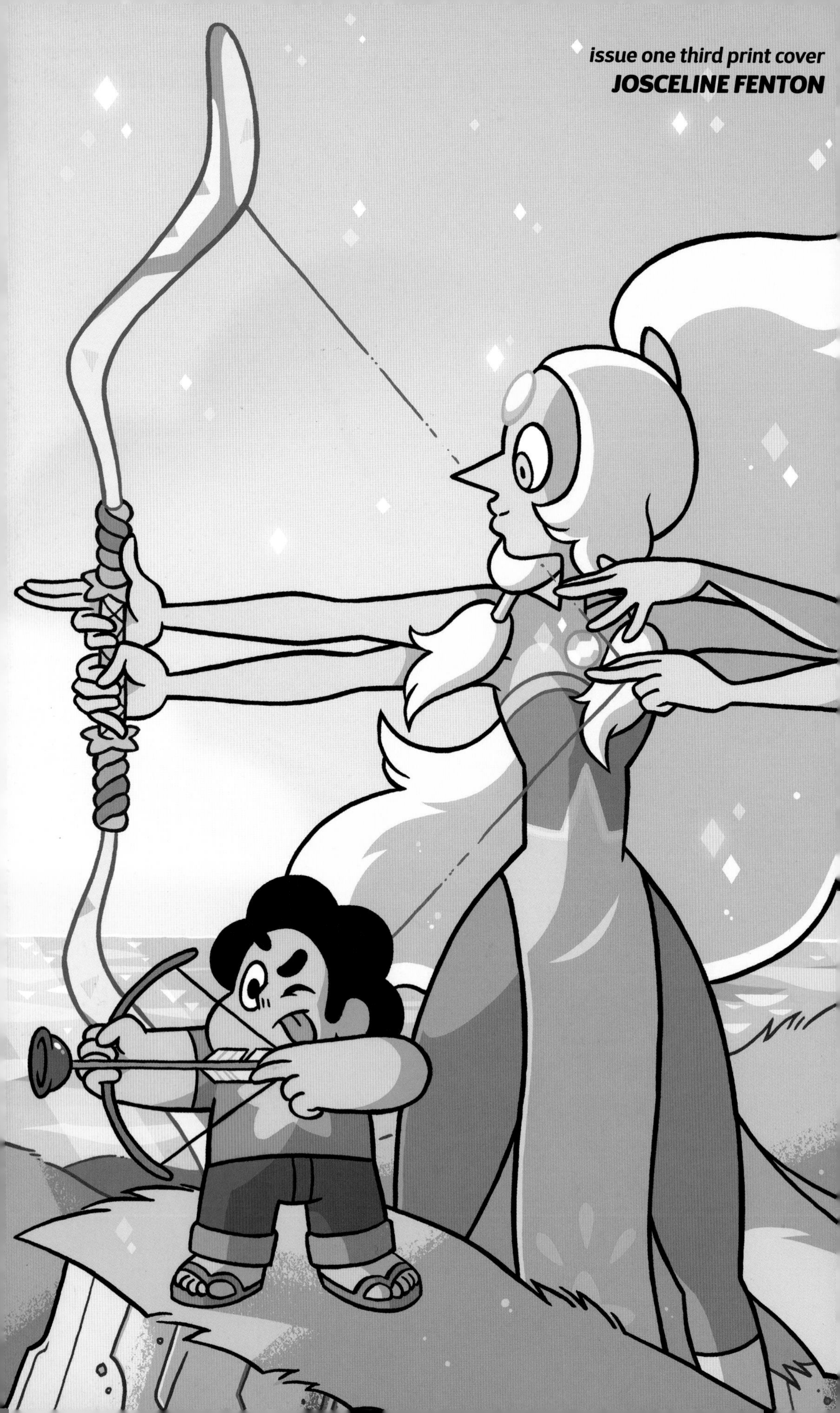

issue one hot topic exclusive cover
SAM DAVIES

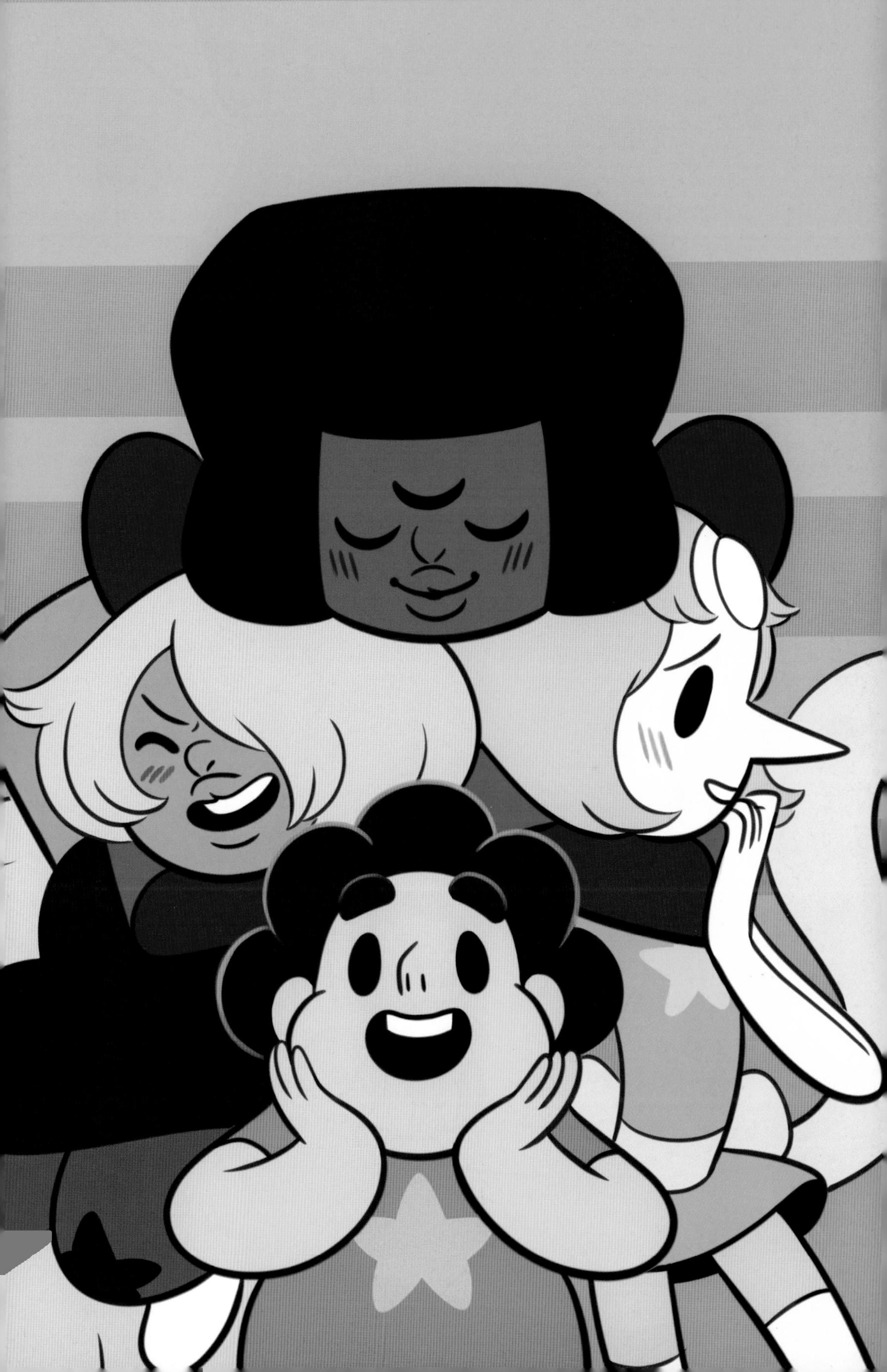

issue two main cover
KAT LEYH

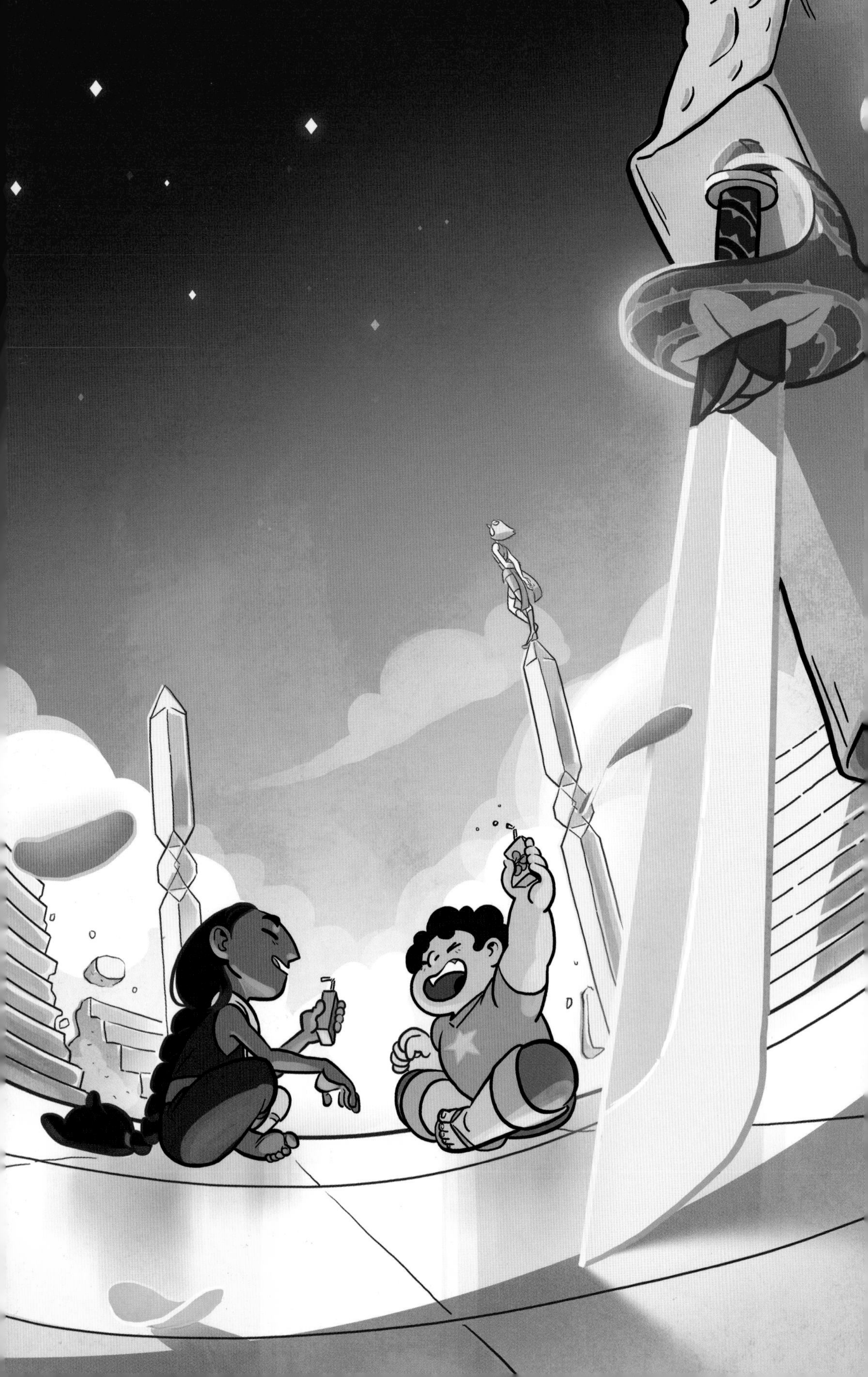

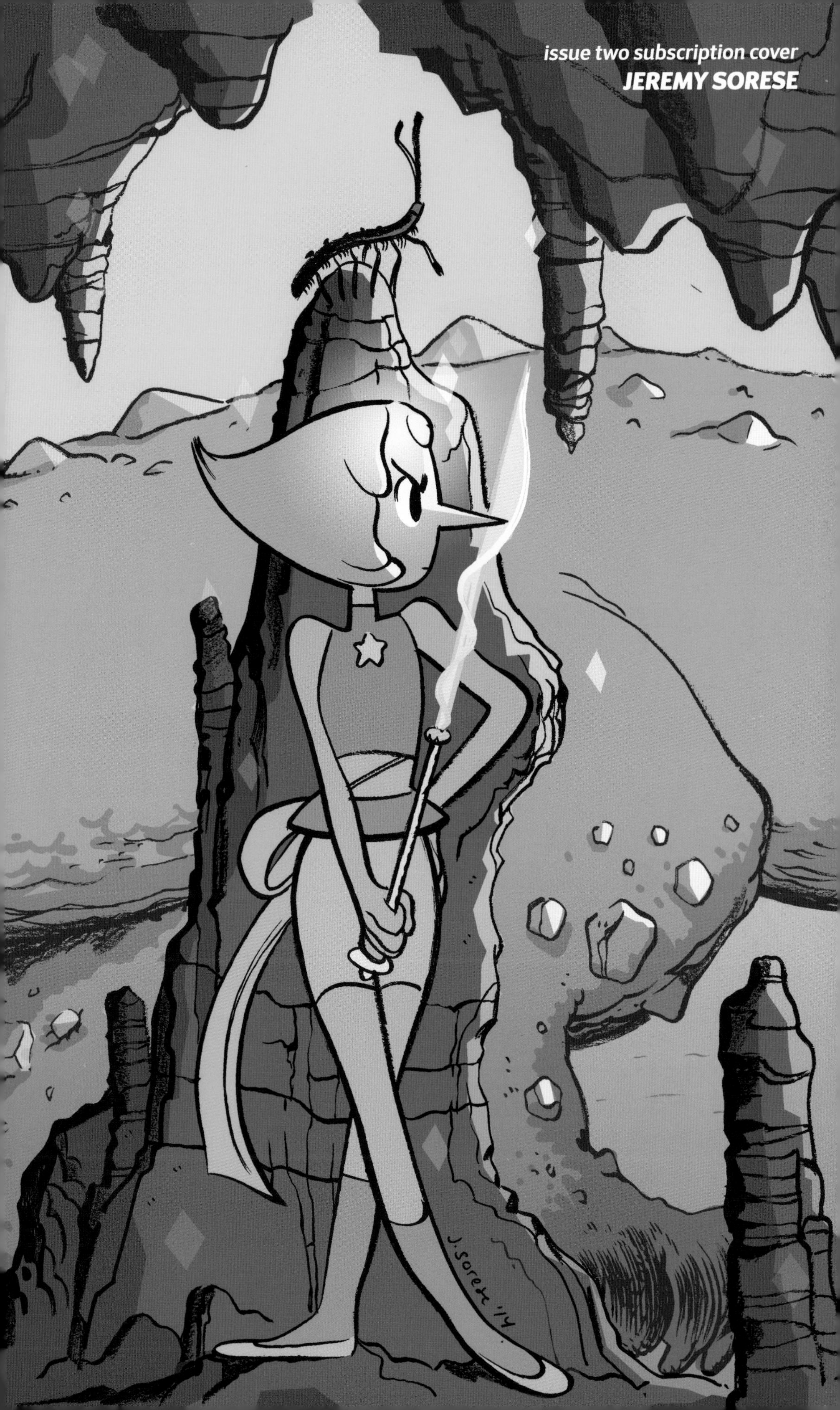
J.Sorese '14

issue two subscription cover
JEREMY SORESE

issue two variant cover
MILDRED LEWIS

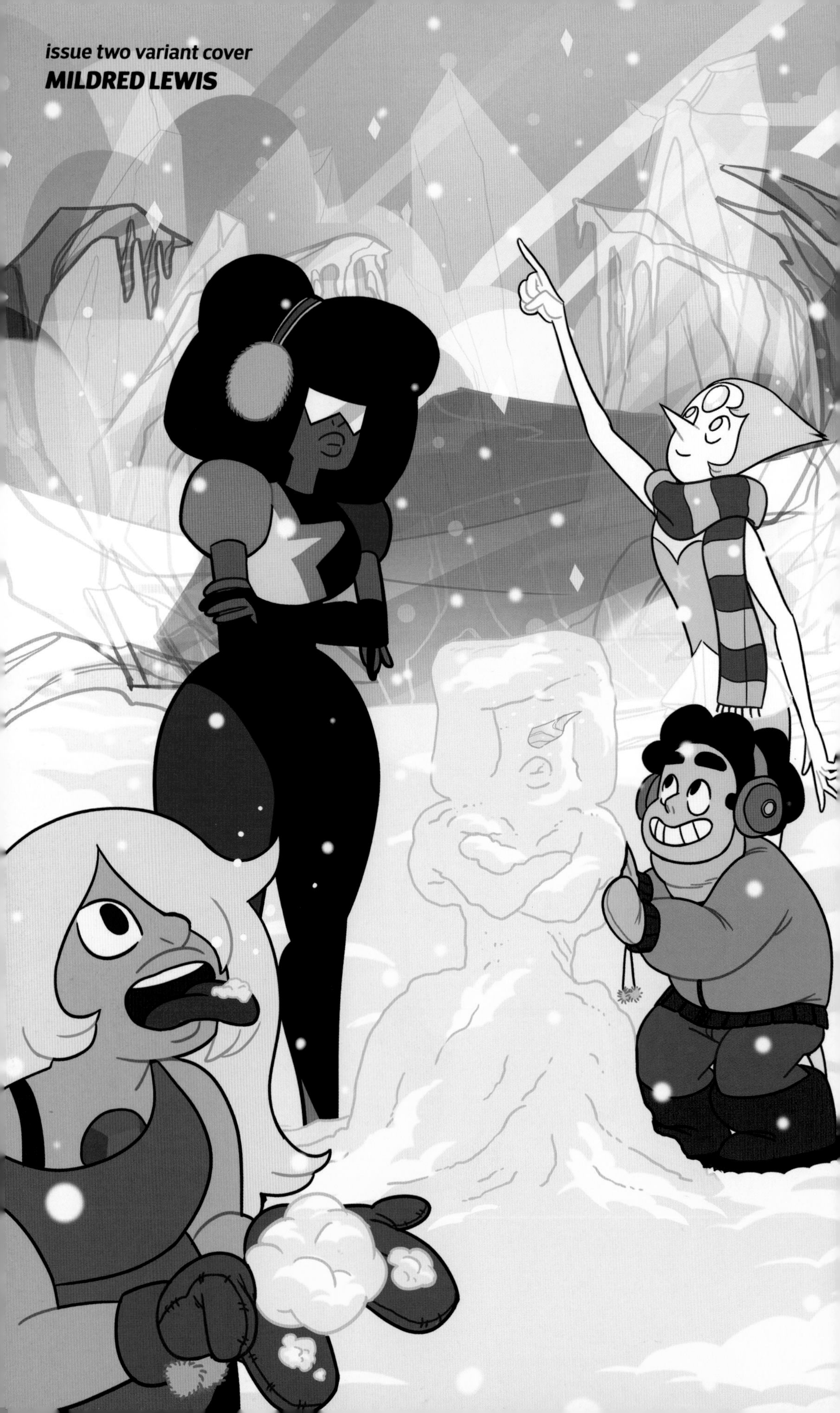

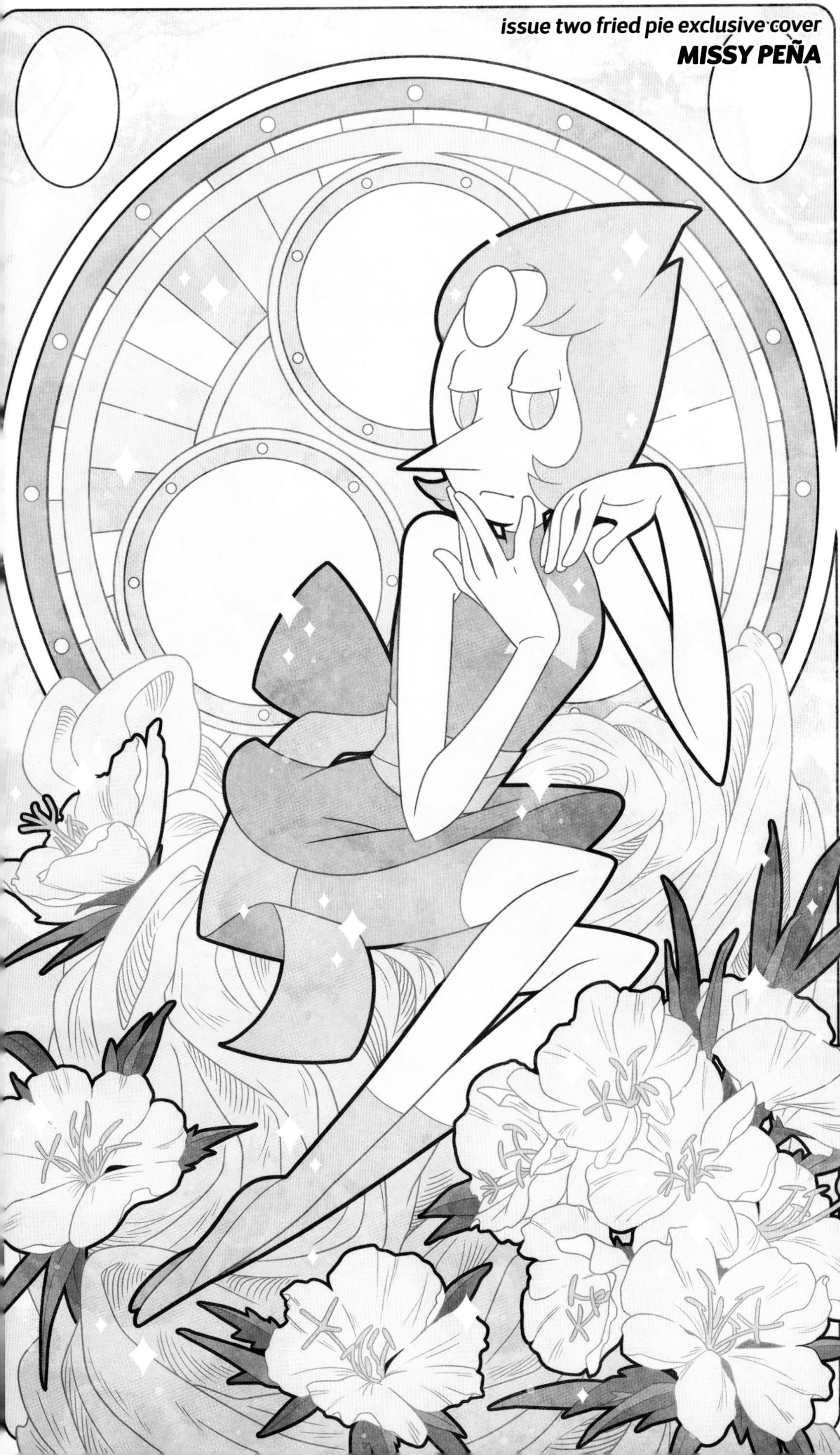

issue two fried pie exclusive cover
MISSY PEÑA

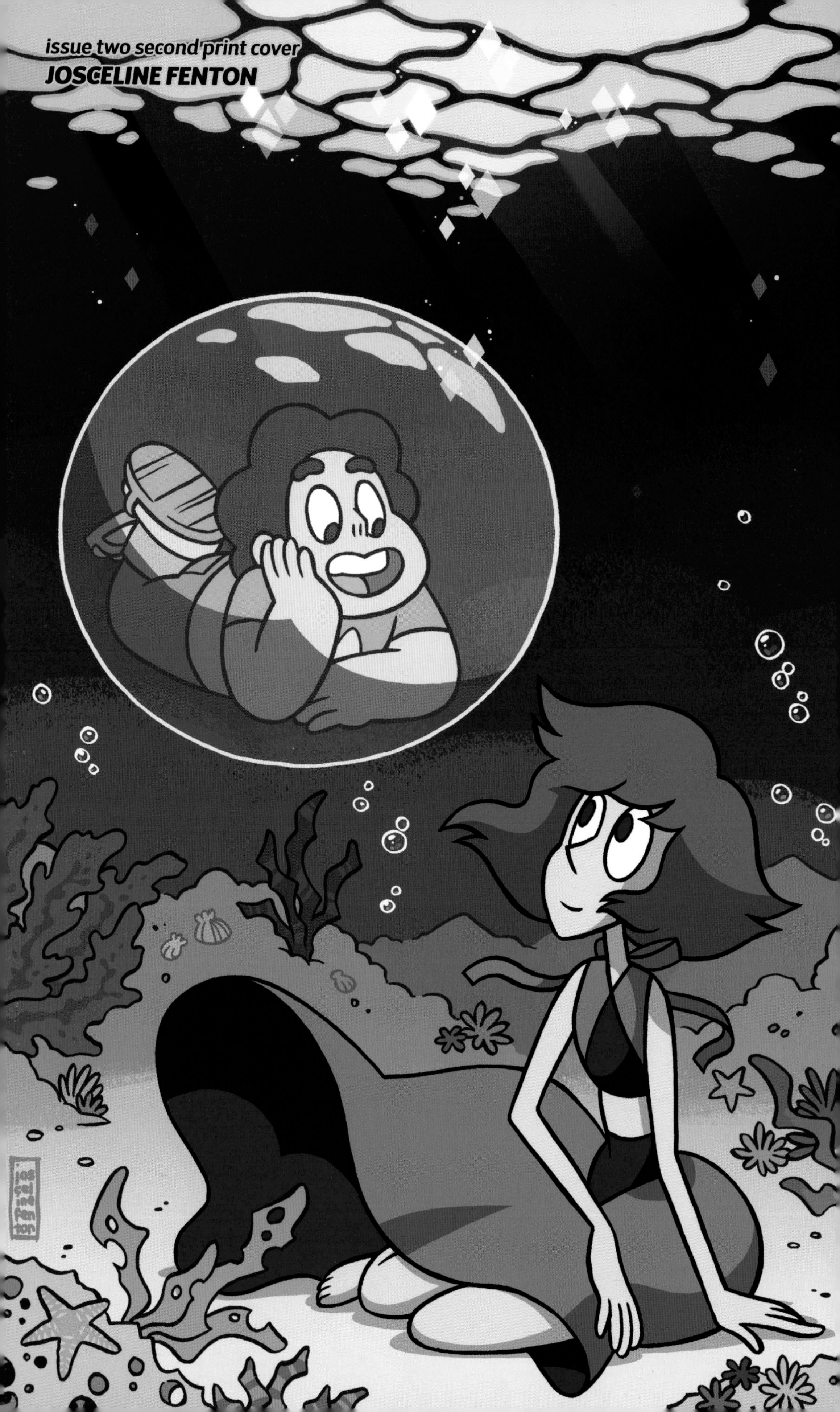

issue two second print cover
JOSCELINE FENTON

issue two hot topic exclusive cover
SAM DAVIES

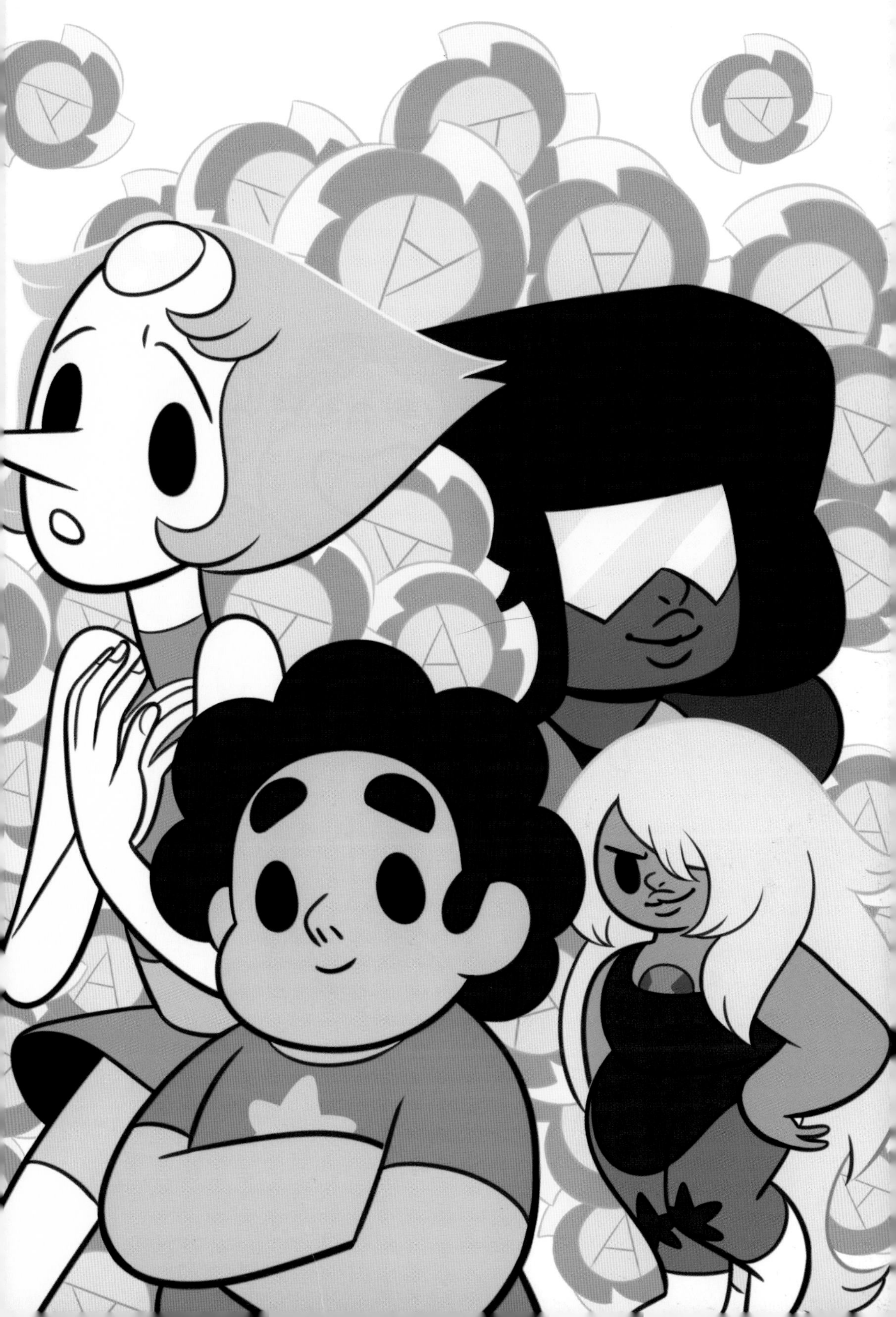

issue three main cover
KAT LEYH

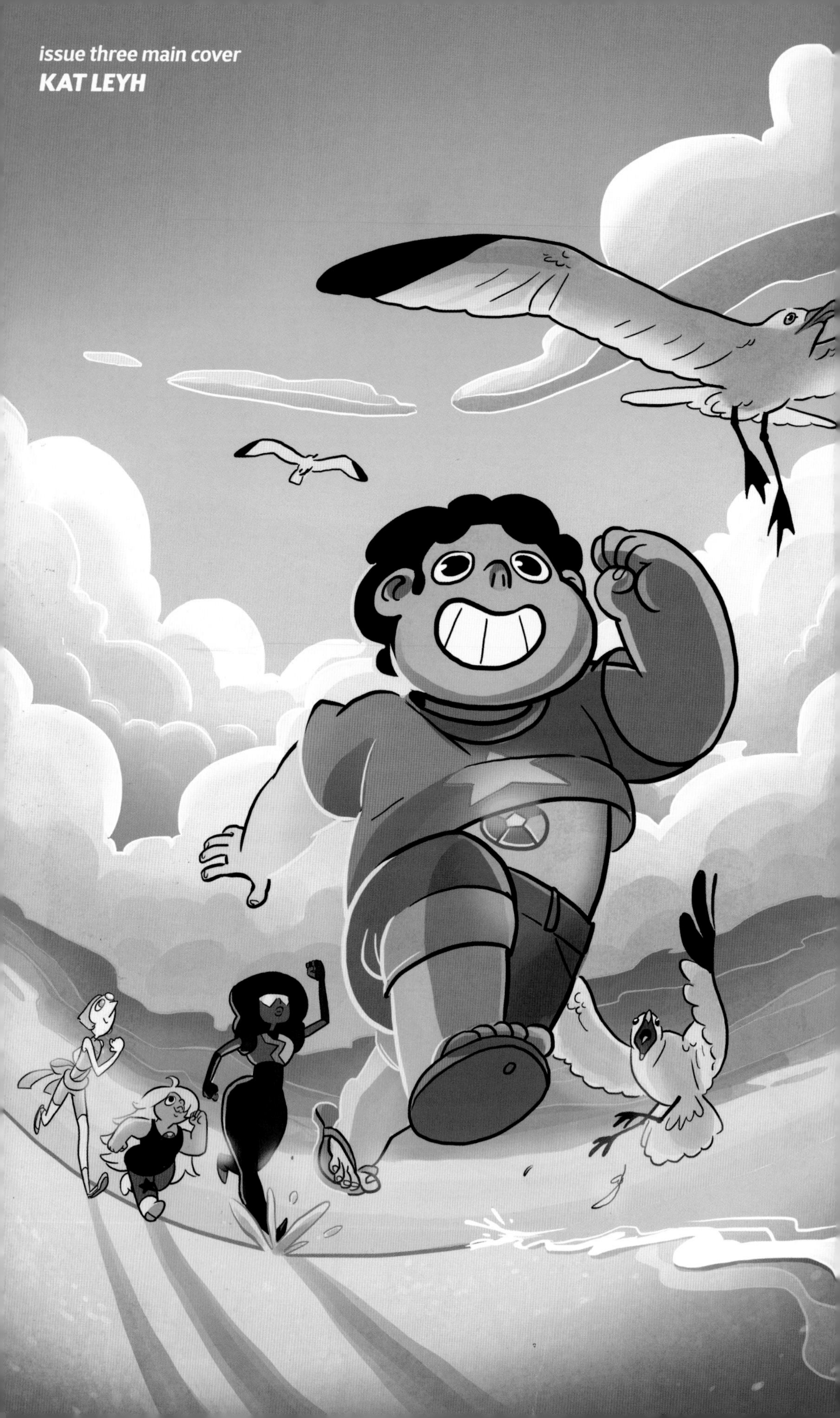

issue three subscription cover
JEREMY SORESE

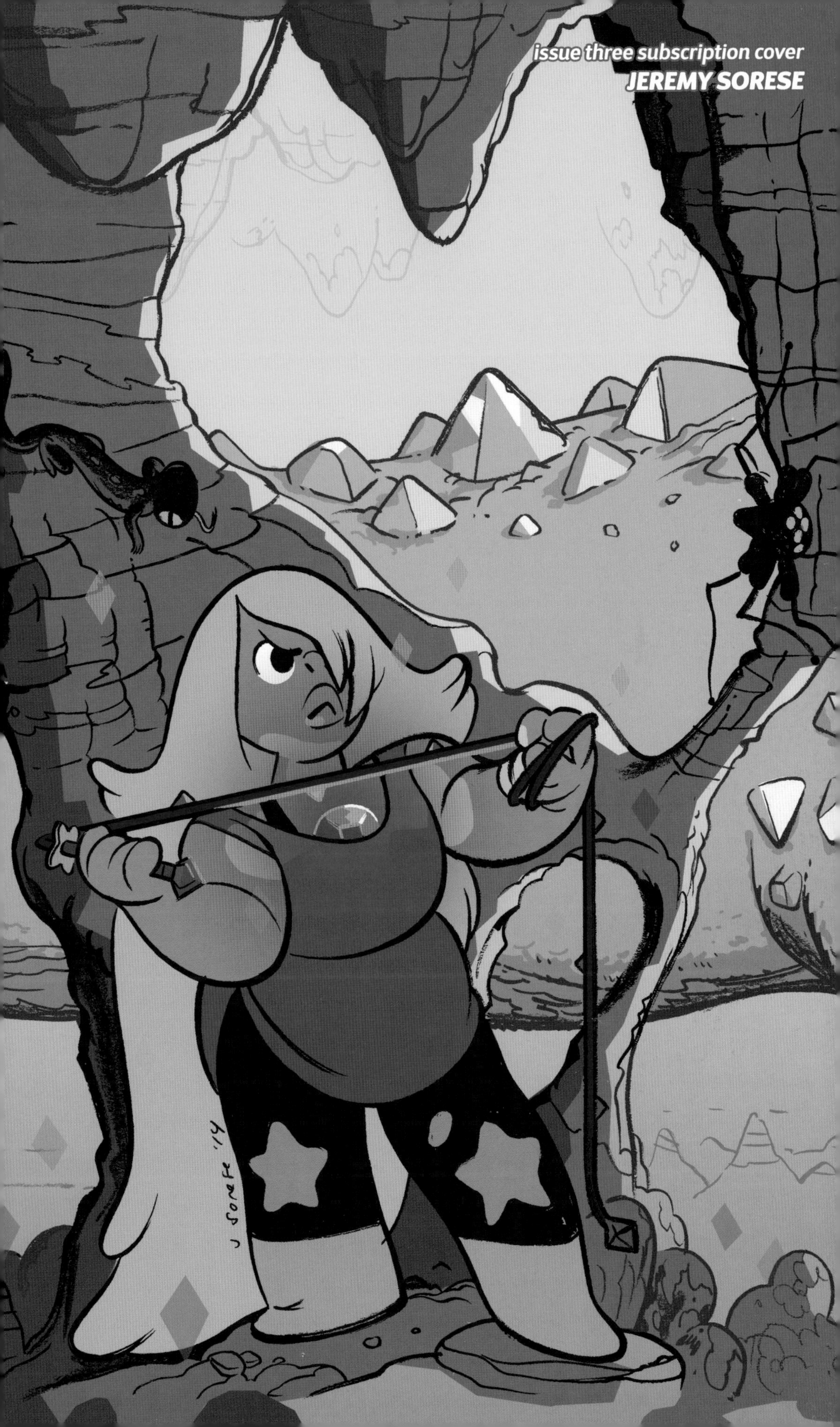

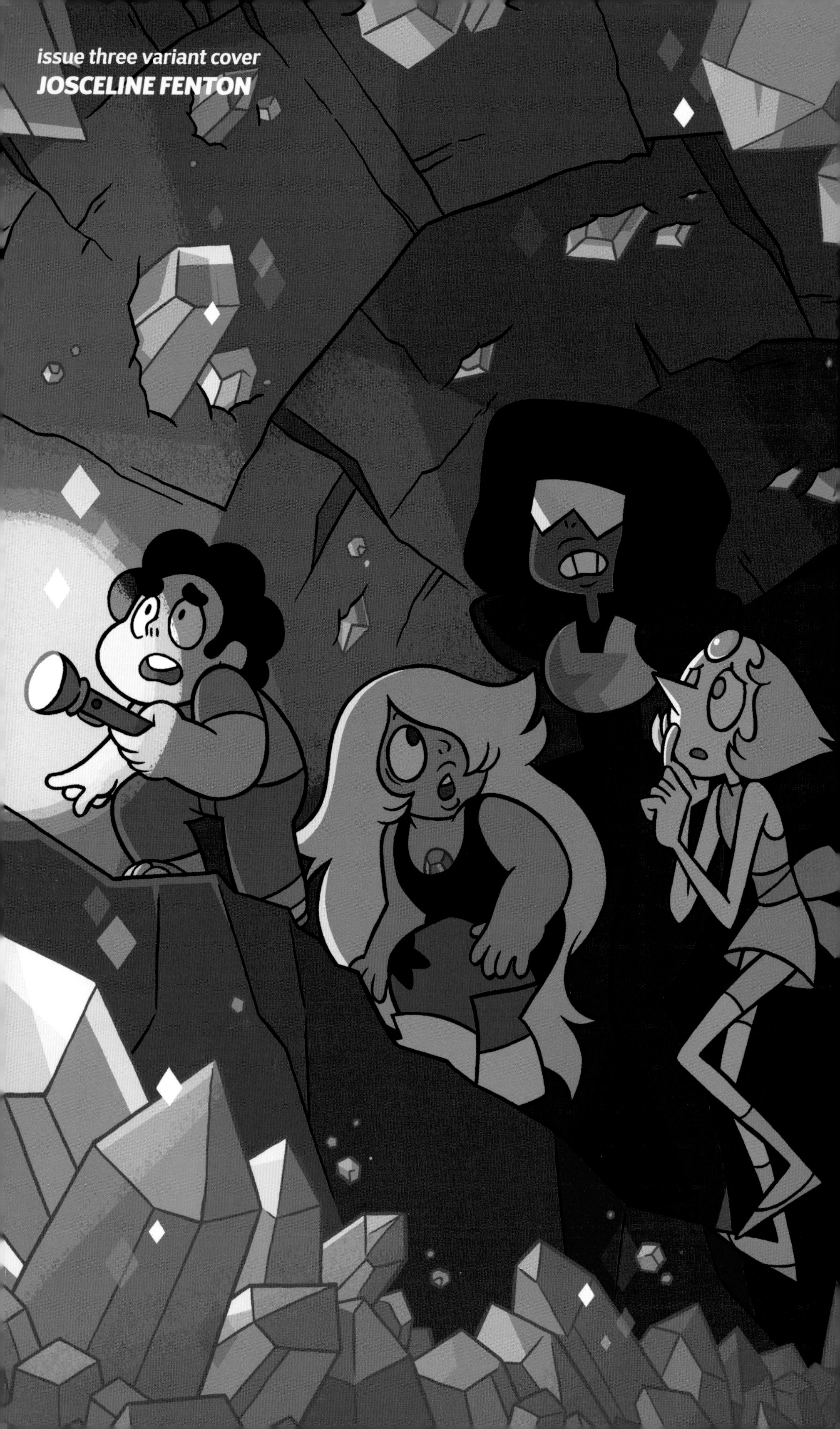
issue three variant cover
JOSCELINE FENTON

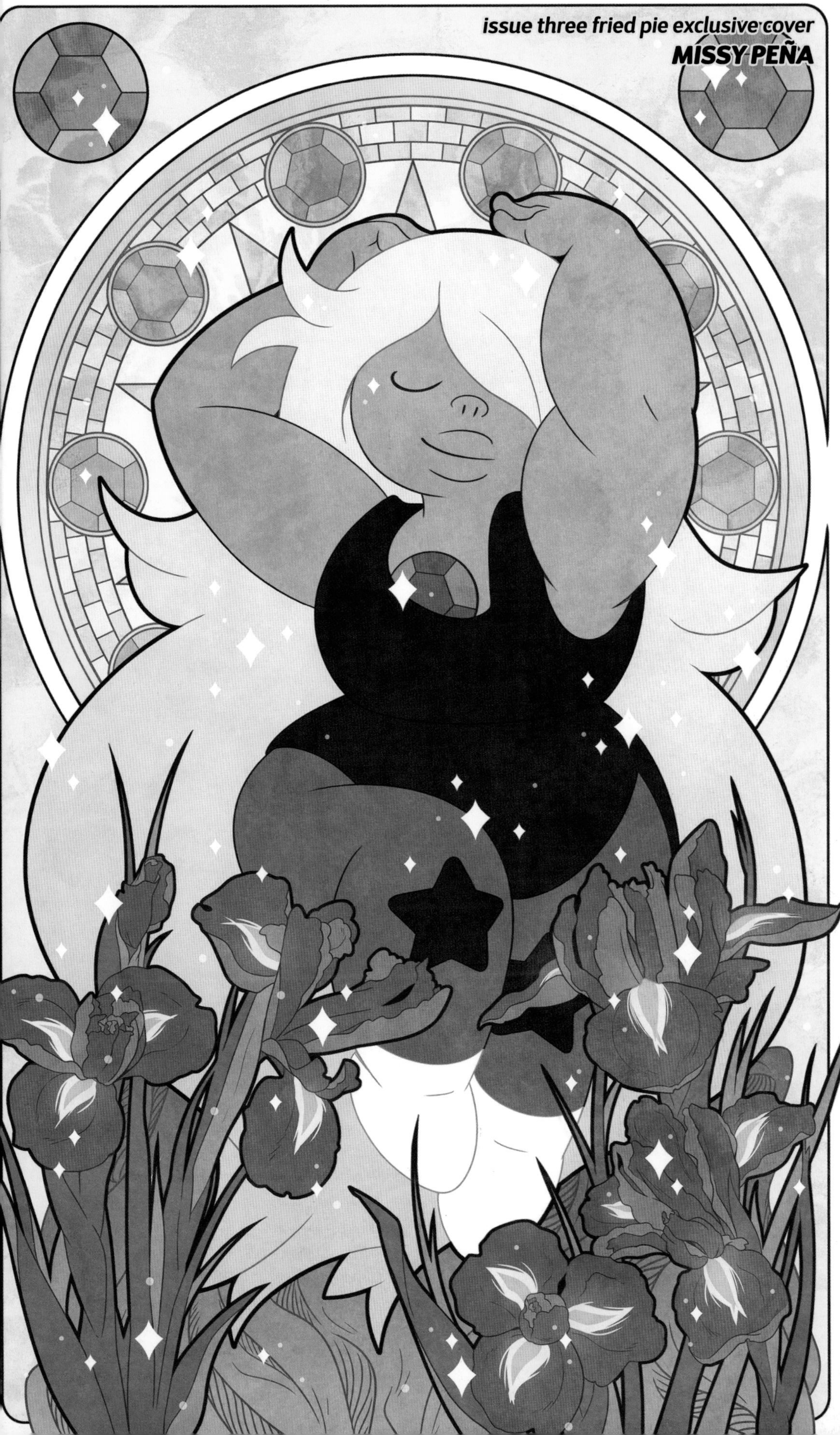
issue three fried pie exclusive cover
MISSY PEÑA

issue three hot topic exclusive cover
SAM DAVIES

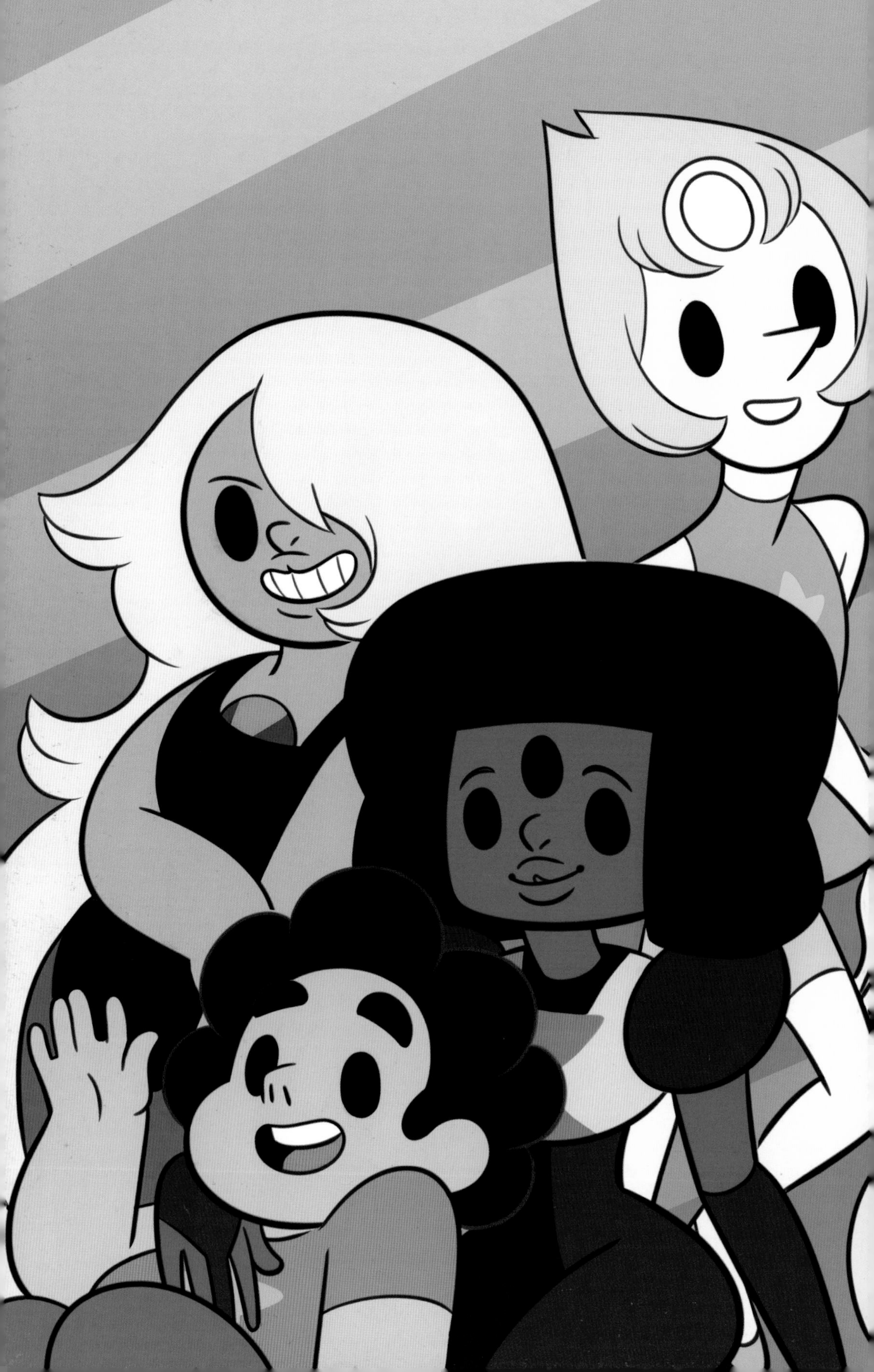

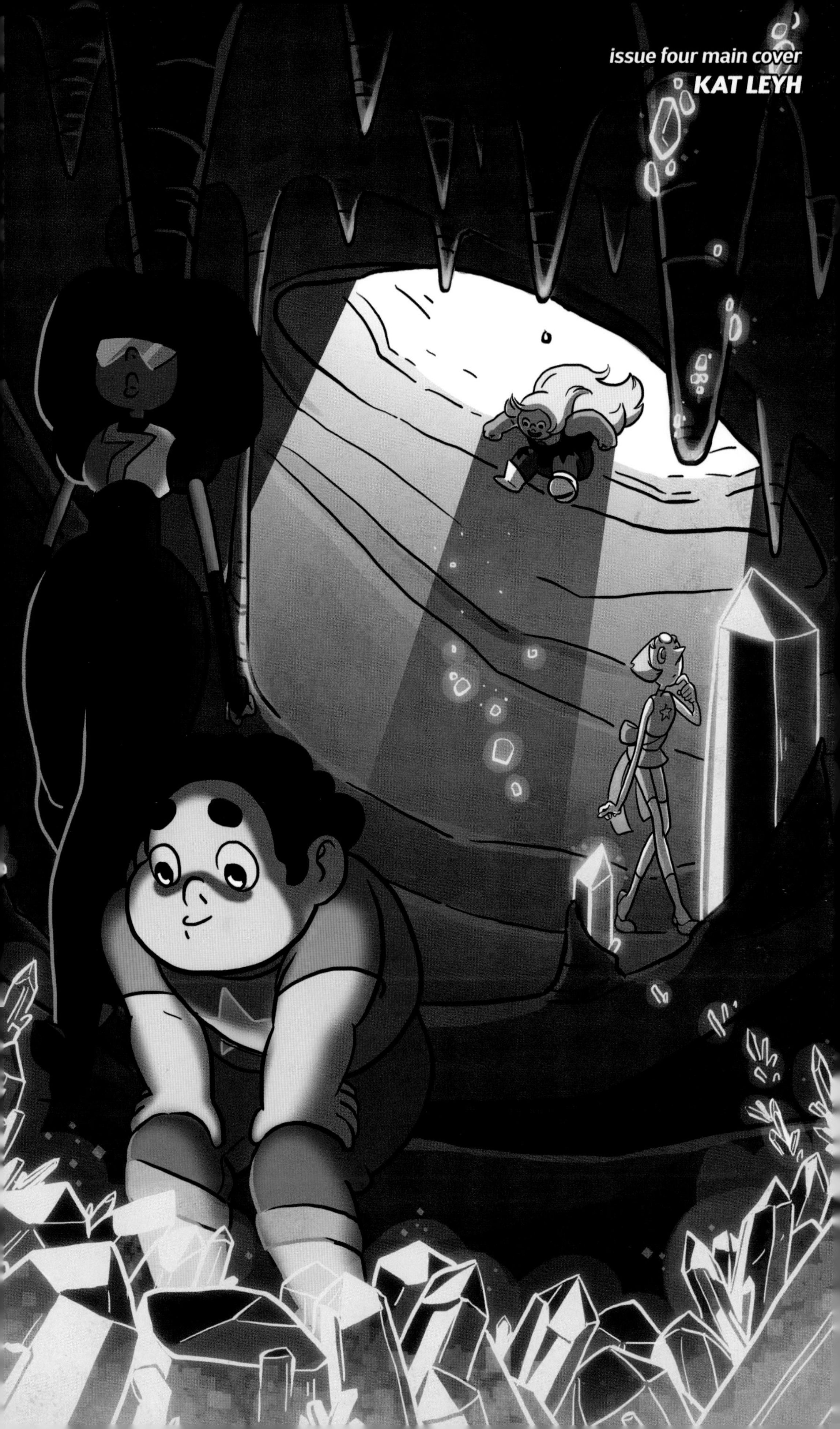

issue four main cover
KAT LEYH

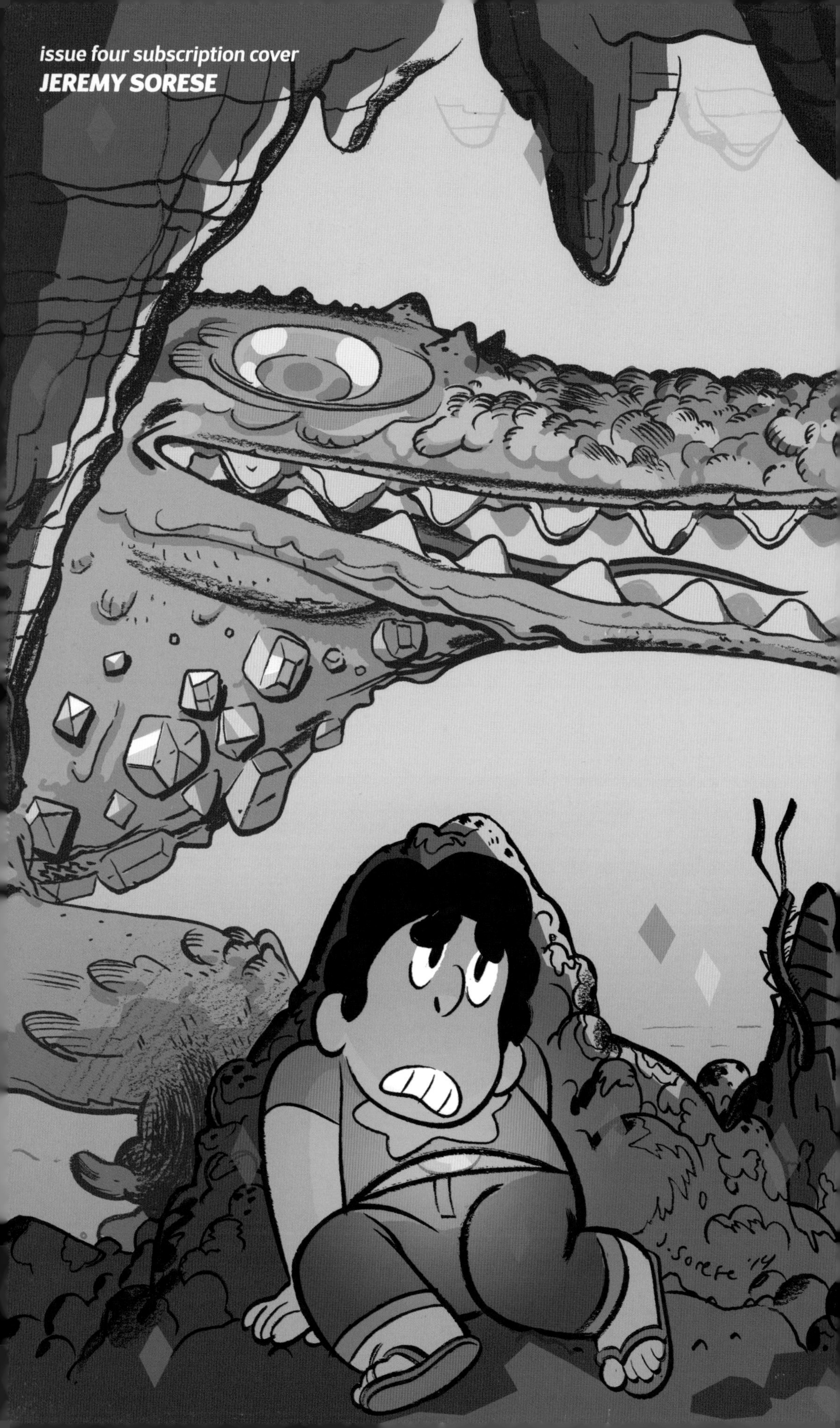
J. Sorese '14

issue four subscription cover
JEREMY SORESE

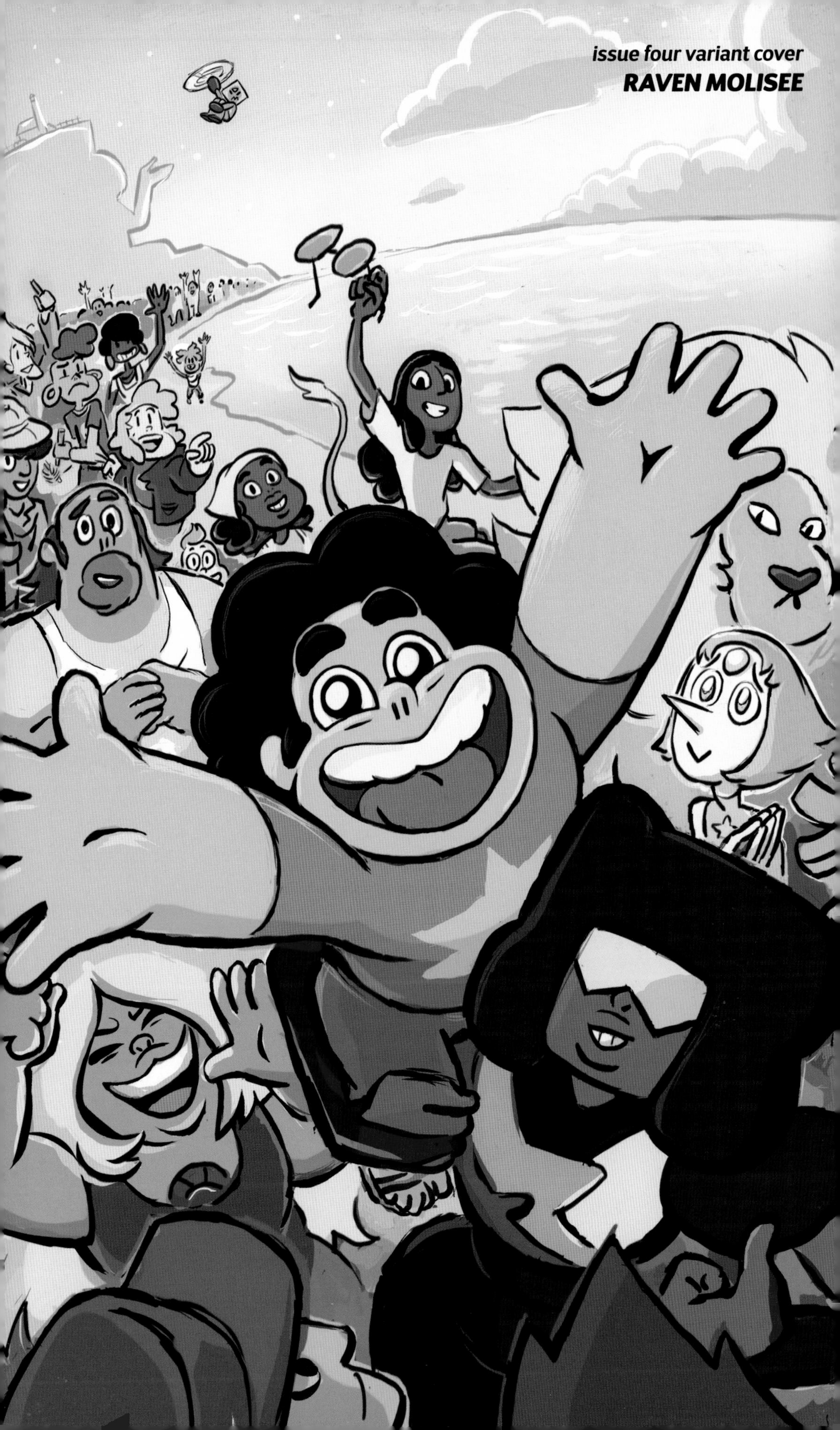

issue four variant cover
RAVEN MOLISEE

issue three fried pie exclusive cover
MISSY PEÑA

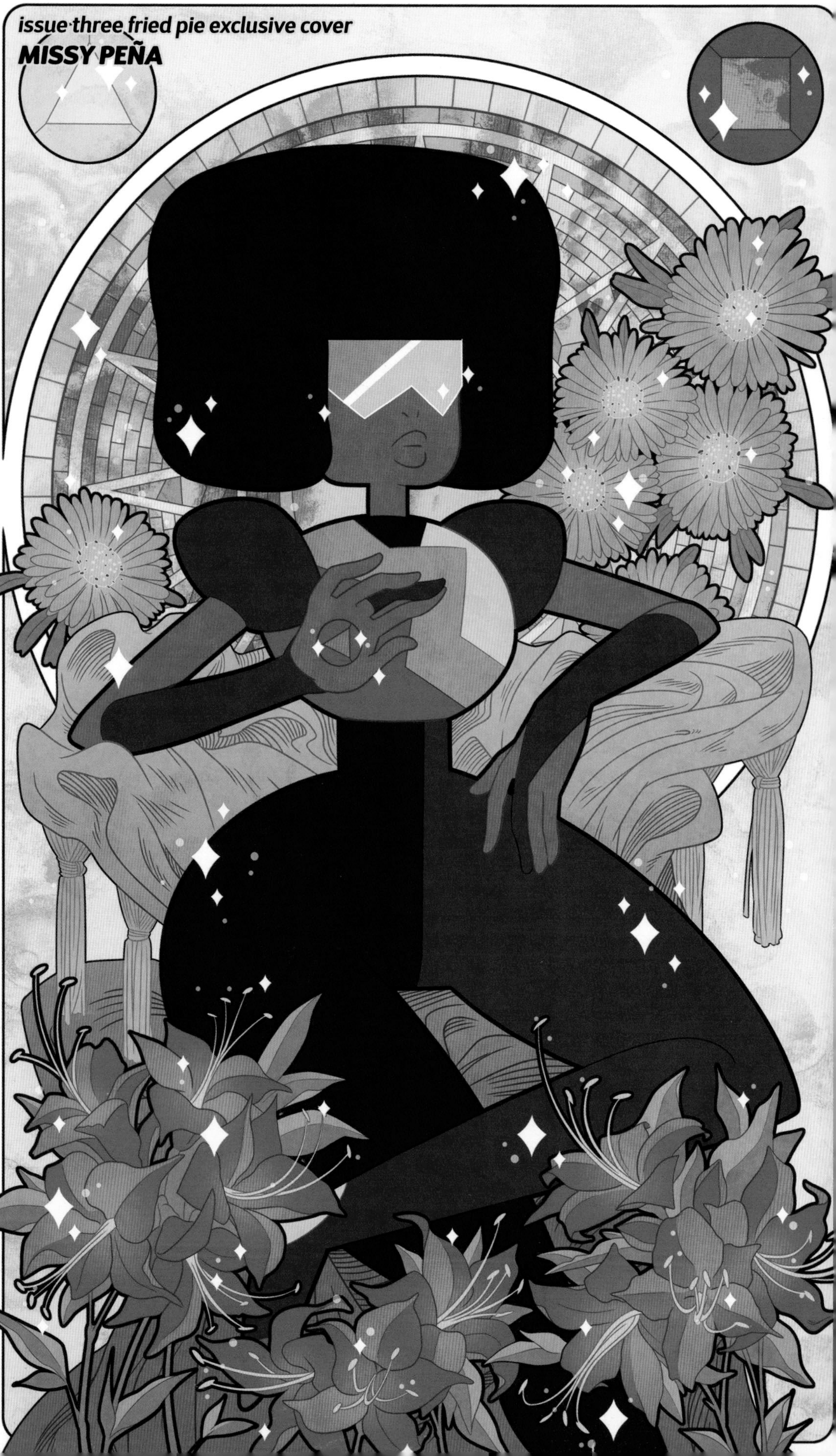

issue four hot topic exclusive cover
SAM DAVIES

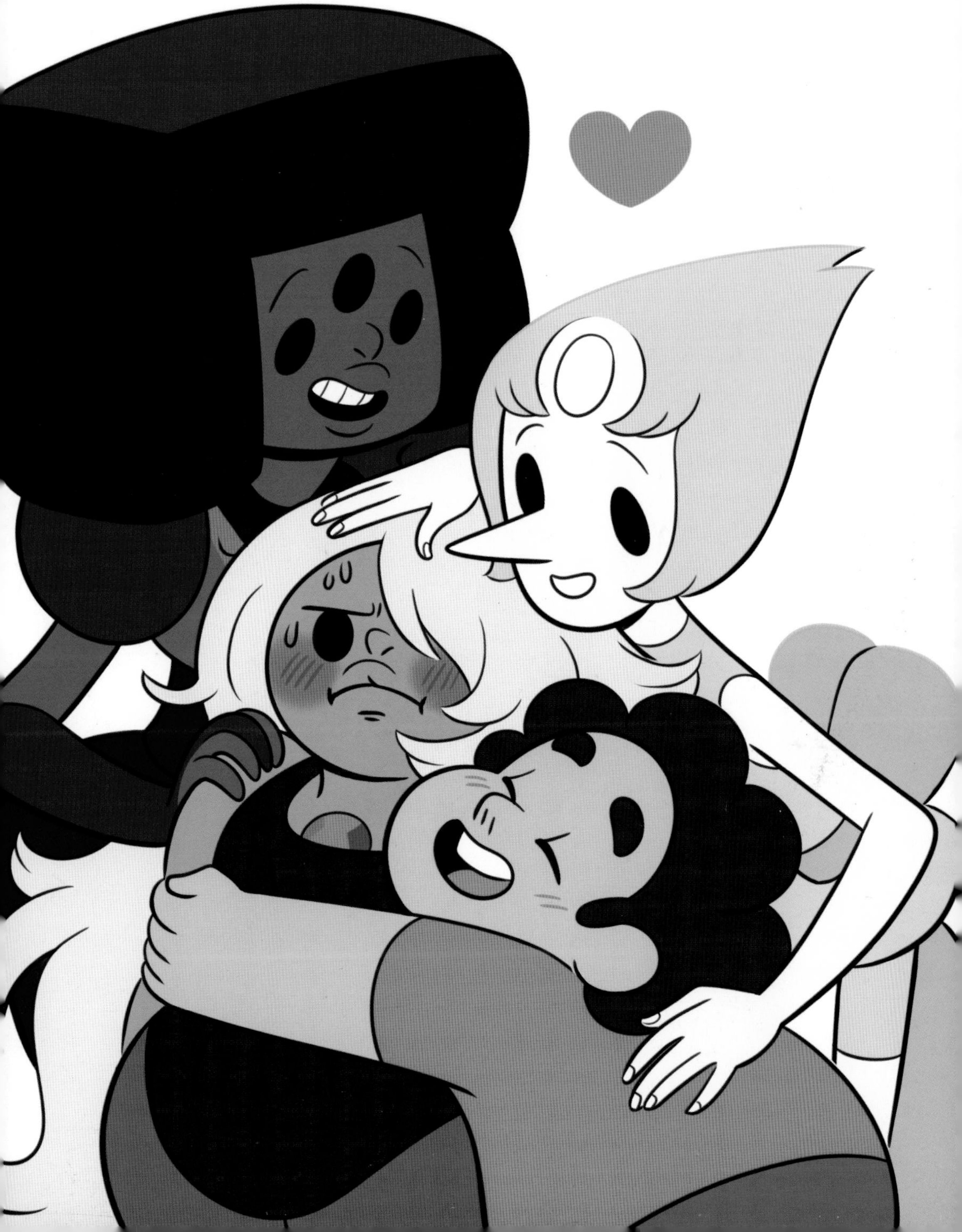

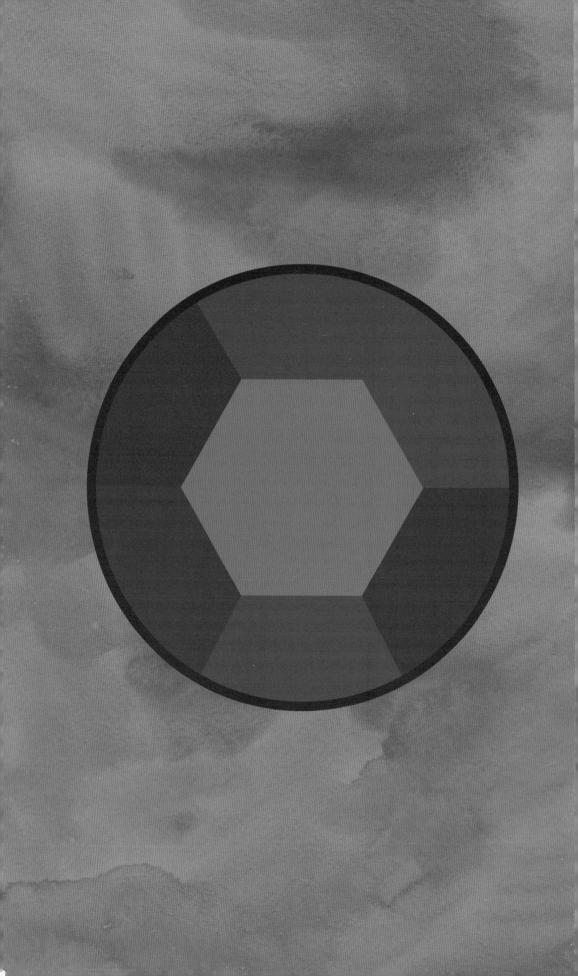